WUHAN DREAMS

The Pandemic Begins

WUHAN DREAMS
by
Jerry Cimisi

ISBN: 978-0-9999038-2-7

Library of Congress Control Number: 2022907844

The ambiguity shrouding this whole crisis makes it all the more difficult for the mind to adjust to; runners can only pace themselves if they know how far the finish line is and yet in this race our finish line is just a prediction, an educated guess. —Aysha Taryam

There have been as many plagues as wars in history; yet always plagues and wars take people equally by surprise. — Albert Camus, *The Plague*

===

"I saw strange things...."
"You didn't put them in your reports."
"I wasn't sure.... You would think I was crazy."
"You're not doing this to stay sane."

        *   *   *

"Maybe the first carrier of any disease is an anomaly."

        *   *   *

The psyche chooses its disguise for survival. Though a disguise implies the opposite of appearances was once hidden. Perhaps the disguise eventually effaces what was hidden. The disguise becomes the essence.

        *   *   *

"So if thoughts have energy, and energy is matter, are thoughts matter?"

        *   *   *

Aren't all mysteries a path to uncover lies?

Dr. Sun's research on the origins of SARS-CoV-2 is based on a paper written by Li-Meng Yan, Shu Kang, Jie Guan, and Shanchang Hu: "Unusual Features of the SARS-CoV-2 Genome.," etc.

WUHAN DREAMS   *Jerry Cimisi*

Chapter One: Zhen Li

1.

Zhen Li maneuvered the lunar rover along the large Von Kármán crater basin on the far side of the moon. Though if the simulation often made him feel he was directing the rover, in truth he was following either live or recorded tapes of its passage. He had been doing this for so long this dead, colorless world seemed natural to him now; he found himself looking to the other monitor at the face of Earth, an image brought to his eyes by the *Queqiao* satellite, positioned 65,000 kilometers past the moon, and considered it surreal that he was actually on the world the satellite revealed, not the lunar surface that had become so familiar to him by constant, virtual passage.

Simulation blended into reality through the long lunar days. When it came time for the rover to power down during different periods of that day, resting like a desert animal in the heat, and Li left the room in which he seemed to live 384,000 kilometers from Earth, he walked into the immediate world of that planet like a man waking from a dream whose repeated intimacy clashed with the world in which he could actually walk.

Wuhan. This city of eleven million people, with some of the most unusual architecture of the 21st century, and which this past October had played host to the International Military Games, was suffering its own otherworldly transformation.

Passersby were wearing surgical masks—and looked at Li, who was not, with wariness, apparently judging this full exposure of his face as a defiance and a threat.

Li was not being defiant. His superiors on the project, whose overlapping and sometimes shifting power confused him, pressed him intently on his time (his "education," as they put it) in the simulation room, and other aspects of the program, but as of yet had not spoken to him at all about the new respiratory virus that was spreading through Wuhan. Perhaps, if unconsciously, they saw Zhen Li more of the moon than of Earth, as he often did himself, and so did not consider he would be touched by the sudden situation in the city, and gave little thought he needed to be bound by the new rules of plague.

In fact, on these streets, Li was the one who felt a threat. The masked bodies who averted their eyes from the unmasked Li, or who looked sternly at him as if he endangered their safety, seemed a sudden switch in human activity whose possibilities were unpleasant. That this "switch" was not of their own doing, but an acceptance of what the authorities had imposed on them, gave their acquiescence a further, ominous aspect.

Li had to walk a bit to the bus that would take him to his apartment outside the city limits. As a taikonaut he was one of his country's elites but, he did not have car. *Absolutely ironic*, he thought: *I will travel to the moon in a rocket, drive machines on its surface, but in my own country can only be a passenger on a bus.*

His brother often needled him (though a little less so now, as it seemed certain he might be headed for the moon). Li could have joined him in business—finance, import, export; it seemed Hau did everything. Hau had a big house and two cars. And a stunning wife. Li was single. "Married to Chang'e," Hau laughed, referring to the mythical goddess of the moon—and the name of China's lunar program.

Li stopped at an intersection and witnessed something that astonished him. The police had put up a roadblock and were stopping cars. Each driver and any passengers had to exit, have their temperatures taken by a man wearing what Li could only describe as protective clothing worn when handing dangerous biological materials. He watched a middleaged couple stand worriedly outside their car during this procedure. In a moment the temperature taker gave a nod to the police, who instructed the couple to get back inside the car; they were allowed to go.

But the next driver, alone in his car, did not fare so well. He was young, perhaps only a little younger than Li. He stood by his car nervously—and coughed twice. And as he did, he gave a look that said, that hoped, no one had noticed this. But of course, everyone had. The man in the hazard suit swiped the small instrument across the driver's forehead; and in a moment he nodded sternly to the police.

One of the officers made a gesture, as if to characters who must abruptly take their place upon a stage, and three men in hazard gear, not only on their bodies but covering their heads and faces, appeared as if out of nowhere, grabbed the man roughly. He cried out as they dragged him to a large van or small bus and threw him inside.

Li was shocked. He had heard that the government was forcing those who were ill into quarantine, but he hadn't expected it to be effected like this.

One of the officers looked disapproving at Li's unmasked face, and asked sternly, "Where is your mask?"

Li's answer was to display his government identification. The officer looked at him fixedly, the eyes over his own mask stern, trying to find a way, Li knew, to bully him.

"Everyone's wearing a mask now," the officer finally said. "Do you want to get sick? It's the law."

"I haven't been told," said Li. He knew he sounded childish. The officer could only regard him as some idiot protected by the government.

"I'm telling you."

Li didn't have a response for that. He tried to redirect the issue. He pointed to the car still blocking the road. "What happens to his car?"

The officer looked back at him as if Li had asked a ridiculous—and forbidden—question. "It will be taken care of." As if on cue another policeman got in the car and parked it alongside the road.

As Li was watching this, the officer who was so plainly disapproving of Li was gesturing to someone who went into a police vehicle and who emerged with something and walked over to Li. He extended a mask.

The officer before Li said, "Take it."

Li took it slowly, as if not wanting to be complicit in his own violation.

"Wear it," said the officer, turning his back on Li, perhaps not wanting to see if his order was being challenged. The man in the hazard suit was taking the temperature of another driver. Li walked on, masked now—and as if he had been randomly, roughly, marked by an event that had abruptly upset the ascetic, austere nature his simulated forays over the moon's far side had cultivated.

When he got on his bus his masked face matched those of all the other passengers. That is, no one looked at him with mistrust now; he appeared one of them. But Li felt the mask a disguise, hiding a personal inner rebellion (if not quite the right word) which would upset the safety the other passengers tenuously held by their compliance.

The bus took Li to almost its last stop, where a suburb was interrupted by apartment complexes of twelve and fifteen stories. Li, who had grown up on a rice farm far from Wuhan and other major cities, looked at his living in such small and crowded places as a sacrifice for his passage through China's space program. Occasionally, he would go up on the roof, look at the sky, especially at night, as he had when growing up, seeking the familiarity of the celestial. Of course, the skies here, if not as bad as right in Wuhan, were polluted with the lights of early 21st century Chinese civilization, but on clear nights there were enough brighter stars to be seen, giving Li a peaceful connection to the celestial worlds of his childhood.

Because Li's working schedule was determined by the lunar day and the *Yutu-2* rover's periods of activity within it, he did not have the hours of regular commuter. But today, his return home happened to coincide with the typical end of a worker's day; he arrived at his apartment building after the early dark of winter had just taken over from a grey twilight.

He made himself dinner and watched the state-run news. There was a good deal about the virus, and the measures the citizens of Hubei province must now undertake.

Despite what he had witnessed at the traffic stop, that poor driver being literally dragged away to some official quarantine center, and the masked populace now on the streets and the bus, Li felt that this threat was apart from him. It would be an annoyance he would have to pass through going back and forth to the simulation site and his long sessions roving the surface of the far side of the moon.

But then, he looked at the mask the police officer had given him; Li had placed it on a coffee table. It rested on this surface with a seeming rigidity that belied its actual texture. He realized he had begun not to think about it during the bus ride, had walked to his apartment with it on, rode up to his floor on the elevator—with other masked people—and had removed it without thought.

As if I'm used to it, he thought. *Already*.

He literally shook his head, not pleased at all with the situation.

Meanwhile, the TV was saying....

2.

Li had always been fascinated with the stars, the planets. He had always wanted to go "out there." As a boy he had eagerly read about the history and present missions of both the American and Russian space programs.

It was an attraction that had begun even before he consciously sought such knowledge. Or so it would seem, from what he had been told by his parents about the first years of life—which one little recalls and can only know by the tales of others. Of course, there were photographs, videos, but the essence of what the child was, had been, was told by the child's elders. Growing up, and as an adult, it would be for the child to interpret those tales.

Li was told that when he was a few months old his mother would nurse him to sleep under the summer sky, his eyes closing upon the face of his mother and the stars. In the following summers, a year old, two years old, she would take him again outside before bedtime, and both his parents said he would raise a hand to the night sky pointing "at the lights of heaven," his father had said, sometimes saying things in child-speak, as if privately naming what was above.

His mother had also recalled, "I remember the reflection of the moon in your eyes."

Of course, his parents could not imagine their son being trained to go to that very moon. They both had come from a long line of farmers, workers, peasant—that Mao, the founder of modern China, had so idealized. Though they had decided it would be good for their son to have a life that was apart from the toil they had known.

Unlike their parents and grandparents, they did not have many children. It was the era when China, trying to stem the size of its population, decreed official incentives for families of two children or one. Or rather, not so much incentive as punishment for those who went past two. Whether Li's parents had planned for just two children, or the reproductive dice just rolled that way, they had never communicated to Li, who enjoyed having one older brother—even if he was definitely of a different nature. Li was the child who, in the warm months, would stand barefoot in the wet rice fields, enjoying the openness and the sense of things growing, while understanding his future would be away from this life.

Li made himself dinner, only half paying attention to the news in the background. When he sat before the screen with his food, a newscaster was blandly stating some facts—at least they were considered facts for the moment—about the beginnings of the virus.

"It appears the first known case of this virus, an unknown Patient Zero may have been traced back to December 1 of last year, in Wuhan. No one could have suspected that first case, and those that followed, would result in the situation we face this month, especially in Hubei, centered around Wuhan. As many of you know, experts believe they have traced the source of the virus to the Huanan Seafood Market, which authorities closed January 1. We know from experience with earlier viruses, that a virus can jump from animal to human, and it is believed that is the case here.

"This is a new type of what is called a coronavirus, identified from a sample taken from a patient at Wuhan Central Hospital. At first this was thought to be a reoccurrence of the SARS virus—Severe Acute Respiratory Syndrome—but this did not prove the case. A number of doctors have been admonished for spreading false rumors. All that could be determined at that point was that this was a virus whose main result is a pneumonia of an unknown cause."

"The virus was obviously the cause," said Li to the TV.

"On December 31 the Wuhan Health Commission confirmed 27 new cases, a small number yes, but by January the virus had spread outside of Hubei, though the province is still the epicenter, especially Wuhan.

"On January 20 almost 140 new cases were reported in one day, including two cases as far away as Beijing. The data we now have shows that more than six thousand people had been infected with the virus by then. A few days later, the British medical journal, *The Lancet*, stated the virus was being passed through human transmission. If it had been animal in origin, and had been suspected to have been passed into the human population by eating animals from markets such as those in Wuhan, where live animals are slaughtered on the premises, this is *not* being transmitted by eating animals, but simple contact with other people. *The Lancet* report also strongly recommended protective equipment for doctors, nurses, hospital workers and that the virus had the potential to become a pandemic."

Pandemic? And Wuhan its origin?

Li thought about all the people with masks. The Chinese, especially in major cities, often wore masks because of pollution, but what Li had seen today was a response that had a visceral unease, a state driven by the authorities and a new unknown virus.

The phone rang. It was Fan, Li's girlfriend.

"So you're home from the moon."

"For now. Just got in."

"But you always go back."

"Someday I'll go to the real moon."

She said this all the time; he said this all the time.

"I never understand why you would want to go somewhere where you can't breathe."

"Didn't we have this discussion before?"

"Since you first told me you wanted to go 'out there.'"

Li smiled. "That's years ago, now."

Two years ago, Li had been ordered to attend a lecture Fan was giving, on the uses of nanotechnology in space flight. If the focus of her lecture had been the uses of the qualities of materials at the most minute levels, and literal machines that could be constructed that one could view only through a microscope, she had thrown some asides of how all this could be connected to the equally minute qualities of animate life, suggesting that certain bacteria and even viruses could be melded to nanomachines in much the same way human beings are fitted with prosthetics. Li could not fathom how exactly how latter vision might advance space flight, but he was stricken with the obvious genius of this young woman who was as attractive as her visions were advanced.

He had spoken to her after the lecture, and to his own surprise, had overcome his usual reserved nature and asked her for a date. Her initial response had been to laugh and for a moment that had made him feel foolish, but her subsequent acquiescence had eventually led to something he had not at all foreseen in the focus of his training: a romance. "Well, a romance of sorts," Fan would say.

Perhaps it was an odd pairing, or perhaps not: Li the fledgling taikonaut, Fan the all too brilliant young lady who worked on the new and strange borderland of molecular biology and nanotechnology.

Li soon became very drawn by this young woman, who, alongside her brilliance, seemed to meet life in a literally fearless manner. Her name fit her personality: it meant "dangerous," or "lethal."

Li told Fan about the driver getting taken away at the traffic stop. "I have a nice quiet time on the moon, and then I see—"

She suddenly said, "They are going to quarantine Wuhan—all of Hubei."

"What does that mean? How do you know?"

"It's worse than you think it is."

"I don't know how I think it is. I just, today—"

"There were government officials at the lab. They think the virus got out of the lab."

"I wasn't even thinking about that, but did it?"

Fan worked at Wuhan Institute of Virology, a Biosafety Level 4 facility, one of the few of its kind in the world, where some of the most virulent pathogens were studied—and, some suspected, bioengineered. Much of the work there was secret, so it was inevitable such a rumor was widely believed.

"Who knows? I haven't heard anything. Not that someone would tell me. I haven't seen anything to make me think that happened."

Fan had been conscripted—and that was precisely the word, Li thought—to help design nanotechnology that would further the study of viruses. A virus is so small that it falls between the wavelengths of light; in other words, it cannot be seen by the eye, even through the most powerful optical microscope; it is "seen" only through an electron microscope, that uses electron beams to create an image and is effective down to .2 nanometers, a thousand times more powerful than a light microscope. Thus we "know" these pathogens only through electronic representations.

Fan would talk about machines so minute they could be seen—and constructed—only with a microscope, while she spoke about how space craft could carry nanomachines that could construct other nanomachines to perform essential tasks in orbit or when landing on other worlds, the cargo of such marvels of so little weight leaving yuhangyuans (universe travelers)—or taikonauts (space sailors)—more room for not only their bodies, but the supplies they would need for sustenance. Fan even speculated that in the near future these nanomachines would be able to mold inanimate materials into the animate, and perhaps even plant-like substances that could be food sources.

"After all," she said, "Once on earth there was just the inanimate, that somehow evolved, became animate: primitive organisms, then colonies of such, then plants—"

Fan said so many fantastical things that grasped Li's imagination, but the most striking thing that she brought to his awareness was that while he, since childhood, had been drawn to the worlds and lights above his head, while all his perspective was that large, vast universe "out there," the nano world this wondrous woman described was just as vast, a universe he had largely ignored. Of course, through his scientific interests and his education, he knew of the atomic and subatomic worlds, but Fan made them alive, beating vividly in every molecule in existence. So intrigued was Li by this awareness, that he might have said Fan, through this wide-ranging lecture, had erupted a sudden outlook within his consciousness that lodged in his brain like another eye with which to look upon the world.

Of course, it was Fan who really had that eye, and surveyed existence with that sight. But she had made Li aware of a vision he had not used. And as if he needed to keep the creator of this new awareness close to him, then and there, without putting the words through his head, he knew he must be her lover.

Well, being a young and not unhandsome yuhangyuan in training also wielded attractions to the opposite sex. After her lecture he was one of the many who stood in line to speak with her. When he finally reached her presence, his enthusiasm mixed with a desire he made no attempt to hide, Fan was both flattered, wary, and drawn. They had an almost awkward dinner together two days later, in a sense parrying each other with swords of science: the intricacies of the nanouniverse with the pressing mission of Li's exploration of other worlds.

Li tried to bridge these universes, connect them with the remark, "Someone told me about an old American comic book he'd read, about people living on subatomic worlds, worlds that would be as big to them as the Earth is to us. Do you think that's possible?"

She laughed. "Do you?"

"I asked you the question. I don't think so, but.... Well, human beings were astounded when they found living creatures swimming around in a drop of water, creatures they could never have known or seen without a microscope, so…maybe it's not impossible. And maybe we are like the people living on atomic particles: the Earth is just like an atom, the smallest part of a world we call the universe—which itself could be—"

She stopped herself and laughed, flung out her arms and said, "Who knows?"

He laughed, too, and then segued from the esoterica of science to conversation more common for a young man and woman trying to get to know one another: talk of the workplace. Then again, their workplaces being what they were, science was never far apart from any of their conversation, whether at the beginning of their relationship, or now.

Li found that Fan had more than a little interest in American comic books. For some reason she was very drawn to American popular culture. "It's just so legendary," she said. (Li thought that a peculiar way to put it.) Fan knew English and told Li she had seen many American movies and even TV shows.

"These men that came today," said Fan, "went around questioning every department."

"So they talked to you."

"They did. But I think I confused them so much—they really knew nothing about nanotech, just viruses. II think they thought me innocent."

"Innocent of what?"

"Releasing that virus."

"So it did come from the lab?"

"No one really knows."

"I thought it was decided it came from that market."

"It could have come from the lab to that market. Or came to the lab from the market. Viruses move around—because we carry them and we move around."

"What is your opinion of the source?"

She paused a moment, then said, "I have to wait for more evidence." She quickly added, "It's a coronavirus—like the cold virus, like SARS, but it's a different one. It seems it spreads very fast, very contagious. Things are going to get bad, that's what I feel."

"In what way?"

"People are getting sick, some very sick."

"Are you worried about—?"

"That I'll get it? It's possible, but—maybe it's all not real enough yet." She laughed, a forced laugh. "Take me to your moon—there's no virus there. Or maybe there will be. Maybe we'll carry it there. Imagine having a virus in your spacesuit."

"I heard there are more bacteria and viruses in our bodies than human cells."

She said, "That's true. So maybe we are the pathogens in a host we can't...we can't comprehend. They are the host, not us."

He could feel her shaking her head over the phone. "When am I going to see you?" he said.

"You're one who's always on the moon."

"You're the one who's always late at the lab. I have to be back at the simulation early. Tomorrow night?"

"That's good. Unless those inspectors drag out the day again."

"Just make sure they are not suspicious of you."

"Why would they be suspicious of me?"

"A lot of people who work for the government are not too smart. They get suspicious of brilliant people."

"So you still think I'm brilliant?"

"Even more so than when I met you."

She laughed. "Well, I'm glad you're not stupid."

Her echoed her laugh. "Just 'not stupid'?"

"No...and I'm afraid you might be wasting your mind on the moon."

"How is that a waste?"

"Men: they want adventure, don't they?"

He thought a moment. "To be the first—to go."

"But when you get there—what?"

"Who's to know? That's the adventure."

Li dreamed that night of the police officer thrusting the mask at him. He did not put it on right away as he had on the street—so obediently, it appeared—but instead held it in his open palm, and as he did, he noted the most subtle movements in the material of the mask, as if it had some type of pulse. He realized it was the nanomachines of Fan working through the texture of the mask for some purpose he could not know. He slowly put the mask on, felt the pulse of the unseen nanoworld, while the officer was yelling, "What are you waiting for? Go! Go!"

Li moved on, through Wuhan, his face not so much caressed as become the terrain for the continual throb of the nanomachines. He worried that they would move into his flesh. He wanted to take the mask off, but with everyone else masked on the street, he felt it would be unwise to do so. But he became increasingly worried that these machines would literally eat into his flesh. This was still the situation as he boarded the bus that would take him home—as he thought, "I only have a little way to go—"

And he wondered if the masks of the other passengers worked at their faces, too, and they bore it with obedient stoicism.

At that point he awoke in the dark, shaking his head, telling himself, "I'll have to tell this to Fan." Though at the same time he thought he would be embarrassed to tell her. Why, exactly? Dreams can be like this. Surreal, foolish: in which we worry over things that can't happen.

3.

China had had plans for a space program back in the 1960s. The country would join (or not so much join as match) America and the Soviet Union in putting human beings in space. But the cruelties and chaos of Mao's Cultural Revolution wrought havoc throughout any technological prowess China might have produced in that decade. And Mao's assertion that the Russians had slipped into neo-capitalism did not help: through the 1950s the Soviets had been supplying China with missile technology. The subsequent Sino-Soviet split ended that.

The Chinese did put a satellite in orbit in 1970 and the next year Project 714 was on the boards: plans for putting men—and women—in space. Nineteen candidates were chosen. But Project 714 was one of the many that did not bear fruit.

Mao died in 1976. His rival and successor, Deng Xiaoping, declared the Cultural Revolution reactionary. It was not until 1986 that another manned program was established: Astronautics Plan 863-2. This would evolve into Project 921 in 1992.

It would not be until the beginning of the next century that China put a human being in space—Yang Liwei, on October 15, 2003, with a fourteen-orbit mission that lasted for 21 and a half hours. In orbit Yang assured his wife with "I feel very good, don't worry," and ate packets of shredded pork, Kung Pao chicken and eight treasure rice (a glutinous rice desert, with lard, sugar and eight kinds of fruits and nuts) and of course sipped Chinese herbal tea. Viewers of state TV saw Yang waving a flag of the People's Republic of China and of the United Nations.

Yang was also supplied with a knife and tent in case he landed off course.

He came down in the grasslands of Inner Mongolia. He emerged from his space craft with bleeding lips; he had had a hard landing.

He received the title of "Space Hero" and would have an asteroid named after him—as well as a fossilized extinct bird, *Dalingheornis liweii.*

In 2007 the unmanned *Chang'e 1* orbited the moon, as did *Chang'e 2* in 2010. *Chang'e 3* (2013) and *Chang'e 4* (2019) landed on the moon with a robotic rover.

In 2018, China put *Queqiao* in orbit 65,000 kilometers past the moon, in a position to receive and send messages from the moon's far side and Earth. *Queqiao* means, literally, Magpie Bridge—after the Chinese folk tale of cowherd boy and weaver girl. Their love was not allowed and so they were banished to opposite sides of the heavenly river—the Milky Way. The cowherd is the star Altair and weaver girl is Vega. But once a year, on the seventh day of the seventh lunar month, they can meet on a bridge of magpies that spans the Milky Way. The earliest version of this tale goes back 2,600 years.

After *Chang'e 4* landed on the moon, it sent the *Yutu-2* rover across the immediate vicinity of the lunar surface. Yutu means "Jade Rabbit." This rover was modeled after the *Yutu* rover of 2013. The rover was expected to last for several years. *Chang'e 4* landed on the moon January 2019; by December it had broken the record for lunar roving, previously held by the Soviet Union's *Lunokhod 1* that had begun exploring the lunar surface November 1970 and had lasted for eleven months.

Zhen Li, one of China's possible voyagers to the realm of Chang'e, awoke feeling heavy and stiff. He was a young, athletic man—he had participated in the past October's international military competitions that had been held in Wuhan—and he was not used to waking to a body that seemed difficult. It was a different feeling than the almost welcome feeling of over exertion in one's muscles after a day of particularly strenuous effort. With a long exhalation and sigh he recalled his odd dreams and attributed the sluggishness of his body to the strangeness his imagination had suffered during the night.

He was about to close his apartment door behind him when he remembered his mask. He retrieved it with annoyance and distaste. If it was not uncommon to see many different types of people wearing these medical masks, people who were feeling the discomforts of air pollution, people who were sick and thought it right-minded not to spread it to others, and people who did not want to breathe in any malaise others carried, Li had never been one to wear a mask. He probably could not have explained why. But he had the instinct he should put on this newly given mask before getting on the elevator.

He was right. There were three other people in the elevator, a middleaged man, an obvious businessman type, and a mother and her son, who looked about nine or ten. The businessman wore a mask, a dark blue one; the woman wore a mask of light blue; the boy did not have a mask. And the man was tactfully admonishing the mother: "He should not go out without the mask."

She gestured, embarrassed. "He takes it off. He took it off three times." She waved a light grey mask in her hand. "I'm going to have a policeman tell him."

The boy looked up at his mother and the man, smiling. But it was a smile that didn't hide a bit of worry. He wasn't sure if his rebellion could still exist without harm being done to him once he was brought outside his building into the world.

Li was annoyed with both the man and woman; he felt he understood the boy's rebellion and dilemma.

Li and the others from the elevator exited the building one after the other—Li was deliberately last. The businessman quickly crossed the street. The mother and child went down the block, and it seemed the mother was successfully forcing the mask on her son.

Well, for all their rebellion, children fear to stand out. Everyone on the street was masked. *What happened to this world, while I was training to be on the moon?* Li asked himself. This mysterious, new, unnamed virus did not seem—at least yet—a real threat to him.

Again, his bus was packed with masked faces.

The curious thing, thought Li, that even though he was masked, he felt exposed, apart, standing out from the rest of the masked crowd. He didn't really understand why. He did not like to brood on psychological ambiguities, especially within himself.

The bus stopped at a corner just past a Buddhist temple. Of course, being a frequent rider on this bus, Li well knew its route, knew this temple was there, but he little regarded it or thought about it, save for the few times there were bright robed acolytes outside, as there were today. Being winter they had more on than their robes: jackets or thick sweaters; and all wore pants under their robes. A few had woolen hats on their shaved heads. They seemed engaged in some group activity among themselves, a song or prayer or chant; Li faintly heard some unintelligible babble through the thick bus window.

And each of these Chinese followers of Buddha wore masks. It gave a bizarre aspect to their activity, whatever it was.

As the bus continued on its way, Li turned to look back at the Buddhists. He tried to read something on their faces, something he could comprehend. He could never understand the lure of seeking some peace—enlightenment—in a perspective apart from this world. *Existence is all we've got,* Li would tell himself. It seemed these acolytes sought some delusion, illusion, whatever as an excuse to not face the struggles that all living beings face.

These followers of some ancient sage—did they admit to the rule of the contagion their masks were supposed to thwart? Apparently they acknowledged the enforcement of an edict that had just come down upon Wuhan and its outskirts. Or were the masks, any kind of trapping of this life one and the same, to be shed, wholly disregarded, upon that first step into Nirvana?

Li wryly considered: *How would they act in a spacesuit, exploring the moon? Would they recognize the goddess Chang'e?*

Not that Li, a scientific young man, had much truck with myth, but Chang'e, the moon goddess, did mean something to him in a visceral, irrational way. He was the space navigator who would reach her lands.

On the edge of Wuhan, Li got off the bus at an industrial park. He walked toward an inauspicious three-story building. On one side was a shoe manufacturing company, on the other side a warehouse and retail store for vitamins and herbal supplements.

He entered the building with no problem; it seemed anyone could walk off the street and enter here. Though that was deceptive; by now Li well know the position of the security camera and armed guards (who seemed like harmless government workers) scattered throughout the front of the building.

He did note that everyone he saw wore a medical mask.

It was when he had to take an elevator down to the training floor that Li had to use the first of the security cards before a digital reader. A red light turned to green and Li stepped on the elevator.

He rode the elevator down alone.

When he exited on floor below, he used a second card to enter a corridor. There was no one here either.

He stopped at a door, drew out a third card. Why couldn't there be one card instead of three? It was annoying, but he imagined a three-layered security was fitting here. And there was a discipline involved: to manage three cards instead of one.

The door opened and there were the two guards, Lin and Yang. Well, they weren't exactly guards, but Li thought of them that way. Lin was masked, Yang was not—and they were talking about wearing or not wearing a mask. Lin was saying, "You put yourself in danger and you can infect others." Yang, a bit guiltily, said, "I told you, I just forgot it."

"And no one reminded you all the way here."

"I had a few…looks. Don't forget I walk here. Outside, it's not like on a bus."

The mention of "bus" made Li think of the masked Buddhists for some reason. That image was interrupted by Lin saying, "See Li has a mask."

Yang said, with a little mockery, "Well, the future of the space program depends on following procedure." Then, as if to ameliorate that apparent sarcasm, he said to Li, "You're a man of science; what is going on with this sickness? They say it's a virus."

"That's all I know. But I came out of here yesterday and it was like I *had* been on the moon—for a while. Everyone had a mask—"

Yang: "Well, your last session was a long one. You should be at home on the moon by now."

"Almost, almost." Li smiled, but it was a wan smile; there was something about this pair that always made him a little uncomfortable. And there was a question about them he had been brooding over—and he suddenly asked it.

"What I don't understand…the two of you are always here when I come in…but when I come out, you're not here. No one is."

Ling shrugged. "That's the way it's ordered."

"But I understand you making sure it's me when I come here— security." (He didn't say: *Who else would have those three cards?*) He went on: "But what if…I don't come out? Something happens to me?"

Ling laughed. "What could happen on the moon?"

"I'm serious," Li insisted.

Yang said quietly, as if gently telling a child something obvious but not quite pleasant, "Li, you are watched."

"Watched?"

"You're surprised? How could you think you're not watched? You walk on the street—a camera at every corner. You think at a facility like this—?"

Li was suddenly realizing how stupid he'd been. Of course, his training sessions were being monitored. He knew they were being recorded, but watched in real time— Yes, it was understandable, but it was an intrusion on what had become a very personal endeavor.

He sighed, "So if all this watching—why are you two here at all?"

Both shrugged in unison, masked Lin, unmasked Yang, who said, "Maybe they just need witnesses that you entered."

Witnesses…as if to an accident—or a crime. "I would think coming out would be just as important."

Lin spread his arms. "Perhaps it isn't. We can't know everything."

Li was frustrated and disturbed. Everyone masked, including himself, that conversation with Fan, this absurd situation with Lin and Yang…. He entered the simulation room, returning to the world of Chang'e.

The *Yutu-2* rover was exploring the Von Kármán crater, in the 1,100-mile wide South-Pole Aitken basin. The surface was as fine as sand on Earth, a layer of regolith that the rover's radar determined extended for 40 meters, though farther down in the regolith were boulders, and below that alternating layers of coarser particles with fine.

Regolith could be gravel, broken rocks, and sand that lies atop bedrock. On Earth, soil, the organic living earth that supports life, is the top layer of regolith. The moon has no organic soil; it's all regolith above bedrock—with the exception of steep crater walls, and some old lava channels that expose bedrock.

It had been a surprise not to detect any basalt, which would have been left at the bottom of the crater after a meteor impact. It was surmised that the layers of regolith had formed over basalt by further impacts, which would have also broken up any boulders.

And the fact that regolith went down 40 meters overturned previous findings and hypotheses. The Apollo missions had drilled down about three meters. It was generally thought the lunar regolith did not exceed ten to twenty meters.

But perhaps, for as yet unknown causes, the far side of the moon was very different.

Li's experience in the simulation room was both meditative and focused. But today it took him a bit longer to join his attentions to his mission. He was brooding over this aspect of being "watched." He subtly—or so he thought—glanced this way and that, then chided himself that he was expecting to see cameras as obvious as those on the street.

And then chided himself that he should be bothered—for he was—that his presence was being monitored. Anyone living in early 21st century China should regard surveillance as matter of fact.

Absently, as if to distract himself, he increased the magnification of the view the rover presented. The lunar surface flowed before his face as if he were inches from it. He breathed slowly; the surface of regolith became a soothing abstract.

Then Li was pulled out of his malaise by what the rover was seeing.

There seemed...he strained to see...almost, yes, it seemed, structures, something that had that aspect, in this magnified area of the regolith: as if seeing buildings from a height. Not that he believed he was seeing actual buildings, but some odd pattern in this portion of the surface—

It was gone. *Yutu-2* had passed onward.

Li was able to replay what he had just seen, and had to replay it again and again until he once more saw the pattern: like a city or town seen from the air. He was able to increase magnification a little more, but not much; the impression of buildings was still there—and yet, somehow, it was elusive.

He stared and stared. The image of what this seemed was like something that was, well, mocking. He rubbed his eyes. He almost looked about again, at the cameras he could not find, but caught himself.

He was able to save that image; he would refer to it later. He returned to the passage of the rover, unmagnified, and spent the rest of his session with what had become common lunar sights.

Before leaving the simulation room, Li was to write a brief report of the session. He made no mention of the tiny "buildings."

Exiting, he passed through the room where Lin and Yang had greeted him. Previously, he had shrugged off the anomaly of their absence; now he felt as if he had been deliberately left alone to…witness something quite odd.

About to step out of the building and exit the lobby that gave no indication of the subterranean link to the Chang'e mission, Li had the thought "they" could well know he'd seen some city-like vision in the regolith—and not reported it. It could be a test.

He shoved that thought away and walked to his bus with its masked passengers. As the bus drew away from the industrial park and toward the suburbs, Li noted, three separate times, drones flying fairly low over a street. These mechanical flying insects—Li always thought of them as huge mechanical bugs—made Li uncomfortable today. Like cameras in the city, drones overhead were not an unusual part of everyday life, though they were certainly not as prevalent as cameras.

As twilight came on and the bus drew near that vague border of metropolis and suburb where Li's apartment complex stood, a bit incongruously, like a vestige of the city, Li noted an old woman emerge from her house slowly, and with the stiffness of age and begin to walk. Abruptly, out of the dimming air, a drone swooped right above her, glinting in the streetlights. Even through the thick window of the bus Li could hear a loud, very loud command from the drone—about wearing a mask. The woman looked up, utterly frightened. She seemed to Li old enough to have been a child at the beginning of Mao's peasant revolution—and now the 21st century was berating her from above. She threw a hand up over the lower half of her face, as if she could hide what she lacked, how she had "defied" the orders of the authorities, while the drone continued its unfeeling, harsh command, coming down even lower and following after the woman as she ran as fast as could, half stumbling, back to her house, and threw herself inside.

This all happened in the space of seconds. Li was shocked at the helplessness of the old woman and the inhuman insistence of the drone—which hovered just above the woman's house, shooting out some final declaration before it darted away, to seek out another transgressor. He and others on the bus turned their heads to take in this final scene as the bus went on. Many passengers shook their masked heads, whether indicating the woman had been foolish to not wear a mask, or showing disapproval of the drone (which of course represented the authorities), Li could not know.

When he got off the bus, he looked up more than once as he walked to his apartment complex, expecting some condemning drone, even though he was masked. –Because he felt some rebellion in himself that was more intentional than the old woman's, one which could be "read" from the height of a drone?

4.

Li called Fan. "It would be nice to go some place to eat—"

"Are you serious? You really think that's safe now?"

"You didn't let me finish. It would nice, I said, that's all. After being on the moon all the time, it would be nice to—"

"Do something on Earth?"

"Yes. But the with the city like this…." He told Fan about the old lady and the drone.

"That's awful. She could have had a heart attack. I'll come over, bring some food. I'll see if Cheng wants to come."

"Why do you want—?"

"I think you'll be interested in what he has to say."

Chang Cheng was a colleague of Fan's at the virology lab. He was about ten years older than Li and Fan and highly esteemed in his field. Li, being a normal young man, would have been more than a little jealous at Fan's friendship with this not unhandsome and successful man, were it not for the fact that Chang was gay—a fact that was not exactly widely known. Although modern China had decriminalized homosexuality activity in 1997 and as of 2001 no longer considered it a mental defect, Chinese society still had an uneasy relationship with its homosexual brethren.

Waiting for Fan and Chang to arrive, Li watched the news. Apparently, the government was revising—at least admitting to—the number of cases of the virus. Until recently the numbers officials had released were very low, while it was obvious the authorities were worried about something much more serious. The newly released figures were much larger than only the day before, indicating they had been climbing all along.

Fan and Cheng arrived while Li watched further televised scenes of a Wuhan peopled with masked bodies. After giving a slight nod in greeting, Cheng said immediately, "Tomorrow they are going to lock down Wuhan, everything around it."

But Cheng was like that, more polite than friendly, and abrupt with facts. He was a tall man, with the thickest hair, even for an Asian, and a manner that usually conveyed that the only thing essential between him and others was an exchange in which everything discussed was accurate, without the normal human exaggeration or dissembling.

Li: "Tomorrow? You know that for sure?"

"No one comes in and out of the city. No buses, cars, trains, flights. All highways closed. Everyone to stay in their houses, with exceptions of certain government workers."

"Stay in their houses? People have to come out for food."

"I'm not sure how that is going to work."

If Li had questioned how people would get food, what he was really thinking was how this would affect his lunar training. He gave Fan a look that might have meant: *Say something to make this more clear.*

Fan was a petite dynamo, with a face that many had said—Li included—was of a perfect beauty. To that Fan had remarked to Li, "Almost like people mean it's beautiful, but not sexy." Li would disagree with that, but Po Fan lamented the lot of the complimented. She wore lipsticks of odd but intriguing colors and kept her hair in what she told Li was a retro shag style from America—copied from an old movie of the 1970s. "Jane Fonda, in *Klute.*"

"A half century ago," Li had once said, "and from another country, and I'm supposed to know that connection?" It wasn't surprising that Li had no knowledge of old American movies or actresses, though it was an ignorance Fan suffered with amusement, as if he lacked a normal perception that others could easily access. She loved movies, especially from America, but from other countries, too. She had recently dragged Li to *Parasite*, a South Korean film that was being shown almost clandestinely in Wuhan. Li, son of hardworking rice farmers, had understood the struggles of the poor family in the film, but did not quite approve of the way in which they had duped the rich family to secure positions with the latter. Li had some integral sense of rightness, of being truthful (in a way not all akin to Cheng's notion of truth). Fan had affectionately mocked Li's "good Chinese" turpitude. "You are the perfect universe space worker. You approach the stars with the correct moral attitude. What did you tell me taikonauts are supposed to be? 'Rigorous, prudent, meticulous and exacting.' That's definitely you."

Li had smiled at that, but had been slightly offended. Those four qualities were certainly admirable, but Fan has pronounced them with a bit of mockery. "So it's bad to be like that?"

Fan had laughed: "The rest of us can't be like you, so we're jealous."

"It's accepted knowledge at the lab," said Fan stressing the lockdown was imminent.

"How long do they think—?"

Cheng said, "This is too new to know."

As she had promised, Fan had brought some food and went into Li's small kitchen to prepare it. Fan was an exceptional cook. Cheng had once chided her that she had paralleled her accomplishments as a scientist with fulfilling a traditional woman's role. She had joked, "I tried to resist that stereotype, but really didn't want to."

While Fan had chided Li that he had little interest in anything other than the space program. Li could admit to this, but did not see it as a fault. He was focused on a goal; he could enjoy other things in life, but ultimately they were passing distractions, even if sometimes pleasing. "So, am I a passing distraction?" Fan had said. But not like other young woman might have said it, coyly, insisting her man give a satisfactory answer. In fact, she had said it like a question Cheng might have asked: simply desiring a correct answer.

Li had smiled: "Not just a distraction, and not passing." Then had added, "But I might be passing to you. What if I wind up on that moon base—for a while?"

"And when is this base going to be?"

"It's planned in the next decade."

"In the 2030s..." She seemed to muse over that year as if a future more an alternate reality than one definitely ahead. Then had said, "We won't be young then."

"We'll hardly be old." Being a taikonaut, Li kept himself to a vigorous physical regimen. He was strong, and could not imagine a decrease in that strength, or an ageing that decreased that strength.

Fan dismissed that future with the pronouncement of a sage: "Let's see what the next year is, not the next decade." That was fine with Li— who actually wondered, as much as he was drawn to going to other worlds...would he really want to stay on them for long periods? He had more the spirit of an adventurer than a colonizer: to make a fantastic journey, then return to share its marvels.

While Fan cooked, Li related to Cheng the story of the old woman and the drone. Apparently, this had really struck him to the core. Cheng nodded with an interior expression, as if he drew something from Li's witnessing that Li himself did not divine. He glanced repeatedly at the news on the TV, which Li was now ignoring. From this too Cheng seemed to be drawing something only he could discern.

There was no further talk of the situation in Wuhan at the beginning of the meal, with both men remarking how much they liked what Fan had prepared. She was vegan and repeatedly surprised Li at how much he liked anything she cooked. If Chinese cuisine easily lent itself to a vegan path, Li liked his meat and fish. But he missed neither in Fan's meals.

Though eventually matters at hand were discussed. Fan said, "Cheng's been at the lab since—?" She looked to Cheng.

Cheng thought a moment. "Almost ten years—2011."

"You told me something very interesting, what, two days ago?"

Cheng made a gesture that—uncharacteristically—seemed to say the "when" did not matter.

Fan: "Tell him."

Cheng had apparently been brought here to impart something to Li, but he pursed his lips, as if undecided. Again, a bit out of character.

Then he said: "It's basically established—well, believed—that this is a zoonotic virus: something that jumped from an animal to human. We got the genome of the virus very quickly—by January 10. Zhang Yongzhen at Fudan University in Shanghai used an American gene sequencing machine from Illumina. So only two months since the first cases, yes, it seems November now, the first case, and we have the genome.

"These types of viruses don't necessarily hurt the original host, but in jumping to another host can be very...virulent."

Li: "That's why they closed the wet market. So it did come from there."

The so-called wet market was where live animals were sold for food. Some were slaughtered right after a customer picked them out; others the customers took home, birds and dogs or whatever in cages, then slaughtered later that day, or the next...

Cheng said, "It *seems* this is a bat virus. But the bat in question—I've heard from those who investigated the market and no such bat has been sold there for some time. And this bat's natural environment is 900 kilometers from here."

Li: "But you're saying it is from a bat."

Perhaps neither of the men noted Fan purse her lips at the mention of the market, and a stern look cross her eyes. She had once said to Cheng, "That market makes me shudder."

There was a pause. Fan looked at Cheng as if she fully expected him to say something she knew would make her uncomfortable, but which he had to speak of, nonetheless.

Cheng gave an odd nod, as if to affirming to himself the accuracy of what he was about to impart. "Last year, the American National Institute for Allergy and Infectious Diseases funded work at the lab—and elsewhere—for what's called gain of function research on bat coronavirus. This was a program that had followed another similar program. Many cold viruses are coronaviruses; so is SARS. This new virus is related to SARS, but different. We had that SARS outbreak in 2003—"

Li: "I was a kid. I remember my parents talking about it. They were saying it wouldn't come out to where we were, in the country. You said, 'gain of function.' What's that?"

"Exploring, well, to be exact, manipulating viruses to study their potential for infecting humans, increasing that potential. This is not done with the intent of infecting people, but as a protection, in case—"

Fan: "In case the virus got out of the lab?"

Cheng said, "There is no indication of that—yet. But if you just look at it…there is a possibility."

"What do you think?" Li asked.

Cheng shrugged. "The work was done here. The outbreak is here. Too much connection."

The three were quiet a moment. Li said to Cheng, "You just said there were two programs."

"America's National Institute of Health started a program in 2014. It was an overall view, a sort of survey of bat coronaviruses. That ended last year, when the second program, or I guess you could say, the second phrase was started. There was an extension of cataloguing, but also the gain of function work. It's still going on. To predict spillover potential—let me read it to you."

Cheng took a folded paper from his pocket. "It's the proposal for the program. 'We will use S protein sequence data, infectious clone technology, in vitro and in vivo infection experiments and analysis of receptor binding to test the hypothesis that divergence thresholds in S protein sequences predict spillover potential.'"

Li said, "I'm guessing that 'spillover potential' means going from animal to human."

"Yes. The S protein is the spike-like proteins the coronavirus has to latch onto the cell. SARS, and I think this version, too, attaches to the ACE2 receptor in the lungs—and other organs: heart, gut, kidney, nose. The nose is likely how the virus gets in first."

Fan said, "Explain exactly what ACE2 is."

"Before I explain that: S proteins have two segments, S1 and S2. Both have to attach to the cell. ACE2 is angiotensin converting enzyme-2. The ACE2 receptors in the body breaks apart two forms of the protein angiotensin to keep blood pressure stable. Whether with SARS or this virus, there is the question of blocking the ACE2 receptors, but that regulates blood pressure. Actually, we still don't have a perfect understanding of ACE2."

Li asked, "So how are these patients being treated now?"

"Antivirals, oxygen, ventilators, corticosteroids, hydroxychloroquine, interferons, convalescent plasma infusions—with not too much success. It seems the patient gets better or doesn't regardless of what we do. And traditional Chinese medicines." Cheng abruptly smiled. "My mother was very…adept at this. Very modern woman, but she felt she knew better than doctors. She told me that Qi is the energy that maintains the whole body. There is good Qi and bad Qi. There is an old herbal medicine, Yupingfeng San, for lung ailments. It has astragalus, fangfeng and atratylodes. Astragalus improves lung function. There are studies that definitely show Yupinfeng Sang helps the immune system."

Li: "Is that really effective for the virus?"

"Some esteemed colleagues swear by it."

Li felt there was a hint of mockery in Cheng's "esteemed." He asked, "What do you think?"

"We don't have full data on it yet. But I have seen my mother...help many people. There is certainly a science to those old medicines."

"What does your father think of that—the old medicines?"

"He thought some were good, others not. He was a language teacher—English, French—"

Fan said, "I thought your parents were in finance."

"For a long time, now. And doing very well. But when I was younger, my father with his languages—sometimes I thought there was something too...Western about him. Now I think we have to know everything from all over the world. We're the oldest culture, but too much in our history we thought the rest of the world barbarians."

Fan said, "I think India is the oldest culture."

Cheng laughed, but it almost seemed a rebuke. "Well, each of have our timelines."

Li found something quaint about Cheng's manner, something formal. He had the feeling it would be hard to get close to something essential in this man.

So he sought to get something more personal from Cheng. "How did you mother learn those medicines?"

Cheng sighed and looked genuinely sad. "Her parents were intellectuals driven out to the farms during Mao's cultural revolution. They were both in the medical field. I guess they turned to the medicine of the country. They passed it on to her."

Fan shook her head. "Imagine a country trying to suppress its intelligent class."

Cheng: "It seems governments need to exercise some sort of cruel power to feel in charge."

Li said, "Are we being cruel to people who are sick now?"

Cheng actually looked puzzled. Li told him about the driver who was dragged away. Cheng said, "I understand there are quarantine centers. Nothing ominous."

Fan said, "Just taken off the street like that to who knows where? And you know all those rumors of organ harvesting."

"No one is going to harvest organs from sick people."

Fan looked shocked. "You approve of taking organs from healthy people?"

"I didn't say that. I was just..." He seemed frustrated. He tried to smile. "Just being factual."

Fan said to Li, as if in mock aside, "He prides himself on being rational."

Li said, "I think I was even more disturbed about the old woman the drone chased back to her house because she didn't have a mask."

"That's not a good image," Fan conceded. "But I guess that's for her safety."

Cheng said, "I don't think the population in the West would put up with what is happening, going to happen in China. I know there will complete lockdown of Wuhan, maybe all of Hubei in a day or so. They were talking about it at the lab."

Li: "What does that mean, though?"

Cheng shrugged. "Severe restrictions in movement. To what extent—"

Fan said, "But with the Spring Festival starting, that's going to be difficult."

The Chinese Spring Festival, or Chinese New Year (based on a lunar calendar) is a seven day holiday. Fireworks are set off the instant the new year arrives, the color red (auspicious) is everywhere, and there is the traditional family reunion dinner. Each year is marked by an animal sign corresponding to the Chinese zodiac: 2020 (4718 Chinese traditional calendar) would be the Year of the Rat. Li had noted little red rat toys and dolls and the stores.

Fan said, "I read that the Year of the Rat will be very good for those who take advantage of circumstances that come their way this year."

With a wan smile Cheng said, "This year is not beginning with good circumstances." He abruptly added, "I'm very worried about a friend of mine…. Dr. Sun. He told me just a few days ago the city, the health officials in Hubei are trying to play down the number of cases, the danger of this situation. The last two days I can't reach him."

Fan and Li were silent. They knew that sometimes people who rocked the boat of government disappeared in China. Or at least their voices did.

Looking at the expression of worry on Cheng's face, Li wondered if Cheng was "involved" with this doctor. It was perhaps a typical hetero response: if a gay man talks about another man, there must be some connection more than social.

Fan offered, "He might be…busy."

Cheng shrugged. He seemed to backdrop whatever he communicated tonight with an ambivalence that left Li unsatisfied, as if something cryptic needed to be deciphered, though he realized there seemed so much uncertainty in the air. He asked, "What are symptoms of this virus?"

Cheng said, "Like a flu. It could be not so serious, or it can become pneumonia. That's the worse stage; it attacks the lungs."

Li: "The Qi."

Cheng: "You don't believe in that?"

"I don't say I don't, I don't say I do."

Fan said, "I definitely do. The flaw in so much of modern medicine, is it can only regard what it sees. There are things the eye doesn't see. In China we recognized that. I hope we don't become too 'modern' to disregard it."

Li made a sort of grunting noise, then reminded Fan about how much he had been impressed with her lecture the first time he had ever seen her, as a prelude to saying, "You work with things the eye can't see. At least I can go outside and look up at the moon."

Fan said to Cheng, "He wants to be the first Chinese on the moon."

"You've told me. That's a great goal." Cheng looked at Li as if only now assessing if that aspiration were realistic.

Li wondered just what Fan had told Cheng about him. He seldom thought about what other people thought of him, but with Fan it was different.

Talk of the moon and the unseen recalled to Li what he had beheld at his last training session. So, he told Fan and Cheng, "This section, this small section, looked like the smallest buildings—as if a city had been miniaturized. It made me think: remember that conversation we had about people living on atoms—that could be worlds, universes to them?"

Cheng gave him a look that might have said: Is the would-be taikonaut seeing space illusions? Li was a little annoyed by that look. Fan laughed and said, "What you probably saw was an optical illusion. You've seen drawings in which things are shaded so they look like they are coming out of the page at you. I bet these were minute depressions with slight shadows and it looked to you like structures raised up."

Li said, "It was just so…regular. Artificial."

He felt Cheng watching him, waiting for Li to accept this rational answer. A little flustered and embarrassed (*I never should have brought this up*—), he just said, "Well, it could be."

Cheng said, "Isn't all of that recorded? You can just look through your last session."

"But often access seems…sporadic. That's the only way to describe it. I would have to specifically ask."

Cheng smiled, in a way that seemed genuinely friendly. "And you can't say you think you saw a tiny city on the moon—"

Li gave a resigned sigh. "I'll just see if the rover covers that area again." But nonetheless he harbored something unsatisfied.

In a while Li, Fan and Cheng drifted away from all this and watched a local program on the coming festivities for the New Year. Li abruptly remarked: "That old superstition—events that happen on the new year set the...tone for the year. So whatever the predictions for the Year of the Rat, if you're in a hospital—or the whole city gets locked down—"

Cheng said flatly, "This is only the beginning of this." He had a far-off inner look, apparently musing on something he didn't want to articulate.

Fan took Cheng home. Before leaving, Cheng shook Li's hand. He had firm grip, stronger than Li would have suspected. Fan and Li kissed; Li didn't like Cheng watching.

Fan and Cheng put on their masks and left. Li sat alone, not watching the TV as it droned on about the New Year, the Year of the Rat. If restrictions were put on Wuhan, how would that affect his training?

He turned off all the lights in his apartment and went to a window where he sometimes looked at the moon when it was prominent in the sky. Then remembered this would not be one of those nights. With the end of the last month of the year there was just a sliver of the moon left, and that would not be rising in the east until a little before dawn. The time of the new moon, or as he always said to himself, of no moon, was just ahead: the new year, 4718.

It is believed the Chinese calendar was invented in 2637 B.C.E. under the reign of Emperor Huangdi. It is based on the phases of the moon. A year has twelve months, but a leap year has thirteen months. A normal year has 353, 354, or 355 days; a leap year has 383, 384, or 385 days.

The date of the new moon—when there is no moon in the sky—is the first day of the month, unlike the Hebrew and Islamic calendars, which begin their months when the crescent of the new moon is visible. Leap years happen when there are thirteen new moons between the eleventh month of one year and the eleventh month of the next; a leap month is inserted in that year.

The calendar works on sixty-year cycles. Each year is assigned a name based on two factors: one is called Celestial Stem, the second is Terrestrial Branch, with the names of the animals of the zodiac. The current sixty-year cycle began February 2, 1984.

After the revolution of 1911, the western Gregorian calendar, first brought to China by the Jesuits in 1582 (when it was first used in Europe) was generally adopted in China.

Being so drawn by the celestial, Li had always been pleased (if not exactly the right word) that the ancient Chinese calendar had been based on the moon. In senior middle school (the equivalent of high school in the U.S.), Li had written a paper on ancient calendars. Fan's mention of India being a very old civilization made him recall that the Hindu calendar was also based on sixty-year cycles. It is believed this is derived from five revolutions of Jupiter around the sun and the cycle of the Nakshatras, or lunar mansion in Hindu astrology. A lunar mansion or lunar house or lunar station is a segment of the ecliptic through which the moon passes in its orbit around Earth.

Li, looking out that window that showed no moon, in fact no stars at all this evening, wondered if he really would walk on the moon that had directed time for some many ages for so many cultures on Earth.

His sleep was unsettled. He dreamt Fan was walking through the lab—which Li had never been in—saying to herself, "I have to find Li's buildings on the moon." She looked through electron microscopes that showed nothing Li could recognize (he was seeing everything through her eyes): they were abstract nanoworlds. Finally, in a room that was entirely bare, she was calling Li on her iPhone; it kept ringing and ringing but Li did not answer—while at the same time he was home, hearing his own phone ring, but could not find it. The dream segued, as dreams do, to Li in his lunar simulation room, looking at the banal surface of the regolith, while suddenly someone was banging on the door, yelling that Li had a phone call. He turned away from this vision of the moon and shouted, "I can't now! I'm looking at the moon!"

He awoke in the dark, literally shaking his head. He had the impulse to call Fan, but he didn't want to disturb her in the middle of the night. He wished she had not come over with Cheng; she might have stayed over. He liked those mornings, when he awoke with her, her smile an extension of her sleeping body, and feeling his own smile as she veritably cooed to him, "Are you sure you're going to come back from the moon to see me again?"

Chapter Two: Po Fan

5.

Shortly into the ride as Fan drove Cheng home, she asked him, "So what do you think of my taikonaut?"

Cheng gave her a fleeting smile that was gone in an instant. "He is very focused."

"So you could see that."

"I felt that, yes."

"That's too true. It's the moon all the way with him. It's like he had one course since a kid and that's where he's going."

"Well, when you give yourself an unusual direction and stay on it—"

Fan paused as she made a turn, then said, "Sometimes I feel it's almost as if...he sweeps the human aside."

"You're very self directed, too."

"Am I? Sometimes I think I'm moving in my field at the direction of others, not myself."

"Well, where do you want to go?"

Fan hesitated in reply. "It's not as much where I want to go as where I think the science needs to go."

"Isn't that the same thing?"

"To apply nanotech where it has never been applied."

"You're not doing that now? With viruses?"

"It's been done. Though it's still new enough."

"Very new. You may be doing something with this virus."

"That would be interesting. That would be...a challenge." After a pause, she said, "It's spreading, isn't it?"

Cheng nodded. "It's pretty established that it's person to person contagion."

"Isn't that all coronaviruses?"

"Yes, but when it's a new virus— But it seems it's following that.

Though it can be devastating—in some cases, anyway."

They were quiet. Fan said to him, "Are you afraid of getting it?"

"I think I would be if I worked in a hospital."

"Apparently it finds people and *puts* them in the hospital."

Cheng gave a soft laugh. "I guess we're the scientists who watch the new phenomena attack others—as if we look on from above."

Fan slowed down to make another turn. At the corner, a man in a ragged coat was slumped against a building. A police officer was apparently trying to hand him a mask. The man crunched it into a ball, stuck an arm out as if to push the officer away. The officer stepped back and spoke into a walkie-talkie.

Cheng shook his head. "They will be taking him away."

Fan drove on. Cheng looked back at the officer and the crouched man, adding, "Things will be getting more strict. Very strict."

Fan said nothing. She was disturbed at this brief, somber scene they'd witnessed. The apparently homeless man was metaphor for the population that would be helpless before the virus as well as the authorities.

Nearing Cheng's home, they were quiet. Finally, he said, "I always meant to ask you: What is a young woman like you doing driving a car like this?"

Fan had a Qiantu K50. It was not only an expensive car, but Fan was among the minority (if a sizable minority to be sure) to own a car in China. China is the biggest producer of cars in the world. There were about 240 million cars in China, certainly no small number, but when you take the country's population of 1,435,000 and compare that ratio to the 279 million cars in the United States with its 330 million people, it was apparent car ownership was still not the normal state of affairs for the average Chinese citizen. Li did not own a car; neither did Cheng. Of course, being in or around the hub of a city such a Wuhan, there was plenty of public transportation available.

Fan said, "I told you, my father's an officer in the military. There are certain perks. Connections where you can get things less expensive."

"The new ruling class."

"I thought the money class is the ruling class. The financiers."

"Maybe they are both the ruling class. My family is...the money class. My parents were a little disappointed I became a scientist. My father was a teacher when he was young, then, I don't know how, he went into finance. He always said, 'The blood of China is money.'"

"And my father says China's strength is the military."

At the end of the second decade of the 21st century, China had 2,035,000 personnel in the People's Liberation Army, with 510,000 in its reserves, appreciably ahead of India, with 1,444,500 active forces, and the U.S. with 1,359,450.

Fan went on, "I had a discussion like this with Li. He told me his parents—they were rice farmers—that China's strength is its people, its workers."

Cheng laughed. "We see our own world as the strength of the country."

After a moment Fan said, "I thought we were almost to your house."

"Almost. About two kilometers."

"Sometimes I forget how big Wuhan is."

Wuhan covers 8,494 square kilometers. In comparison New York City is 790 square kilometers. If there was plenty of public transportation, to get from the city's outskirts to its center, or from one end to another, was a journey.

It is a city whose population has boomed over the past half century. In 1970 there were two million people in Wuhan; in 2020 there were 11 million. Much of that increase had been through an influx of rural people coming to taste and own a piece of urban life. Which often is not easy. Rural workers, with a dream of owning a house or apartment in the city, might often buy in Wuhan—and China's other major cities—but remain working in distant factories or farms, creating the all too common phenomenon of "empty home."

Cheng had purchased one of these empty homes, after a rural family had given up trying to arrange their life and finances to move to Wuhan. Li had once asked him if he had felt "bad about taking advantage of someone's difficulties." Cheng had bought the house for a very good price. He had replied, "I relieved them of what had become a burden."

Fan's response had been: "I guess that's probably true." She'd said that with a smile, as if excusing a friend from something from which she might not have excused another.

After dropping Cheng off, Fan had a half hour drive to her apartment, halfway back across the city. She considered calling Li, saying she would come back to his apartment, but that would be a long trip, and it was late; and she was distracted from that thought by what she increasingly felt was a sense of eeriness from the streets of Wuhan. While driving and talking with Cheng, the only interruption that indicated the immediate nature of the city had been the briefly seen vignette of the police officer and the apparently homeless man. Alone now, Fan definitely felt something large and ominous growing in the city.

There weren't many people about; the handful who were, were masked. There was definitely a sense of...expectancy. Certainly an uneasy one. As if the few bodies out here on the streets had to accomplish some movement before any movement was curtailed.

Or was it just simply a fear of this new contagion that had grown more threatening as the New Year approached? Fan thought: what was more threatening, the government or the disease?

Her father, who had reached a high rank in the army had once told her, "It's not bad for people to fear the government a little."

Fan, a teenager at the time, had said, "Wouldn't it better to respect the government than fear it?"

He had laughed. "You're a new generation. When I was your age, we were still pulling a new country together out of a very old one. Yes, respect; but also a little fear. It's a balance. Sometimes you need a little more of one than the other."

Her father had been among the troops the government had called out to quell the protests at Tiananmen Square. The press for greater freedom in post-Mao China, perhaps mirroring the increasing anti-communist movement in eastern Europe, resulted in a seven month period of martial law (May 20, 1989-January 10, 1990) and most notably the June 4 massacre in which perhaps 10,000 demonstrators, many of them students, had been killed; the true number could never be determined, Even bystanders had been killed. A day after the massacre, a lone man stood in front of a tank, blocking its passage—in fact the first in a line of eighteen tanks—and, if briefly stopped the advance of a military that could crush thousands, if not one single human body. But the crew of that tank stopped for that man, and he spoke with them, apparently about the concerns and nature of his protest. Then other demonstrators, fearing the eventually violent outcome, pushed the man out of the street. "Tank Man" left his moment in history as anonymously as he had begun it.

Fan's father had been among the crew in that tank.

"I wasn't the one who talked to him, but I heard all of the conversation. I did understand his...perspective. But change does not happen as an eruption."

Fan had said, "Mao didn't disrupt China? The revolutions in America and France—?"

Her father had smiled at her innocence. "Fan, things have grown too large, too large...."

It was too vague an answer for the precocious Fan. Her father would not repeat the remark after the collapse of communist regimes in eastern Europe as the year drew on, and Gorbachev's abolition of the Soviet Union two years later.

Fan was in her mother's womb during the June 4 massacre and was born early the following year. "That was the year everyone was worried about Saddam Hussein invading countries in the Middle East," her father had remarked to her more than once. Fan felt she had some visceral connection to the upheaval of nations.

Because of her father's military career, his family had lived in several places. Fan had seen China's great cities, and its outback. It was natural that as a child she did not like these "disruptions"; at the same time, Fan felt she had gained a perspective of her country other youth did not have.

In regard to Tiananmen Square: to this day China will break into anyone's internet connection who receives or sends the words "June 4th Tiananmen Square massacre." Users are given the message: "According to the relevant law and regulations, the search results cannot be displayed."

This censorship of the past has had the effect the government intends. Thirty years after the protests and the massacre, only fifteen percent of Beijing university students could recognize the "Tank Man" photo.

And thirty years after that upsetting time, Tiananmen Square was stage for the stupendous 70th Anniversary of the People's Republic of China, October 1, 2019. In a celebration that enlisted thousands of people in a 90-minute display of fireworks, dancers and speakers. It began with "Ode to the Red Flag," with 3,000 performers carrying light panels that showed the national flag, and children saluting the flag that soldiers sternly guarded.

Fan attended with her parents.

The performance of the dragon dancers lived up to expectations. Fan had always liked this old Chinese tradition, a practice that had begun in the Han Dynasty 1,800 years ago. Dragon dancing could involve single men in a dragon costume, or two men, or a line of people, each holding the long part of a dragon's body in an undulating, choreographed movements. In Chinese culture the dragon was a symbol of good fortune, long life and wisdom and dispelling bad spirits. Since a child, Fan had loved this "fantasy creature," as she had called it when a little older. Her parents would give her little dragon toys and she filled her room with them. She even still had a few of them, in a corner of her bedroom.

Her father, three decades older than the soldier who had been in the tank that "Tank Man" had stayed in 1989, was a high ranking officer in the military by the time of that 70th anniversary celebration. His status had granted his family a wonderful vantage point to view the ceremonies.

And it was a marvelous ceremony—as Fan's mother often repeated throughout. And as much as Fan had appreciated the dragon dancers, she found the fireworks spectacular, especially the ones that looked like red flowers with spikey petals. Months later she would connect those spikey petals to the spike-like proteins of the new virus.

Fan went to the rear of her apartment and opened a window. She called out for her cat, Mystery. She had let him out in the morning just before leaving for the lab.

Fan's apartment building had four floors; Fan was on the second floor. In the back of the building was a courtyard bordered by other similar buildings. Fan's building had a lattice work of ivy that rose up from the edge of the courtyard, past her floor.

And soon, there was Mystery below, a black cat, mewing. For an instant a light from somewhere caught the opal of his imploring eyes.

Smiling, Fan called down. "Come on, come on."

Mystery was a feral cat that Fan had taken in just before the previous winter, so she knew he could take care of himself on the streets and the alleyways of his immediate world, but she was always a little relieved to see him at the end of the day. Unless it was raining, snowing or extremely cold, he wanted to be outside. He had no problem weathering a normal winter day.

Mystery mewed again, and began climbing up the ivy. Fan smiled. His presence pleased her so much. In a few moments he had reached the windowsill and she gathered him into her arms. His body protested a moment, then accepted her embrace. He had the loudest purr of any cat she had ever known.

Fan fed him and watched him eat. She said, as she had before, "I wonder where you go." Mystery appeared to pay no attention to her. Fan added, "And I wonder where you came from." Mystery continued eating.

That was why Fan had named him Mystery. Prior to last winter, Fan had been feeding him in the courtyard. There was a back exit from the building that accessed the courtyard. One day in summer Fan had noted the black cat, not full grown, moving about the grasses and weeds. She had called to him. He disappeared. She saw him the next day. He looked in good condition; she did not know if he was someone's cat, wandering around, or a stray. This time he came toward her a bit, mewed, then darted off when she tried to get closer.

The next day she bought some cat food on the way home from work, and presented him (she knew he'd be there) with it on a paper plate along with a small bowl of water. She backed away and the cat came to the food and ate hungrily. "If he's got a home he's getting a good second dinner," Fan thought.

Fan brought food to him late every day and gradually could stand a little closer to him as he ate. She was leaning more to the fact that he had no home. She decided he definitely did not when one day in autumn she came home late from the lab and in the earlier darkness of the season she heard him mewing from the back of the building. She opened the window, looked down. He looked up at her plaintively, or scolding. He was plainly saying, "You're late. I'm hungry."

This continued through autumn. By now, Fan could stand right by him as he ate. One day he let her pet him for a second or two, then, eventually, for a little longer. By the borderline of autumn and winter he would actually follow Fan around the courtyard, sometimes mewing, and with a very loud purr. But he would not let her pick him up.

She realized she was going to have to take him in. Fan had no idea if this cat had any shelter anywhere at all. She began to put the food out by a cat carrier, then at the edge of the carrier, then further inside. He got used to eating in the carrier.

In mid December, a bad snowstorm was forecast. The evening before the storm the cat was mewing in the courtyard even before Fan got there. He seemed so hungry Fan did not even put down put down the carrier in the usual place, but just put it down in front of her as soon as she got outside. The food was in the carrier, he went in; she waited a few moments, then shut the carrier. He made a lot of annoyed noises as Fan went back up to her apartment.

Inside, he sniffed around cautiously, suspiciously. Fan wondered if he had ever been inside at all. As he settled—or more accurately positioned himself—in a corner of one room, she placed a tray of cat litter there and said, "You're a mystery, you know." And so that was his name.

It was not surprising that on this night, as this new pathogen threatened Wuhan, that it entered her dreaming.

Fan tried to fall asleep but sleep eluded her for a while. She wondered if this new virus would create a great epidemic. But that was perhaps just a surface concern upon something a lot deeper.

Of course, Fan had been drawn to what she liked to call the depth of things. Nanotechnology, forming nanomaterials, nanomachines, working on the level of literal molecules, in the realms of a billionth of a meter, appealed to her sense of plunging into the very heart of matter.

Viruses are certainly denizens of the nanoworld, so small they fall in between the wavelengths of visible light, and can be "seen" only with an electron microscope; they reside on the border or the animate and inanimate. They can be as small as 20 nanometers (billionths of a meter) to 300 nanometers. With genetic material surrounded by a protection coat, they come "alive" only when they latch onto and penetrate a living cell (which is many times larger than the virus), take over the cell's DNA to produce other viruses, until the cell bursts with innumerable new viruses which in turn will infect other cells and begin the process anew. Thus all viral infections increase their infestation exponentially

Fan had come to the Wuhan Institute of Virology because more and more she had focused her work on the melding of viruses and nanotechnology. Her university thesis was "The Future of Viral Nanotech," expounding on the increasingly applied concept of "viruses" being used as a platform to synthesize the creation of new nanomaterials.

Fan had her own surreal dream that night. She was at the lab, watching a huge screen on which an electron microscope image of a coronavirus was displayed. For years there had been extensive studies at the lab on coronaviruses, which included the common cold and SARS. The purpose of these studies was to assess how viruses that were found in animals might "spillover" into the human population.

The coronavirus is round shaped, with spike-like protein projections—the S protein—which it uses to latch onto a cell.

In Fan's dream the virus particles became three dimensional, seeming to come out at her from the screen. She instinctively stepped back. But the viruses were not coming for her. As the viruses became three dimensional, the streets of Wuhan, its nighttime streets, were suddenly a backdrop, and the viruses twisted and moved and began to roll down those dark streets, like tumbleweeds in the old American westerns Fan had seen.

The streets were empty, except for a lone man crouched against a building, his head buried against his knees. It was the man she and Cheng had seen tonight. As the tumbleweed viruses approached him, he raised his head, as if he had sensed or heard them. To Fan it was all soundless.

The man wore a mask. The covering across his mouth and nose seemed to emphasize the expression in his eyes—of incredulity and horror. He began to rise, but before he stood up his body was buffeted by the viruses. He was covered with them. All that could be seen of him were flailing arms. Then Fan did hear a cry, of a policeman rushing toward the scene. He began striking at the viruses with a club, while shouting "Do you have your mask? Do you have your mask?"

At that point Fan awoke from this dream whose meaning was all too obvious. Cheng had said this apparently new virus was related to SARS and it could become an epidemic. The streets of Wuhan and its citizens were threatened, and perhaps, at least for the moment, all the authorities could offer was the flimsy protection of a mask.

6.

That morning Fan drove cautiously through streets that seemed tensed for desertion. The masked pedestrians appeared ready for some type of attack, or flight. She had taken her mask with her (how could she forget a mask after that dream?), but did not wear it while in the car. What would be the need of that? It was on the seat beside her.

She encountered a traffic stop like the one Li had described. Despite herself, a pang of fear shot through her.

An officer and a woman in protective medical gear were outside her window. Simultaneously the officer and the woman pointed at the mask on the seat. Fan put it on, stepped outside the car to have her temperature taken. In the instant the instrument swept across her forehead, Fan had the thought, *At least it can't read my mind.* She was a little taken aback at thinking that. She certainly wasn't having any subversive thoughts.

Fan's temperature was normal. She got back in the car and kept her mask on as she drove away. In her rear view mirror she watched another driver emerge to have her temperature taken: another young woman, like Fan. As this scene receded in the mirror, Fan felt herself watching a retroactive diminution of what she had just gone through. Fan had to make a turn, thus losing sight of the scene, before she could witness the outcome of the traffic stop.

At the lab, masks had always been used, along with a lot of protective gear; as much to protect the staff there from possible contagion by the many viruses studied, as to keep the researchers from "infecting" the viruses. Fan often thought it a bit surreal, how these very disparate worlds of human and virus were both connected to one another, yet were held at bay—at least here in the lab.

Speaking further of masks: Fan was currently using tobacco mosaic virus, a rod-shaped virus, as substrate for both organic and inorganic nanomaterials to make fabrics, in particular medical masks. To put it in a crude, but not inaccurate way, Fan used the rod-like virus as nano-knitting needles to weaves her microfabrics.

"It figures," she had once joked to Cheng, "woman's work. I've brought stereotypes into nanotechnology."

Tobacco mosaic virus or TMV, is an RNA virus, and was literally the first virus to be discovered. In the late 1800s scientists were homing in on a disease that could infect plants, much like a bacterial infection. Yet there was evidence this agent was non-bacterial; the infected sap of these plants could pass through filters that caught all the known bacterial agents. And this sap could still infect other plants. It was not until the advent of the electron microscope that TMV could be "seen." Those first images were in 1939.

TMV was also the first virus to be crystallized; and remained infectious even after crystallization. Rosalind Franklin, who worked on the discovery of DNA with Watson and Crick, had hypothesized that the virus rod was hollow and its RNA single stranded. She would prove correct. Franklin never got credit for her work until decades later.

TMV infects not just tobacco plants but nine different plant families—tomatoes, peppers, cucumbers, ornamental flowers, etc. Research in TMV help set down much of the foundation of virology.

If the lab outwardly seemed normal today, there was, as on the streets of Wuhan, a definite unease. All Fan could see of many of her coworkers were their eyes—which were often behind thick plastic googles—but the flashes of expression she saw there were enough. She wondered if she betrayed similar ocular emotions.

Around midday one of the administrative heads led a group of four men about the lab. Fan knew these men were outsiders, some type of officials. "They're looking for a leak," she thought. She knew the talk was that the virus had either come from a live animal, possibly from the "wet" market, or the lab. She inwardly shrugged: Maybe both, in a way. A virus that had been researched at the lab had been carried out by an employee, brought to the market. She didn't believe—though it was possible, not likely, but possible—that a bat or bats that had been used as experimental animals at the lab had actually been sold to the market. Though what would be the motive for that? Hardly money. Just some evil, diabolical intent? She had heard of people deliberately poisoning food supplies and medicine. There was no explanation, no rationale for such evil.

And if these men, so shrouded in protective gear to which they were obviously unaccustomed, were looking for the source of such evil, or at the very least trying to assess such possibilities, there was certainly something ominous about their presence. Fan knew these types could inform—or get others to inform—on those that would be deemed the guilty party or parties.

She had had more than a few discussions with her father, who always defended whatever China did. "Why, when something bad happens, does the government always look for someone to punish?"

"When something bad happens, someone usually caused it."

"But don't accidents happen—that are no one's fault?"

"But it's people who allow the conditions for an accident to eventually happen."

The conversations would go on like that. Fan, always frustrated, would conclude with something like. "You just can't see what I'm saying because you don't want to. The government can be very wrong—"

He would neither deny nor agree, but said, "What would we all be without the government?"

Yes, the government made this wonderful and modern scientific lab that I'm working in, Fan thought—with American funds backing a good deal of bat virus research, but…if something dangerous comes out of our research….

Fan explained to one of the officials what she was doing. He was a small man whose solemn eyes seemed relieved Fan was engaged in nothing that could be linked to the virus that was threatening Wuhan and the entire province of Hubei. In fact he was pleased when he understood that Fan's research could result in more superior protective equipment for medical personnel.

"We may need that," he said, nodding, almost happily it seemed.

Somehow that seemed almost ominous to Fan. At any rate, as the official and his colleagues went on to other departments, other researchers, she found herself thinking, *I guess I'm lucky—for now.* Then she asked herself if she expected to be unlucky in the near future.

There was a difficult future coming, a very near future, she intuited, whose details few could discern.

During her lunch break Fan looked out upon the trees that were before one section of the lab. Sometimes she would go outside during this time, but on this mild midwinter day, she sensed she would feel too exposed, a lone lab worker outside a facility that many people felt might be the cause of this mysterious and sudden outbreak.

Instead, Fan sought out Cheng in the cafeteria. She told him about the official visit. He said, "They haven't come for me yet. But I'm sure they will."

"Well, you worked with the bat lady. They'll want to know all about it."

The "bat lady" was Fan's off hand name for Shi Zhengli, the lab's leading virologist (perhaps the leading virologist in China) who had literally entered countless caves throughout the country to study bats and their viruses, which could possibly infect humans.

Cheng said, "She told me recently that she brought three strains of bat coronavirus into the lab. One has a 96 percent similarity to SARS. One has about 80 percent similarity to this new virus. She made that 80 percent seem a distant match, but that doesn't seem so distant to me."

Fan said quietly, "Did this new virus come from the lab?"

"You ask as if you think I know."

"You're in a better position to know than I am."

"Possibly...but I really do not know. Didn't we have this discussion last night at your boyfriend's apartment?"

Fan had the sense that "your boyfriend's apartment" veiled almost a disapproval Cheng harbored against Fan's involvement with Li. But maybe she was reading more into this than was actually there.

"We talked about it, but—"

"But not to the point of interrogation?"

"Cheng, are you angry with me for some reason?"

He replied stiffly at first, then smiled and said "No." That "No" seemed to break some floodgate of a mood whose source Fan could not discern.

Cheng said, "I'm just—this situation in the city—the suspicion here—"

"Have you heard from your friend—the doctor?"

"No." (This was a different "No.") "Something isn't right."

Fan said gently, "Are you and—what's his name again?"

"Sun Bao. If you're asking are we...involved: no."

Fan half nodded to herself, as if settling a question. She caught Cheng noticing this. "Just asking," she said.

"Nothing wrong with that."

Fan gave a placating smile. "We're all feeling tense. Driving to work today—I got caught in one of those traffic stops where they take your temperature. It gave me a long moment of...concern."

"You were going to say 'fear'?"

"Maybe fear, yes. When Li told me about that yesterday—taking that man—where do they take them?"

"You won't find that on the news yet—official quarantine zones."

"Zones?"

"Places. You can't get out for two weeks or so. Then if you're not sick, you can go. Well, that's what I heard."

"What if this virus really gets out of control?"

"I think it's at that point now."

"And it could get worse?"

After a pause, Cheng said, "Yes." After another pause, he added, "Shi has said that the viruses she's brought back are just the tip of the iceberg, that the viruses are out there in the world whether we like it or not."

"Out there in labs or—?"

"In nature. We have to go find them, study them before they find us."

"Maybe we brought the virus from nature into here and then out there again. Someone could have brought it to the market."

"There are none of those bats there, I understand."

"Well, it's good it's closed."

"Even if the virus spread from there in the beginning, it was out in Wuhan well before they closed it."

"That market is the reason I'm vegan. I only went there once, and the horror of it— Not that it should really be more horrible than those big businesses that kill a thousand animals an hour; it was that that mix of wild, terrified animals in their cages, cages on top of each other, the fish in barrels, the animals slaughtered so casually at the customer's wish; and, just as bad, customers walking away with live animals that would be killed minutes before dinner. Just all those bodies, those eyes—"

She was quiet. She looked at Cheng as if he suddenly had to, in this moment, see with her eyes, and feel with her feelings.

Cheng said, "I understand." But did he say this more because he was simply at a loss at how to respond than any real sympathy?

"Cheng—and this is not just directed at you—if everyone understood, everyone wouldn't do that."

"Perhaps we accept that for some to live, some have to die."

"You mean for the few to live, many have to die. This country has a billion, four hundred million people; how many animals do you think we have to kill to feed that?"

"I don't know."

"I don't know either—I don't want to do that horrible math." She added, "Maybe the virus feels the same way; it feeds on us; it multiplies through us."

"You're saying the virus is sentient?"

"Not the way we think of sentience. But we have a prejudice with that. You know when they talk about finding other intelligent life in space? What if there is intelligent life we can't recognize because it's so different from not only what we think of as intelligence, but we think of as life? I read an old science fiction book from America about a situation on a spaceship where what was thought the host of the virus was really the disease and the virus was the host."

Cheng smiled widely. "A matter of perspective. You like a lot of American things, don't you?"

"Maybe I do. The movies, I know."

"And what in the American psyche intrigues you?"

"You think I'm intrigued?"

"You must be."

"Well, but it's cliché: more freedom for the person than the state?"

Cheng said, "Maybe that's an illusion the rest of the world believes too much; maybe an illusion for the Americans, too. If people think they are free, but they're not, as long as they think that way, they're easier to control than if they don't feel free but are afraid of the state."

"So do we have freedom here?"

"Only so much. Only so much. Enough to have a decent life. Unless—"

"The government makes you disappear."

"Is that what you think happened to Dr, Sun?" Cheng said, with seeming challenge, but which hardly disguised concern.

"I'm sorry Cheng, but that's the simplest explanation."

Returning to the nano-borderland of virus and human materials, Fan had the thought if she could work a weave with this new virus and nanofibers, she could create a sort of vaccine cloth: a virus cloak that could protect against infection from the virus. Of course, this was a brief instant of fantasy: immunity had to be created *within* the body; nonetheless she felt herself just short of grasping some revelation about the nature of this new virus and a possible protection from it.

That afternoon Fan saw the probing officials two more times passing through different parts of the lab. None gave evidence they recognized her. With all her protective gear, it was easy for her identity to be subsumed among the many researchers they surely had spoken to, in their search (it was presumed) for the possibility that the new virus had its origins at the lab and or had escaped from the lab.

She had a short conversation with Cheng at the end of the day. He said, "They told me they had monitored U.S. intelligence reports that had monitored the lab—I was surprised they were telling me that; reports that suggested the lab had experienced some 'unusual event' in October. The intelligence they monitored indicated a marked decrease in cell phone activity in certain areas of the lab, indicating, well, to them, the possibility of some...disruption."

"They're telling you information they got from spying on America spying on us?"

"That's what it seems."

"I didn't notice anything unusual in October. Did you?"

"No. But neither of us know everything that goes on in this place. And that's what I told those men. But they pressed me as if I should know." He looked as if he were wondering what to say aloud; what he did say, after a pause: "They are looking for someone to blame. And the worse it gets the more they will look—and find someone. The government never looks for innocence."

Fan recalled one of those conversations—debates?—with her father, and him saying, "The most important thing for the government is results." He had said this with enthusiastic pride. Fan had taken this as just another slogan of his continued pride in his country. Now that remark meant something else to her. If the government were looking for someone to blame…a lab virologist like Cheng would be a perfect candidate.

Though she did not voice her fears to her colleague. Cheng returned to his work, Fan to hers.

She was leery of leaving the lab at the end of the day. She sensed that events in the outside world would be accelerating. Sometimes she considered her time at her work, absorbed in her nano universe, a day-to-day vision the rest of the world was ignorant of, similar to Li's lunar training: removed from the everyday to a plane of existence it was hard to convey to others. It became a personal realm—and, in some way, a sort of sanctuary.

Removing her lab gear sometimes felt as if removing a protective skin, leaving her exposed. She felt that all the more today.

The grounds of the lab were quiet. Fan sensed this was the proverbial calm before the storm. Whether rightly or wrongly, the Wuhan Institute of Virology was the center of what appeared to be a new epidemic.

And for the first time Fan wondered if the new virus would spread throughout China and then to other countries. Could she really be at the epicenter of something that virulent?

Contrary to her expectations, the highways and streets she drove along returning home did not seem different than in the morning—at least visually. There seemed no increase (or decrease) in masked pedestrians, traffic stops, but the general sense of tension seemed palpably stronger, of a populace and authority getting ready for a very difficult time.

She noted a traffic stop far ahead of her and turned out of her way to avoid it. What if she had developed a slight fever during the day? One's temperature was higher at the end of the day than in the morning. What was the cut off temperature at which one would be removed to an official quarantine center?

She arrived at her apartment without being kidnapped by the government. She wanted to call Li, but he had told her he had a longer than usual training session today. She had joked with him before, about him not getting cell phone reception on the moon. She considered that she did not even know the location of Li's lunar simulation center; he had told her at the beginning he was not allowed to reveal it to anyone; she had not pressed a lover's prerogative. Until now she had not really given that another thought, now she worried that if some general catastrophe ensued, the only place she knew of to find Li was at his apartment; if he was "on the moon" he might as well be literally on the moon as far as contacting him was concerned.

The news she watched that night would give no hint of calamity—but again, there was the sense of it throughout. A stern middleaged woman informed viewers that officials in Hubei were moving "swiftly and professionally to contain an outbreak of a new type of pneumonia."

The Fan reflected that "pneumonia" was a known condition and did not sound so threatening. But just the words "new type" had to add at least an uneasy aspect to the situation. Had that been an unconscious addition by the newscaster or the official announcement subliminally undermining "swiftly and professionally"?

She assuaged her worries with her dinner: natto and rice, bamboo shoots and winter vegetables. Dessert was a doughy sesame seed covered sort of pastry that she often made for herself and which Li particularly liked.

Often, after the break of leaving the lab and having dinner, Fan would review her day's work in her mind, drifting back to her nanoworld. She had a sudden thought about plant and animal viruses. A plant virus never infects an animal (that includes humans) and an animal virus never infects plants. But could a plant virus, like TMV, become a vector for a coronavirus? A vector as in the sense of literally being attached to an animal virus—a carrier, not a host. And could plant viruses be engineered to be a sort of microbiological glue that could "pull" a coronavirus away from human cells? Again, this might be equal fantasy to her "virus cloak" (or mask), but Fan felt herself looking at some horizon to which she wished she could draw closer, a line of vision that was like a destination past a difficult sea.

Chapter Three: Chang Cheng

7.

Cheng wished the inspectors/interrogators would have come to him early in the day; he had to bear the tension of anticipating the searchlight these officials would try to direct upon him in order to affix blame. But blame for a virus? Cheng thought wryly, *I have nothing to do with what nature creates.* He doubted this new coronavirus had been artificially created in the lab—or elsewhere. Though it was possible, he had to concede, this virus may have been under study at Wuhan and had somehow, accidentally gotten past the grounds of the lab.

The four men had confronted (that seemed a fitting word) Cheng in a small room, their protective head gear pushed back, revealing disparate faces directed on Cheng, who had first kept on his surgical mask, though he too had pushed back his protective hood. Perhaps he had left the mask on to hide the expression of his mouth as he spoke his words carefully, guardedly.

"We understand you are very familiar with bat coronaviruses." said a short, heavy man, who had a resonating voice that made him seem larger.

Another said, "Basically it's your field."

Cheng nodded, uttered a brief assent as a third man asked, "You have worked extensively with Shi Zhengli, we understand."

Cheng guardedly, replied. "I have been working with Shi Zhengli for many years."

"And she has been doing this for years before that."

"Yes, she has. I would go out to the bat caves with her. We would catch the bats—"

"Are they hard to catch?"

Cheng thought that question and the previous irrelevant. But perhaps, like lawyers in a courtroom, these idle-seeming questions had a purpose to entrap him. He sighed and answered, "Before night we would put a net across the opening of a cave where there were bats. When it got dark the bats would try to go out and feed, get trapped in the net. We'd take blood and saliva samples, fecal swabs."

The fourth man, who hadn't spoken before, shook his head with a laugh and said, "I wouldn't like to handle those things."

Cheng said, "They're harmless, small. After the samples we'd let them go. In the morning we'd go back to the cave, collect urine and fecal samples."

"And this virus comes from these bats?" It was the fourth man again, who had changed his tone from an almost puerile dislike of bats to a question that sounded as if it required an admission of guilt or innocence.

"It seems. It seems." Cheng wanted to sound ambivalent. But it was at this point he took off his mask. Perhaps he dared these men to challenge him now. He would relate his perspective truthfully.

"When Shi Zhengli first did this, she was trying to discover the origins of SARS. It was some time before they found…evidence. Another lab—which one I don't know—had come up with a way to test for SARS antibodies, a test that had been used with people. It worked with the bats. Her research team found three bats that had SARS antibodies. Eventually we found that the presence of the virus itself in the bats was not long lasting, but the antibodies were.

"I went with Shi to many bat caves. Many were in mountains. A lot of climbing—all over the country. There was one particular cave, Shitou Cave, near Kunming. We studied those bats there for five years. We found hundreds of bat coronaviruses. Most of them harmless, like the bats."

Cheng wondered why he had to emphasize, a second time, the bats were harmless. Was he transferring his own "innocence" to these night creatures?

He went on. "Though there were enough viruses—dozens—that were related to SARS. They infected human lung cells in a petri dish, and caused SARS, or at least SARS-like sickness in mice. Hong Kong researchers had found that wildlife traders in Guangdong had caught SARs from civets—which was the first clue this virus had come from animals. That was what got the search started for coronaviruses that could jump from animal to human. The viruses found in the horseshoe bats were a 97 percent match to the those from the civets.

"There have been other viruses—Hendra virus, Australia, 1994; Nipah virus, Malaysia, 1998, one went from horses to people, the other, pigs to people. But we had found, before SARS, the original carriers had been fruit bats. The other animals were intermediate hosts."

The small, heavyset man said, "Do we need to eliminate these bats?"

So he's an idiot, Cheng thought. He said, "Any time you eliminate a species…it always has a bad—tragic—effect on the entire biology of the ecosystem."

"That is what everyone says now. But if this virus, this new coronavirus is so dangerous…."

There was a pause in the room. Cheng was inclined to shrug, but restrained himself. Another man said, "This cave, with all the virus bats, how far from people, a town?"

Cheng said, "There are villages near enough. It is a very productive area. Oranges, walnuts, berries. In 2015 we collected blood samples from two hundred people in four different villages. Six people, three percent, had antibodies for SARS—or I should say the SARS-like viruses we found in the bats. None of them said they had any SARS-like symptoms or had anything to do with wild animals. Though all said they'd seen bats in their villages.

"These traces weren't uncommon. A few years before that we found six miners in Mojiang Hani Autonomous County had something like pneumonia; two had died. We took samples from that mine for almost a year, I think; we found coronavirus in six different types of bats. Some single bats had many different virus strains."

The fourth man said, "So the miners go sick from those bats."

"No, they didn't. There was a fungus there; that was the cause. But the miner's illness led us to discover the bats with the virus. Though the mine was shut; eventually the miners would have caught the virus."

"And all these viruses you found—are here, in the lab, now?"

Cheng studied this speaker, who had a lean face. Cheng would have called it a hungry face, or at least a face that seemed to need a food it rarely ate.

Cheng nodded. "They're here. All here. Nothing has escaped. We've been very secure. And in fact, when we reviewed the viral samples from the first patients of this virus, none matched the viruses we previously took from the bats. I'm saying 'matched.' It was none of the viruses we had taken. But the new virus was 96 percent similar to one of the viruses we found in the horseshoe bats in that cave in Yunnan. It was 79 percent and 89 percent similar to two other bat virus samples. It was apparent the bats were the source of the virus.

"The supposed source is the market, since these bats are not in this area by hundreds of kilometers. But it seems that 14 of the first 41 cases had nothing to do with the market. I saw a report that five of the first seven cases had nothing to do with the market. To me that means human to human transmission. In fact, a human may have brought it to the market. There have been conflicting reports as to whether bats were being sold there or not."

Cheng added, "The pangolin also harbors coronavirus." (The pangolin has often been called a scaly anteater. They have been illegally hunted for Chinese traditional medicine preparations.) "A number of pangolins taken from illegal traders had lung infections from the virus and died. The virus in pangolins is a close match, but the virus in the bats is closer. *Nature* had an article two years ago that pointed out the bats could be the source of a new epidemic outbreak."

One of them asked, "Why are they called horseshoe bats?"

"Their noses have this fleshly structure—a nose leaf, it's called. It protrudes. Not very pretty. A section of the nose looks like a horseshoe. We're not exactly sure of its purpose, but it probably helps in echolocation. You know, bat radar."

Then it seemed two voices were addressing him at once, or rather overlapping, like a sort of spontaneous duet. "You have become very esteemed in your field, Mr. Chang. Almost as much as your colleague Shi Zhengli." Before Cheng could reply to what he felt not so much a compliment as a threat that the position he had reached in his field could always be tenuously regarded, one of the officials added, "Perhaps in some years you will be her equal." It was a remark in the same vein, Cheng thought.

Then: "So we assume you are involved in what goes on—occurs—here."

"Well, in my department—"

"Of course, we know there are things you do not know."

There was a slightest pause. Were they going to tell him—or make him guess what he could not know?

The heavyset man said, "We are allowed to tell you that we have been monitoring American intelligence that tries to monitor what happens here."

Cheng: "The Americans are spying on us?"

"Of course. They have funded some of the research here—your research—on coronavirus."

Cheng said tightly, "Yes. In the spirit of scientific cooperation, I felt."

"That is always the ideal," the official said unctuously, "but it would be naïve for us to think that is completely the case."

"I don't feel I am naïve."

"We're not accusing you of that. Or of anything."

Until you have something to accuse me with, Cheng thought.

The fourth man (why was Cheng thinking of him that way—because he'd been the last of the four to speak?) said, "What we have learned from, let us say, spying on their spying is interesting—and curious. First there are periods when there is virtually no cell phone traffic in the lab, compared to normal traffic."

Cheng said, "It's a big place. There may have been problems of reception in some areas."

The man nodded. "Always possible. But it seemed too consistently a problem."

"I can only say I didn't have any problems. Or hear anyone speak of…any problems."

"It's fortunate for your department." This was said as if Cheng and his department had escaped some vague perfidy through some ill defined malfeasance.

"And then," the fourth man said, "there were roadblocks, to one of the lab's entrances for a few days in October. What was that about?"

"If I remember…some large equipment was moved in and out. Emergency generators—old ones being removed, being replaced with new generators."

"Did you know that for sure? Or you were told that?"

Cheng paused. "I can't say I know that directly. I didn't inspect what was being moved…."

"So perhaps it might have been something else."

Cheng shrugged. "It's possible. What do you think it was?" So at least he had asked a question of them.

One of the men sighed and said, "We do not speculate. We are trying to gather information."

"I am telling you what I know."

The heavy man smiled a fake smile and said, "We appreciate that."

Cheng pursed his lips. The official took that as a negative reaction and added, "We really do."

"You have to realize," said Cheng, "emergency generators are very important. If we lose power we cannot maintain the proper air pressure to ensure that nothing we are studying here escapes. The air pressure inside is less than the pressure outside. If something escapes—"

"Such as this new virus?"

"Any pathogen. I don't meant escapes from the lab, but accidentally is not properly contained, it cannot get outside, cannot move from lower pressure to higher. The higher pressure outside keeps it inside."

One of them nodded. "So simple and so important."

Another said, "Accidents still happen. The other lab in Wuhan, the Center for Disease Control and Prevention, also studying bats. A researcher there was attacked by bats—and they urinated on him. He had to quarantine himself for two weeks."

The official added, "The market is less than three hundred meters from that lab...and right across the street from the hospital that handled the first cases of the virus."

Cheng had not heard of that incident, but before he could respond, another said, "Were there any times in October and November—or December—that you were not here, days you weren't here on your regular work schedule? Days you might have been unaware—?" He drew out the last word, left it trailing.

"I told you I was not aware of any change, decrease, increase in cell phone usage, I do remember the moving of equipment—not that I really knew what the equipment was."

The heavyset man: "You were asked if there were any absences— illness, vacation, away from the lab for research? Explore any further bat caves?"

Cheng knew he'd been trying to circumvent any question of absence. "I was not here for two days during the International Military

Games. I went to the games." Before he could be asked a further question he said, "A colleague had a friend who was competing."

"Oh. So you showed support."

"Yes."

"I thought perhaps you simply liked to view the athletics."

There was some barely veiled inference here. At least there might be. The state and society in general were not as cruel toward homosexuals as it had been in Cheng's youth, but it was still not accepted as normal. Did these men know of his "condition" (as he had once heard it referred to)? They would put him in the stereotype of the homosexual erotically contemplating the physique of male athletes.

"It was a tremendous spectacle, but I don't normally go to...competitions."

"It was your colleague—and her friend."

"Yes." *Her.* So, they knew. He said, "The extent of my sporting life" (why was he using that odd phase?) "is to sometimes take long bike rides. I think over...science—or to get away from it sometimes." At the same time, he was wondering if he should add—

They did that for him. "Your colleague Po Fan."

"If you know these things you don't need to ask me."

There was a smile in return. "We're not trying to—"

"Toy with me? Intimidate me?"

The foursome seemed surprised at Cheng's sudden challenge. Another man said, "Mr. Cheng we are just seeking information. And sometimes we wish for you to tell us what we might know but aren't sure of."

"And why is this about the games important? I went with Po Fan. Her friend is a taikonaut in training for the lunar missions. He was competing."

"Her friend." It was said with a tone showing they knew this was more than friendship.

Cheng spoke Li's name before they could. "Zhen Li."

"A promising young man. I think he finished third in some competition."

Cheng: "Fourth, unfortunately."

"Well, at least he'll be fit for the moon. The games, October 18 to 27…The first known case of the virus was in the middle of November. So it must have been here in October. The games were here in Wuhan. We have to consider it possible it was brought here by athletes from another country. America? Whether accidentally or on purpose."

"You know I can't help you with that. What would America gain by—?"

The heavyset man: "If you think a moment you'll give yourself the answer to that naïve question." Again, that's naïve."

"Kill a few of us without going to war?"

"You're still being naïve." (Were they trained to speak down to him?) "An epidemic would harm our economy. What does America most want to do—especially with this current president?"

Like many scientists Cheng thought the barbarities of politics and nationalism unfortunate facts of life science had to work through and around. He made a gesture with his hand that was in place of a shrug. He said, "It's a crude way to do it. Unreliable. Any biological agent, a pathogen will not stay within one particular border."

The fourth man asked, "Do you think we have an epidemic? Now?"

"If people are being scolded by drones because they do not have a mask, I think someone thinks it is an epidemic." If Cheng had not seen this happen, he did not doubt the story Li had related.

It seemed that all four of the men nodded, though hardly in harmony. One of them said, "It's almost certain all of Wuhan, all of Hubei will be quarantined—soon."

"How will that affect the lab?" Cheng asked.

"I don't know if anyone can say at this point. You want to keep working, I'm sure."

Another said, "Of course you are needed…with this virus."

Cheng felt that sounded as if he was being ordered to clean up a disaster in which he had some hand. He said, stiffly, "I will always do what I can." He had wanted to make that sound more ironic but failed, he thought.

After his visitors left Cheng could not focus on his work. Factors other than science had thrown him awry.

Both of his parents had accused Cheng in childhood of seeking "the safety of science" as his father had put it, instead of the "real problems of life" (his mother's words) the realm of finance offered—demanded. His mother had been the business manager of a luxury hotel, his father had performed brilliantly in what Cheng had always considered the vague realities of stocks, futures, bonds, and hedge funds.

He had grown up in an atmosphere of wealth, with Korean servants. Perhaps because the everyday trapping of wealth was commonplace to his life, he thought little of them. At any rate, he did not see wealth an end in itself, as his parents seemed to view the matter. He was hungry for knowledge; he excelled in science. In particular, the world of the virus, both potent and beyond the faculty of the human eye, drew him—especially when he learned that viruses are so small they fall in between the wavelengths of light. He began to explore their variety and mystery. He remembered saying to himself, *So we only see them through our instruments—we don't actually physically see them.* In a sense, it was if dealing with the metaphysical

Wavelengths of light range from 400-700 nanometers. Electrons from the outer regions of atoms have a wavelength of one nanometer. As light is focused and magnified in an optical microscope, electromagnetic coils perform a similar function with electrons in an electron microscope, giving the eye an electron micrograph, a sort of photograph or TV image.

So as Cheng's parents lived largely in the largesse of the world, Cheng focused on the unseeable—which, nonetheless, influenced the world so much. As it was doing now.

Not that Cheng's parents discouraged his course. Becoming a brilliant scientist was, of course, something of note. But perhaps they saw their son's course as more an escape than an embrace; a course, as Cheng's mother once intimated, "that suits the way you are."

His parents came to recognize—resignedly—Cheng being gay, and apparently connected it to his "burrowing" (his father's words) into the unseen. If most virologists were surely not gay, in their son's case, the parents saw some sort of metaphorical mirror between that nanoworld and the unseen reason their son had "chosen that way" (his mother's words).

Of course, Cheng's parents were children of the latter half of the 20th century, decades after China had been pushed from old ways toward a modern world superpower.

Through most of Chinese history homosexuality had been generally accepted in society. It was not until the revolution of 1911, and the increasing adaptation of a more western outlook, that gay men and women in China were regarded without favor. Though the rainbow flag is not a common symbol in China—perhaps in part due to the country's own queer population not wanting to be unduly directed by what can be seen as western influence. Thus, even among the marginalized, a xenophobia toward the outsider can be prevalent.

If the same sex life had been decriminalized in 1997 and no longer considered a mental disorder since 2001, that declassification was never officially recognized by the ministry of Health. In 2016, the State Administration of Press, Publication, Radio, Film and Television banned all homosexual material from TV.

But such bans have also been confronted by enormous pushback. On April 3, 2016, one of the country's most popular microblogging platforms, Sina Weibo, declared that all content of violence, pornography and homosexuality would be banned—a policy, the platform said, that was prompted by the Network Cyber Security Law. This declaration was met with a good deal of anger, not just among the gay community but others. A post by someone declaring "I am gay, what about you?" was read 2.4 billion times and shared by three million users in less than three days. On April 16 Weibo reversed itself: it would not ban content related to homosexuality.

China's Network Security Law, which went into effect June 2017, bans pornography but makes no mention of homosexuality.

Cheng was certainly aware of all this, and realized he was—by being what he was—part of a culture that was alternately being more accepted yet still more than somewhat apart from "accepted" society. But the focus of his life, science, and, in particular, virology, made him a "member" of a literal minority that drew more of his psyche than the larger cultural clash between hetero and gay norms. Perhaps there was almost an elitism in his attitude of being apart from the madding crowd, but this was, simply, his nature.

Before leaving the lab that day, Fan stopped by to see Cheng. He was just returning his attention to his work—further DNA sequencing of the new virus; he was in fact a little annoyed that he was being drawn back from his work, a respite from the officials' visit. But as this was Po Fan; he had to give her a smile, albeit a wan one. He related a condensed version of his exchange with the four men. Fan offered to drive him home; Cheng told her he would be staying a while. "We'll talk later," he said, trying to offer her a more friendly smile, returning to the world that fell in between the wavelengths of light.

The winter night had taken hold when Cheng finally left the lab. In fact, he caught the last shuttle that ran from the lab to areas in Wuhan where one could catch a variety of public transportation. There were only several colleagues on the shuttle with him, all masked, as he was.

The shuttle brought him to where he caught a bus. After a short ride he took a railroad train to the suburbs. He usually enjoyed the train ride. He really disliked the subway, closed in and tunnel-like, but the above ground train, in which he could look upon roads and houses as the train sped on, was relaxing, a progress of the familiar that soothed him. Though the visit of the four men stayed with him. He did not like the taste of the government looking over his shoulder.

He looked about at the other passengers, all absorbed in their own thoughts and tensions, all masked. Some looked down at newspapers or their phones. Cheng had the sense, *We are all heading toward something.*

At his stop, those disembarking with him seemed to scatter quickly, as if this evening there was a pressing necessity to reach home as soon as possible.

It was only a ten minute walk to his house. In a moment he, too, was walking quickly, alone now, in the winter evening, also wanting to simply reach home.

Because Cheng had come from a moneyed family, along with the fact that by now he had a decent salary, he had been able to purchase a house, not merely an apartment. It was not a large house, but certainly it was roomy enough for him. It was always a welcome sanctuary, with tall evergreens in front that gave him privacy from the street and bushes along the borders of the property that added further privacy.

Cheng ate some leftovers for dinner, while he studied various as yet unpublished reports about the virus. There was a structural loop in the S (spike) protein that differed from other coronaviruses; perhaps this made it easier for the virus to hook onto and enter a human cell. This was perhaps the reason the virus was so contagious; it was more successful at transmitting itself. The S protein is the largest structure on the virus and it divided into two polypeptides, S1 and S2. S1 consists of a receptor binding domain (RBD) that binds to human receptor ACE2.

A definite surge of tiredness swept through Cheng. He shook his head, moved his focus not to the particular, in this case the new virus, to the general.

A virus floats along the surface of a cell, as if actively seeking a foothold. (Well, who knew the inhuman aspects of viral "intelligence"?) The outer membrane of both virus and cell are composed of lipids and proteins. Lipids are linear molecules of fat and water that are the sole reasons membranes maintain their shape. As fat and water do not mix, lipids are alternating layers of fat and water—bilayers. Viral fusion proteins (in the case of the coronavirus, the S protein spike) insert into the bilayer. Membranes are about half limpid and half protein by weight. Proteins are much heavier than lipids, so to keep this half and half ratio, there has to be many more lipids than proteins. If the virus binds to specific receptor molecules on the cell, that alone does not create entry. The cell and virus would remain simply attached, but the latter could not invade the former unless the fusion proteins disrupt the continuity of the lipid bilayers cell, causing it and the bilayers of the virus of the virus to become one bilayer and create a fusion pore through which the virus enters the cell. At first this fusion pore is very, very minute, in the order of one nanometer, while the virus seeks to insert a hundred nanometers into the cell; so, the pore has to be expanded. It is thought that the energy for pore expansion is much greater than that of the hemifusion of the virus to the cell.

How does one measure the energy of a virus?

The new virus is a retro virus, using RNA to make DNA; usually it's the other way around. It is the viral DNA that is injected into the host cell.

Cheng recalled how intrigued he had been when he had learned—long ago, now—that viruses plainly have a role in remaking the human genome. Retroviruses can move segments of genes from one organism to another; about eight percent of current human DNA is derived from retroviruses.

He leaned back, rubbed his eyes. He envisioned humans being remodeled with the virus from bats. Then he laughed at his mind's-eye image of a black caped Dracula, out of those old American movies Fan liked so much.

What if we owed our intelligence to thousands of years of viral invasion? Cheng smiled to himself. Humans and viruses: a love-hate relationship. For humans it's consciously just hate, but perhaps for our genomes there is an inevitably biological embrace.

The ringing of Cheng's landline broke his roving imagination. It was Dr. Sun's mother.

"Dr. Chang, I hope it's not too late—"

Cheng had no idea of the time. He looked at a clock. It wasn't that late, really; but he was realizing he felt so tired, He sighed, "No, no."

"You sound tired." The woman's voice was one of worry, but she was being polite, considerate.

"I was just going over some work. Any news?"

"That what I wanted to tell you. Although it could be just rumor. Another doctor called me; he said my son was being held in secret quarantine. Do you think that means he will be let out soon?"

"I certainly hope so." But Cheng did not feel as hopeful as he tried to sound. Dr. Sun had been persistent—and loudly so—about the government, at least the government here in Hubei, suppressing the severity of the outbreak, of under reporting the number of cases.

"Have you heard anything?" she asked.

"No, no I haven't. I would've...told you right away." But if he had heard bad news, would he have told her "right away"?

Anyway, the fact no one had seen or heard from Dr. Sun for three days was bad news enough. Cheng spoke some vague assurances—if you could call them assurances: "The government is being very zealous, pulling people off the street, quarantining them, not really caring, it seems to notify families. They care more about keeping order than anything else, but I wouldn't think—"

Though he would "think." As when the topic had come up when talking with Fan and Li, everyone realized that people do disappear in China if the government is "displeased" with them. He wanted to be comforting with Dr. Sun's mother, but didn't think he succeed very well. And he himself was very worried. He had developed a lot of affection for Dr. Sun Bao. In fact, it was an affection that was sexual, too. He was not sure of Dr. Sun's sexual preferences, who appeared to have no apparent attachment at the moment to anyone and had never talked about anything sexual. If Cheng sensed possibilities there, he also realized they could be more based in his own desires than any reality in Dr. Sun.

Cheng had been drawn from his realm of science, the virus and its ways, to this his concern over the disappearance of a man who had confronted the official handling of this specific virus. The world, this outer world, was not pleasant.

He assured the doctor's mother he would call her if there was any news he could impart. It was sad the way she thanked him. Cheng dragged himself (that's exactly how it felt) to bed.

Like Fan and Li, he too dreamed. He was in the lab, surrounded by the four men, who were positioned equidistant from one another, as if they were points on a compass, so that he had to continually turn his head to face each of them as they spoke. It was hard to keep track of what they kept shouting at him, not so much accusations as declarations:

"The lab shut itself down!"

"We must consider you were not at the games!"

"The friends of Dr. Sun may be unfortunate!"

"We're sure what was moved in and out of the lab was not normal equipment!"

Cheng responded to these bursts of words, but even in the dream he could not understand himself. It was as if he were babbling, trying to piece together something important that he was not at the moment capable of uttering coherently. Then, as abruptly as they had shouted these—and other—things at him, the officials left; though it was more as if they had vanished then left. Cheng was alone, but emotionally battered.

The scene shifted. Cheng was walking through the lab, which was empty. His footsteps were uncommonly loud. He found himself in one windowless corridor that was very dim; up ahead was a fluttering of wings. Bats. It took him a moment to realize this—or, rather, admit to it. He braced himself as the sound of wings came toward him; in another instant he felt the rush of light bodies passing over and around him. He was repulsed, then surrendered to it. *They won't hurt me*, he thought.

Then the bats were beyond him, gone. He considered it was night, their feeding time; they were out of the lab, out in the world. He wondered if many, if any had the virus. He did not consider if this contact with them had infected him. He was then on the enclosed walkway that connected two parts of the lab, raised a story above a road below. It was still night. He could see lights only in the distance, far from the lab. *We're finished; it's the end of it*, he thought, but exactly what "it" was, he did not know.

He awoke, a bit shaken by this dreaming, but relieved it was only a dream, not a surreal reality he had been afflicted with. Then in the dark he smiled ironically. Reality was surreal enough at the moment. He gratefully returned to sleep, dreaming no more.

Chapter Four: The Dark Side of the Moon

8.

Zhen Li did not forget his mask when he left in the morning. He did this unconsciously; he was in fact thinking of the moon, not of Earth, not of Wuhan—until he stepped out onto the street, saw the masked, tensed citizens. So he had to think of Earth, as well as the moon; and was anxious that the present situation in Wuhan would affect his training. Fan had talked about a coming lockdown, a citywide quarantine; but surely, he, working on an important government mission, would not be kept from completing it....

He wanted to separate himself from the passengers on his bus, but his eyes kept straying toward them. Many seemed to look ahead, unseeing, communicating an unease equal to Li's. The rest were at their phones. There was one old man reading a newspaper, sometimes his hands shook and the paper fluttered. He heard a man saying to a woman next to him, his wife apparently, "But what is happening now?" She turned to her husband, in a manner both scolding and reassuring, but Li could not hear what she said.

He was distracted by a text from Fan: "People from the government, asking questions."

He texted: "What questions?"

She didn't answer directly. "They seemed to find my work useful."

Li's banal reply: "That's good."

"I'm sure they will be giving the virologists—Cheng—a hard time."

"Yes."

"So you're having a long day?"

"That's the schedule."

"Call when home."

Once more Li entered the plain looking, three-story building in the industrial park, went through the procedure with three security cards and once more was confronted by Lin and Yang. This time, Yang, like Lin, also wore a mask.

"He gave in," said Lin.

Yang said, testily, "The evidence was enough to warrant caution."

But before Li could enter the sanctuary of the lunar simulation, there was something new in the routine. "We're taking your temperature," said Lin.

"Why?" Though this was really a rhetorical question.

Lin aimed the instrument at Li's forehead. "It's…99.1—but that's acceptable."

"What is not acceptable?" Li was worried his temperature was nearly a degree and a half above what was normal for him. His temperature was always around 97.7. (A doctor had joked, "You're the perfect almost normal.") Li had recently read that the long-accepted standard of 98.6 was from a century ago, when lower community health standards left many with chronic minor infections that continually raised the body's temperature. The norm for the 21st century should actually be below 98 degrees.

Yang said, "Anything 99.5 or higher, we have to worry."

"'We'?"

Yang responded, "Us. We have the responsibility to…." He didn't seem to want to finish.

Lin cut in. "You're fine. Just a little above normal. Go in."

In moments Li was once more looking at the comforting, unremarkable surface of the moon. He followed the course of the rover like a man absently sightseeing. He wanted to clear his head of the "outside" world.

Then he recalled the area where he thought he had seen raised, minute buildings, as if he had been looking down on a miniature city.

He wanted to see it again; and he did not want to see it. It would be better if he came to realize that momentarily his imagination—well, let's say the human need for patterns, to put natural formations into an artificial construct—had made him sure of something that wasn't really there. After a few minutes of not seeing the area, he was thankful for not seeing it.

Then it was there again. He sighed. He blinked his eyes. He thought of Fan's explanations: that he had seen natural depressions but through an optical illusion they had appeared raised structures.

He increased magnification. But these "structures" were so small they became blurred—and still looked like blurred structures. He tried to play with the levels of magnification, decreasing it, increasing it slowly, to reach some point at with it would be clear enough and magnified enough to reveal something further about what he was seeing. But he was continually frustrated.

He looked away from the screen, looked up, tilting his head, trying to relax his neck and eyes. He looked back again. He still beheld the enigma. He had talked with Fan about minute beings living on atoms, but this was just a fancy; he really didn't believe that. If only he were actually on the moon, could reach out a hand, touch what he was seeing— But he was here Earth, contemplating a mystery 384,400 kilometers away.

He considered: could this be a test placed before him? To see if he reported it or not? To see if he could resolve what appeared to be impossible? –While at the same time he thought the word "impossible," he was thinking: what if some extraterrestrial race had left a miniature model of a city…for him to discover?

If awed by the wonders of the celestial, Li also considered himself practical. If it was likely that other life forms existed throughout the vast universe, he was hardly convinced of the validity of alien abductions and the like. He could concede there could be some reality, some truth to a small percentage of the innumerable accounts of UFOs that have been reported worldwide since the end of World War II. Though he thought any explanation for that a reality far from the beliefs in gray, bulbous-headed aliens, which to him seemed too much like ridiculous creatures from American science fiction movies of the 1950s that he had once watched with Fan, who seemed contentedly amused by the crude special effects and ridiculous storylines.

Li drew away from the "city," as he was describing it to himself, and roamed about the lunar surface. He would return to this enigma later.

With other would-be taikonauts. Li had attended a lecture at which he had heard some very eccentric stories about humans in space. The professor, a thin, energetic man, had plainly delighted in the tales he related.

"The Chang'e program realizes the mental, emotional and psychological aspects of going into space can be as daunting as the physical. Perhaps even more so."

And so Li heard that in 1984 three Soviets cosmonauts witnessed what they described as "space angels," luminous figures of light that were in view for some time. On the 155th day of their mission on the *Salyut 7* space station, they were surrounded by a mysterious orange light that seemed to them to come from outside the station and permeate right into it. The light was so bright the crew was momentarily blinded. When they regained their sight, they looked outside the portholes to try to see the source of the light. They feared something had exploded outside the station. What they saw was seven angelic-type beings. They communicated to ground control these apparitions had faces and bodies that looked human and which kept pace with the space station for a full ten minutes before vanishing.

The three cosmonauts would not be the only witness to space angels. On day 167 of the mission, they welcomed three other spacefarers, from the *Soyuz T-12* spacecraft. Shortly after their arrival the space station was once more bathed in the bright orange light. Once more cosmonauts peered through portholes and saw the figures. One cosmonaut reported they were the size of an airliner. If the cosmonauts did relate this bizarre occurrence to their superiors, they were ordered not to speak of it. The surreal events did not come out until after the collapse of the Soviet Union.

When discussing this incident with another taikonaut candidate, he told Li of another story he had heard about the Soviet program. An anonymous "Cosmonaut X," had related that on a spacewalk, he and another cosmonaut had experienced telepathic "whisperings." They had been told to return to Earth, that Russia was not ready to go into space. The story goes that the "whisperer" told the cosmonaut things about himself, his past, that no one but he could know.

Of course, an explanation for such events can be that, removed from the usual sensations, the usual grounding of Earth, especially for long periods of time, hallucinations and delusions can occur. Was that happening to Li, after repeated sessions on the moon?

Hardly likely, he thought. He was not going through extended stretches in the simulator. He was constantly returning to Earthly life. Then again, perhaps the continual juxtaposition of the lunar and the Earthly was unhinging his perceptions.

If Li had been enamored of the celestial and had dreamed as a boy of being a universe space worker, at that time the moon seemed a more prosaic destination than Mars. (He would tell his friends he wanted to be the first man on Mars.) The moon was common and close—and Americans had already been there. But by now he was thoroughly fascinated by the moon, which plainly had figured both mythologically (hence the very name of the Chang'e mission) and physically in Earthly life. Everyone knew how the months had been based on the moon, how it affected the tides, but the moon's importance in the life of Earth and its inhabitants was integral beyond the awareness of most people.

The moon is the fifth largest satellite in the solar system. The four larger moons all orbit much bigger planets than Earth: Jupiter's Ganymede, Saturn's Titan, Jupiter's Callisto and Io. The moon is one quarter the size of Earth, so the ratio of moon to planet is by far the greatest in the solar system.

It is this size that affects the way the Earth orbits on its axis, a wobble that changes the tilt of poles slightly through the course of thousands of years. This slight change is not a disruption but a regulation. It is thought that without the moon, the Earth could tilt as much as 85 degrees every million years, resulting in severe climate change, wreaking havoc on evolutionary progress. The equator would be where the poles are and vice versa.

Li tried to quickly go through the video library of the rover's progress. Li put in the coordinates of the "city," but he came up with no previous video of the tiny region. He could request better magnification of the city, though would have to explain why. He could not imagine relating to anyone in the program that he was seeing a tiny city in the vagaries of the lunar regolith.

I might as well tell them the moon is hollow, he thought.

That was a fringe idea that had been kicking around for decades now, a good half century, one which was "disproved" by the general scientific community, but which had a continual life in this millennial era of, well, space angels.

H.G. Wells published *The First Men in the Moon* in 1901, a novel about a hollow moon, but modern science definitely regarded that as fiction well into the 20th century. If most scientists still think this fiction, more than few became puzzled at the data the Space Age had brought into consideration.

Analysis of material from both the American Apollo missions and the earlier Chang'e rover missions, suggest that the moon is much older than previously thought, formed only fifty million years after the formation of the solar system. Originally it was thought that the moon and Earth had formed out of the same accretion disc of matter, but it seems the moon is very different from Earth.

The moon has much more titanium than Earth. Some of the moon rocks the Apollo missions brought back contained as much as ten percent titanium; on Earth the highest percentage of titanium in minerals on Earth has never exceeded one percent. In addition to having an abundance of mica and brass, the moon bears radioactive elements such Uranium-236 and Neptunium, *which are not found naturally on Earth.*

In addition, it was discovered that the moon rocks were magnetized. It had been thought the moon never had a magnetic field. Earth's magnetic field comes from a rotating, electrically conducting liquid iron core, but it was thought the moon did not have a sizable enough core to create such magnetism. Unless this magnetism had been created artificially. The moon is a quarter the size of Earth, but the mass of the moon is only 1.2 percent of Earth, and the volume is only two percent of Earth's. Way off what should be expected.

In 1970, two Soviet astronomers, Michael Vasin and Alexander Shcherbakov, hypothesized that the moon is a space craft created by an extraterrestrial intelligence. (Those Soviets, Li thought: space angels, telepathic alien whispers and the hollow moon.) They published an article in a popular magazine, *Sputnik*: "Is the Moon the Creation of Alien Intelligence?" Vasin and Shcherbakov postulated that the moon had been inhabited by its creators for many years.

Vasin and Shcherbakov pointed to the formation of lunar craters, commonly believed to be created by the continual bombardment of meteors freely striking the moon, which has no atmosphere to prevent so that all but the largest would burn up through friction with air. The moon's craters were mostly too shallow and flat and some even had convex bottoms. While small meteors made depressions like cups, the larger ones went deep enough into the surface to strike an artificial hull underneath.

The Soviet astronomers would have welcomed information that was soon revealed from the Apollo missions—and would have taken it as confirmation of their conjecture: the moon literally rings like a bell. The same year of the article in *Sputnik*, there was an article in *Popular Science* about how the moon reverberated like a bell during moonquakes, both natural and manmade.

Apollo astronauts had placed instruments on the moon that recorded seismic activity from meteors hitting the surface, to explosions that were set on the surface, to the crash landing of rockets. It was found even the sun's heat, thawing the frigid lunar surface as lunar night became day, engendered seismic activity. In some cases, the moon literally rang like a bell for an hour, a quite unexpected phenomenon.

While there are theories about how the moon was created and wound up in a gravitational orbiting harmony with Earth, none has been conclusively proven. The most widely regarded is that the Earth was hit by an object the size of moon, ejecting material into space, that eventually formed the moon. This was also an explanation for the moon's lesser density. The material ripped out of Earth was from the mantle, which is much less dense than its core.

Naturally there are the ancient legends. The Zulus say a hollow moon was placed in the sky by two brothers who had fish-like, scaly skin. The brothers stole it from a fire dragon. The moon was egg-like. They emptied it of its yolk and placed it in the sky, near Earth. Before the moon, the Earth was everywhere covered in a watery mist; the presence of the moon caused all this water to rain down on Earth. The great flood of which so many cultures speak? The scaly brothers of the

Zulus recalled the Sumerian Enki and Enlil, who were depicted in fish-type raiment and who were said to have brought the first civilization to Earth.

Water. Always the beginning of life. Or sign that it once was? It was not until forty years after the Apollo missions that NASA announced there were caches of water in the rocks brought back from the moon. In fact, *Apollo 14* had reported a cloud of water vapor over the lunar surface. At the time NASA had explained that tanks of water the astronauts had brought had ruptured. Though the tanks contained no more than a hundred gallons of water, which did not seem adequate to have created a cloud of water vapor that covered a hundred square miles and lasted for fourteen hours. NASA's analysis of the moon water forty years later showed it had twice the levels of a deuterium isotope as water on Earth. It was postulated there were 600 million tons of water trapped on the moon, a wealth of water seemingly at odds with the lifeless surface that Li surveilled.

Of course the biggest fringe theory at all was that the Americans had never been to the moon in the first place. Li saw this as so illogical, so nonfactual, he could hardly regard this as even open for debate. Once as a student he had—against his better judgement—gotten into an unpleasant argument with one of his peers whose anti-Americanism was suited to the assessment that NASA had pulled a hoax on the whole world in order to say they had bested the Russians to the moon. Li, who was certainly not "an American lover" as his peer accused him of being, respected scientific achievement and abhorred the righteous ignorance that was being spewed at him nonstop. The student said, "What about that picture of the flag, that's being blown by the wind? There's no wind on the moon," Li told him that flag had bent wires running through it to look as if it was windblown. "If they wanted to fake something, do you think they'd be so obvious?"

"So you believe everything they say." Li had been so frustrated.

People believe what they want to believe. He responded that the rocks brought back from the moon, studied by scientists all over the world (who would have to be, absurdly, in on the "hoax") were clearly not of Earthy origin. He went to say that the Americans had left reflectors on the moon that Earthly lasers could bounce off (to more precisely measure Earth-moon distances): additional proof which the other continual shrugged at. (The Soviet unmanned Lunokhod probes also left two reflectors.) Li eventually just broke away from this idiocy, and never again engaged in such puerile confrontations.

Li wondered, this day in the year 2020, if that student, well into adulthood now, still believed no one had been to the moon. He thought to himself, well if America got there first, China will be there next, the first nation in the 21st century to land on another world. –And on the unexplored dark side of the moon.

Now Li was consciously avoiding the region of the minute city. Soon he felt himself going through the motions in his "progress" over the lunar surface. Prior to coming upon the city, he had been fulfilling his training diligently, but the aspect of this anomaly had disrupted his, well, disciplined reason, leading him to recall some wild speculation, from space angels to a hollow moon, a spaceship created by aliens. It would be exciting indeed to discover that this world, which has so woven itself into life on Earth throughout all of remembered history, had an intelligent intent: an interstellar vehicle that had stalled in its travels, its crew now long deceased leaving the largest monument one could conceive.

But the moon was too "perfect" for Earth for this to have just been an incident of Earth being the moon's "last stop." It had often been remarked that it was almost beyond the realm of coincidence that the moon, when seen from Earth, had the same size in the sky as the sun, which made total solar eclipses possible. Well, in a universe of trillions of worlds, a coincidence like that could happen somewhere, but…

Li literally shook his head. He looked at the time: Wuhan Earth time, and lunar time. The new moon of the Spring Festival was beginning, which meant the far side of the moon would be fully illuminated—but Li felt detached from either reckoning. Speaking of artificial worlds: *he* was in one, isolated before the vision of the surface of a moon whose nature had grown more mysterious the more science knew, while being a citizen of a city that was hardly mysterious, but beset by an epidemic.

9.

Li was to begin another stage in his training, to which he looked forward, but which also made him a little anxious. He knew his progress in this would be monitored in real time.

In these first sessions he had replayed the many journeys of the *Yutu-2* rover with the Von Kármán Crater, giving the experience that he had been seeing through the robot eyes of the rover. Now he was to simulate his own journey across a bit of this landscape: as a taikonaut might space walk outside a craft or the space station, Li was to walk across the moon. It would not be that far, but far enough so that the rover would be a small object on the horizon.

And if this was a simulation, if Li would be safe in his special chair in the training room, there would be a realness to it. There would be no other lights on in the room; only the screen that showed a simulacrum of Li in his space suit, the image of himself he desired to be, a lunar traveler of the near future.

This simulacrum did not step out of a landing craft, but was merely *there*, a sort of scientific immaculate conception, alongside the rover. The lunar Li slowly began to move away from it, taking cautious long strides in the moon's light gravity. Part of this exercise was for Li to monitor his movements, so he did not "over jump," as one of his instructors had put it. As he moved forward, in more or less a straight line as he saw it, he turned back now and then to see the rover grow smaller with distance. The moon being one quarter the size of earth, the horizon was proportionately smaller: 4.66 kilometers on Earth, 2.43 kilometers on the moon. –That's if you are standing on a plain. The higher up you are, the farther the horizon extends. Atop Mt. Everest, the horizon is 336 kilometers away!

Li was to continue on, ahead, until the rover was just visible.

The monotony of the landscape made it hard to judge distance and time. There were small, very small craters here and there, and various slight undulations of the lunar surface, as if a surface of sand that had been slightly molded by a long ago wind, a wind that was no more and then had left the surface that way, these millions and millions of years. The nature of this lunar land was alternately soothing and worrisome to Li. Alternately he put himself fully *there*, and then had the displacement that he watched himself from, projected himself from an Earth that was an utterly different world than this lunar realm.

He stopped, turned back. He could barely discern the lunar rover. He was relieved. Had he just gone a bit farther…. He started back, trying to control his long strides even more, trying to suppress his eagerness to get back. This feeling was not to his liking; he saw it as a failing; as, even, a fear. A need to return to the proximity of this landmark of his own world.

Soon he was standing back by the rover. He had the sensation the return journey had been faster than when he had gone forward from the rover. And found that was the case. In a moment his simulacrum, his lunar self, vanished—and that gave him an unpleasant feeling: that he could be so easily disembodied, disposed of… The screen in front of him was filled with a line, not at all a straight line, of his progress. Because he had only turned back to look at the rover now and then as he moved away from it, and because he traveled across a surface that gave few distinct landmarks (and any that might have been called such were unfamiliar to him), his progress had been a sort of spiral, in fact nearly a circle; so when he had stopped and started back, with the rover before him as a steady and constantly seen marker, he had actually been returning from a point that was almost directly "behind" the rover from which he had started. Li recalled learning that a person lost in unfamiliar woods will wander in a circle and eventually come back to the same starting point. This was another failing on his point, he thought, no matter how understandable. He looked on the spiraling path of his progress with chagrin. It defied the focused image he had of himself.

At this point he took a break. He ate his lunch, which in fact Fan had prepared for him. One or two days a week she would bring over her "special culinary feasts," as he liked to call them, put them in his refrigerator, and through the week Li would consume everything she had brought. "Where else are you going to get a nanotech to cook for you? What's going to happen when you're on the moon? Who knows what they'll make you eat there."

Eating her food and thinking of Fan saying that, made Li smile; for a moment he forgot his displacement on the moon, and his none too purposeful path from the rover. He wondered when he did get to the moon (there was no "if" in his mind, only "when,") would the rover still be working? He wanted to stand by it, his real lunar self, looking down upon the marvelous machine (would it be correct to say robot?) that had brought him to more and more of the moon until he would actually be brought its real surface. He would think then of these training sessions, look upon them as the immature beginnings of a journey that had matured into his desired destination.

So, he had really forgotten about the moon only for a moment; the path his simulacrum had taken from the rover and back had really left its mark.

His lunch finished, he resumed the training schedule. His next task was to again walk outward from the rover, but this time to walk past the point when it was out of sight. He knew he had to prepare himself to recognize landmarks, however subtle they may be. Oh, and there would be stars—which he had paid no attention to on his first walk. He could use them as navigation points. Then he remembered why the stars had been no part of his attentions and was embarrassed he had forgotten something so basic.

One of the points the moon hoaxers often bring up is that there should be stars in the photographs that were taken from the moon. The fact that the moon has no atmosphere, which makes the stars we see at night less bright, should make them particularly vivid on the moon.

The previous lunar missions had all been during the long lunar day; but there would be stars for the seeing during those two weeks—except for the fact that just as the brightness of sunlight on Earth prevents us from seeing stars during the day, the brightness of the reflective surface of the moon keeps the eyes from seeing stars. The moon's surface actually isn't that reflective; it has an albedo of twelve, which means it reflects twelve percent of the light that shines on it. But that is enough to make the moon, especially the full moon, so bright in Earth's sky, and that is bright enough to cause one on the surface not be able to see the stars—unless situated under the shade of a huge boulder, letting the eyes adjust to the dimness: then you would see stars. All the photographers taken from the surface of the moon in the era of the moon landings were with cameras using film, not digital cameras. Focal lengths and aperture settings had to be adjusted for the brightness—or reflectivity—of the objects being photographed: the surface of the moon, an astronaut in a spacesuit, etc. Thus the stars are drowned out. There are Apollo photographs of the lunar sky; images just focused on the sky from the moon, images taken for a few seconds (not the less than a second images taken of objects on the surface) which reveal the stars.

Not being able to navigate the lunar surface by the stars in this long lunar day, in this exercise Li would be proceeding from the rover very carefully.

Once more his simulacrum appeared by the rover. This second appearance of "another" self unsettled Li. Before he had merely accepted it, as one would accept an unusual occurrence breaking through the normal round. But this second manifestation of a spacesuited Li (and it was Li; he could focus in close on the helmet, see his own face) gave him an unpleasant feeling that his image could be so freely recreated that he, the "real" Li, was merely a template.

He began to move forward. But wait, he suddenly thought: this should be easy. His footprints should be easily traceable. Footprints remained forever on the moon. Why hadn't he looked down before, when he had been circling the rover instead of heading right back toward it? But when he turned around to look at the footprints he had just left in this thin, grainy surface, there were none. As accurate as this simulation was, it lacked this. He was annoyed; they had forgotten to add this essential bit, this reality. Or was it intentional? Did they want him to journey across the moon solely on his ability to detect landmarks in this moonscape? Was this a rigorous test? Yes. He moved on.

Li of course could end this simulation any time he wanted. But he could not avoid it. He would have to go back to it until he completed it successfully. And would not look good for his candidacy for the moon mission if it took him many tries. He took on the attitude that this was real, that he was indeed on the moon, that his life depended on watching where he was going, memorizing every banal detail of the surface, and finding his way back.

After walking to a point at which he could no longer see the rover, he was to walk on for another five minutes, then turn back.

Then the sudden thought: he did not know how much oxygen was in his suit. He assumed it had to be hours. The Apollo astronauts had enough oxygen to last seven hours. In this simulation Li had no dial outside the suit or inside his helmet to monitor oxygen. Another thing "they" had intentionally forgotten?

Li had trained with spacesuits before. The air in a space suit is 100 percent oxygen, not the twenty percent one breathes on Earth; so, in a very real sense there is more air—for as long as it lasts—inside the suit than in Earth's atmosphere. Before suiting up, a taikonaut has to breathe this pure air for some time to remove nitrogen (which makes up 80 percent of our atmosphere) from the body in order to avoid nitrogen gas bubbles when pressure is reduced, or "the bends."

Li walked on. He tried to memorize small rocks or boulders. He bent down to pick up some rocks, place them in an arrangement that would serve as a return marker, but found his simulacrum's hands could not grasp anything. He blew out an exasperated burst of air. The visor of his helmet momentarily fogged. So *that* they got real. Or, rather, allowed.

The surreal experience of watching himself proceed, focusing on that simulacrum to the point where he felt it himself, that he was within that moving figure with all his senses and purpose, almost became transcendent. He left off his frustrations. When he looked back— frequently enough—at the rover, seeing it shrink in his perspective, it seemed now a marker he did not fear to depart from.

Looking at the scatter of rubble in the crater, and the occasional boulder, he remembered a philosophy professor speaking about our conceptions of life. "We want to meet intelligent life in the universe— or at least many of us do. But why are we so sure we will recognize life *as* life, let alone recognize intelligence? We will be bound by our own biological perceptions, by our virtually innate paradigms." (Li could not know that, almost simultaneously, Fan had mused on this.) The professor continued, "Now a lot of people have said that; that's not original, not profound. I'll add some additional questions. How about the matter of time? Aren't we bound by that? Suppose, say, rocks are alive, but existing on a time scale of millions of years; they move, they express their lives on such a vast time scale that to us they seem still, lifeless. Imagine that their weathering is like our faces, our bodies as we age."

Li had been intrigued. He would have described himself as practical and scientific, but at the same time he was always open to consider the possible, no matter how much it seemed beyond the accepted facts as we knew them. Hadn't all great advances challenged and gone past what had previously been accepted?

It was Li who offered another extension of what the professor had postulated. He said, "So when we mine minerals, break rocks for our uses, we are murdering rock life? We move so fast they can't stop us? They can't even comprehend what is happening to them? They, because of their time scale, can't even see us?"

The professor had laughed a happy laugh. "That's what I like: think things through to the next step. Who knows? Maybe rocks are alive, maybe not. I'm saying our perceptions of life are limited—by our limits."

From that recollection, Li recalled a discussion between Fan and Cheng, about whether viruses are alive or not. Bacteria, fungi, protozoa, plants, insects, animals—all are certainly alive. But a virus, outside a host cell, seems inanimate; within the cell it comes to life.

Fan had said, "If the virus shows life inside the cell, maybe what it is doing outside the cell is like hibernating: waiting for a favorable season."

Like the professor laughing happily at how Li had extrapolated a vision of living rocks, Cheng had chuckled. "Is it that being outside the cell is the virus' winter? You've given seasons a new definition."

"Well, we think of winter as the time hardest for life. When people first existed, they weren't living in places that had winter."

Cheng said, "It's moving into places that had more physical hardship that caused us to develop technology."

"Then why did civilization first develop in very temperate areas? Not too hot, not too cold?"

Cheng laughed again, "I think we're going far afield from viruses."

As Li was going far afield from concentrating on his moon walk. He turned to look back. He could not see the rover. How long had it been out of sight? Had it only been a moment? Or several minutes? He was supposed to walk on for five more minutes after he could no longer see the rover, but now he could not pinpoint that point. The record of this exercise would show that point, but Li, in the midst of it, could not know. Could they, his watchers, know the point when he knew? He decided to walk on for another five minutes. He was tense now, hardly at all transcendent; certainly, he had left reverie and recollection.

He looked at the watch on the wrist of one hand several times as he walked. He considered there should also be a watch configured to lunar time, and for a moment lost himself calculating how that would work. Then he realized he was not paying attention to the detail of the surface. With a sigh he stopped when five minutes, five Earth minutes had passed.

He turned to look back; but was he really looking at the direction he had just passed? He began his return, counting on both memory and luck. If only he could have used the stars.

He was relieved to see a big boulder he had passed a while ago. So he was on the right track to return. In fact, the boulder was so big there was no way he could have missed it. And it was big enough to cast a shadow of utter darkness in the bright lunar day. It was not a round boulder, but more vertical, with one side roughly round, another side diagonally slanted, with an almost flat surface. It was this side where Li crouched in its shade—and waited, as his eyes adjusted from the bright surface to this new darkness. He looked up and did indeed see stars. Apparently the creators of the simulator had supplied stars. Not footprints but stars.

Of course, with just this one vantage point, Li could not assess any accuracy of passage. But enjoyed (not quite the word, but close) crouching in the boulder's shade and looking at these suns beyond the moon. Then he found himself imagining the chill of that dark lunar shade coming through the suit. The daytime temperature on the moon goes up to 260 degrees Fahrenheit (127 Celsius); at night it can go down to minus 280 degrees Fahrenheit (minus 173 Celsius). The boulder's shade would not quite plummet the temperature down to the frigidity of the lunar night, but it was enough of a stark descent. The spacesuit of a Chang'e lunar traveler was constructed to keep its wearer comfortable in both these extremes of temperature; but perhaps there would be some sensation of great cold or heat right outside the wondrous construction of the suit. And Li was imagining there was some sensation of cold in this boulder's shade; and then considered how much he had been drawn into the recreated reality of the simulation.

While he was examining the fact that he was imagining the cold of the shadow to the point of actually feeling it, he noted something on one small portion of the boulder's surface. Li squinted, peered closer, the hard surface of his helmet's visor centimeters from what he now anxiously studied. There was a stream of irregularities on this surface, as if water had worn this surface into stony rivulets eons ago. But his "rivulets" seemed more than that: almost like a sort of writing, or some abstract artwork. Or to another eye perhaps not so abstract.

Not again, he said to himself. The mysterious minute city, and now this…"writing"? Or was it more like a diagram?

He frowned. He looked away from the markings, back to the stars. There were more stars now; the longer he had been in this patch of darkness the more his eyes had adjusted to seeing these suns.

He looked back to the markings. They were still there, of course. *Are they taunting me?*

Maybe it was just like the famous face on Mars: looking like something it wasn't, due to a moment's angle of light and dark.

He reached out a spacesuited hand to touch the markings, forgetting that he had not been able to grasp rocks in this simulation when he had wanted to place them together as a signpost on his lunar walk, But now he could touch the boulder's surface with this thickly gloved hand, material so thick he really could not feel the indentations and rises in the stone, but just that he was touching something.

Oh, so they provided for that.

He gave a very long sigh, for a moment slightly fogging his visor. When that cleared, he tried to memorize what he saw, just as he had sought to memorize the surface he had passed over. The simulated spacesuits were provided with no cameras.

But could he, the Zhen Li in the simulation room in Wuhan, review this session's passage, studying the markings again?

He left the star filled dark of the boulder with regret; this was so real… And resumed his return, with a tension he tried to use to focus on memory.

He walked on. Sometimes he felt himself lost—and had visions of himself walking hundreds of kilometers across the lunar surface. (Could the markings have been a map? No, they really hadn't looked like a map.) Perhaps the simulation would not care about an oxygen limit and just let him wander, until he admitted defeat and had to start this session all over again—while at the same time burdened with the brooding of one who has discovered an enigma, he felt he could not relate to anyone in the program.

And then he would note something on the surface he had definitely passed and feel a sort of relief, but a relief that did not relieve him of the fact that once again he had beheld something that so definitely *appeared* artificial…in the surreality of the simulation.

Yet there was true relief when he saw the rover in the distance. He almost started to run to it, but caught himself. He had gotten the knack of walking in the lunar gravity, one sixth that of Earth, but he knew that to try any increase of speed would disrupt that rhythm disastrously.

Soon he stood by the rover. *Fellow moon travelers*, he thought.

The session ended. The screen went dark. Slowly Li segued into a man who had been tested and yes, as he had said, taunted. There had to be some purpose in this. And he was convinced, viscerally, that somewhere in the Von Kármán crater there was the inexplicable minute city and the boulder—a tablet?—that had shaded his simulacrum.

10.

His simulated excursions on the lunar surface had exhausted Li. He was glad when it was time to leave the training room.

Once again, Lin and Yang were not outside when he left. Li always felt them odd guardians to the room (he did privately call them guardians; it amused him for some reason), their presence created by some necessary absurdity that always exists at some level in whatever the government does. He considered that perhaps a logical purpose for their presence was to assess his mental state before entering a training session. In that case two assessments would be better than one, giving a more complete psychological profile. But if that were indeed the situation, they would be required to be there when he left, to assess him afterward. Of course, they never seemed to make any formal assessment of him prior to these sessions; there would just be a gut feeling as to his manner, etc.

Such thoughts flitted through Li's mind briefly; he accepted the presence—and absence—of Lin and Yang as nothing more or less than they were simply there, or not; there was nothing positive or negative about it.

Passing into the lobby of the building before exiting, Li did note it seemed less peopled than usual. Those he did see wore masks. Well, that was expected. As he had many times before, he wondered what went on in the floors above. He had the feeling that whatever it was, it had no connection to the space program. The training room had been placed in here covertly, among whatever disparate functions the building offered. Li had the feeling that scattered through the country were similar secret rooms in innocuous buildings in which other candidates for the Chang'e program were being acclimated for the moon. This was just speculation, but Li felt a certainty about this. Normally, whether in the American and Russian space programs, those who would be sent into space were trained together in one or several established locations. He had in fact visited the Yuri A. Gagarin State Scientific Research and Testing Cosmonaut Training Center at Star City of Moscow Oblast, a heavily forested region near Moscow that was established in 1960 to train the Soviet Union's space men and women. ("Oblast" is an administrative division; the word can mean zone or province or region.) Li had been fascinated by the replicas of prior Soviet spacecraft, and found he drew an essence, a spirit of historical purpose from visiting Gagarin's office and had paused before his bust, the first human in space. Li felt a communion with the man who, in 1961, had orbited Earth in a craft that was certainly primitive by 21st century standards. Ironically the first man to fly free of Earth plummeted from Earth's skies to his death seven years later, in 1968, on a training mission in a Soviet MiG-15 fighter jet.

If future taikonauts from other countries had trained at Star City, Li's visit there in the company of several colleagues had been more sightseeing than training. Li had appreciated the history of the place. The Soviets had forged ahead in the Space Race in 1957 by putting the first satellite in orbit. They had put the first man in space in 1961. They had put the first woman in space in 1963. They had achieved the first spacewalk in 1965. Yet the Americans had beaten them to the moon in 1969, effectively ending the Space Race. But by the end of the 20ᵗʰ century, with the American shuttle program ended, U.S. astronauts had to hitch rides on Russians rockets to get to the International Space Station. Li knew that now the Americans were apparently returning to space on their own, via a collaboration of NASA and private enterprise; but in the space race of this century, Li considered that China would have the upper hand. Certainly China would return humans to the moon before any other nation.

If the lobby of the building had seemed quieter than usual—but then Li was leaving later than usual—the streets, in the early winter dark, seemed a bit more active than usual. It seemed as if there were a lot of people shopping. All masked, of course. Well, with these rumors of a lockdown because of the epidemic, people were understandably stocking up on food, supplies that would be necessary to comfortably pass through a quarantine.

He waited for the bus with some of these shoppers, who held full shopping bags. When the bus came, he took a seat by a window and a middleaged woman squeezed in next to him with two thick bags of goods. He tried to give her a bit of room by shifting a little closer to the window, but she gave him a look—her eyes darting above her mask—that seemed to say she was annoyed at his presence rather than being appreciative he was being polite.

He tried to call Fan, but he had difficulty getting service. He heard one ring, but that was it. And Wuhan had been among fifty cities in China that had installed an extensive 5G system that was supposed to provide better cell phone service, connectivity, etc. It was a huge technological rollout that was not supposed to be in effect until the end of 2020, but it had gone into place ahead of schedule; in Wuhan it had been in effect since November 2019, with more than 5,000 base stations (expected to increase to 50,000 by 2021). Of course, Li reflected, the more advanced technology is, the more problems can beset it. He recalled once reading that just as it is dangerous to be in a city during a severe earthquake, that while such a natural disaster ravaging the normal flow of life can cause many deaths, to a primitive society with simple shelters, the quake would be suffered as a disruption, but probably not a disaster. They would not have to pick people out of the rubble of buildings; they would have no sophisticated communication networks that would have to be repaired. The more a civilization requires technology, the more it suffers when that technology is befouled.

Getting off the bus and walking to his apartment building, Li wondered if the severity of this viral outbreak would increase. Cheng had been so certain about a citywide lockdown. Would Li still go to his training? He had the wry thought, *It will be easy to quarantine myself on the moon.* That brought a grim smile to his face as he entered the building, just behind a woman who had entered from another direction. She gave Li a quick look; he was not sure he recognized her. A mask could confuse identity unless the wearer was well known to the viewer. But he certainly noticed the abrupt wariness in her eyes; she literally darted away from his presence, up a stairwell. Well, contagion makes us fearful of others. A sign, he thought. On the bus people had sat next to each other, acknowledging the official decree to wear masks: it was something they had to do. But if this were really serious…the presence—the proximity—of any "other" could be dangerous. The other signified contagion.

Well, he was glad to be in his apartment, to leave his moon simulations. He slowly ate his dinner—again, something Fan had cooked for him: spicy bean curd with peppers, onion and ginger. He had to admit that her vegan dishes were savory. As he ate, he reviewed some training materials. Even after going through a long day of training, Li liked to look at this material; perhaps it simply gave him the comfort—the reassurance—that he was among the select few at which this was directed. Fan sometimes chastised him about his "narrow interests." She subtly—or not so subtly—tried to "expand" his appreciation of other things. Well, she had certainly got him interested in her vegan cooking—at least he was interested in eating it; and he could enjoy (in varying degrees) watching her old American movies. But these new enjoyments aside, he would say to her, "The more I fix myself on what I want to do, the more likely I will be able to do it."

She had said, "I focus on what I do. But when I go away from it and come back, I am able to focus better."

He had said, smiling, like the proper gracious lover. "You're my diversion that refreshes me."

This mock gallantry had been so uncharacteristic of steadfast, fixated Li, that Fan had laughed. And yet it had not seemed affected. They were two very different personalities, yet somehow there was a connection. Was it simply that they were young attractive people who were doing something very unusual? How many people in the entire world were training to go to the moon? How many were weaving nanomaterials into viruses?

The phone rang. As he had been thinking of Fan, Li was sure it was her. But it was an abrupt, commanding male voice. Li knew who it was, not expecting a call from this person; indeed, never having received a call from him, Li had to take a long moment to realize it was his lunar training supervisor, Yángé Huizhong.

"You had a long session today." Before Li could affirm that, Yángé said, "I will be reviewing the video." Li knew they always did, but being told this seemed, well, threatening. But he believed he had acquitted himself well. Then he was hearing Yángé tell him, "At 10 a.m. tomorrow morning Wuhan will be quarantined. There will be extensive restrictions. In some places only one person from each household will be allowed to leave to buy food. Only a few food stores will be open. Most businesses will be closed. Only essential personnel will be allowed to travel in the city. You are essential personnel. If you are stopped—and probably tomorrow you will be—show them your identification. You will soon be issued a special pass for this period."

Li said, "For how long will this be?" Though he knew it an ignorant question.

Yángé reacted to it as such. "This is unpredictable. It depends on how effectively people comply. As you must be sure to comply with all health measures."

"Of course."

"The training you have received is invaluable."

"Of course." In other words, the training they had given him was invaluable, not his life.

Then Yonge's voice changed, became less commanding. "Zhen Li, you are among our most promising men. You are important. Please be careful. This could be a dangerous time."

Li naturally assured Yángé that he would be the epitome of caution, obedience and self preservation. ("Rigorous, prudent, meticulous and exacting.")

"Good, good. Simply report for your training tomorrow."

Literally seconds after speaking with Yángé, the phone rang again. It was Fan.

"You tried to call me?"

"I was on the bus; I lost service." Li related what he'd just been told.

She said, "I haven't seen it on the news yet, but everyone's expecting it. But if it's tomorrow, they should be announcing it all over. I can't imagine the lab will be shut."

"I hadn't thought of that. My training will continue."

"Well, you're not going to be contaminating people on the moon."

That phrase "people on the moon" made Li recall the apparent hieroglyphic on the large boulder. Before he could consider mentioning it to Fan, she said, "I'm going to call Cheng, see if he's heard. I'll call you back."

Li waited for her return call. He considered what Wuhan would be like, a city in quarantine.

When Fan called Cheng, she found he had already received a call much like Li's. "I will be—I have to be—there tomorrow," Cheng said. "They said to me, 'This is a virus, you're a virologist.' So I'm wanted. As far as I know, everyone in the lab is cleared to come.' He added, "In a way, you've become a virologist, too."

"In a limited way. I'm nowhere up to your speed."

"It'll be a challenge." Fan heard him sigh. "But I wish it could just be science. I know they haven't been releasing the full extent of the cases, the full numbers. And how restrictive will they get? Even with us, eventually."

"How bad do you think this will get?"

"It will get worse, I'm sure."

"Bubonic plague?"

Cheng gave an odd laugh. "That would be too…historical. Let's just say it's an epidemic."

Fan called Li back. She told him she was coming over. Li was surprised; it was late. "I'll drive both of us to work tomorrow."

"Sure." This pleased Li but also made him uneasy. He got a sense that Fan felt something so ominous going down that she needed to be with him before it exploded into the everyday.

Fan was always more emotional that Li. "You're too distant sometimes. A lot of times. Like the moon." Li would smile. He knew there was truth to that. He normally felt most people overreacted to so much in life. While Fan would say that Li's intense focus on his moon mission was *his* overreaction.

Though as Li tried to return to his training manuals, he found that for the moment he did not have the focus for it. He waited for Fan's arrival in a sort of vague suspension.

When Fan did arrive, there was nothing vague about her. She hugged Li tightly. In a few moments they were in bed. Though it seemed Fan's body expressed more worry than passion. "Is it the end of the world?" joked Li.

"It feels like it." Fan said this seriously.

In these moments of nudity Li beheld Fan with a particular quiet awe. She was lithe. Her body seemed flawless. His eyes travelled over her flesh with a dichotomous appreciation: a natural lust on one hand, and a tranquility her beauty inspired. Her face, attractive enough, seemed transformed into something further, something more compelling as he beheld her entire body.

And then there was this: In a process that Fan had invented, and whose science Li had never quite understood, Fan had imbued her skin with a dusting of innumerable metal particles that glinted with her movement and the change of lighting. "Some nano, some a little larger," she'd said. The glinting or sheen was quite subtle; it was something that you had to pay attention to, like picking up on minute flakes of color in a rock. But it gave her an intriguing iridescence, a unique quality to her flesh. "A lot better than a tattoo," Fan had said. She considered tattoos too common and usually unimaginative.

Where Chinese society once considered tattoos the mark of criminals, the country's millennial generation had more than embraced this body art—which, Fan, had remarked, she usually found unappealing. As for Li, if of this new generation, he had no desire for a tattoo. Fan had joked, "You're just not modern, Li."

He'd replied, "Going to the moon isn't modern?"

"You know what I mean. You go into the future with a strict old fashioned sense."

But Li did admit he liked what he called, "Your nano iridescence." Though he had also said, "Isn't putting metal in your body not exactly healthy?"

Fan's response, "It's such a small amount, and spread so thin, it doesn't affect the skin at all. Doesn't keep my skin from breathing." She told Li about the famous James Bond film, *Goldfinger*, in which a woman died after having been covered entirely in gold paint. "Skin asphyxiation."

When Li was in bed with Fan and the particles in her flesh seemed to flash a sort of pulse with her movements in the dark, the sort of light that seemed to disappear even as you saw it, it sometimes gave Li the sense that this woman was beyond his grasp, just as this elusive sheen of flesh avoided being fixed by the eye. Fan had called Li's persona distant and "out there," while he would tell Fan, "It's almost like your body's elusive," no matter how immediate it was to his hands.

And so, when she said, "You seem to get a hold of it easily enough," Li's response was, "But even so, it's almost...unearthly."

"I think that's transference."

Then she had to explain to him what transference was; the conversation led into a discussion of why western psychological tenets that focused on individual angst and achievement had little hold on the collective-driven psyche of the Chinese.

Li grew bored with that dialogue and gently raised one of Fan's arms in the dim light of the bedroom, as if displaying to not only himself but Fan the elusive visual play of the particles. "Someone would say your body is unsettled."

"No. That's only what your eyes put upon it."

Li shrugged, laughed. Fan's iridescence was attractive to him. It was like the light of minute fireflies emanating from her body. And there was the sense that as she had taken it upon herself to mark her body in a special way, it gave the wordless message that whatever perceptions others might mark her with could not permeate her own portrayal of herself.

At the same time, there was the sense from Fan this night of a surrender to whatever would come, an abandonment to the sanctuary of this moment before tomorrow's storm, which made her more beautiful and immediate to Li.

On Fan's part, she was always pleased with the totality of Li's body, which was athletic and muscular. Whether in bed, or watching him in the recent military games, she was drawn to his strength and well as a grace she believed he did not realize he had. Li's face, that many might have considered average, had a special handsomeness for Fan because of his perpetual focused intensity; now, as a beginning or end to his nude body, it seemed just the right face for the rest of him.

They lay quietly afterward, in the dim room, a lamp with low illumination in one corner.

"Asleep?" Fan whispered.

"No…. I was thinking…." His words floated upward, on a slow breath. "When I was in the simulation today, I saw—now you're going to think I *am* seeing things: on this boulder, marks like writing—"

Fan gave a laugh and propped her head up with an arm bent at the elbow. "Wait, first you see this 'city'…on the video from the rover. Now you're beyond the rover—so what they have you going through is definitely a simulation of the surface. And in this made up...scene, whoever made it put mysterious writing?"

"Doesn't make sense, I know."

"Do you think it's possible…you spend hours in this imaginary world—but it's connected to reality…and maybe you start to see things?"

"Do I seem like someone who has delusions?"

"No, but even you— You're doing something that most people don't go through. I know there's still a lot we don't know about the experience of being apart from Earth. Even if you're not actually off Earth, in that room— Well, doesn't it feel like on the moon?"

"It does. I feel like my perceptions are split. One part of me knowing I'm on Earth, the other feeling I'm on the moon." He was quiet; he looked away from her, at the ceiling, as if seeing a celestial ceiling, not an earthly one. "The training—it's to realize two things: going to another world…but bringing the Earth with you."

She whispered, "Because wherever you go, if you don't bring where you've begun…."

He looked back at her, smiled. Was it a sad smile? She didn't know. Almost, she thought later, a forgiving smile: she couldn't possibly understand. He said, "Someday, people are going to be born on another world. They won't have anything of Earth in them at all."

"If they're born of people that come from Earth, they will have that—and genetic memory."

"So how many generations do you think it'll take for people to feel totally apart from Earth?"

"There'll be blood memory, but I think by the time your great-grandparents came from Earth, people will belong to a new world." She abruptly added: "Could you see yourself living on the moon, some other world, never coming back?"

"Probably not. I want to go out there, come back."

"Be the hero that tells us of the journey."

"I don't think I can ever really express the journey. And not as a hero, no. Explorer. That's a human tradition."

"Why do human beings want to go where they are not?"

"The other side of the mountain, the ocean; the other side of the sky. Look at you: you go down into the infinitesimal. Another place."

"But I can step right out of it and be here. You want distance: to go."

"I don't really analyze myself. I just do."

"You're young yet."

"And you—?"

Her smile was self-deprecating. "Why are we going on with this? We're avoiding…the virus out there."

"Is that what we're doing?"

"That's what I'm doing." She sat up; she sighed. "There was something on the news—just a few minutes…about the bats. Were they at the market or not? You get different stories. It was my father taking me to those markets that made me vegan. It was horrible. Those frightened animals packed in cages, waiting to be killed. They all knew it. Or knew they were in such a horrible situation, a *distortion* of existence that we had forced on them—something they knew they couldn't live in. Like if you woke up and—"

"Was on the moon."

"The moon isn't horrible to you. It's where you want to go. It's your choice. When we choose something, even if it's bad, becomes bad, we chose it. Don't you understand, we've got this virus here because of what we're doing to animals. The virus from those bats—those bats don't live anywhere near Wuhan. You heard Cheng say that."

"Did he?"

"If he didn't, I am. We kill all this flesh and we bring it to our flesh—" She stopped, looked at Li. They had exchanged the requisite "I love you," but she felt neither of them were sure of that, that each had simply performed a declaration necessary for further intimacy. And in this moment, if Li was being considerate of, attentive to, her passion about animals, she knew he could not move alongside her to its depths. He was for the journey to "out there," bringing to new worlds all the old rough ways. Was that roughness needed to proceed "out there?" They were joined by science—that was a depth they had. But she had another dimension in which he could not join her. She was satisfied now to work along the border that separated them, to pull him over that border as much as she could.

Li was looking at her peacefully, waiting for her to continue. She said, "I didn't know, until this, that if bats carry viruses, they really aren't affected by them. They don't develop the immune inflammatory response that attacks human beings."

"We need bat antibodies then."

"They did studies—I'm sure Cheng, working with the bat lady, knows all about them—with the horseshoe bats years ago to see if they could detect SARS antibodies. They couldn't. They also concluded that coronaviruses—I don't know about the one we have now—could pass from bats to humans."

"I thought you just said we're getting this from a bat virus."

"The study was about the SARS virus, not this one. Though it's closely related."

There comes a point when lovers are tired of talk, even tired of love. They slept.

Fan dreamt of the markets her father had taken her to. He smiled, even laughed at the horror she expressed, at her tears, thinking—he said as much—that this was all very much like the reaction a nice little girl would have; but older, of course, she would outgrow it. "You'll be married and shopping for your own family someday," he said.

She had hated him for that. Her relationship with her father was a constant shift in the weather of love and hate. She knew he did love her, and she had to love him for that. He would have given his life for her. But she did not love, in fact she hated how he stood by tradition, the threatening aspect of the military: hated how much he loved things as they were. In fact, he would say, "The world is the way it is because it works that way. Many things in it are difficult, but it would be more difficult if you tried to change it into something else."

And so, this night, next to Li, she dreamt of being a child in the market, being horrified as she been when a child. Her father was there, perhaps right by her, looming large, and yet he was a distant being to her. She went from cage to cage, to the animals caught in the wild, to the animals raised in backyards, to the barrels of fish that swam in irregular circles in that small confinement, not looking up at the world of the creatures who had confined them but ahead, as if there was still the possibility that, in the next instant, there could be freedom. And yet the fish knew, all the animals knew (as she had told Li) they had been put into an unnatural realm that could have no good end and could only have horror before that end.

She whimpered in her sleep. Li, asleep beside her, did not wake. Fan's dream went on: she began to open the cages. There were cries of outrage from the humans all around her. Frightened animals swirled at her feet. But the fish, what could she do with the fish? She was a little girl; she could not lift the heavy barrels to water; she could not pluck each fish out of the water and bring them to—

Her father was shouting her name.

Fan awoke with a start. She sat up slowly, breathing slowly. The still form of Li helped to calm her. It was almost as if his still form physically blocked the horror and images of her dream. She sighed, laid herself back down.

11.

Li too, had his dreams. He was in the training room with Yángé Huizhong. Li had been in Yángé's presence twice; in the dream, Li immediately felt this an ominous visit. The official was sitting by the screen on which had played out Li's lunar world. He was a small, shaven-headed man in his sixties. There was a greyness to his face, but to Li it did not betoken ill health but a sort of gravity earned—achieved—through some hardship over years and gave him a commanding manner. Before Li had been in existence, Yángé had been through a place and time Li could not comprehend, only sense.

Yángé was saying, "You found strange things on the moon."

Li: "I *saw* strange things. I don't know if they are really on the moon."

"You didn't put them in your reports."

"I wasn't sure…. You would think I was crazy."

"You're not doing this to stay sane."

Li was both offended and disturbed by this. "You don't want me sane?"

"We want a change of mind. We do want you to see things—differently." He gestured to the screen, which was dark. "You have to be prepared."

"For what, though?"

The man gestured to the screen again. A moonscape appeared, so vivid, so immediate. "Look, look," he said.

Li leaned forward, straining his eyes. He supposed it was the Von Kármán crater, but he could not be sure. "What am I supposed to see?"

"Keep looking, it will come."

Li awoke, searching through his mind for something more of the dream, but he could not recall it. "Keep looking, it will come." It seemed a warning.

As Fan had awakened and looked at a sleeping Li, he returned to wakefulness and looked upon Fan. He loved to watch Fan's face in sleep. She seemed so peaceful, and calm. Li could not know that an hour or so ago, Fan had been through the tortured dream of the animal market.

Li settled back. It seemed a while before he fell asleep. He wondered if the announcement had been made public that the lockdown would go into effect at 10 a.m. in the morning. If it had not been made public by the evening did that mean everyone would find out at dawn, hours before it was to begin? Li did not know that the lockdown was announced to sleeping Wuhan at 2 a.m., when relatively few would be awake to receive it, via TV or radio or the internet. But like the virus that had caused this extreme measure, it would begin with just a few people, then the fact of it would spread to more and more people. In fact, in these predawn hours, Wuhan was stirring, being awakened with the news, and there were people leaving their homes, seeking buses and trains. The city was a nocturnal hive that had been abruptly stirred by a danger of containment. The winter's late dawn would find more "commuters" than normal; by ten o'clock, 300,000 people will have left Wuhan and the neighboring vicinity, refugees of a pathogen of the nanoworld.

In the suburbs, far from the heart of the city, Cheng somehow had a sense of this. Around four or so in the morning, after awakening to use the bathroom, he could not go back to sleep. He had the intuition he should look at his phone. There were messages: "Lockdown by ten am!" He scrolled the internet. He got out of bed, went to the livingroom, parted the curtains and looked out on the dark street. There was no movement, no one passed there. But as one hears the hum or buzz of a hive of insects just out of sight, from the direction of the city he seemed to hear (actually more felt than heard) the movement of many, the center of the hive of Wuhan stirring, awakened by a threat. Sighing, trying to shake off a palpable tension, he returned to bed, forcing himself to seek rest, as if he had to not be tired, to have as much strength as possible for the coming day. He wished he did not have to go the lab that day—and yet he found himself saying, as he did fall back to sleep, "This is the challenge."

Fan and Li left together in the morning, driving through a city that was a dichotomy: people leaving it, and people closed in their homes. Stores decorated for the Spring Festival lunar New Year were closed.

Masked police were everywhere. Before they had gone very far, they were at a traffic stop. A brusque officer tapped on the window. The couple expected to have their temperatures taken, but the officer was demanding identification. The lockdown would go into effect in another half hour.

The officer, about the same age as Fan and Li, was obviously surprised—and disappointed?—at the identification presented to him. Surprised that this young couple had such important government positions. He returned the ID, vaguely nodding, then made an abrupt gesture to someone at a distance, and said to Li and Fan, "Wait." He had one last bit of authority to exert.

At first it was hard to discern if it was a man or woman who approached the car in protective medical gear, and swiped first Fan's forehead, then Li's to take their temperatures. Instead of going around to the passenger side of the car, she (it was a woman, after all) stayed at the driver's window and Li had to lean across Fan, his head twisted upward, to have his temperature taken. The instrument poised at his forehead seemed a threat. But a very brief one. When the instrument was withdrawn, Li wondered if there had been enough time to accurately take his temperature. He thought the woman was just going through the motions of her duties.

The woman signaled to the officer that Fan and Li were clear to go. He gestured—as if angry—the couple could proceed.

With that scene behind them, Fan said, "Are we going to have to prove our existence every day?"

"Maybe." The combination of having to produce identification, and the awkward way in which he'd had his temperature taken—or not taken properly—unsettled Li more than it should have, he thought. But he offered, "Well, they're trying to contain it. That's good, isn't it?"

If lips could shrug, Fan's did. "I have a feeling it's going to get more draconian."

Li did not know that last word. Fan explained, "A guy named Draco, legislator in ancient Greece. There used to be just oral laws, what people said; he replaced all that with written laws that could only be enforced by legal courts. In other words, you wouldn't have a questions about what the law was."

"That sounds good."

"In principle. But a lot of his laws had heavy punishments for small offenses. So draconian means severe—usually beyond what's necessary."

"And you think they're going to go beyond what's necessary?"

"Doesn't the government always do that?"

Li said nothing. When Fan did engage in any discussion touching on the political, she usually had harsh things to say about the way things were in China. "We have a great, modern country—after all, you're going to the moon—and we have people with backward minds running it."

Li tended to regard life in China as having unavoidable unpleasantries or even wrongs that were outweighed by having "a great, modern country." Fan would chide him, and sometimes was actually angry he "accepted the way things were," just because things were good for him. "Like my father."

She added, "Maybe as long as you're going 'out there,' it doesn't matter what it's like here. But *here* is where you're going to be for most of your life—unless you're going to be a moon colonist."

"I told you: I want to go there, come back. Maybe Mars, come back."

"And while you're going and coming back, here in China—"

"Don't things always move to better ways—eventually?"

"Thing go up and down. China has concentration camps for Muslims."

China had established what it called—in true communist fashion—reeducation camps, interning anywhere from hundreds of thousands to a million Uyghurs, Kazakhs, Kyrgyz and other Turkic Muslims, as well as Christians and some foreigners. Ostensibly created because of the "people's war on terror," the camps were beyond the oversight of the country's legal system, with individuals held without being charged.

The camps began in the Xinjiang region in 2014, after several years of violence between the native Uyghurs and Han Chinese who had moved into the area. In 2009 a riot in a factory there caused more than a hundred deaths. In subsequent years radical Uyghurs killed many Chinese citizens in a series of terrorist attacks, apparently sponsored by the Turkistan Islamic Party, clearly an organization that had been recognized as terrorist by not just China but Russia, Turkey and the United Kingdom, as well as the U.S and the UN.

Fan had said, "China uses that excuse—"

"Are real terrorist attacks an excuse?"

"An excuse to round up everyone you don't like—like America does."

"Fan, I have a feeling it's not so simple."

"You're accusing me of not looking at—nuance? You're one who looks at things in black and white—like on the moon."

"There's color on the moon—in nuances. Sometimes I think you resent me and, well, the moon. As if you're jealous of it."

"Jealous of the moon? Your Chang'e?" She had laughed, and it did not seem an affected laugh. "Well, on the moon, you just have to worry about…getting around there."

Li had laughed back, but more in exasperation. Fan was earthbound, he was not. That was all there was to it. Sometimes, when he looked at the famous Apollo pictures of Earth, he thought on that globe was all the petty conflicts and the real suffering, the foolish histories of the human race; and there, on the moon, the austere lands of new beginnings. Of course, all Earth travelers there, and those to other worlds, would bring that Earth history with them, but there was a chance to shed it, begin something new. At least that was how Li looked at it.

At any rate, that morning Fan was driving Li to a major steppingstone to "out there." When they pulled into the industrial park Fan said, with surprise, "It's here?" She has never been to the site of Li's "workplace."

"Sometimes the government doesn't want to announce itself."

They kissed. Li put on his mask and went into the building. There were definitely less people in the lobby. Li went through the usual procedures with his security cards allowing him further entrance into the training zone. Lin and Yang, masked, were there to meet him. For a moment Li thought they looked like a pair of big puppets.

Lin said, "An unusual day outside, isn't it?"

Yang said, "You must have gotten the last bus. I hope you have arrangements when you leave."

Li realized he was going to have to ask Fan to pick him up at the end of the day. But that might be inconvenient for her. Like Li, Fan often did not come and go from the lab at the same hours every day. And for the first time Li wondered how Lin and Yang got here every day. "I will figure something out. Unless one of you can take me home."

The pair gave overlapping laughs that Li found unsettling. Yang said, "I don't think that will be possible. We will have to arrange something for you."

"Well, that's good, if you can," said Li slowly, feeling (irrationally, he considered) he did not like looking to Lin and Yang for favors. He didn't want to think now about what he'd have to do at the end of this session. He began to move to the door that would give him entry once again to the all too real simulation of the moon.

"Wait," said Lin, reaching for something in a drawer of his desk. "We have to do this first—" He waved the same temperature taking instrument the woman at the road stop had used.

"I just had this done half an hour ago."

"We have orders. Anyway, you know you're all right." He gestured to Li to lean forward. He felt, as he had in the car, this was an awkward moment. Was his forehead going to be scanned many times a day from now on?

Lin moved the instrument across Li's forehead, drew it away, looked at it. His eyes widened. "You definitely have a temperature. This is no good."

Yang was now peering at the reading, and echoing, "No, that's no good."

"But I just had...." Li's protest faded; he knew the woman at the traffic stop really had not taken his temperature correctly. But he was not feeling feverish—just, well, unsettled.

Lin: "But you said you just had it taken."

"Yes."

Yang was saying, "Maybe this isn't working." Lin responded, "We took our own temperatures." Yang nodded in affirmation, as if he'd forgotten.

Li realized he was going to be sent back home, quarantined. But he was immediately informed of something that would have made that situation desirable. "You will have to stay here," said Yang.

"Here?"

"In the simulation room. You have a bathroom. You will be given something to sleep on. We will have to arrange for food—"

This was all too bizarre for Li to absorb. "I can't stay here."

"That's the procedure," said Lin.

"I need to call Yángé Huizhong."

Lin and Yang looked at each other. "That's not possible now."

"What happens if I just walk out?" There was a long pause. Now Li felt hot, felt not himself, confused as to what he should demand for himself, unsure of how to react to this. Lin and Yang looked at each other. Lin had placed the offending instrument on the desk in front of him.

"Take it again," said Li; that was all he could think of at this moment.

"I'll do it," said Yang. He swiped Li's forehead. He shook his head slightly as he looked at the reading. "Two tenths higher. One hundred point one."

"I can't be sick," said Li, irrationally. Then he was thinking of Fan and Cheng, who both worked in the lab where it was possible the virus had originated. He thought about being in bed last night with Fan. But of course, the virus could not take hold that quickly. Then again, how did he know that? This was a new virus.

"It's probably nothing," said Lin. "Like when you don't feel well for a day. But the way things are now—you have to comply."

"But if I just leave, go home. I don't feel sick."

Yang sighed. "We can't let you go."

Li wondered if the pair would physically try to stop him. Even if it was two against one, the pair didn't appear strong enough to detain the very athletic Li.

Yang added, "It would not be good for you to defy this. Fourteen days. Just stay here. You will be taken care of. You want to go to the moon; this is just momentary…."

Li felt utterly defeated—by both his body and this surreal turn of events.

Lin said, "We will inform Yángé of the situation."

Li took in a deep breath. He walked into the training room. He had entered here before with enthusiasm, but the removal of his freedom now made it seem he entered a surreal prison. The absence of choice changes every perspective.

And so Li began another training session. A session he would not be leaving for fourteen days. The length of a lunar day. Or night. He felt literally exiled to the moon. He sat before the screen for a while before turning it on. He looked about the room he was to inhabit for two weeks. He realized he had never really taken it all in before. He had been focused on the lunar world. He sat at a long desk on which the large screen transported his attention and his senses to the far side of the moon. There were no windows. There was lighting that mimicked natural lighting and whose level he could control. There was a bathroom—and now he was very thankful there was a shower in it. He'd wondered at that before. He had the paranoid thought: *Was this planned?* Ridiculous, of course: an outbreak of a new disease, just to lock him away?

He resigned himself to begin the training session. He returned to Von Kármán 's crater. Soon that familiar austere landscape, one that more and more he had developed a feeling of connection to, made him half forget his circumstance, or at least push it to a part of his thoughts that he did not have to consider too deeply for the moment. Outside this building Wuhan was locked down, no buses or trains running, no planes in the air, and inside here he wandered in a world apart from Earth, but one that looked down upon Earth, as the moon—as Chang'e—looked down upon Earth.

Long, long ago, the Earth had been beset by ten suns that made the earth parched and unbearable. Yi, husband of Chang'e, was an archer who shot down nine of the suns, leaving the one necessary sun. His reward was to be given an elixir of immortality. But he did not drink it down; he gave it to Chang'e; he did not want immortality without his beloved wife.

Yi went out hunting one day and his apprentice Fengmeng burst into Yi's house and tried to force Chang'e to hand over the elixir. To prevent Fengmeng from getting it, Chang'e drank it. And then she flew up to the heavens and chose the moon as her eternal place to live; she wanted to live near her husband, in sight of Earth. Yi of course was immensely saddened and began what would become the mid-autumn Moon Festival, by displaying the cakes and fruits that Chang'e had loved on Earth. The festival is celebrated on the full moon of the eighth lunar month. An outdoor altar is set up facing the moon. On the altar are pastries for Chang'e to bless.

Though another version of the story, perhaps an older one, has Chang'e stealing the elixir from her husband, drinking it, and then flying to the moon so he could not follow her.

Which myth is "true" perhaps depends on the needs of the one who imparts it.

Chapter Five: Lockdown

12.

Fan endured two more traffic stops on the way to the lab. Each time she tried to give the officer who stayed her an ironic smile behind her mask, emphasizing her expression with her eyes, but she felt no reciprocation. Surely the police weren't happy about doing this drudge work. And how long would it go on? Though both times when she was handed back her ID—and also when she had been stopped with Li— she sensed a disappointment from each officer, along with more than a tinge of resentment: that someone so young had this official "clearance." She was clearly someone of importance, allowed to go here and there in the midst of an emergency, while these officials of a menial level were stuck in this repetitive policing of the streets. The temperature check that followed the scrutiny of her identification seemed to her an attempt to thwart her passage.

At the lab there was another temperature check. Fan wondered at her forehead's constant exposure to these instruments—something that will be going on for some time, she realized. Even if the instruments did not actually touch her, was that sanitary? Speaking of that, there was sanitizing going on everywhere, more than usual in a place that was very conscious it dealt with pathogens. While the usual crew of scientists went about their daily work, there were a horde of cleaners with cannisters of disinfectant from which slim hoses with metal nozzles at the end sprayed out something meant to destroy any possible contagion. Fan hated the smell of most commercial disinfectants, and often thought that over exposure to them could be worse than whatever they were used to combat. Many of her fellow researchers had no such qualms, and walked among these brief bursts of disinfectants as they might walk through a mist of rain outside. Especially the unusual number of visitors in lab coats or even protective gear that Fan knew were not native to the lab—official sentinels, she surmised, of scrutiny and disapproval, to make sure the Wuhan Institute of Virology was not some place that could endanger the country, spreading who knew what. Retreating to her own place of work, Fan took a few moments to scan the news on her phone. The *People's Daily*—state run—had posted on Weibo: "Come on Wuhan, let us win this disease prevention war together!" Fan gave herself an ironic smile now, fully understanding she, along with everyone, had entered a bizarre stretch of time.

She tried to push that away with work—at the same time connecting her research with this sudden invasion of a new virus. A few days ago, she had come across an article translated from the *Arabian Journal of Chemistry*, about using Squash Leaf Curl China Virus as a nanotemplate to create gold and silver nanomaterials through the use of gold chloride and silver nitrate. Her field of meshing nanotech with Nature's nanotech of viruses was becoming more often attempted and, hence, recognized. Her own Tobacco Mosaic Virus was being "woven" (as she liked to think of it) with nanoparticles of recycled plastics, mostly e-waste that had come from the e-trash heaps of China, where literal mountains of discarded PCs, laptops, cell phones and so forth were arranged and sorted by the poorest of the poor, suffering from the pollution of that plastic and metallic debris as heat was applied to separate components. This merger of the natural and the manmade nanoworld could, as she had mentioned to one of those official visitors, yesterday, be used for protective medical gear: masks, operating gowns and the like.

At the same time, Fan could imagine—well, fantasize—that her creation was like something woven out of an art that would be like magic to most observers, like some magic cloth in a myth. She smiled once more to herself, certainly not an ironic smile this time, but one of private pleasure. Nurturing this mythological perspective as she contemplated the electron micrographs of the samples she had woven thus far, Fan drifted into seeing patterns, almost figures, as if her weave were an impressionistic artwork that barely held itself to the recognizable. There were figures on horses, a lake, trees. Of course, she did not accept this vision as literal, just the fancy of her imagination, like seeing things in clouds. But clouds, however large to the eye, constantly change to other shapes: Fan's minute weave held. Or did it? It was so intricately small, so tightly woven, with so many "strands," that the eye could shift just slightly and see something else entirely. Now the weave seemed to depict a high cliff, with small birds in the sky.

Fan shook her head, put the micrographs down. She was getting like Li, with his minute city on the surface of the moon, and his "markings" on boulders. She had asked him if he had considered his focus on moving through simulations of an otherworldly landscape had caused him to see things; perhaps the same thing was happening to her. But not really; she could play with her imagination, know it was play; she was not, insisting, like Li that what was presented to her eyes was actually there.

She suddenly thought: how is Li going to get home? There would be no public transportation later today. She would need to pick him up. Could she find that place again where his training was held? He had said the training room had no cell phone reception, but there had to be a point during the day when he could reach her.

She put it out of her mind for a moment.

Cheng had made it to the lab just before the lockdown went into effect. He assumed there would be some transportation provided for him at the end of the day. Though he considered he might be naïve to think so. But surely his work, and how it related to the epidemic, would grant him special considerations. Then he told himself there was really no way of knowing how things would fall out. Passing closed stores decorated for the Spring Festival, noting the crowded train stations, thronged with those who were escaping Wuhan, he had to recognize this was a new moment, bizarre and surreal, and who knew how it would play out.

Though soon after his arrival he was quickly assured (if that's the word) about how the government regarded the worth of his presence and inferred that his everyday needs would be looked after. The official who came into Cheng's office did not seem like the interrogators who had accosted him yesterday, but someone measured and concerned that Cheng "should be supported in everything" he did in relation to combating the virus. He introduced himself in sharp, sudden fashion, so quickly that Cheng did not quite catch the name, and he did not ask the man to repeat it. He wore a Mao-type jacket, but more stylishly cut. His wearing of a mask added another aspect to this ensemble of traditional Chinese gear. Cheng found that curious and amusing, and so the official perhaps did not understand Cheng's slight smile as he said, "We recognize your expertise in coronaviruses, so you are very necessary to us and it is expedient that you proceed on this situation as tirelessly as possible." This seemed more like a political speech to excel for the greater good than a personal exhortation. Cheng never cared for such officialese, but he smiled back at the man and nodded, who immediately added, "Is there any new understanding about this virus?"

"Well, not since yesterday." If this man was under the four who visited him yesterday, Cheng realized he was connecting him to them; there had been nothing new yesterday, and it was the same today.

Although there was a difference; the official related that the virus appeared to be infecting more people each day. "It's exponential," he stressed. "I'm sure you understand that."

He almost said that as if Cheng did not understand and so it had to be explained to him—or, if not explained, a dire fact stressed to the point that one had to act without the luxury of fully understanding.

"I know how viruses are," said Cheng flatly. "Essentially our tact now is to find, before there can even be a vaccine, how we can prevent the protein spike from linking to the human cell and what better therapies we can give the sick."

The other seemed to look upon the first part of Cheng's statement with approval, then frowned at the rest. "Therapies, yes, but we have to stop it before that." There was the impression that concentrating on methods of treating the ill were a defeat; the virus had to be conquered before it could cause illness.

The conversation, if it could be called that, went on a while, with nothing of substance really being said, though there was the banal reassurance that Chang Cheng was highly regarded—and there would be transportation provided him to and from the lab during this "unfortunate circumstance."

Sometimes, whether it was a banal friendly conversation between himself and someone, or a workplace "official" exchange like this one, Cheng in a sense stepped outside himself and became a disinterested listener who found the conversation nothing more than an agreed upon insanity that both parties had to adhere to in order to keep from admitting—at least recognizing—that the basis of all they spoke about were the constructs of a life of madness that one had to unfortunately accept. So, Cheng found himself drifting into this perspective shortly into the exchange with the Mao-suited man. Actually, this was less an "exchange," and more of Cheng listening to this apparently respectful assessment of his worth and responding with safe and expected replies—a circumstance of rhetoric and its reception to which this visitor was habituated. Chang wondered if everyone in the lab, down to its biohazard custodians, was getting such special considerations. Well, if half of the lab personnel did not have cars, and public transportation was now shut down, and the government wanted to—

had to—keep the lab running, apparently there was little to do, but "aid" everyone at the lab with a guarantee of ease of coming and going. –Unless, Cheng had the thought, eventually we will all be locked down in the lab, "sheltering in place" until the collective genius of the Wuhan Institute of Virology was able to combat the virus. As much as he saw the lab as a sort of second home, as the place in which he could exercise his skills and scientific imagination, Cheng could not look upon such a prospect with any willing acceptance.

He said as much to Fan when they met for lunch.

"I don't think any of us would like that," she said. "I could see battling through a long weekend, but permanent, at least indefinite imprisonment—" Cheng laughed abruptly. "What's so funny?" asked Fan cocking her head, poised with strands of a seaweed salad in her chopsticks.

"Not funny—but that's what I'm imagining: imprisoning all the brains here."

It was Fan's turn to laugh. "Well, a woman always wants to be appreciated for her brains." When Cheng looked at her with a quizzical smile, she added, "It's a line from one of my American movies."

"What is this American fixation you have?"

"I don't think it's a fixation; it's an interest: in a curious, certainly influential culture. Why do you think American movies are the world standard?"

"Are they really?"

"Possibly a little less now, but certainly it was America who brought this to the world."

"But…a gift or a diversion?"

"Diversions can be much needed gifts."

Cheng smiled. "I can't say I'm much for movies of any culture."

"Yes, you're too intellectual for popular entertainment."

"You're mocking me."

"A little. But speaking of other cultures, you're eating with a fork. You always eat with a fork—like an American. Like the west, anyway."

Cheng shrugged. "Since childhood. It seems a more practical way to bring food to your mouth: prongs that go into it, grasp it, instead of between two sticks. It makes me think primitive people ate like that, with little twigs."

"But our twigs are polished and slim—and you grow up with the art of them."

Cheng chuckled, echoed her: "The art of them."

"Yes."

"So, what is it with America?"

"Maybe I can't explain it. Li always asks me. Maybe I don't want to explain it to myself: I'm being a disloyal Chinese."

"You never struck me as a nationalist."

"I'm not. I have the ideal—maybe we'll get to it in five hundred years—we'll think of ourselves as Earth people, like in those science fiction movies, instead of all these one hundred countries. I had this discussion with my father once—more than once."

"The military man? I'm sure he was of a different opinion."

"He said if you had a one world nation, a one world government, and you didn't like the government, you'd have no place to go; you couldn't leave."

"Well, there's truth to that."

Fan suddenly said, very earnestly: "Do you feel good, being Chinese?"

"I don't know what it would be to not be Chinese."

"You know what I mean: living in this China, the way it is."

"I have a lot of misgivings about the government." Cheng actually looked about him as he said this, as if this not very forceful criticism could be overheard and held against him.

Fan of course caught this. "You afraid you'll be hauled away?" Then asked: "Any news of your friend, the doctor?"

"No, none so far."

There was a pause. Fan had finished her lunch. She looked thoughtful a moment, then said, "Speaking of American entertainment: I was watching this, well, compilation of America's old comedy shows. They are called sitcoms. Short for situation comedies—"

"Situation?"

"That means each of these shows is set in a specific setting, with recurring characters. The compilation was meant to show how what Americans found funny in each decade reflected attitudes in society."

"And what do they find funny now?"

"I don't really know. This covered fifty years, 1950 to 2000. That's a lot, though, half a century. There's this scene I saw—a show from the 1960s. About this rural sheriff and his deputy in a place that became a synonym for old fashioned life and good simple people: a town called Mayberry. But the name's not important. This sheriff and his deputy really don't have any crime to handle. They have this town drunk who gets unruly a lot and they put him in the jail in the sheriff's building, he sleeps it off, they give him breakfast in the morning and they send him on his way."

"I suppose with one drunken person in town they can be kind."

"Oh, they treat him like one of the family. So the deputy gets it in his head that he is going to help the drunk with his drinking problem. He's going to use psychology. He says to the drunk we're going to have to see how your mind works. He shows him one of those inkblot tests— throw ink on the paper, fold it, open it. Say whatever you see, first thing that comes to mind."

"The Rorschach tests."

"I think they're more like a game than serious. Anyway, he shows the drunk this inkblot and the man says, 'It's a bat.' 'A bat!' says the deputy. 'It's a butterfly.' The drunk says it looks like a bat to him. The deputy says, 'What kind of person are you, wouldn't you rather see a butterfly than a bat?' The drunk says, "No, once in a while I want to see a bat.' The deputy says, 'That's your problem right there, you prefer bats to butterflies.'"

Fan and Cheng both laughed. Fan said, "With what we're going through now—"

Cheng: "Now we have to prefer bats whether we like it or not."

Fan smiled, "I think we're going to get very tired of bats."

"The little creatures, what they unleashed." Cheng shook his head. "It funny you mentioned—or I mentioned—Rorschach. He invented that whole procedure in 1921. He studied mental patients and controls—three hundred mental patients, so I guess he found the mental patients could be determined by what they saw in ambiguous forms. Rorschach died the year after he invented all this. Actually, he thought this was good test for schizophrenia, he didn't mean it to be a general personality test. There is, in fact, a 'butterfly or bat' inkblot test. I'm not sure what your choice—what you see—indicates about your personality. Of course, there are cultural differences. And it's more highly regarded—used—in some countries than others. The British don't use it, the Japanese love it. I don't know about the Chinese; we don't love psychiatry so much. We have the Communist Party to assuage us."

"Well, it's interesting what people see in something." Fan told Cheng about what she had "seen" in her nanomaterials—and about what Li said he had discerned in the simulation training.

"You know *you* are putting patterns there; Li thinks he is actually seeing something."

"Too much time on the moon?"

"Probably. What's going to happen when he really gets there? He might be disappointed. Or see some really fantastic things."

13.

When Li settled in to begin the training session, a message came up on the screen in place of the lunar landscape:

"YOUR TRAINING BEGINS A NEW PHASE TODAY.

Did "a new phase" mean him being quarantined?

SIMULATION WILL BE FURTHER ENCHANCED.

3D? Holographic?

AFTER A REVIEW OF PAST SESSIONS YOU WILL BE FURTHER IMMERSED IN THE LUNAR LANDSCAPE

Further immersed….? To begin how and when?

Then across the screen flashed scenes Li had been through—at least he recognized many though did not recognize some. He did not see the "city," but he did see himself wandering about on the surface. The "review" ended with a long look at the *Yutu-2* rover, box-like, the essence of machine, the essential robot traveler into space. But what camera was looking at the rover? Li guessed this itself was a simulation. The rover appeared like a condensed monolith, indifferent to human efforts, certainly human gaze. Yet Li found himself fixed on it for a time, as if he waited for some literal movement from it, some, well, sign.

What came was not so much a sign as an abrupt transformation. The training room disappeared. Instead of a large screen depicting the lunar landscape, the room *was* the moon—the room was not; it was all the moon.

Li stood, a man transformed, standing on the moon, space suited. From his helmet's visor he looked down at his arms, his torso, his legs. He slowly lifted moon boots from moon dust and placed them down. He made footprints. He reached down and picked up a handful of regolith and brought it to his face. Unlike previous simulations in which his hands could not effect any lunar grasp, he could indeed hold whatever piece of the moon he could grasp.

He was understandably astounded. This was beyond any science that was known. Had he been drugged? He had not eaten or had anything to drink since arriving here this morning. He tried (and tried is the word) to fix the reality of Lin and Yang, the earthly guards—gods?— of the training room, but he had the sudden and distinct feeling that they had left reality, at least his reality. Or he had left theirs. He pictured the building that housed the training room, he pictured roads that led to it; he was trying to affix his everyday reality—but that everyday existence seemed of another world, not the world he stood upon.

He turned around slowly. With just this simple movement he could feel himself in the lighter gravity of the moon. He turned slowly, as if at some point there might not be the moon in his vision. But the moon—and the bright sun beating upon it—was everywhere. The 180-kilometer reach of the Von Kármán crater was everywhere. Of course, most of it was beyond him, lost beyond the shorter distance of the lunar horizon.

Li tried to arrange his thoughts—and physical perceptions—in a linear, concrete fashion, confronting the "magic" of this surreal transformation with a stream of facts. He needed to ground himself, fix himself upon the "real." The Von Kármán crater was in a larger crater, the South Pole-Aitken basin, 2,500 kilometers wide and 13 kilometers deep. The northern part of Von Kármán was the walled plain of Leibnitz. There is a central peak at the midpoint of Von Kármán where the crater was formed after which lava had flooded the surface, leaving the southern portion of the crater flat and level.

Theodore von Kármán was a Hungarian-born mathematician and physicist. Even before the Nazis took power, he had been concerned about the tenor of the times in Europe and came to America. At Caltech he was the Ph.D. advisor to Qian Xuesan, who would work on

America's Manhattan Project, return to his homeland and become the founder of the Chinese space program.

Li had reviewed these facts as if they could help orient him as to what to do next. As for literal orientation, if he knew the name of the place in which he stood, he was in effect, in the middle of nowhere. Was he expected to proceed in one direction or another? In which direction? Would some voice come into his helmet, directing him? He actually half expected it. But that would be ridiculous. Or would it? He had to hold on to his thoughts to keep from getting not so much confused, as distracted. There must be something *he had to do*.

And then, quite minute, he saw the rover in the distance.

That gave him a veritable surge of hope. He had been standing before the rover the instant of his transformation—and had apparently "come to" far from it. He would go to it now.

He began to walk, then quickly had to adjust himself, clumsily, to the kangaroo hop of the moon's low gravity, the hop he had seen in films of the Apollo astronauts—the hop his simulated self had executed fairly well. During this not very long trek—if he was clumsy, he was keeping a good pace—he became more conscious of the sensations of his body, the movements of his muscles, and the insistent heat of the sun just outside the protection of his suit. He decided it was more a realization of the heat just outside this advanced protection than actually feeling it—it was like a distant threat that was not quite reaching him but could easily do so if something went wrong. Spacesuits were designed to protect the wearer from the 500-degree difference between lunar day and night. But for a moment Li trembled at what seemed frail protection: what human handiwork could withstand such cosmic brutality?

Li stood before the rover. How long ago had he stood before it when the transformation had taken place? Had it been on a short time ago?

Or much longer? He was not trusting his time sense.

As he had before, he stood before the rover for a time, as if waiting for—something.

And then he was in the training room again; the moon had disappeared. On the screen was:

THIS HAS BEEN THE FIRST PORTION
OF YOUR ENHANCED TRAINING
DUE TO THE NEW SITUATION OF QUARANTINE
THE PROGRAM WILL BE ADJUSTED ACCORDINGLY
AFTER A PERIOD THE NEXT SESSION WILL BEGIN

Adjusted accordingly? After a period? What is going on? Li looked about the room, absorbing its reality. Then he noted a tray of food had been left for him. This actually shocked him. The tray was warm. So while this room was the moon, someone had entered, someone not "on the moon," had left this food. That meant that the effect of this room being transformed was wholly in his head; there had not been some holographic transformation of the room. If there had been, whoever had entered would have been seen by him—

But wait, was he figuring this out right? There was some point in this, some aspect, he could not grasp.

Then he saw the cot in the corner of the room with a small mattress, sheets and blanket on what liked a foldable aluminum form.

This really unsettled him. Food, a bed—brought in here while he had been in the midst of the Von Kármán crater.

If his mind hadn't been captured and played with…. Had there been some diverting warp in space time: him on the moon, while the room had remained the same, and others had entered, two realities that "they" could both diverge and coalesce.

But of course he had not actually been on the moon; it was just a further extension of making the training more real.

ENHANCED

He felt this should have been explained to him, that he should have not just been thrust into it.

But perhaps that was part of the...test. To see if he could take whatever they thrust at him.

He looked at the door. He got up, went over to it. It was locked.

He had expected that.

He went back to his desk and ate his food. He looked at the clock. It was well into the afternoon. When was the next session to begin? What "period of time" would pass before—before what? Simply be on the moon again? He continued to eat, savoring the reality of the food. That was it, he realized. All along, he had been subjected to more extreme bends in reality. He was not simply training to go to the moon, but to be able to handle displacements in his reality.

My reality? Well, everyone's reality, isn't it?

Again Li tried to ground himself by returning to the "facts" he had pushed through his head during the all too real stimulation. He considered that both Van Kármán and Qian Xuesen had come to America and established themselves as brilliant scientists. But because Qian was Chinese there was a conflict the times made inevitable. He had been given security clearance to work on the Manhattan Project— even though before that, in 1940, army intelligence suspected him of being a communist. But apparently, he was needed at the project and continued to hold a security clearance. Then in 1950 he announced his intention to return to his home country. The Cold War had begun, and if America regarded the Soviets as their main enemy, the newly created regime of Mao in China was not looked upon well, either. In a conversation with undersecretary of the Navy Dan A. Kimball, Qian said he did not want to build bombs that would kill his countrymen. That statement put him under a loose house arrest: he was not allowed to leave the country. During this time, he wrote *Engineering*

Cybernetics, published in 1954, dealing in servomechanisms, the separate controls of multi-variable systems, von Neumann's theory of error control and perturbation theory. Qian fully showed the genius that would later help him design missiles and rockets.

During the five years he was in detention, Qian was under continuous surveillance, but was permitted to teach. There was a long and secret diplomatic negotiation between the U.S. and China for his release. Eventually he returned to China in 1955. It was rumored that the U.S. had exchanged him for eleven American airmen that had been held prisoner since the Korean War. Kimball would later say America's treatment of Qian had been a big mistake; he was no communist.

Li thought about how the passage of so much of science in the 20th century led to America. Look at Werner Von Braun, who been developing the V-2 missile for the Nazis; America takes him in after the war (along with many other Nazi scientists), and America beats the Russians to the moon. And now, two decades into the 21st century, it is to those Apollo missions we owe our knowledge of what being on the moon is like.

Though this century would have China in the forefront of space, Li was sure. Already the Chang'e program had claimed the far side of the moon.

Li had wondered more than once why had China chosen the far side of the moon for the Chang'e program. It would have made more sense to establish China's first foothold on the moon on the side that always faces Earth. There was the simple fact of communication. To place rovers and eventually a manned expedition on the far side, China first had had to place the *Queqiao* satellite beyond the moon, to relay communications to Earth from the far side.

Li was a focused and intelligent young man; but often his psyche, so focused on pushing himself to excel at whatever situation he was placed in, did not see the enveloping blood and beat of the society in which presented the tasks he would have himself accomplish. When he would ask himself about China's reasons for choosing the dark side, he would of course arrive at the obvious: because no other nation had landed there. *Chang'e 3* had touched down on the far side in 2013, and *Chang'e 4* in 2019. To do something others hadn't done was answer enough. And yet for some reason Li had to keep reminding himself of this reason, as if national pride at being first could not be a full explanation.

But perhaps that was only a quirk of Li's personality, to seek something more than socio-political honors.

At any rate, his country would be "satisfied" with pioneering the far side. A paper run by the Chinese Communist Party, *Global Times*, had editorialized:

"Unlike mankind's mania in the past, the Chinese people ultimately harbor the dream of shared human destiny and practice open cooperation. We choose to go to the back of the moon not because of the unique glory it brings, but because this difficult step of destiny is also a forward step for human civilization!"

Li was student enough of the history of the Space Age to sense in that "we choose to go to the back of the moon" an echo (if perhaps unconscious) of President John F. Kennedy's declaration to put a man on the moon by the end of the 1960s: "We choose to go to the moon in this decade and do the other things, not because they are easy, but because they are hard, because that goal will serve to organize and measure the best of our energies and skills, because that challenge is one that we are willing to accept, one we are unwilling to postpone, and one which we intend to win, and the others, too."

Li always wondered what those "other things" were. At any rate, Kennedy spoke from nationalistic pride; in this century the Chinese, at least officially, were claiming "a forward step for human civilization."

In fact, a number of nations had already contributed their science to the Chang'e program: Sweden, Germany, the Netherlands and Saudi Arabia.

While the Americans in the 1960s had had their ex-Nazis.

But all governments have their sins. At the moment Li, in quarantine because of the new virus, and suddenly in the surreality of "enhanced" lunar simulations, did not so much feel he was at the forefront of progress, but more a victim of it. Not that he would have applied the word "victim" to himself, but that he was being confronted with a rigorous, even harsh test.

And wait: did he really have a fever? For a moment he forgotten the reason why he'd placed in quarantine. He hadn't felt sick earlier today, and he didn't feel sick now. He pressed a hand to his forehead. He wasn't sure if he was warm or not. And shouldn't he be worried? This virus could be serious. If he actually did not have the virus, how soon would he exhibit symptoms? And his training would be disrupted....

Li suddenly recalled that the last Chang'e mission that had brought this lander and the rover to the moon contained a small, sealed biosphere of Earth life: the Lunar Micro Ecosystem, a three kilogram cylinder with seeds and insects eggs, an experiment to see if plants and insects could form an ecosystem in an enclosed environment on the moon. The seeds were of cottonseed, potato, rapeseed, and *Arabidopsis thaliana* (a flowering plant). Yeast and fruit fly eggs were the other half of the ecosystem. The experiment was designed to test if such a contained biosphere could maintain an ecosystem on the low gravity of the moon as well as the radiation it would be exposed to without the protection of an atmosphere.

The hatching fly eggs would produce carbon dioxide, the germinating plants would release oxygen. The presence of yeast would regulate the oxygen and carbon dioxide, while decomposing waste from the flies and dead plants would be a food source for the insects.

Within hours after landing on the moon, the seeds were watered and the temperature set at 24 Celsius—slightly more than room temperature. In less than two week the potato, rapeseed and cottonseed had sprouted. But the very next day the very frigid lunar night has set in, and it proved impossible to raise the temperature enough in the biosphere to preserve the life within. The experiment, intended to last for a hundred days, was cut short.

Did the insect and plant life, not possessing human consciousness, die of the lunar cold without awareness? Or was there, Li considered (and not find it strange at all he was thinking this way) some sense of doom and end that this nonhuman life possessed?

He shook his head; he needed now to focus on earthly matters. Li tried, though he knew it was useless, to call Fan. No service. But she would not know what happened to him. And he would not know how she was faring in the epidemic. There had to be some way he would—should—be allowed to contact at least one person. Wait: he had forgotten that Lin and Yang had promised to see that Fan and Li's family were contacted. Li normally called his parents once a week. If they did not hear from him they would fear the worst, especially as he was at the epicenter of the outbreak.

People do drop out of sight in this country, he thought: vanish. There was Cheng's friend, Dr. Sun. Was he in some state ordered, isolated, lockdown?

14.

Shortly after lunch, Cheng got a call from Dr. Sun's mother. Someone had told her he had been hospitalized with the virus, but the hospital would not confirm that when she called.

"I went to the hospital, but they told me patients with the virus could have no visitors, it wasn't safe. And even though I was there and stood in front of I don't know how many people and pleaded; they would not confirm if he was there or not." Her voice was strained, fearful, tearful. "You have a professional status. They would tell you, wouldn't they?"

Cheng was at once grateful (a poor word, though) that there was possibly some concrete word of Dr. Sun, and worried that he had been stricken with the virus.

"Which hospital? I'll go there."

"Oh, thank you, thank you," she said, tears overcoming her words.

Cheng was literally about to leave the lab—and abruptly leave his grave duties which the Mao-suited man had impressed on him—when he remembered there was no transportation to be had. He had been told he would have transportation (of what type undefined) to and from work, but first, it occurred to him just whom was he supposed to tell when he was leaving, and, secondly, he knew to ask for transport to try to find a friend in the midst of this lockdown would doubtless be a request not only looked upon without favor but refused.

He sought out Fan. He knew other colleagues with cars, but realized she was the only one he trusted.

Fan looked up from her micrographs with at first the displacement of being drawn from her own interior world to his presence. Cheng later thought that if he could have captioned her look it would be, literally, "Who are you?" It would be a recollection that amused him; he understood it. Often, to shift from entire concentration on one's work to an intrusion was like going from one distinct world to one less distinct—and annoying.

But Fan coalesced her displacement quickly into grasping Cheng's need. "Sure, let's sneak out."

Cheng inwardly cringed at that description. He normally walked in and out of the lab when he wanted to, but today they would indeed be "sneaking out."

. . .

It was a grey raw day. That was nothing unusual for Wuhan in January: usual daytime temperature in the forties, nighttime at freezing. The months when heat is most required is when the air is most polluted with the burning of coal; this city of 11 million in the 21st century, with some of the most modern of architecture along with the venerable, still used too much of a 19th century technology to warm its citizens.

Who were utterly locked away. Fan and Cheng saw literally no one on the street and few cars on the road. They passed a lone masked cyclist on a bridge. Was he pedaling to a distant destination? There were no police in sight to stop and question him, take his temperature. Fan and Cheng had arrived at the lab in the morning with the knowledge that the border, the hour of the lockdown was nigh; now they were seeing its result. It was indeed as if almost all life had been sucked from the city. The lone cyclist appeared like the survivor of a cataclysm, bearing a final sign of life. Cheng found himself watching the cyclist until Fan made a turn and this lone traveler was out of sight.

At the hospital the security guard in the parking lot peered sternly into the window at Fan and said, "Patient?" He saw two people in personal protective gear. Making the assumption that Fan was driving someone who needed hospital care, he gestured at Cheng—who took the lead on this, flashing his identification and saying, almost pompously, "Wuhan Institute of Virology. We are here in a professional capacity." Simultaneously Fan produced her identification. The guard studied the ID cards uneasily, then looked back at Fan and Cheng. He made a movement to the phone in his booth: "I should—" But Cheng was bold: "This had been arranged. We are here to see Dr. Sun." Fan almost smiled at how authoritative he sounded. It would be unlikely the guard knew the names of every doctor working in the hospital; he would certainly have no idea that Dr. Sun was a patient. In another minute the guard was giving Fan and Cheng a frustrated wave to proceed.

"We could have been stopped right there," said Fan as she pulled into a parking space.

"For some reason I don't think so."

"I think that smile means this isn't the first tale you're going to tell people."

"I will say what is necessary. You could think of some things, too."

"You look more official. It'll work better with you."

"Your assessment I think is correct."

When they entered the hospital Cheng was ready to play the same role to the security guard at the information desk, but the woman there seemed besieged in the midst of several people and Cheng and Fan walked past her, as she said to him, "How are we going to find him without asking?"

"We'll ask, a bit more further in."

Fan would recall that "more further in" like the memory of proceeding through a crowded maze. The protective gear she and Cheng wore was not as complete as most of those working the in hospital. Not only were their bodies covered, and their faces masked, but many of the doctors and nurses wore hoods that sheltered the sides of their faces and wore googles that fully covered the eyes. Everyone had on medical gloves. Consequently, there was the sense just from that that Fan and Cheng were not from the hospital community—and yet still had some professional capacity. So they were not unduly questioned when they asked a nurse as to the whereabout of Dr. Sun Bao. "A colleague," said Cheng, at once casual and with concern. The nurse looked up at him, the eyes above her mask not questioning his right to this knowledge, but apparently searching through her beleaguered mind to affix the name to the patient. Fan saw, and for the first time realized, how beleaguered indeed the staff was here, how severe this virus really was. There did not seem to be enough room for the sick. They lay on gurneys in the hallway, some silent, some calling out for attention, other conferring with a doctor or nurse. Fan noted one old man clutching at the arm of a nurse, who was tactfully trying to disengage his grip. Who would want to be gripped by a contagious person? Fan thought. Finally disengaging the hand with an abrupt jerk, the nurse, perhaps feeling guilty, patted the old man on the shoulder and said something to him—probably a promise to return—and then lost herself in the corridor of patients, doctors and nurses. While the nurse, who was trying to affix in her mind the information Fan and Li sought, seemed to be reworking her memory through corridors, and rooms of the afflicted—until she suddenly said, as if memory had rushed upon her like a torrent—"Oh, Dr. Sun. But you can't see him. He's a patient."

Fan said quickly, "We know that, but we're—"

"Even family. He is contagious."

Cheng: "We can stand—at a distance. It is very important." Again Cheng produced his identification, with Fan following suit.

And yet the contagious Dr. Sun was in a room with two other patients.

Fan and Cheng stood at one end of the room with its three patients: an old man, a middleaged man, and Dr. Sun in the middle bed. The middleaged man was sleeping, loudly snoring in irregular blasts. The old man turned his head and regarded these visitors quietly, while the nurse said, "Just for a for minutes. Make sure you don't go close." Though Cheng seemed to be disregarding her presence; Fan smiled at the nurse and assured her, "We will stay right here." In fact, she very much agreed with the caution, the necessity of procedure to thwart contagion. She certainly had no wish to catch the virus. She was here as a favor to Cheng, who seemed less fearful of the sick; several times he had stepped toward Dr. Sun on the bed, then caught himself before the nurse could give him a warning look. Though what was really going on in Cheng's mind when he caught himself was not worries about contagion (though he should have worried) but how sick Dr. Sun was, a man apparently in his late thirties (Cheng never had known his age) covered by a sheet up to his neck, his mouth covered with a mask and some type of oxygen-carrying device at his nose. Only the eyes and forehead seemed free of obstruction, and the eyes seemed half closed most of the times, flickering to open wider a little, than flickering into that half lidded state, like a man drifting on the shorelines of sleep and semi-wakefulness.

"He is very sick," the nurse asserted, as if she had to excuse the appearance and state of her patient.

Fan said, "So is it safe for them to be here?" She gestured to the other two patients. The old man blinked at the fact that Fan was including him in her statement and gesture; the faintest smile passed over his face, as if one of at once pleasure and irony.

"They're both sick," said the nurse—with the new virus or from some other cause, she did not say. What's the difference if the ill are together? she seemed to be saying. Fan did not pursue it.

Cheng softly called out Dr. Sun's name. There was no response. But just as Cheng turned to the nurse to ask about Dr. Sun's condition, he stirred, and tried to sit up. The nurse rushed over to him, speaking to him rapidly, in alternating tones that scolded him and sympathized with him. Dr. Sun settled back in bed. As if his movement without rising had tired him extremely—or was it that he realized he did not have to deign to speak with this visitors. –Though when Cheng called again, he raised his head, turned to one side of the room, then the other, as if focusing the ability of sight, then looked hard right in front him, where Cheng and Fan and the nurse stood. He seemed to take some long breaths—you could hear the hiss from his oxygen apparatus; a thin tube ran from a tank to his nose;—and slowly did sit up a bit...just as Cheng asked, "Bao, how long have you been here?"

Instead of a direct answer there was a laugh—a sad, difficult one—through the mask, and his own question: "How did you find me?" But it didn't seem he expected an answer. He added, vaguely, "I can't find myself here." It was a statement with several levels. It appeared to disconcert Cheng and intrigue Fan. The nurse frowned. Then Dr. Sun was saying, "They finally put me here. That's all they could do. They had to—" His head turned to the side again, as if that was a painful admission. He had turned in the direction of the old man who blinked back quietly, as if in agreement, or with the detachment of an observer who was not at all involved in what had stricken Dr. Sun, but had merely happened upon this scene.

When Dr. Sun turned back to the trio in front of him, he seemed to have gathered himself, stepped aside from whatever vagueness in which the virus had gripped him, though vagueness laced his story. He began broadly, with the larger story, something apart from himself, but a story in which he had become its center. "They're lying about the numbers, the cases. I went to everyone...I could. Officials." He said that word as if it were a breed of creature that life was afflicted with, and which had to be approached with urgent strategies. "They looked back at me" (Fan thought that a curious phrase) "as if I couldn't...count. It would be too shocking for the people to know, that was what they meant. Why was I surprised?" Cheng, Fan and the nurse, too, could feel the wan smile beneath the mask. In fact, Dr. Sun touched the mask, perhaps assuring himself the smile was there. He slightly shook his head. It made a faint whoosh against the pillow, which apparently was plastic, not fabric.

"What happened," he said, slightly wheezing, was that I went to too many people. I took videos—and too many people saw the videos. The people—and them. I was trying to convince one of them, desperate at that point, and naïve, the numbers you have to look at the numbers, admit to them, release them so we can all— I was going on. And then I was shown to—and I was still talking, still trying to convince—a room, some place, where I was told—ordered—to stay while 'all this' would be investigated further. I was probably the first person to be quarantined because of the virus who did not have the virus. Then, anyway." He coughed subtly, almost delicately, as if not trying to make an ironic point.

Fan noted a distressed look on Cheng's face. He moved toward the bed. It was almost as if, Fan felt (for no reason she could have explained) that Cheng was facing some sort of guilt at the distress of his friend. And possibly more than friend—despite what Cheng had told her. She didn't know any details of this friendship, but it was plain Cheng was pulled toward this man. Who regarded Cheng without any particular emotion (it seemed) from the eyes just above the line of the mask. In fact, the old man appeared to regard Cheng with more interest; he seemed puzzled, in a sad way, trying, like Fan, to unravel an inexplicable thing he sensed. While Cheng was regretting things not said; and even though he had told himself in the past it was not likely Dr. Sun was gay, and even if that, had any romantic interest in him, he felt he had allowed his friend to move into a situation in which any overtures would seem tasteless in light of the emergency the virus had brought to everyone, personally and collectively. Cheng, paused in some uncertain emotion, not knowing what to say, or if he should say anything, seemed in a sudden center for a dynamic that could have no resolution. It was a quandary he was perhaps saved from by the nurse, who had certainly been absorbing everything Dr. Sun said, and without surprise, for she had experienced the day to day of what the virus had wrought and how the silence of the authorities had helped the infection to spread—the nurse gestured to Cheng to step back, or at least not step any closer. Cheng looked at her as if he'd forgotten for a moment she was there, then gave her an expression of apology and even obedience, but did not move back. There was a sort of compromise: he would not move any closer to the bed, but he would not move back. The nurse shook her head, frowned, but did not insist Cheng keep wholly to the rules. After all, in her eyes he was an official visitor.

Following a pause—in which he possibly finally sensed something of Cheng's heart and mind—Dr. Sun said, "I was in this room—I really don't have any idea where it was—in the back of some official building—I mean I could find the building but not the room—one day someone I had not spoken to came to me—he was wearing a Mao suit, but cut in a modern way, like a 21st century version of a Mao suit—" Dr. Sun did not notice Cheng shaking his head slightly, making somber connections. "He told me my assessment was more or less accurate— he seemed to stress the 'less' more than the 'more'—and that the government would be looking at the virus with 'a different path.' But he added—very coldly—that I had been 'gravely wrong' in posting videos online. I was 'worrying the people without solution.' He told me the video had been removed. I told him everyone has to recognize the problem before there can be a solution. He just shook his head at that—as if I were a naïve child, patted me on the shoulder—I didn't like that—and left, telling me, 'We will take care of you.' I did not like the sound of that, either."

He pushed his head further back on the pillow and looked at the ceiling. He had to relieve himself for a moment of the presence of others and their sympathy. But a sudden snore, a series of snores from the man on the other side of him, drew his look to human intrusion. He reached a hand up to the bridge of his nose above the mask and massaged it with apparent deliberation, as if it recalling he had an oxygen tube there and that he had been distracted from its continual annoyance.

"I was there another day, and I guess they were taking care of me, feeding me, but I was waiting for something...unpleasant. Then something unpleasant did happen: I got the virus. Did I have it before they brought me to that room? Did I get it from one of those men that came to talk to me, that brought me food? The one with the Mao suit?" (Fan noted a little flinch of expression on Cheng's face.) Dr. Sun shook his head against the pillow, or was he simply scratching the back of his head? "They came to see me—confront me—like I was in a hospital. Then I got worse, and they brought me here. Left me here. None of them have visited. As if I am not a danger—now. Was I then? Will I be? But Cheng, you haven't told me, what exactly is the situation— now? I'm sure it's not good. But how much not good?"

Cheng had almost started at being directly addressed. Until that moment it seemed Dr. Sun had a barrier between himself and others: his sickness, his protest against the secrecy of the authorities had set him apart from everyone, certainly those in that hospital room. But by that question Dr. Sun had rejoined the sphere of others. Cheng, feeling the attention on himself, was not sure what to say right away. The old man looked to Cheng, expecting something important, something vital. Fan almost opened her mouth to speak, but then Cheng quickly said, "It is difficult." (Why did he feel he had to be tactful—wasn't "difficult" a tactful word?—and not blunt?) "Did you know Wuhan, all of Hubei, is on lockdown?"

"I was expecting that. Not an auspicious new year."

The nurse said to Fan and Cheng, "I am sorry, you should be leaving."

Cheng nodded. "We appreciate— Just a few more minutes."

The nurse tilted her head a little, weighing. "Another minute." She tried to say it sharply, but it was more kind than otherwise. "He's not well. None of them—" She gestured, indicating not just Dr. Sun but the patients on either side. The old man had settled back on the bed; he paid no attention. The other patient continued to snore. Dr. Sun seemed to nod slightly, too, agreeing. "I have patients I have to see." She turned quickly and left.

For the first time, Cheng acknowledged the old man. He apologized for the intrusion. "We had to find my colleague," he said, gesturing to Dr. Sun. The old man returned this statement of duty with his own gesture: he understood. He stretched himself out and closed his eyes. Cheng introduced Fan to Dr. Sun. With the hand that had massaged his nose and which he'd kept outside the blanket, he gave a weak wave.

Softly, Fan said to him, "How are you?"

Dr. Sun gave a weak laugh. He raised the hand then let it fall. "As you can see...."

Cheng: "But you'll recover."

Dr. Sun: "There's that hope." It was an answer that for a brief moment considered possibilities, not certainties. Thus there was the sense of another sort of smile behind the mask. "I have to struggle with all I know. And I don't know if I should worry more about the virus than...the authorities."

Cheng asked, "They haven't been back?"

"Not since I've been here. I guess they think I'm harmless now. But if I get better—will it be that room again?" Though he didn't really say this as a question. He took in a difficult breath. In sudden sympathy, Fan felt herself tense with the effort. "It's not good—or maybe it is— fighting something you know too much about. Though we really don't know enough."

"Everyone is working on it. Everything is mobilized now."

"Finally."

"A lot of that is to your credit."

Dr. Sun coughed. "It would be nice to think so; but I imagine it's more that the situation is just too...large. There is a point where no one can ignore...." He drifted off. He concentrated on breathing.

Cheng said, "I would think they would have you in here alone."

A weak laugh. "So I'd be more vulnerable?"

"Because—contagion."

Another laugh seemed to mingle with a slight cough. "We're all—here—" He spread both arms outward, lifting the other from under the cover. The old man, who seemed to have no longer been paying attention, nodded at that. "At this point, all the same," Dr. Sun added. "And it's better, the company." After a pause: "We don't talk too much, but we bear it together." Another pause. "Not that I've been here that long. It only seems longer."

Abruptly the nurse was in the doorway again. She said, impatiently, "It's more than a minute."

Fan was placating. "We're leaving. We're sorry. We were worried."

The nurse shook her head, shot out a long sigh. "I will be back here in two minutes." She quickly disappeared.

Fan looked to Cheng, who nodded back, then said to Dr. Sun, "We'll be back." Fan noted that he apparently included her in future visits.

Dr. Sun raised a hand in more of a salute than a wave. "Make sure neither of you come back as a patient."

Cheng nodded quickly, like a child taking a parent's advice. As he and Fan left, she turned to wave at both Dr. Sun and the old man. The other patient still slept, but he was not snoring now. There was a sense of suspended quiet in the room, as if an event had just passed through its confines, then departed, leaving an aftermath no one, either visitors or patients could yet divine.

Fan and Cheng quietly moved through the hospital, got lost twice looking for an exit, had to step through corridors lined with patients and passed rooms in which doctors and nurses moved in and out of with urgency. Both had the sense that they were working with difficulty through a labyrinth in which illness dictated one's path and the exit of which—to life—was not easy to achieve. When the two finally reached the main entrance once again, Cheng said to Fan, "I have to keep in touch with him, make sure he's being treated." Fan looked at him, said nothing, thinking that was Cheng's hope, but the reality might be something else, was in fact likely to be something else.

Before they got into her car, Fan said. "Are you going back to the lab? It's late already."

Cheng frowned, looked at the low winter sun. "I'd like to go back, yes. Unless you—"

"No, I want to go back, too. I need to—" She sighed. "I've been thinking of a new—well, I will tell you later."

Another sort of quiet settled between them as they drove back to the lab. On the way to the hospital, they had taken in the surreal aspect of locked down Wuhan, but they had also been seeking their destination. Now, returning from it, their mission in a sense accomplished (if it had left them with unease), they more absorbed the spectacle of the great city silenced by an invisible pathogen. Cheng was thinking he became fascinated with virology when he had learned, around fifteen or so, that viruses were so minute they fell in between the wavelengths of light and so could not be seen even with a normal microscope. And yet this infinitesimal invisibility had brought Wuhan to an abrupt stop. The closed shops with their New Year's decorations particularly brought this home. A tradition of celebration going back countless calendar years now stilled by a virus, that parasitic creature of protein and ribonucleic acid. While Fan's thoughts were not too unsimilar. As a child she had loved the bright red decorations of the New Year's Spring Festival, the shops with gifts and sweets, and the pleasure her parents took in her pleasure in bringing her into these wonderful places. That was indeed innocence then, when the holiday and the turning of the year was a happiness that was ignorant of the commercial, when it was all about family and presents. Of course, when older, she understood the more venal aspects of this time, but she could still partake of its graces. But now all that was checked, by a pathogen that was a true denizen of the nanoworld. She recalled Li's miniature city on the moon, about how they had talked about worlds within atoms—and then remembered:

"I have to pick up Li. He won't be able to get home." Cheng looked at her as if that consideration was bizarrely apart from any aspect of the moment. "I have no idea when he finishes today. When we get back—but he says there's no service in his training room."

"I'm sure he'll call you when he gets outside."

She sighed. "I wish we knew how long this is going to last. I think it's going to get…stranger."

Cheng nodded. He found himself looking for that lone cyclist, as evidence of human movement (other than himself and Fan) through this unmoving city. They passed a man emerging from a van, unloading boxes of food in front of an apartment building, provisions for the sequestered. The man turned a masked face toward Fan's car as they passed, and he gave an abrupt wave, recognizing them as among the few who had ventured out into—were allowed to venture into—the stilled city. Fan waved back; Cheng gave an enigmatic look. Here was indeed another sign of human activity, but it was activity created out of the lockdown. The cyclist they had seen earlier was an individual passage, apart, a passage of the self—or so Cheng imagined it….

15.

Re-entering the lab, both Fan and Cheng felt they would be immediately accused of having stolen away from important work at hand. But no one said anything to them. Until Cheng, back in his office, checking messages, was abruptly visited by the Mao suited man, who said, in an affected friendly way, "I was looking for you."

Several responses went through Cheng; he chose a bold one—that might also sound casual. "I was visiting a friend in the hospital."

"A hospital isn't a healthy place to be—now."

"No. Especially as a patient."

"Your friend—the virus?"

"Yes."

"But I thought...visitors weren't allowed."

Cheng looked down, as if considering his next words. He looked back up. "Certain visitors. You visited him...before."

"I...visited—?"

"Dr. Sun."

"Oh..." The other said that slowly, then quickly smiled. Perhaps he had solved a puzzle—or was presenting Cheng with one. "H he is a friend?"

"Yes. He had disappeared. His mother asked me—"

"A mother would be worried."

"I was just about to call her, tell her—"

"What though?"

"Why does that concern you?"

"But you know it does."

"Yes. You visited him. Threatened him?"

That smile again. "Your friend...was not cautious. How well did you know him?"

Cheng did not like that was asked in the past tense. And he detected an undercurrent in that question, possibly hinting at Cheng's sexual preference. ""I'm not sure how well. But when you say he wasn't cautious, he was trying to...."

"Yes?"

"Tell people what was happening. Tell the government."

"You don't think our government knows--?"

"It knows. As everyone does now. Why did you want him silenced?"

"Information has to be done properly."

"Information is 'done'? What does that mean?"

"Let us not spar like this. It belittles us both."

"The government belittled Dr. Sun. Violated him."

"That is a strong accusation."

Cheng said nothing. He wondered if something would be done to him. The man cocked his head and smiled—as if saying: *Where we go from here depends on you.* What that meant depended on how Cheng would react to what this emissary of the government wanted from him. This man had told Cheng earlier today how valuable he was; that meant he was to be "used." But in what way?

Cheng almost said, "I don't know your name," but changed that to the more assertive, "What is your name?"

"I told you this morning."

"You spoke too fast."

"I could understand—you must have a lot on your mind. Having to search for—"

"Then tell me again. Or is a secret?"

"No secrets, Mr. Chang. I'm Dong Chao."

For Cheng it was a small victory (not so much victory as an assertion of a defense) that he had drawn this from—demanded from—the Mao suited man. "And what department of the government are you from?"

"I don't need to tell you that—you don't need me to tell you that. Let's just say it's related to intelligence."

"That I don't understand. Or maybe I do."

"There are many facets here, many facets. What we are interested in right now is mutations of the virus."

"We're all interested in that."

Dong Chao leaned forward. "This is what we really need for you now. Already the virus is taking on—or becoming, that's more accurate—different identities."

"Identities?"

"My phrase. Being in my field— The word doesn't matter. One of the first patients diagnosed with this has remained infectious for six weeks now. He is about fifty, did not have a bad case, was barely sick, a little cold—which was not good. It would have been better if he had stayed in bed. Because he continues to test positive for the virus after two weeks, three, three and half weeks, thirty days, thirty-five days, forty days. He will be tested again tomorrow. That means he is shedding the virus, giving it to others. If we have a city of even a few of these—"

Cheng was both intrigued and alarmed at this news. If there was one carrier like this there were probably others. Whether it was many or a few.... But even a few could spread the virus exponentially. He said, "But the government has been assuring everyone the virus wasn't contagious."

"We didn't have all the information we now have."

"That was a convenient lie. That put everyone in more danger. So it turned out not to be convenient."

"Have your—anger. You and your friend. He's in the hospital now."

"What does that mean? Did you put him there?"

"Me?"

"Your intelligence."

"Please. We are going off the point. We need you to research this mutation, to give us...information about this—and other possible mutations. How the virus can possibly change, what those changes could mean."

"That is very hard to forecast. A change in a protein—we don't know what it means just finding it, it's connecting that mutation to results, what it does in the body."

"I understand, I understand. It's not a simple task. That is why you...are special to doing this."

"Do you tell all the other researchers they are special?"

"Only a few, that have earned it."

"And I begin when, how?"

"I think you know how to begin. You will be provided with all the research—so far. It's not that much. I imagine you will be providing the bulk of it."

"Myself?"

"Bring whomever you want into it. But you will be heading it."

"Well, it's a challenge." Cheng slowly nodded. "Of course, I will proceed."

Dong smiled. "Good, good."

"But let me ask you this—"

"Yes?"

"Is that a designer Mao suit? Paris?"

Dong gave a genuinely pleased laugh; he apparently did not take it as a dig. "No, Italian. A lot of Chinese, you know, work in Milan. So, I had a connection. It's a variation on a traditional style."

"Would Mao have considered himself traditional?"

"What was new then is tradition now." Dong suddenly seemed in a rush. "I will get the research to you. We will speak again."

"I'm sure."

Cheng looked after the vanished official. So much seemed to have happened just in one day. He sat at his desk, looking over some recent research on the virus. There were the colored graphics of the virus, its round body one color, the protein spikes another. These simplified renderings communicated a sense of the "body" of the virus, but they were, to Cheng, like drawings in a children's book, that gave a basic sense of form but lacking an essential nuance. He considered this something like the illustrations of atoms from a hundred years ago: a sort of solar system with electrons in oval orbits around a nucleus.

Then he suddenly remembered: Dr. Sun's mother.

Her great exhalation of relief, overlain with continued worry when

Cheng told her he had visited her son in the hospital, was for a moment too great, too emotional for Cheng to gather it all in. He suddenly felt himself responsible for what could happen now to Dr. Sun—even as the doctor's mother said she would call the hospital. Cheng cautioned her that the hospital was not allowing visitors due to possible transmission of the virus, adding he had gotten in to see Doctor Sun because "I have some official capacity." (He inwardly winced at describing himself that way—as if he might be connected to Dong Chao and his Mao suit.)

"But at least I can talk to him on the phone."

"I'm not sure. They don't allow cell phones and I didn't see a phone in his room. You can call the nurse's station…."

"They've got to let me talk to him."

"Whatever happens, I will keep you informed," said Cheng, feeling this poor woman would not be able to reach her sick son.

He sat awhile at his desk, his head in his hands. Then, as if his call to Dr. Sun's mother had caused a ripple in the universe of phone calls, he received a call from his parents in Beijing. After the urgency and worry of speaking to his friend's mother, the more measured concern of his parents was welcome. His mother said, "We'd say you should have left Wuhan, but this is your game, and I'm sure you're needed."

"In fact, I'm being told I'm very special here at the moment," he said with self deprecation.

His father said, "Just don't wind up in one of those hospitals. We just saw the news."

Cheng did not mention he had just been visiting one of "those hospitals"; instead, he asked, "How is the news in Beijing looking at this?"

His father began to reply, but his mother shouted over him: "Your deserted city looks like the end of the world." Cheng could hear his father sigh at this. His father said, "It seems what is necessary to control it is being done."

Cheng said flatly, "Yes, that's being done." He did not add that if what was "necessary" were indeed being effected, the question of "control" was unsettled, unpredictable.

Right after that conversation he received an email from Dong: the reports on the mutated virus—and the directive to visit the unusual patient, along with a number at which he could text Dong.

I will go, but I am not a doctor, was Cheng's text.

We have doctors for him. I want a virologist to look at what this patient seems.

To, Cheng "seems" was an odd word choice. *When?*

Tomorrow. No later.

Cheng realized that as a scientist he was used to approaching a phenomenon in his own time, studying it a manner and at a pace in which he worked best. Now phenomena, outside events were pushing him to work in a manner and pace that was not of his own choosing but that was molded by events. How was this all going play out?—for him?

Not long after, at the end of the day, Cheng talked to Fan. She told him she had not heard from Li yet. She was more frustrated than annoyed. "Maybe he's in lockdown on the moon," Cheng lamely joked. Fan grimaced and shook her head, asked Cheng if wanted to leave, she'd drive him home. Cheng told her, "I've been promised transportation, but I'd rather ride with you. I'll look over this material at home."

He told her about the patient who had tested positive for six weeks now.

"One person—a few people—like that could infect hundreds."

"Yes, it could be more serious than—" Cheng stopped himself; he had the sense that degrees of seriousness would all seem the same horror in the end.

"Anyway, I wanted to talk to you. I had an idea today, and you're the one who can tell me if it could work."

Cheng laughed. "Don't make me responsible for you, too."

They were getting in her car at this point. Fan said, "What do you mean, you too?"

Cheng tried to make light of an apparent Freudian slip. The visit to Dr. Sun, his meeting with the official, being charged with research of mutations, his conversation with the doctor's mother: today he had become *responsible*. He felt an actor given a role for which he had not auditioned. He laughed and said to Fan, "I just meant a lot of things have been thrown at me today." He told her about talking to Dr. Sun's mother."

"Well, you are going to have to keep track of what is happening with him."

"It's not that I don't want to—"

Fan said carefully, "Cheng, I know you told me that—"

"I admit I'd be interested. But I'm not thinking about that at all now. He's done something brave. He needs to be protected. And I don't mean from the virus."

Fan nodded, drove on for a few minutes in silence.

The last light of the winter day was the thinnest strip in the west. Actually, both had left work earlier than usual. In January it would be completely dark when their day at the lab was done. The yellow-orange that was left of sunset was like a surreal, far-off wound that showed at the horizon of highways, and at the end of streets lined with closed shops. Some of the shops had one low light on coming from somewhere in the back of the shop, while their signs outside in front were dark; other stores had their full outside lighting above dark shops. For Fan it was really sinking in. The lockdown announcement in the middle of the night, driving to the lab that morning—it was an abrupt, if expected change. Driving to the hospital earlier she'd felt like an explorer traversing a strange landscape. Now she had fully absorbed the fact that this was familiar landscape, transformed—transformed for who knew who long, and by something that was immediate to her work.

She said to Cheng, "What I've been doing, the TMV substrate, the recycled plastic—"

"Your nanoweave. We'll all be wearing masks from it."

"What would you say about this mask: with a protein from this virus as substrate?"

Cheng smiled. "Sounds like a mask vaccine."

"That's what I was thinking."

"Breathing in that material would create antibodies?"

"Would it?"

"I have no idea. Sounds possible. Though I have a feeling the standard answer would be no."

"Aren't there vaccines administered through the nose?"

"With precise doses. Yours wouldn't be…exact."

"But continual wear—"

"Well…it's an imaginative idea."

At home Cheng found himself smiling at Fan's imagination. "Who knows, she may be on to something brilliant," he said aloud to himself.

He had the feeling that each day would bring something new to consider. For instance, today, just when he and his colleagues figured the structure of the virus had been set, there is a mutation. Probably it would only be slight—in structure, that is, but that slight change could increase its rate of contagion.

He slowly began to realize how tired he was. Seeing his friend in that hospital bed had had its effect on him. Sometimes he knew he fell into the common delusion that being on the scientific side of this epidemic gave some sort of protection against the virus that the average person did not have. As if just *knowing* more were a protection. Of course, doctors and nurses in hospitals were like soldiers on the front lines: they were exposed over and over again to the enemy's fire. For a surreal instant Cheng envisioned innumerable viruses bombarding his medical colleagues in trenches. And then asked himself: *Am I going to get this—thing?*

And was a virus, who needed a host to "come alive," a thing or creature? It was a question he had often asked himself, both ironically and soberly, a question with no definite answer. Ultimately, he would say, it did not fit our definitions of either the animate or inanimate.

He thought about the virus travelling a good deal past Hubei province, and not just throughout China, but into other countries. Of course, that was what viruses do. Someone from Wuhan, or many people from Wuhan, in the early days of this, had been infected, not yet become sick, and traveled to other parts of China, and to other countries. In the 21st century (and well back into the 20th) an infected person could get on a plane and in six hours or twelve be thousands of miles away, be halfway around the world, presenting the virus with new hosts—and, thus, creating a pandemic.

Cheng cocked his head in contemplation at this thought. He had not, until this very moment, considered this new relative of SARS could be the pathogen of a new pandemic. It was a surreal thought that he could be at the epicenter of something that could ravage the globe.

But was "ravage" too strong a world? Time would tell.

The prospect of an infected person bringing the virus far and wide, of the virus becoming more contagious, led Cheng to thoughts of AIDS. He had said to himself in the past that if he had been a young or middleaged gay man in the 1970s, while the virus was taking hold in thousands of gay men, but not yet manifesting (a long term mechanism still not understood), or in the 1980s when it did, he would have at least some chance of having contacted it. The human immunodeficiency virus (HIV) had run like a fire through the world's gay male population, if more so in the west than Asia. Cheng had not been promiscuous as so many of those first AIDS victims had been. He had recalled reading that the first 2,500 AIDS cases had had sex with an average of 90 partners. And speaking of spreading a pandemic by airplane: there was the infamous "Patient Zero," the French-Canadian airline steward who allegedly had had sex with 2,500 people. To be assailed with the intimacy and proximity of so many foreign bodies. It was no wonder that one's immune system would be assaulted. Of course, Cheng knew there were cases of HIV that had come from much less intimate repetition.

China had had many less cases than, say, the U.S.; then again Cheng well knew the Chinese were always reluctant to reveal the full extent of anything negative, especially a disease, among their population.

He remembered details about AIDS in China in the 1980s, but he had learned them so long ago…. He opened his laptop for some cursory research.

Officially the first AIDS case in China was in 1985—the year, Cheng knew, when AIDS fully exploded in the American media, driven by the death of actor Rock Hudson. Fan, ever the source of all things U.S., had filled him in on this. At any rate, through the first years of the 1980s, China was the unfortunate recipient of blood products from America, especially blood products to treat hemophilia. If the Chinese government would quickly come to regard AIDS as a product of a degenerate lifestyle, the truth could not be denied that AIDS had been brought into the country by America—American capitalism, by companies who in fact knew that their blood products might not be safe.

Cheng read that at the end of 1984, there were 7,699 cases of AIDS in the U.S., with 3,665 deaths, a staggering mortality rate. There were 762 cases in Europe. By the end of 1985, there were 20,000 cases worldwide.

So America had brought this scourge to the world. It made him think about the possibility that America had deliberately brought this new virus to China during those military athletic games this past October. But the evidence at present strongly indicated the virus had originated in China.

Cheng sighed. *Let us hope it was not from the lab.*

Apparently, at least as the official story went, AIDS in China was not widely spread by gay men, but more by intravenous drug users. By the end of the century between 60 and 70 percent of those with HIV in China had contracted it in this manner. In fact, from 1985 until the end of the '80s, only 22 people tested positive of HIV in all of China, 18 of whom were foreigners or what were considered "Overseas Chinese." AIDS was seen as "loving capitalism disease." The Chinese believed their country largely free of the "perverted practices" of the west necessary for the disease to spread.

The decade of the 1990s saw a rise in infections due to unsafe practices in blood donations clinics, which in fact the government had to shut down for a year or so before they could reopen with new health guidelines.

If this century had brought not a cure but treatment for AIDS to the extent that it was no longer an automatic death sentence, Cheng considered this new virus still did not have the mortality rate of AIDS—or SARS. But it appeared more and more contagious. The face of Dr. Sun came to mind again.

That night Cheng dreamt he was searching through the streets of Wuhan for the Patient Zero of the new virus. He knocked on doors. Those who answered his knock were distressed and wary and gestured him away, offering no knowledge of what he sought. Many cursed at him. Many doors did not open. But then the dream shifted, and he was in a room, a drab room, maybe it was a kitchen, with the winter light from one window falling roughly on a man of about fifty sitting on an old wooden chair and he was telling Cheng, "I don't know how it happened to me. I was fine, I was fine, I was healthy," while very visible and innumerable viruses—the rounded, spiked coronavirus— were seeping out of his body like a tide, sliding down his body, flooding onto the floor, making a swelling puddle that was seeping toward Cheng, who found himself stepping backwards, toward the other end of the room. "But you can help me," said the man. "They sent you. They sent you."

Cheng woke from that dream with a start, ran his hand over his face, fell back to sleep with a sort of relief. He wanted to sink into hours of dreamlessness before he would have to face morning. He was given that dreamlessness; at least he would recall no further dreams when he was awakened with the wan morning light.

Fan was also tired that evening. And distressed she could not reach Li, worried that he had not called. He must be locked into a long training session on his simulated moon. How strange that he lived in a lunar world for hours every day while still on Earth. –And now on this Earth of Wuhan, in the midst of an epidemic.

From the courtyard below she heard Mystery. Watching him climb up the ivy to her window, Fan thought again, "Where do you go?" And then made a connection: Mystery was like Li, going "out there," then returning from the unknown. In fact, yes, if Li were a cat, he'd be very much like Mystery....

She would have to tell that to Li.

Her parents called. Her mother expressed a normal concern—which was a great deal of concern, the situation being what it was. "Is it safe for you, in that lab?"

"Probably the safest place in Wuhan." This could hardly be true, but Fan said it so convincingly.

"At least you're not working in a hospital. Can't you just leave for a little while, come here?"

Fan's father, nearing retirement from his military career, was stationed in northeast China.

"You know no one can get out of the city." And Fan realized that even if she had the opportunity to, she would not have left Wuhan. There was a challenge here for her, for her work.

"It horrible. Horrible," her mother said.

Her father tried to act less worried than her mother, but Fan sensed his concern. As usual siding with the established order, he said, "It seems they're taking the right precautions."

"I think so." But who could really know, at this point, what was "right"?

"If it's contained, it will pass—soon, I hope. But I know they don't tell everyone the full extent of the situation. Just how bad is it?"

Fan sighed. "It's not good. But when you compare the number of cases with the population—" She knew she was sounding formal.

Her father seemed to accept that. He made some remarks about the weather where they were, asked about the weather in Wuhan, and that was it.

Fan found herself nodding off soon after dinner. She did not want to go to sleep that early. She made a brief attempt to watch the news, but felt she knew more than what was being shown.

Sleep—and dreams—did overcome her. She dreamt she wore a huge, trailing cape of her viral nanoweave around her, as if a royal cape, and she moved through the lab while others complimented her on this unique garment. In her small office she hung the cape on the wall, spread it out like a tapestry—and it became so: in the weave she made out figures, buildings, country scenes. She found herself straining hard before these images, straining to make a story from them, a message she was meant to absorb. Then into the room came one of the official visitors from the other day, the one Fan had told that her nanoweave might be used as a material for masks.

"Oh, you made so much," he said. "But we have to cut it up."

Fan cried out as the man began to shred huge pieces of the nanotapestry with some type of electric scissors, tearing through the images she had been trying to interpret. She rushed at the man, grasped his hand. He tried to pull himself away and cursed at her. This was so different from his original happy and pleasing attitude that Fan actually felt hurt, even betrayed. She awoke feeling herself in the aftermath of a physical struggle that had stabbed deeply into her psyche.

There in the dark, breathing slowly, remaining troubled by the dream, she reached for her phone and tried Li again. No answer.

Chapter Six: Lunatic

16.

Li was surprised—shocked—when the door to the training room suddenly opened, and two figures entered in full protective gear. There was a shot of fear: was something horrible going to be done to him?

"We're bringing you what you need," said one of them. It was Yang's voice. So it was Lin and Yang. Li was abruptly relieved. But still in a remnant of shock over his situation. He wanted to ask questions, to complain, but simply watched the two men go in and out of the room, bring a cot, a small refrigerator, a hot plate, plates, chopsticks, a pot and some clothing.

Finally, Li said, "Wait, I have to ask—"

One of them stopped and said, sternly: "What?" It was Lin.

"What is happening to me here?"

"You are quarantined. We told you. We are making you comfortable."

"The training has changed. It's as if—"

Lin: "We don't know anything about that. We have our job, you have yours."

Yang: "We were told to tell you, if you get sick— Wait, we didn't take—" he approached Li with a forehead thermometer. Li instinctively back away. "Stop," said Yang. Li stopped, held his breath as Yang swept the instrument across his forehead, an inch away.

Yang and Lin both looked at the reading together, as if it were something they had to confer over. Lin said, "Three tenths of a degree less. That's good. But—there will be someone to give you a test for the virus—though the tests are not that reliable yet. Even with a negative result you will be here fourteen days."

The pair also placed a phone, a landline, in the room, connected to an outlet Li had not even noticed before. It was Yang who said, "This is for when they need to reach *you* officially. You cannot make calls on it."

"Who is going to call me?" Both Lin and Yang shrugged simultaneously, gesturing they were unable to answer. Li said, "I have to reach my parents. And a friend."

Yang cocked his head. "A lady friend?"

"Yes." Li said this flatly. He did not want to show any vulnerability.

"Give us the numbers. We will call—or have them called. To let them know you are safe. That is all we can say."

Li hesitated to give this odd pair any such information, but he had to take a chance. "So you promise you will call."

Yang: "They will be contacted."

Lin: "You think we would lie?"

Li in fact did not trust the pair. Would they call his parents and Fan and say bizarre things? He said, "It's important they know, so they won't—"

"Worry, yes, of course," said Yang. Li sensed a smile behind the mask. Whether it was a trustworthy smile or not….

Soon Yang and Lin had left. Their very prosaic if odd presence made his recent very real-seeming experience of being on the moon all the more strange. He was caught in a maelstrom of thoughts: of what he had just been through, his need to get in contact with his parents and Lin, the fact that he was in a locked down city in quarantine in what must be the strangest place in the city.

And then the phone rang.

As the expression goes, he practically jumped out of his skin. The phone had just been put there and now it was ringing. He had been shoved into world, some sort or realm that wasn't real—or not operating in the way the real world had operated all of his life. He walked over to the phone and picked it up. He tried to say "Hello" without emotion, but the word was too drawn out to seem natural. He seemed to hear a slight echo of his voice from the other end—and heard nothing in return for a beat. Then a voice came through: "Zhen Li, you have been doing well." The voice was so precisely modulated as to almost seem artificial, but there was a strength, at least a confidence, that was visceral and thus fleshly.

"Who is this?"

"That doesn't matter. You are to just listen. You have been chosen for the most advanced tests. Keep in mind in the subsequent sessions—which may come upon you without warning—you are to pay close attention to what you find unusual" (as if being "transported" to what literally seemed the moon was not unusual), "and pursue it. Decipher it. Resolve it."

"What am I going to find unusual?" He was thinking of the miniature city, of the markings.

Another pause. "We cannot give you…forewarning. That would defeat the purpose. Explore. Decipher." (That world again. Did they mean the markings?)

Li found himself sighing. "I wish this could be clearer." Then he regretted saying that; it was too much an admission that he was not in control.

"Keep this clear," said the voice—almost in a friendly and encouraging manner (almost): "We need you to tell us things *we* do not know."

Li could not help saying, "I didn't think this was the way to train for the moon."

"This is not the old American missions of fifty years ago. Half a century. Just to go, land and return. In our new century—but the century isn't so new now, is it?—in our time we have much more to work. We are going to the moon in a different way."

The caller hung up. Li sat back. He did not quite feel himself. He wondered if he were sick; he wondered if he were hallucinating in some way. He wondered if he was an unwilling subject of an experiment. Then he considered that putting human beings on the moon was always an experiment. And he had never thought of it in that way before. And considered: Was this quarantine a ploy to put him in this situation? Had he been lied to about having a temperature? He put his hand to his forehead. It felt normal. Was this all set up to keep him here every hour for two weeks so he could be subject to— What, exactly? Though in a way he knew. He would "walk on the moon" again—whether in an hour or a minute…. And the prospect gave him both a bit of fear (it was so real but of course it was not real) and an anticipation he welcomed, if warily. He would be moving through something, a technology that was certainly unlike anything of which he knew, and perhaps through a deliberately mind-altering experience whose nature he could only dimly assess.

Was it possible for him to take control of anything in this process? He went to the training monitor. Already this seemed an old path, one he had—through circumstance not of his choosing—been left behind. In the instant before he turned on the dark screen he wondered if this itself was a transgression. He could not keep himself from looking to one side of the room, then another, looking above, along the line where the walls met the ceiling. Surely he was always being watched. Of course, nothing met his gaze—and the monitor came on.

He saw the scenes of the moon he had reviewed before. He realized he was looking for the enigmatic city, the markings. "Decipher," the voice had said. Li realized he was just thinking of that voice on the other end as a voice, not so much a man behind it. Normally we place a face and body behind a voice we hear, say, on the phone, the radio; we imagine the body we feel behind the voice. But in this case Li could not connect any image to the voice. And then he wondered if the voice was not human at all: a computer program. A robot, he thought, wryly. But it had responded to him—though not exactly. It said what it had to say, practically disregarding anything he had interjected.

And then, on the screen, he saw himself on the moon. He started. This had never happened. He watched in shock. And realized this was a record of the most recent session, when the entire room had become the moon.

He watched himself with fear. It was as if the rover had recorded him. Well, the rover could have and— *No, no, am I crazy. The rover is on the moon. I am not.*

None of this is possible. None of it makes sense.

He moved to shut off the monitor. But his own image held him. He watched himself move upon the surface of the moon, making awkward kangaroo hops, watching himself as a man might watch of a film of himself walking down a street, a film that had been taken without his knowledge, so the man was as he was, without any consciousness of the camera. The result was unsettling. There was the sense that this lunar traveler might not be up to the task.

Li switched off the monitor. He found himself waiting. He felt his forehead again, as if searching for fever. *Do I need an excuse of illness—to explain this?*

The day moved on. That was exactly how he felt it: moving, but in a sluggish way. He had nothing to distract him, nothing to read, his phone was useless, there was no television or radio. He was tempted to switch the monitor back on, but he did not want to see himself again, in bizarre simulacrum.

He could only wait.

He was in some half state, not really half asleep, but removed, or trying to be removed—and suddenly he was back on the moon.

This change from one world to another not so much woke him up, but triggered what appeared to be an automatic response, like a runner sprinting off at the sound of the starting gun—or a machine abruptly switched on? But he did not consider this almost Pavlovian response. He stood on the great plain of the crater, slowly turning about, scanning the near horizon of the moon, Not too far off were both the lander and the rover. He made his way over to them, at first awkward again in the moon's light gravity, then feeling he moved with much better control. He stood before these marvelous instruments his country had sent to the moon.   And realized he looked at them now as if he were truly connected to them, was in fact an integral part of their purpose. The lander, the rover, him: a triad. He nodded to himself. Something wordless had been apprehended and assessed.

Though if Li was being pervaded by a wordless connection to these achievements of his country's science, he was also, for some reason, recalling facts—as if to ground himself amidst this extraordinary "teleportation." The name of the rover, *Yutu-2*, or Jade Rabbit, was the name of the goddess Chang'e's rabbit and had been chosen by an online poll. The rectangular, six-wheeled rover, a meter and a half by one meter, a meter high, 140 kilos in weight, was powered by solar energy. The rover had ground penetrating radar, which could probe to a depth of 30 meters. The previous lunar rover, intended to last for three months, functioned from December 2013 to August 2016. *Yutu-2* was intended to function for a longer period.

The cost of the entire Chang'e 4 mission was equal to building one kilometer of subway.

Atop the flat surface of the rover was a panoramic camera that could rotate a full 360 degrees. As he faced the rover, Li saw the camera fixed on himself. It had probably recorded his approach.

The rover also bore an energetic neutral atomic analyzer to investigate how the solar wind interacts with the lunar surface and which could possibly determine how water might form on the moon.

This suddenly struck Li as something he was supposed to focus on: water. It had been long assumed that the moon was an arid world, but through the era of the Space Age several possibilities allowing for the existence of lunar water had been advanced. Remnants of ancient water could be frozen in crevices of craters, along rims of craters, forever shadowed. There has been inconclusive evidence of bound hydrogen at the lunar poles. It is also possible that bound hydrates and hydroxides can be bound in lunar rock. In 1976 a Soviet probe took samples at various levels of the lunar regolith and returned to Earth. This lunar material was found to have one tenth of one percent of water. In 2008, India's Moon Impacter Probe apparently found water ice in Shackleton crater.

Water could also have been created on the moon over ages of being hit by comets, asteroids and meteors bearing water, or by hydrogen ions of the solar wind's impact on minerals containing oxygen.

Li was recalling more about this water on the moon connection. He had always looked upon the moon as an austere, barren world; whatever traces of the things that made Earth the place for an abundance of life were too minimal to matter—like the taunt of a possibility that could never be realized. But he was now recalling a lecture he had attended before he had become a taikonaut in training, a lecture about the geography of the moon in which the speaker had spent a good deal of time focusing of the aspects of lunar water, stressing the importance of its existence in establishing permanent bases and colonies on the moon. "It could be a resource whose magnitude we cannot realize. It would be prohibitive to ship water from Earth."

At the time Li thought a response to which another student asked: "Can't we just *make* water when we have a base on the moon?"

The lecturer said, "If we could do it just like that, we wouldn't have water shortages and suffer droughts in different places at any given time. You don't just take two hydrogen atoms and an oxygen atom and shake them together. To get them to join into making water you need a tremendous amount of energy, a process that might not be cost effective and could also be very dangerous if the process is not controlled properly. The easier way to 'make' water is to draw it out of the air. On humid days the air can be as much as six percent water. We can pull this water out of air—that is, we can do this on Earth. But on the moon there is no water laden atmosphere. But if the moon has these other sources, even if they are minute, in the aggregate it's large. A moon base, a colony will not be a billion people. If we can extract water from the moon for a few hundred, a few thousand people to sustain themselves, that will be very important, very essential."

Li began moving away from the rover. He thought about that split, leaning boulder from whose shadow he could see the stars in the lunar day. Could there be a trace of frozen water in a place like that? And, of course, he thought of the markings.

But how could he find that place again? And why was he suddenly seeking water? He had thought about what the rover was equipped to do; the possibility of finding water was among those capabilities. And so, like some old-time fortune hunter, was he also seeking this bounty?

As if he could hear sound on the soundless moon, he turned at the sense of something behind him. The rover was following him.

Hasn't the rover been everywhere I could walk? The rover would know where to go. He turned around, got behind the rover. The rover stopped. Li waited. The panoramic camera swiveled about, regarded Li. He had the feeling he was being regarded by an intelligence. Of course, he would say it was the intelligence watching him through the rover, but he was more than a little experiencing the common reaction of regarding a machine that apparently reacted to him as having its own motives. He nodded in his helmet—as if, he thought, communicating a silent command to a dog to move on ahead. The camera swiveled away from Li. The rover moved on, not straight ahead, but angling off in another direction. Li followed. While considering this was not real, none of it was.

I am being hallucinated. How?
"Hallucinated?" As if *he* were the hallucination?

Had Li been like Fan and a devotee of American films, he might have regarded this as sort of an R2D2, *Star Wars* moment. But he was simply trying to work through the strangeness of this apparent progress across the crater floor. And it developed into an awkward choreography; the rover moved slowly, while Li, in moon kangaroo hop, could move faster. What developed was that he was literally hopping around the rover, in an irregular circle, even as he used it— perhaps quite illogically—as a guide.

Though soon he was frustrated with this situation and was about to abandon being the satellite of the rover. And he said that himself, that he was a ridiculous satellite and must look foolish. He certainly felt foolish. It was just then that he caught something out of the corner of his eye. It took a moment to stop his progress—he almost fell flat. He steadied himself, gazed ahead, to make sure he was seeing what he was seeing. It was the miniature, the minute city.

In another moment he stood before it, or rather above it. Its structures were raised slightly above a rough and dusty patch of ground. He knelt on one knee, lowering himself carefully, reaching out his thickly gloved hand. There was an instant when he worried that what he beheld would crumble at his touch—an instant that was filled with a thick flow of thoughts: that this was an unusual natural circumstance that might have been here for ages; that it was an artificial construct, a seemingly impossible one, that had also been here for ages. Then he was touching his enigmatic "city."

Nothing crumbled at his touch. The structures were hard enough. He peered at them closely. He touched something on his helmet that brought a magnifying strip to his eyes. It was shockingly like a city, as if someone, something, had wrought the most minute and perfect organized city and placed it here on the moon. Or had it been "placed"? Was it natural (perhaps not the right word) to the moon?

The structures were not like those of Earth cities, but they were definitely buildings. Or was he seeing something that was something else entirely but translating it into something he knew? Perhaps it was not a city at all—

He peered about the city, which was roughly a meter and a half in length and a meter in width (too much like the rover?), moving slowly about in a crouched position, in fact in such a tight and tightly controlled manner an observer (and there must be one, Li would have asserted) would think him long practiced in lunar gravity.

Then he stood up, stepped back a bit, wanting to take it all in again from this position.

Was it possible that there could have been a species of intelligent beings that were very, very small and had built this, left this? As he was working through the biological possibilities of beings that small being intelligent—wasn't a certain *size* of brain needed for intelligence? But isn't that simply our perspective, or is it a biological reality? What about a city of extraterrestrial insects? Well, we'd call that a hive. As Li was working through something that confronted human paradigms, he realized he considered the city abandoned. It had been left. Certainly there was no activity here.

Yutu-2 was standing right by him. Li started. How long had the rover been there? It seemed to regard the city—its camera was focused right on it—with steady attention. Or that could be simply Li's imagination. He suddenly hoped the rover would not simply move right over it, leaving obliterating tracks over this fantastic city. If its buildings had not crumbled at Li's touch, they would certainly be destroyed by the weight of the rover.

But the rover was still, as if giving the city the same pondering regard Li offered.

Li looked down and now realized that unlike when he had seen himself moving across the moon on the training monitor, leaving no imprint on the lunar surface, now he was definitely leaving tracks. He looked with actual wonder—and, irrationally, a sort of pride—at this assertion of his presence, his passage. –And thought: *Even this detail, they create.*

Having no atmosphere, no erosion or winds and rain, the only thing that could alter the landscape of the moon was a meteorite—of which many, mostly very small, have regularly hit the moon. But barring this, if you put down a footprint on the moon, it remained forever. There were still the footprints of Apollo astronauts, the impact of different probes scattered upon the moon. There might be a future, Li idly thought, when the moon would literally be littered with the ever remaining marks of the passage of human beings, a crisscrossed, scarred world....

Li clicked something at the base of his helmet. As if his very eyes were the aperture of a camera, there was an instant of blackness as the picture was taken. He took a number of pictures of the city, kneeling again by it, many pictures from different angles.

Explore. Decipher.

That was what he had been told. This must be a test. This does not exist on the *real* moon.

But hadn't he first seen the city on the films the rover had taken?

He looked down at the rover. Its dark solar panels, sticking out from either side, looked like wings. He thought for the first time that the rover looked like a mechanical bird, a frail one, that could not fly. He wondered why he hadn't had that image of it before.

He moved away from the city. Would the rover follow? Again, he did not want it to run over the city.

When he had gone about ten meters, he looked back. He rover was still by the city. It was moving slowly, very slowly about it, its camera directed down at the mysterious structures. So the rover "recognized" this was something special to be recorded. Li stopped worrying about the city being destroyed by the rover.

He looked in the distance, to the lander. Should he keep walking on? Wasn't there something he was supposed to—? Oh, yes, water. The shadow of that boulder, with the markings— But he had no idea how to find it again.

Li had to constantly bring himself out of the consciousness of this immediate world he seemed to move in, his involvement with this apparent reality and the reality that he—at least his body was—in a room in Wuhan. In this artificial reality it seemed the unusual had always been placed before him; or he had been placed before it. Or led to it. He walked on, as if leaving both passage and destination to fate, to the gods—to the moon goddess, Chang'e....

And then, he was no longer on the moon, but back in the training room. He was standing in the middle of the room. Where the lunar horizon had been, before him was a wall. This transition back to "normal" both wrenched and relieved him. He was again faced with the impossibility of what he was going through. What they were putting him through. But it had to have a purpose—

He looked about the room in the way he had just looked about the surface of the moon, as if expecting to find something, well, unusual— evidence that Lin and Yang or any others had entered while he'd been "away." He considered that possibility with displeasure. While his mind was on the moon others could have been right here, in parallel presence.

He sat down, considering the facts of the matter. He could not be literally transported out of this room. His body was here. But his mind was taken to the moon—whenever "they" decided. And as vividly as the most vivid dream—with a realism that involved movement and the exact memory of the event after. Even the most vivid dreams did not leave such an aftermath of detail.

They are in my mind....

Well, that was obvious. He resented it; and he marveled at it. Certainly he had been chosen for something wonderous. But was that the word? At any rate, they must know—at least believe—he was capable of handling it, of going through this successfully. Yes, he had been chosen; and the chosen are always charged with difficulty.

Then he saw—why hadn't he seen this right away?—the monitor was on: showing, in slow succession, the photos he had taken of the city. Li almost gasped. It was an entrance of that other reality, the lunar reality he now regularly experienced in this place, here. He watched the slow progression of the pictures he had taken of the city, and was drawn from the fantastical circumstance he suffered—and accepted— to the mystery of these miniature structures. –And was caught by surprise as he saw the rover in the edge of one of these images, one of the wing-like solar panels, as if a dark plane sliced to the side of the city from the abrupt approach of an ominous hovering artifact.

Li smiled at himself. This section of the rover might seem ominous, but overall, the rover had a benign presence—though it could be unsettling when it appeared to regard him as another thing to be studied on the lunar surface.

Li continuously puzzled over the city. It could simply be a model. Wasn't that the obvious explanation? A model for some metropolis— elsewhere.

Buildings, metropolis.... Li recalled reading about the many apartment complexes built throughout China when the economy was in a boom period, and then left empty when the economy suffered a low point. There were stories of homeless encampments becoming entrenched in the empty buildings, virtual hordes of the homeless spread throughout a complex, a poor wretched city formed from its marginal inhabitants—for a time. When the local authorities began to oust these sad residents, there was some sympathetic outcry that caused a pause—briefly—in these evictions. But the owners of these buildings, who had envisioned a city of safe, moneyed tenants, hired their own removal squads and innumerable squatters were evicted; they were homeless once again. Any further sympathetic outcry did not change the situation after the fact.

There were other stories: of the not unexpected sporadic invasions of teenagers using these apartments for sexual rendezvous, for drug use; and there was the story of a politically dissident band of young people trying to set up their own revolutionary group, a sort of ad hoc headquarters. They were successful at establishing a presence for a month or so, but their activities outside their clandestine redoubt led authorities to them and they too were evicted, and a few charged with crimes "against the people," that old communist standby. Li recalled an image he'd seen online of the young dissidents being forcibly removed, the face of a young woman being roughly pushed along by police, her face twisted in a protesting shout. It had given him a very uneasy feeling. Generally patriotic, Li could recognize these spikes of brutality the government often inflicted upon the people it proposed to love. Li had not heard nothing other than vague rumors about the aftermath of this incident. There was the ominous mention of re-educations camps.

Yes, the hearts and minds of the people. This was what kept China together. And had, for centuries. –Or was it not so much hearts and minds as the people acknowledging that the country's rulers, in whatever century, had the power to enact their will.

At any rate, a "metropolis" could serve many uses—other than those which its builders had intended.

The monitor changed. It bore two words:

DECODE

BRAILLE

Li stared at the words for several seconds, then the screen once more showed the city, but highlighted in an odd way. Li stared. There was an apparent purpose in this different perspective. After a moment he slowly said to himself: "Braille?"

The lunar city a braille text? Decode? He didn't know braille. Was he expected to—?

No. In another moment the screen read:

BEFORE RETURN

FARTHER ON

Return of what? Whom? Had, as in China, the city been built for those who, for some reason, had not yet come to it? Or had to leave? And, until then, was he to go "father on"? To what?

So he was to leave the city behind and—Oh, maybe it was *his* return that was being referred to…. Perhaps he was to come back with— what? From where? He had already come here, the moon, from far Earth—

And laughed at himself, as he looked about the room, a banal place (though of technological magic) in plague-ridden Wuhan.

Was he to seek the markings of the boulder? Another braille?

He sat considering all this for some time. Eventually he made himself a meal. He was readied (well, more accurately, tensed) for a return to the moon—but was tired, very tired now, in every way, emotionally and bodily; eventually. he slept.

17.

He dreamed, of cities, apartment buildings, empty apartment buildings that he for some reason was racing through, as if in pursuit of something—or fleeing from something? He went through rooms in which people, seemingly always huddled in corners, looked at him with surprise and interest only for a moment, then who quickly returned to their own purposes. And Li did not regard them with much interest either, certainly with little surprise. He went on, through more rooms, went to other floors, via either stairs or elevators—he was always alone on both.

Then he burst into an apartment that was wholly empty, rushed through a large livingroom to a bedroom whose far wall, that had to be on the outside of the building, was not there; instead, there was the surface of the moon, a lunar vista that rolled to the edge of this world's horizon—and just before the edge of that horizon he could see the lander and the rover.

He stopped, and walked slowly to this sudden rectangular portal to the moon. He wanted to step into it, he feared to step into it. Then there was a noise behind him: someone calling his name. He whirled about, knowing that voice. It was Fan. He was about to exclaim her name in turn, but she rushed past, right to the lunarscape. Li lost his voice, found it, shouted out, "Fan, no!"

She stopped, right before she was about to plunge into this dream portal. "Come on! You have to find it!" And in another instant, she was kangaroo hopping on the moon, without a space suit; an instant after that she had gone off at an angle, the corner of the room obscuring her. Li, shouting, "No!" bounded after her. In a moment the moon was all about him, all the sight of the room had vanished. –And then he awoke.

He sat up, taking deep breathes, anxious. He deeply hoped Lin and Yang kept their promise and got in touch with Fan—and his parents. But what if in just a matter of this day, in a matter of hours, things had gotten even worse in the city? What if both Lin and Yang had gotten sick, were in quarantine themselves? And if that happened what would happen to him? Would be he able to get out of here?

Again, Li thought: *Do I have the virus?* This slight temperature—

but the body's temperature normally fluctuates. And maybe, Li considered, he was being lied to, to keep him here. It had been stressed at the very beginning of his training that even more important than knowledge, skills and physical fitness, was a psychological fitness. To travel to and explore an environment that was so antithetical to human life required a steadfast and unflappable psychology. Fan (who had appeared and disappeared so bizarrely in his dream) had joked with him, "Oh, you've got the perfect psychology for the moon. You'd do your mission if an atom bomb dropped on you."

Li had smiled at that. And then, over his worry that Fan would be worried about him, he worried that she could get this new virus. *What if I do have it and passed it to her?* But he could not believe that something this unfair could happen.

At any rate, in the morning he did not feel sick, only, well, not quite himself either. And maybe that self-displacement was due to his psyche being tried. And certainly it was. But he would confront whatever he had to.

FARTHER ON

He looked at the monitor, which was blank now, but memory imposed that commandment.

He ate lightly that morning. But was it morning? Yes, his phone could still tell him that, even if he could not make calls.

He waited, for his return to the moon. Yes, that was also in that message:

BEFORE RETURN
FARTHER ON

How much farther? And what would constitute "return"? He was always returning, from each session. But this must be referring to a "final" return….

.   .   .

He waited and the waiting made him irritated and anxious. As part of the self control he had developed in his training—though Fan would say, seriously, "You were born that way"—he stilled himself by thinking his pulse was slowing, becoming calmer. He had this "trick," and the one he used when he was trying to push his body through further difficult effort, when his mind would simply tell the body to move that arm, that leg, again and again, that he was infinitely past all tiredness and pain. He had used that in the military games last October, when he thought he would fail; his body fought on. The fact he did not win, didn't even come in second, or even third place, was no shame. Frustration, but no shame. *I'll win next time,* he'd said to himself. *If I'm not on the moon.* He smiled, remembering that. *And here I am. Almost on the moon.*

He looked about the room, as if searching for something that would mark, that would indicate that the change, the transformation was about to begin. Or, rather, return. He told himself that however he seemed to be roaming on another world, he was in a room.

He considered the irony. As a child, standing by the rice paddies at night, that great stretch of open land over which he could see so many stars, he knew his fate was up there. He *decided* it would be up there. The heavens would be his. This vast stretch of the celestial hung over Earth told him there was "more" up there than the world he stood upon. He felt so strongly that vastness, that open course for him, its ultimate infinity.

And yet, here now, he seemed ordered into a narrow passage, no matter how much it was so fantastical, something that appeared utterly at odds with reality.

Li was a very intelligent young man, he was very focused (as Fan liked to say), and if his youthful yearning for other worlds coupled imagination with adventure, perhaps the latter drew him more strongly. The situation he suffered now (was that the right word? Close enough—) tried that imagination by violating too strongly the laws of the everyday. What was happening to him was not merely his being thrust into very real-seeming holograms of lunar existence; his mind was being altered to another reality. –And when he thought those literal words, he rebelled. He considered he was being "infected" with hallucination—but this seemed different, another thing entirely. He moved on this moonscape they had given him, while at the same time he knew that he was in a room—

But wait. Could this be like…a parallel universe? In one universe he was in a room in Wuhan, on Earth, in another universe he was on the moon. But then, it was the moon of *this* universe. Wasn't it? But that model (if it was a model) or a city, the markings of the boulder—were they of this universe—?

And then he was on the moon, this "reality" subsuming all his brooding, whatever perspective through which he tumbled. He was on the moon, bounding carefully over its surface, going "farther." It was a transition which, although he had been anticipating it, seemed to come so suddenly that he was a few seconds into it before he recognized that the training room was no longer in his vision, only the lunar horizon ahead.

He gave a long sigh of acceptance that slightly fogged his visor, then moved onward, Now, instead of willing his body through so much effort, willing it beyond effort as he had done in the games, he was willing it to move onward as needed in this surreal task for which he had plainly been chosen. He briefly wondered if there was anyone else undergoing this "training." Were there others, scattered throughout the country, who moved, as he did, across the moon, and encountered lunar anomalies? –And said the word "training" to himself in a different sense this time. He no longer felt he was being trained. He had gone beyond training. They had deemed him capable of this mission— Yes, he was now *on* a mission. This demanded something from him that no one had ever done. The possibility of others placed in equally strange tasks did not seem possible. They had picked him out, solely, to do this. It was indeed a mission.

But what was its goal?

He almost stumbled in his moon-hopping progress. Suddenly he felt a little less light—as if the moon's gravity has perceptibly increased. He stopped, then resumed, slowly. He definitely felt heavier, if only slightly, but it was certainly enough for him to notice.

He had heard of "mascon" areas that had been discovered on the moon: areas of concentrated mass that actually disturbed the movement of probes that had orbited the moon. These mascons had been identified underneath the "seas" of the near side of the moon; he wasn't sure if any had been definitely located on the far side.

And now he recalled—though was this speculation or fact?—that the center of mass of the moon is actually 6,000 feet closer to Earth than the actual center of the moon. This lent credence—well, let's say support—to the theory that the moon is hollowed out, with some areas more dense than others; it is not an evenly compact solid.

At any rate, Li had not experienced this increase in gravity before. Did that mean he was crossing an area he had previously not crossed? As he had yesterday, he was simply moving forward. Going "farther," giving himself over to fate. He was to "find" what he needed to find.

He thought once more about those wild theories about the moon, that it was an artificial satellite, constructed for voyages of thousands of years. Are the aliens still inside, just parked by the Earth for an eon or so, taking a break in their voyage? Or had their destination been Earth all along?

He recalled learning when a teenager what the Earth would be like without the moon. The presence of the moon slows the rotation of Earth. The planet would have a much shorter day, even as much as short six hours. Ocean tides would be only a third of what they are now. And the tilt of the Earth's axis would not remain fixed at twenty-three and a half degrees. The tilt could change widely, making for very uncertain weather, creating an unstable climate planet-wide that would make the development of life more difficult.

And, of course, there would be no solar eclipses.

How coincidental that the size of the moon as seen from Earth is exactly the size of the sun as seen from Earth. The sun is so much larger than the moon, but so much farther away. But this ratio of size to distance allows the moon to cover the disc of the sun to produce a total eclipse. Li had always heard about this wondrous celestial "coincidence." If the moon were indeed an artificial satellite, would that make the coincidence just as unusual—or not coincidence at all?

But extraterrestrials would hardly have as one of the facets of their purposes to create total solar eclipses. –Unless they were driven by some aesthetic, some cosmic performance art that was too large for us to comprehend as such.

Li laughed out loud, there in his space helmet, heard his laugh in the oxygen of his helmet, and then felt his careful progress a bit lighter; he must have gone past the mascon. What indeed had been below him?

But I'm in a room, I'm in a room, he said to himself, and moved on. Anticipating, expecting—whatever.

He realized after a while he had the sense—more like the sense of a memory—that for a time the rover had followed behind him, but he had left it well behind him. There was the sudden feeling of being left alone; then he wryly told himself that was ridiculous. He was always alone. Yet not alone. Who were the watchers, those studying him, recording him? Were they always the same people? Or was it simply one pair of analyzing eyes?

He found himself descending what appeared to be an eroded wall of a small crater. A crater within the larger Von Kármán crater. But eroded by what and how long ago? The descent was slight; he did not realize his downward progress right away. At the edge of the short lunar horizon, he could see the opposite wall that appeared straight, not eroded at all. Well, eroded was the word he was using because he was looking at all this in earthly terms. But, maybe billions of years ago, the moon had an atmosphere, with a liquid environment.... If it wasn't an artificial construct.

He continued across the plain of the crater. He stopped once to look back at his tracks. He considered there was no way he could get lost; he could always follow his tracks back to— He suddenly wondered if the tracks he made today, in this session—no, he no longer thought of them as "sessions"—if those tracks remained, if his passage from each reconnoitering were still there, to be seen, each time he "returned" to the moon. He told himself he would be sure to check this from now on.

He reached the opposite wall of the crater. It was about a meter and a half high. He moved along the curve of the wall. Along parts of the wall, it seemed he made out what were true signs of a long ago erosion: rivulets in the rock, as if by water. Or lava? The maria on the near side of the moon were supposed to be ancient pools of cooled lava from when the moon was young and very hot, but the far side of the moon entirely lacked these dark seas.

Li stopped suddenly in one place where it seemed these rivulets, if that was what they were, changed—into almost, well, they seemed now like the marking he had seen on the boulder. But not so distinct. That is, they did not seem distinctly artificial. It could be he was reading things into something entirely natural, seeing what he now felt he was supposed to seek.

He stepped back, to assess what he was seeing. He blinked his eyes as the camera inside his helmet clicked. He had made no conscious effort to take a picture. He looked at the rivulets or markings again. He couldn't be sure. Perhaps all evidence of Nature was a script. But that was too fanciful for Li. If someone—some thing?—had left a writing here it would have been after the wall of this crater had formed. Why would an intelligence set down writing on boulders, crater walls? Was it a primitive message of passage? Pertinent information for future travelers? And how far into the future from the time when that writing was set down?

Li was frustrated. Too much wondering, not enough certainty. Though all of this, this moon-life he was irregularly living, had too much uncertainty.

But he realized he was now operating with two mindsets. Before, he was letting the experience, the apparent realness take over, acting to himself as if he were really on the moon, even though he did know he was simply in the training room. But now that latter knowing was running parallel to this "parallel universe" of being on the moon. He had to operate on both levels to do what he was doing successfully. The "watchers" would not want him to deny reality, even while they upended it. Or so he decided. And it appeared they definitely wanted something from him, wanted him to do something concrete in the reality they had created for him. Yes, they had engulfed him with another reality, but there was something in it they wanted extracted— and he had been sent to do it.

He moved along the low wall of the crater. It gradually decreased. He hopped over it and continued, in basically a southward direction. The Von Kármán crater was in the South Pole-Aitken Basin, which in fact is the largest impact crater on the moon and may be the largest of any body in the solar system. After time, Li began to feel the influence of another mascon; and after a time that passed—and he remembered: just last summer American researchers discovered the presence of a huge mass under the south pole of the moon, something equivalent to five times the size of the island of Hawaii. The Americans had been going over data collected back in 2011, when two U.S. satellites had orbited the moon in tandem, mapping the moon's gravity in different locations. It was theorized that an asteroid had crashed into the moon billions of years ago and had buried itself deep beneath the lunar surface.

Well, that was the theory. Perhaps the *Chang'e 4* mission could clear up the matter. Perhaps he—; then he was beginning to feel another mascon. He wondered if it would come in something like waves now: more gravity, less, more, less, etc. But if he was moving in an area of great mass beneath the surface, shouldn't the change in gravity be a constant, continuing, not broken up and wave-like?

For the moment a flat plain was before him. There was a scattering of small craters, more like big holes in the ground, but for the most part there was just this plain. He turned to look back, as he did often now, to note his footprints; and now, he stood a while, looking at their track, tracing them to a vanishing point. He had the sudden thought: of the moon in the future, visited again and again by Earth, a moon with colonies, a moon crisscrossed with tracks that would never weather. He imagined, with amusement, people—or robots—sent out on the surface to rake the moon, to constantly remove the traces of these tracks, though that erasing would leave its own marks.

Marks. Markings. Maybe what he saw at the base of the boulder and among those rivulets was him wanting to see something, translating an odd but randomly natural occurrences as artificial. –Or, of course, perhaps "they" put them there. *To see if I could decode, as they said.*

Then just on the edge of the horizon to which he walked he saw…. Yes, it seemed the tops of buildings. He frowned, tried to increase his pace, but now felt as if the gravity below him was increasing. He was being drawn visually and impeded physically. Not that this was anywhere near the gravity of Earth, but he had by now become adjusted to lunar gravity: here, on the moon, it was what his body expected. (*But*

I am in a room on Earth.)

At any rate, he moved ahead. And yes, what was in the distance more and more seemed like buildings.

He tensed, he stopped. He blinked, he photographed what he saw. Just in case he was returned to the room. He moved on, continually photographing. The buildings rose before him. They looked, at least at this distance, like some of the more modern constructions in Wuhan, a futuristic architecture for the 21st century.

He stopped again, breathing slowly. Was he transporting the city of Wuhan to the moon? Reimagining a lunar Wuhan? And that miniature city (which he'd been told was the raised surface of a Braille communication)....and now this very life size city that he approached. These were definitely no natural formations.

He neared the city. It was a deserted city. There was no movement. No indication of any sort of life being lived here—

Then he was back in the room. Li was startled. And offended. Just as he approached a mystery too large to deny—and the part of his mind that insisted it be tied to the reality of the room mocked his being offended. *Don't let them trick you like this. Play with you. They take you so far, then—*

He looked at his desk, at the monitor. On it was a photo of the city. Buildings with what seemed like windows. Or were those just dark indentations? More...braille?

There was a note in front of the monitor:

PO FAN AND YOUR PARENTS HAVE BEEN INFORMED

He was at once startled and grateful. He hoped it was true.

So someone had stolen in here while he was "elsewhere,"

There was a book next to the note. It was *A History of the Moon*. A great brilliant full moon was on the cover. The author was Arthur Leeds. Li opened it and found it had been originally published in

England in 1995. It had been translated into Chinese in 2003. Bemused—and at the same time feeling this was part of their manipulation—Li opened the book to the first chapter: "Before There Was Even the Moon."

Li's thought was: *So if there wasn't a moon, we had to create one.*

He read:

There are many references in ancient writings to a time when there was no moon. This could be various cultures and writers just trying to refer to a beginning when everything was not yet manifested in existence—both a poetic and reasoning jab into the past, saying everything did not come into existence all at once, but gradually. Or this could be an accurate—if culturally embellished—fact. That at one time there were civilizations fully underway, but no moon in the sky. Democritus and Aristotle wrote that there was time when there was no moon. Aristotle wrote that before the Hellenes inhabited Greece, the peoples who lived there were in a time before there was no moon. Plutarch wrote of a pre-lunar people. Ovid wrote of Greece's Arcadians, who claimed they were older than the moon.

So if there were no moon, were the days shorter then, the climate more unstable, as science says would have to be the case? Li thought.

But, more importantly, in regard to his situation: was his training plainly leaning toward convincing him that the moon was artificial? Never mind leaning—it was bluntly directing him toward such a conclusion. The miniature city, markings on the boulder, the rivulets that could be markings, the deserted city that rose from the lunar plain. Decode, decipher.

Was this an experiment to see how a lunar explorer would handle the presence of alien artifacts? But again, it seemed to him, he sensed it viscerally, that "they" wanted something from him in this surreality they had created but which he alone could produce?

He skimmed through the book. It was the expected recounting of how the moon has influenced myth, religion, folk tales and the everyday of human existence. Plant during a new moon, harvest at full moon. The harvest moon. How the moon affected the supernatural. If it was the expected, nonetheless it seemed an interesting recounting.

Though why give him this particular book, written a quarter of a century ago—and by an Englishman?

Putting the book down, Li smiled to himself. As if he wasn't having his full of the moon.

Again, he had to think about how, while he was "on the moon" someone had come into the room, left the note about Fan and his parents, along with the book. Just bizarre. Did they see his body moon-hopping? They had to see his body. This moon experience was happening just in his mind, he was sure. Maybe his body was just seated or lying down, or just standing in one place, seemingly catatonic. It was an uncomfortable realization that while he was so fully engaged in all his senses somewhere else, he was unconscious to the real presence of another. Someone could walk into this room and kill him—

He shook his head. Why had he thought that? It was an extreme reaction to his apparent vulnerability. He picked up the book again, thinking, *But they want something from me.* But such "wants," if an apparent guarantee of safety, was hardly comforting.

In a chapter titled "Lunatic," he read about the alleged effects of the full moon.

Luna was the Roman goddess of the moon, who rode her silver chariot across the sky at night. And sometimes, as so many people have believed throughout history, Luna causes lunacy—in other words, bad, sometimes very bad, behavior.

If he is considered the father of modern medicine, Hippocrates, in the fifth century B.C. looked upon the influence of the moon in what we today might call an unscientific perspective. He wrote, "One who is seized with terror, fright and madness during the night is being visited by the goddess of the moon.

Li thought of Chang'e and saw no terror there. He read on:

Belief in the mind-influencing power of the moon was so pervasive in 18th century England that those who stood trial for murder could plead for a light sentence if the crime was committed during a full moon. At Bethlehem Hospital in London, patients were shackled and even flogged for the prevention of aberrant behavior during the full moon.

The moon is believed to not only influence mental behavior but influence something as basic as a woman's fertility. The cycle of lunar phases and a woman's menstruation are similar and so it was natural to link the moon and fertility. The connection of the moon to the female is found throughout many cultures, from the Chinese moon goddess Chang'e to Mama Quilla of Incas.

It was a common ancient belief that the moon determined when a woman would get pregnant. An ancient Assyrian text stated that women ovulated when the moon was in the same position as when they were born. Menstruation and menses come from the Latin and Greek for month ('mensis') and moon ('mene').

Modern science had disproved the long-believed connection between a woman's cycle and the moon, in studies that have involved, collectively, millions of women. And yet…it is understandable—and seemingly plausible—that the moon has a direct influence on the hormones and fluids in the body just as it influences the tides of the Earth.

A corollary belief is that the moon has an effect on births, with more babies being born during a full moon. A study for births in New York City from 1959-1973 showed a one percent increase in births during a full moon, an increase that does not appear statistically significant. Other studies have shown no link between the moon and births.

As for the alleged link between crime and a full moon, studies in various major cities have shown a slight rise in crime on some full moon days, a slight decrease on other full moons. In other words, when totaled together, no increase when compared to other days. Although police departments across the world, as well as individual police officers, swear through experience a full moon does indeed bring an increase in crime. Is this a matter of having a crime that happens during a full moon making more of an impression on the police—verifying a perspective, a bias that so many in law enforcement have?

Li skipped to another chapter: "Aliens and the Moon."

It was the 1820s, and Bavarian astronomer Franz von Paula Gruithuisen announced he had observed cities on the moon. He called its inhabitants 'lunarians' and claimed they had constructed complex cities and roads. None of his colleagues could verify his observations. He was laughed at— but eventually a small crater on the moon was named after him.

A much more famous astronomer, Sir William Herschel (he was also a composer) was another who considered there was intelligent life on the moon, as well as Mars. Herschel discovered Uranus, as well and two of its moons and identified more than 800 double or multiple star systems. This diligent scientist who undertook to grind his own telescope lenses and who designed the largest telescope of its time, a forty-foot long reflector with a 49½ inch mirror, believed that he too had seen evidence of life on the moon and somehow saw the setting of lunar life as being like that of the English countryside. He also considered the sun might be hollow and populated.

Li smiled. Brilliant as Herschel was, he had embraced such...fancies. He died in 1822, two centuries ago. Surely, he would have revised his views had he had access to newer discoveries and better instruments. Herschel had a crater named after him on that lunar "countryside," as well as one on Mars, and on Saturn's moon Mimas (which he had discovered). There was also the Herschel Gap in Saturn's rings, and an asteroid that bore his name.

In 1835 the *New York Sun* published entirely fictional articles masquerading as fact, concerning life on the moon. These came to be called 'The Great Moon Hoax.' The *Sun* claimed that Herschel's son John, who had himself become a well-known astronomer, had discovered evidence of the 'lunarians,' who were bat-winged. The articles were illustrated with these lunar bat-men.

There was an illustration of these lunar bat-men: nudes with bat wings flying above what indeed could be an English countryside, with various animals by a stream.

Herschel was actually amused when he found this hoax was attributed to his observations, but in time he became annoyed when he was often asked about the moon people by those who did not seem to know the whole thing had been made up to sell newspapers.

Li put down the book. *So many need to imagine so much about the moon.*

And what he had "seen" on the moon: had that been *his* imagination?

Chapter Seven: Other Visions

18.

Cheng had just awakened when he got a call. The voice did not identify itself. "The car will be there soon—with some information for you. That patient—"

Cheng was about to ask, "What patient?" but the voice was gone.

Cheng sighed, collecting his thoughts. It must be that man who continued to test positive six weeks after he had first been infected.

He'd forgotten about being ferried to work. As it turned out he was to go elsewhere in Wuhan before going to the lab. Soon there was another call—from the car outside. "I need a few minutes," said Cheng. He was told by the driver to take his time; though the driver added, "I'm told to wait a reasonable time for you." That was polite, but almost commanding, Cheng thought. Well, a reminder that Cheng was now expected to follow not just his scientific curiosity but the needs that this emergency demanded. Or what the state saw as those needs.

The driver was a young man in a thick winter coat. He introduced himself as Fu Junjie.

He was masked, of course. He nodded as Cheng got in and handed him a folder as if it were something Cheng had expected. Cheng, masked, too, nodded back. He realized that because of his work at the lab, in which long before this epidemic he was so often masked, it did not seem odd to be interacting with others with masks. He sensed the young driver was not so comfortable with a mask. He tugged at it with resignation.

As the car drove off. The driver said nothing further to Cheng, who looked at the medical records of Du Ping, a 52 year old man who lived with his wife in one of the poorer neighborhoods of Wuhan.

If Cheng wondered why a doctor or nurse were not visiting Du instead of a virologist, the "instructions" in the folder addressed that specifically. "While medical personnel would tend to simply evaluate the condition of this man, the intent of sending a virologist is to ascertain whether there is anything in his environment, along with his habits, which would tend to have the virus linger so long in his body."

Nice in theory, Cheng thought, but unless there is something amazingly unusual with this man, to "investigate" him and his surroundings would glean little useful information. But it seems Cheng's acumen as a virologist was being held in such high regard, he would bring back something that would parse why the new virus continued to find a harbor in the body of Du Ping. Bemusedly Cheng thought sending him into a cave of bats might be more worthwhile. And then he considered, if those forays into caves throughout the country had the purpose of studying viruses that might infect humans, he really had not imagined that one day he would be driving through shut down Wuhan, a city closed away because of a virus from bats.

It was only the second day into the lockdown. But Cheng was suddenly realizing he was looking at the city in a wholly different way. In these last days, as concerns over the virus had grown, the stressed and tensed atmosphere on these streets had been palpable. It had taken Cheng a day to absorb the visceral fact of a locked down Wuhan. Now, with the streets virtually empty, save for those on what were deemed essential errands (as he was, apparently), Cheng saw the city, not its people.

He had grown up in Beijing, surely the most influential city in modern China. His career had brought him to Wuhan, which was a major industrial and technological hub, in south central China, the capital of Hubei province. Last year, in speaking with an American virologist (with Fan as interpreter) who was doing work at the lab for a few months, Cheng had been asked, "How is living in Wuhan different than life in Beijing?"

Cheng said, "From what I know of America, it is like the difference between New York and Chicago. Both are great cities, but it seems New York is the dominant one. Beijing is always the dominant city." Indeed, Wuhan has been referred to as China's Chicago.

Wuhan came about through the joining of three cities, Wuchang, Hankou and Hanyang, the "Wu" from the first city, and "han" from the other two. In 1927, the three cities became Wuhan. Fan, once more knowing all things American, remarked that an article from a U.S. magazine—*Collier's*—had called Hankau the Chicago and St. Louis of China in the early 1900s.

Wuhan's central location gained for the city the description of "The Nine Provinces Thoroughfare."

Before the consolidation of the three cities, Sun Yat-sen's followers instigated the Wuchang Uprising, which directly led to the collapse of China's last dynasty, the Qing Dynasty, and the eventual establishment of the Chinese Republic. Anti-dynasty sentiment and groups had been active in the region for some time.

The first half of the 20th century had indeed been one of national turmoil for all of China. The overthrow of the last dynasty, the Japanese invasion, the American bombing of Japanese strongholds toward the end of the war (20,000 Chinese had died), the rise of the communists and the establishment of the People's Republic of China. The second half of the century had had its upheavals: the Cultural Revolution, in which Mao had targeted the intellectual class; the era of Tiananmen Square, during which Cheng had been a child, though his adult memories were certainly of a more secure and economically prosperous 21st century China—while there had always remained a backdrop , an undercurrent that those in charge could be brutal towards the individual in order to keep (what they saw as) the ideal of the whole, the forward material march of the Republic.

It was a poorer part of Wuhan through which Cheng now was being driven. Without exactly thinking the words, Cheng sadly considered it was somehow fitting: some poor man here was being beset by the virus for an undue amount of time. The poor everywhere bear the most suffering. –Though was this man still "beset"? On one hand he had survived the virus, on the other hand, it would not leave him. Apparently, he had recovered from the illness, but still continued to be host. There was this to consider: if he still "shed" the virus, was it to a degree that it was dangerous to others? At this point in the epidemic there was no way to know at what level of viral load one infected person could be hazardous to another.

Cheng had been supplied with protection against that viral hazard. On the car seat next to him was the protective gear that doctors and nurses would wear when in contact with the infected. When the car pulled up before an ill kept building, the driver turning around briefly to nod at Cheng, he stepped out with a sigh, threw his coat back into the car and with some embarrassment donned the gear out on the sidewalk. Though certainly there was no reason for him to be embarrassed. First of all, there was no one on the street at the moment, a condition that was now common during the lockdown, and moreover Wuhan had become a city in which the appearance of safeguards against the new virus had abruptly become part of life. If for the most part that entailed simply wearing a mask, no one in this city would think it odd to behold someone wearing what Cheng now wore. They would assume, correctly, this was official business of a pressing medical issue.

As Cheng opened the door of the apartment building, he looked back at the young driver, already occupied with his phone, but who gave him a casual wave. In the small lobby he buzzed the apartment of Ping Du—and just realized it was likely he had no idea if this man was expecting him. Well, the voice responding was strong and leery, as if expecting trouble from anyone who sought him. After saying his name in what he thought an official yet casual manner (to be official now had some weight, he thought, and the casual tone would be a relief to the listener) he added, "I'm from the Wuhan Virology Institute. I have been asked to see you."

There was a brief pause in which Cheng expected a normal, reactive "Why?"; but again, Cheng came bearing official weight. There was some mumbled reply he didn't quite catch and he was buzzed in.

Cheng found the elevator wasn't working. He smiled to himself. *Of course.* As if this minor event were an obstacle. He took the stairs to the third floor. He found the stairs somewhat dirty—as expected.

Again, he tried to make his knock both official but not too forceful. He laughed to himself. *It's as if I'm a diplomat.* He was intuiting there was—would be—something of the absurd about his "mission."

A woman he would guess about fifty opened the door. Whatever the tone of Cheng's voice from downstairs or the nature of his knock, she definitely looked at him with suspicion. She was holding a cup of coffee and wearing a robe. Her hair was mussed. It was as if she'd just gotten out of bed, though by now it wasn't very early in the morning. Well, with lockdown, what did people have to get up early for?

Cheng spoke his name again and that he was from the lab. With a twist to her lips, the woman nodded, and gestured back into the apartment. Cheng followed her in the kitchen, where her husband sat. He turned to face Cheng. He too was drinking coffee. From a window there was a soft grey glow of light on the kitchen table, and for a moment Cheng appreciated that light; it felt soothing.

Cheng wondered: *Should I ask them to put on masks?* He decided against it. He should be protected enough.

Du Ping Looked a little older than wife. He gave Cheng a sad smile. Once more Cheng tried to be casual, even friendly. As if he had come to see Du out of genuine concern. "I understand you had the virus— continue to have it."

"Yes," he said it gravely, slightly nodding.

"He was so sick," said his wife, then adding, "he is fine now." As if any association with the virus was not good.

"I was, yes, very sick. But I'm—fine now," Du finished, echoing his wife's assessment of his condition.

Being, yes, diplomatic, Cheng said, "Well, yes, you look fine, but I understand you still…have some of the virus."

Wife: "We have not been going out."

"Oh, we're not worried about that," Cheng said hastily, if somewhat untruthfully. "We just—"

"Are you here to examine me?"

"No, no, I am not doctor. I am just trying to gather—with this epidemic—information."

Perhaps it was the word "examine." Cheng found himself looking closely at the man's face, with its tired, resigned expression. He had had a bout with this new disease and now he was being…interrogated. Cheng could appreciate him feeling exactly that. At any rate, he found himself looking—you couldn't help it—at a mole on the right side of Du Ping's face, diagonally down from the lips, a raised dark brown bump…with, yes, two hairs growing out of it. Cheng almost cringed outwardly when he noted the hairs. Couldn't the man get that mole removed? It couldn't be that expensive. Wouldn't he be covered by the normal health care? Surely his wife couldn't like that feature on the man's otherwise normal face. Cheng found himself sighing—which he transformed into a clearing of his throat. He had the feeling—it was very palpable in this poor apartment—there was no longer any intimacy in this marriage; both husband and wife accepted the course to which life had brought them. Cheng was abruptly overwhelmed by the universal, sad lot of the poor. This was an experience beyond his kin, but he sensed it vividly. Then he had to redirect his attention; Du was saying to him:

"So if you're not here to examine me—?"

"We just wanted some more detail…about your experience."

Du chuckled. "Experience." He seemed sadly amused at this word. "It was not a good one. From a bad cold to—" He frowned and looked out of the window. He blew out a long breath and frowned. It seemed he did not want to speak of the memory of illness.

His wife spoke it for him. "I had to convince him not to work when it got worse than a cold. He does not like to miss work. Then he was in bed. He couldn't breathe. We had to go to the hospital. We had to wait for the ambulance. His breathing was getting worse. But going to the hospital was worse. Better we stayed home. It was crowded. We sat in a crowd of sick people. I am amazed I didn't get sick from that. Then he could hardly sit up. They put him in a bed in the hallway. I worried he was going to die in a crowd."

She looked to him with genuine concern. Perhaps there was something left to this marriage, if not physical intimacy.

Du said quietly. "I was in the hospital for two days. They were about to put me on a respirator. They would have done it, but all of those machines were being used. And when they could give me one, they said I didn't need it." He drew in a breath, as if recalling when breathing was difficult and when it returned. "They asked me to come back, to test, see if the virus was cleared. I still had some left. Other people came here before you, test me again. I still have some virus left. Still. It's unusual, they said. But I am not sick now."

"He is fine," his wife echoed, adding, "People came last week to check him."

Du nodded. "They took blood. I haven't heard—"

Cheng gestured toward him. "You still have the virus. Like you said." Cheng considered he was saying this almost as if Du were orchestrating the situation. Cheng wondered if this man could possibly have been continually reinfected, or at least infected twice. But that seemed unlikely. A reinfection would involve getting over the virus, eliminating it from one's body, then getting it again.

Cheng asked, "You were working, you had a job, when you got sick?"

"Yes." Then Du gave big yawn he covered with his hand, then swept his hands up over his face, pressed against his brow, as if frustrated— and bored—with the subject of himself. In a moment he gathered himself. "I'm a foreman at a warehouse—"

Cheng noted an expression cross the wife's face; perhaps Du was exaggerating his position. Distracted for the moment, Cheng did not catch the name of the business, but its nature was eyeglasses. "Frames. They go all over the world. From America to Africa. And here, too, of course."

"Did anyone else there get sick—that you know of?"

"No. Well, I mean people don't come to work, say they were sick, but if they were, it wasn't this."

"Have you had this job a long time?"

Du sighed. "A few years."

"What did you do before that?"

Du looked at him sharply. "Does it matter what I did before this?"

"Probably not. But I'm just looking for—anything, I have to admit, to explain— This virus is so new, we have to get all the information we can."

"You think I got it someplace else?"

"I really do doubt that, but—" Cheng stopped himself. What if the incubation period for this virus was long? Look at HIV. It could be years before the virus announced itself with lysis, that is, began to reproduce itself, filling cells to the point of bursting, then flooding the body with more viruses, to begin the cycle again. It was still unknown why or how HIV repressed itself so long. Suppose, with this new virus, the people getting sick had actually had it for months, even years?

Though Cheng doubted this. If the new virus was related to SARS, this was not likely. But all possibilities had to be investigated.

He switched his attention back to Du, who was recounting a series of jobs whose essence was similar to his present employment: situations of menial labor or overseeing such labor in which he had achieved some responsibility but could not go past that. During her husband's recounting, the wife's look took on a far-off aspect, as if this listing of employments were a recounting of her life with this man. When Du finished, Cheng turned his attention to her.

"Are you working, may I ask?" Why he felt he had to be more polite to her than her husband, Cheng wasn't sure.

It turned out she was a bookkeeper for one of the largest food markets in Wuhan. That piqued Cheng's attention. Food. Markets.

"I want to ask both of you: have either of you have been to the live market that—?"

"The one they closed down?" she said. "Is everyone sure it came from there?"

"That one, yes."

Du said, "Everyone's been there. Though we haven't for a while."

His wife said, "Last, maybe, October."

Cheng knew the first patients diagnosed with the virus were in mid November. Perhaps this couple has been exposed to something at the market in October. "And when did you get sick, exactly?" he asked Du.

"End of the first week of December, beginning of the second week. Around there."

Cheng considered that was also a bit long of an incubation for a coronavirus, but— Perhaps his wife had brought something home from her market, though her place of business was more in the nature of a superfood store, than a grim collection of live animals purchased for slaughter. Or slaughtered right then and there.

"You said you're a bookkeeper?"

"Yes." Her response was almost haughty. As if he did not believe her?

"So you don't work on the floor of the market."

"I have an office. I hope I have an office to go back to. It's closed. They shut it down. Where are people supposed to get food?" She said this to Cheng as if he had arranged this absurd situation.

"There should be enough places to get food still open."

"But they're not letting us go there."

"I know many stores are delivering." He wanted to get back to her situation. "Did anyone there, where you work, get sick?"

"Not that I know of."

Cheng considered that perhaps the wife had caught it, not gotten sick, passed to her husband. "Did they ever check you, see if you had—?"

"I'm not sick, he is."

"People can catch viruses, not get sick, pass it on."

Then Cheng wished he hadn't said this. There was a look between the couple that, if not exactly animosity, was a revival of old, ingrained, conjugal feuds. Anyway, as far as Cheng knew, all respiratory viruses were passed on only when symptoms arose: coughing, sneezing. Could this new virus be different?

Pointing to her husband, his wife said, "Well, he had it, he's not sick now, but he still has the virus, so can he—?"

"I'm pretty sure he could."

"And you came prepared not to catch it."

Cheng was suddenly aware of something he had not thought of since donning the protective gear outside the car: he must be a strange presence before this couple, here in the midst of their apartment: a true invader. As if he were accused of being impolite, Cheng said, diplomatically, "Everyone has to be prepared to be safe now."

And to placate the wife, he added, "You obviously haven't gotten sick. You must have gotten immunity to it by now."

The woman made a smug, dismissing noise. Her husband said, "Well, all I care is I'm not sick anymore. Eventually, I won't have any virus, right?"

"That should be the case," said Cheng, but he was thinking, what if this man, for some reason we can't know and may never be able to know, harbors the virus for quite a long time, and could be a source of contagion far past normal circumstances? Will he need to be kept locked away from everyone, even after this lockdown is over?

Cheng said to Du, "It is less now, but still enough to—"

"To come and study me."

"We're just trying to…get details. Look, you may be that one in a million case that will really have no bearing on all this in the end, the virus will eventually leave and if you wife did not catch it from you by now, everything will be fine."

"But all you scientists will keep an eye on me."

Cheng gave a little laugh as if this was nothing more than a light amusement that was attached to no cause for worry. "But we won't oppress you with it."

"Isn't that wonderful," said the wife, her hands now on her hips.

Cheng said, perhaps inanely, "We're all making our way through this."

Cheng stayed only a little while longer. He could think of little else to ask Du Ping or his wife. He had had only a little hope of finding out anything pertinent from this visit. He had the feeling that this was just one of those medial anomalies that overall would do little to contribute to fighting this new virus. A curiosity to be noted, certainly to be watched, but beyond that…

Yet, it was so early on in all this. –Early? Was he thinking this just a slice of the beginning that would take everyone on a long, long road? What if Du were a harbinger of many other similar cases? Individuals who could be long term carriers. That would be...difficult for everyone.

Cheng of course hoped this long term carrier would indeed be anomaly. What if Du continued like this for some time? The poor man would remain, isolated, out of work, while the rest of the world returned to normal. –Cheng had to smile to himself at that (literally; he was glad the couple could not see him smiling behind his mask); smile at the thought of returning to normal. Whether that would be in the near or distant future (it was a time that *had* to come), he knew in his gut everyone, in varying degrees, would have to bear some hardship. At the moment, more than those who would be suffering from the virus, he thought of those doctors and nurses in the hospitals who would be inundated with suffering patients. Du Ping before him had suffered at little. Now he seemed fine. He was one of the luckier sufferers—

"Is there anything else we need to tell you?" The wife interrupted Cheng's thoughts. He realized he had been silent, ruminating.

"I don't think so. I'm sure everything will be all right."

Du said, "But you—someone—will be back."

"Well, you should probably be checked again."

"The virus, I know. My visitor."

His "visitor." A virus could be a visitor that commanded. A guest that takes over the home of the body.

He thanked the couple for their time, apologized for the necessity of his visit. Du responded with the smile of the resigned. The wife gave a curt nod. Soon Cheng was back out on the street. When he saw the car waiting for him he had a foolish sense of relief. He hadn't asked the driver if he'd be waiting for him; he had assumed he would. But suppose the driver had other assignments? "I must be really important," he said under his breath, mocking both himself and the situation. He nodded to the driver who looked up from his phone, nodded back. Cheng took off his protective gear quickly, stuffed it back in the plastic bag he had taken it from, settled back in the car. He still wore his mask, of course.

On the way to the lab. Cheng considered that this morning's business might be just one of many other absurd missions in which he would be involved during this crisis. He pushed away the thought—or simply accepted it—as he looked upon locked down Wuhan, the streets for his eyes alone, a city of millions kept away from itself because of a nano-sized pathogen. "My visitor," as Du Ping has put it. How long would the visitor be staying—be in command?

The buildings of Wuhan rolled passed before his eyes, each structure commandeered by plague.

19.

Driving home late, well after the winter darkness had set in, Fan noted the city was still alit. Humans locked in their apartments, their homes. Signs of life that waited. If you just looked at those lights, not the streets themselves, you could almost think it a normal night. Though in parts of the city there were shops that bore only a cautionary back light in their interiors—at a time of when there should be many evening customers in the busy period of New Year's.

What will this new year become? she thought.

She was worried about Li. She had tried to call him again just before leaving. Of course, nothing could happen to him in his lunar training sessions. But she was worried. What would she feel if he were really on the moon? Well, there would be communications from moon to Earth—not this…blackout. She just felt something wrong.

More to push away worry—it was growing, she couldn't help it— she went to bed earlier than usual. In the dark she looked down at

Mystery, curled in his small circular bed on the floor alongside her own. He sensed her look, raised his head and looked back at Fan.

"You could sleep on the bed, you know." As if in answer, he lowered his head, curled further into himself. Mystery did not like to stay on the bed, for some reason. It was as if he felt more comfortable on the floor. Fan had thought: As if he could "escape" more easily. In some way, this too reminded her of Li. Fan smiled and closed her eyes.

And, not surprisingly, dreamed of Li. He was on the moon— whether in his training sessions or the actual moon, she didn't know. But it was lunar landscape he moved across, in his spacesuit—and he came to stand over the miniature city he had told her about. Though in the dream it was not the very small city he had related, but like a child's model of a city, a model made of lunar stone and soil. And as Li bent over the city to study it more closely there appeared what seemed windows in these small buildings; and then there were lights in the buildings. *Beings locked away?* Her dreaming mind thought.

That dreaming mind superimposed the lights of Wuhan she had passed that evening upon these moon buildings. Two cities—with a difference. One, the city of Wuhan, couched itself away from what had just recently been normal life (but seemed a longer time ago than recently), awaiting release, while the city on the moon had to be something older, a beacon of some old, old life that awaited human eyes.

Was Li feeling this? Dreaming Fan looked into the visor of his helmet as he rose from his crouch. He seemed to be deciding something, then moved off, toward the lunar horizon. Fan felt a pang; she felt him moving away from her, beyond her reach—and into something that could be dangerous.

She awoke, anxious. She looked at the ceiling for a time before she drifted back to sleep.

She was more than startled at the ringing of the phone.

Like many young people, she had no landline, just her cell phone. To say it "rang" was to use an old terminology—in the way older people refer to dialing a number. Fan's phone had a musical tone. She had chosen it because its pleasant sound made the intrusion of the world trying to reach her more agreeable. Though in this moment in the dark it was not agreeable at all, but like a warning.

It was not so much warning as...information. Or perhaps the information was a warning.

The voice, a man's voice, did not identify itself, but flatly asked her: "Po Fan?"

"Yes, who—?"

"We are informing you that Zhen Li—" At the pronunciation of Li's name there was start in Fan's heart, as if she were about to receive terrible news. Well, it was not terrible, but disturbing. "He is in quarantine at his training session."

"Is he sick?"

"Fever. That is all. Fourteen days." The voice hung up.

Fan sat up, took a long breath. *He has the virus.*

She took some consolation in realizing Li must have asked she be called. He had to tell "them" specifically to call her. So, he had...communicated.

He's strong. He won't get very sick, she told herself. But this terrible thing was so new. Who knew—anything really—at this point?

Not unlike Cheng, Fan was more struck by the reality of the reality of the situation when driving to work on this second day of the lockdown. Yesterday she had been abruptly confronted by the surrealness of Wuhan emptied of people, almost marveling how the streets had been stripped of the normal rush of bodies; today she was realizing that the unpeopled city was going to be like this for a while.

Of course, the city was not unpeopled; beyond all those windows were thousands, millions of eyes that could look out upon the streets that she passed through—and were perhaps wondering at the purpose—and privilege—of the young woman in her vehicle.

The tenor of the lab was the opposite of the city, in that there was more than the usual roster of bodies—more people, whether in lab gear or suits, than usual. And there was the sense, not surprisingly, of an urgency, a task that had to be fulfilled. But that task could not exactly be defined. To find some secret of the virus that would be its unravelling? It would be an accomplishment just to find the normal parameters of the virus, such as to narrow down its incubation time, to more precisely assess how contagious it was.

She was disappointed she could not find Cheng, or could get no definite information as to his whereabouts. She tried calling his phone; it went to voicemail. Her message: "Are you on some secret mission about the virus?" Yes, Cheng was on a mission, as Fan would find out, though it was hardly a covert one.

She wanted to talk to Cheng further about her idea of interweaving some part of the virus with nanomaterials. She was more than half serious when she mused that a substrate of this virus and whatever nanomaterials at hand might become something in the nature of a breathable vaccine.

If she took, say, the S proteins, the spike proteins….

She made inquiries. Fan was well liked by many in the lab—and, to say the obvious, being attractive and having a pleasant personality helped. Then again, she was not a virologist. Her requests for S protein material were received politely, and sometimes with puzzlement; the most she gained was that it *might* be possible, but with samples of the virus so much in demand for study—

This was why she needed Cheng. He could cut through these polite refusals—which is what they were. He was a respected virologist. She was just in some fringe position at the lab, on the fringe of the world of viruses but not fully in it. *But we are all in this now,* she thought. That was perhaps just a romantic call to arms, but she buoyed herself with that inner assertion.

Cheng returned around noon. Fan waited until he finished the story of his morning before pushing him to push her request. Not that Fan wasn't intrigued by the middleaged man who continued to shed the virus. "If there are a lot of them, we'll never get rid of this."

"I think so far—I hope so far—he's an anomaly."

Fan said, "Maybe the first carrier of any disease is an anomaly."

Cheng's eyes widened. He was about to say that was actually profound, when Fan added the news about Li.

"So he's quarantined in his moon training. Are you worried?"

"Of course. It's too strange. They should have brought him home."

"Well, for everyone else's sake, I guess that's a pretty good isolation. He's a strong young guy. He'll pull through."

"They said he just had a little fever, that's it." To keep herself from dwelling further on Li, she pressed her issue about the S proteins.

"Are you asking me officially, or as a friend?"

"As a friend, of course."

"You want me to steal—?"

"If you have access, you're not stealing."

Cheng sighed. This could be nonsense, it could even be...unprofessional; and it could be a brilliant idea "out of left field," as Fan once told him the Americans would say. He gave Fan a thoughtful nod, without voicing any "Yes." Some hours later he came to Fan's office with a small vial that looked halfway between a liquid and a paste. He gave a subtle smile, a mock bow, and said, "As a friend." He added, "Just the spike proteins. No genetic material."

Fan clapped her hands together and returned his bow, exaggerating hers to the point where they both laughed. "I was never here," Cheng said, he turned to leave.

"Wait. Are you going to need a ride home?"

"I've got the driver from this morning."

"I doubt I would've gotten a driver."

"I'm not so sure. You seem to get what you want."

In fact, after Cheng left, Fan found herself actually brooding—irrationally she told herself—on that. "You seem to get what you want." Cheng might have said that as an objective observation, a compliment regarding her personal drive, and perhaps an offhand criticism, But however Cheng meant that remark, Fan would, more than occasionally, asked herself: *What do I really want?* It was not that she questioned whether she doubted her passion for nanotech, that world below the world we know, or say, in other matters, such as her involvement with Li; it was that she questioned herself in the manner of: *I want these things, but what do I want* from *them?*

Fan gave herself an inner smile of acceptance. She was sure Li never questioned what he loved: his desire to be beyond the Earth, to be among the celestial. *He loves Chang'e more than me. At least he needs Chang'e in a way that—* She shut down that train of thought. What indeed was her relationship with Li? Love? Need? Just the youthful comfort of another body? As for Cheng—she doubted he asked himself such questions. He was plainly satisfied with his career, was fulfilled by its challenges. Then again, perhaps it was presumptive of her. He was a good friend, was open with her—to a degree. He certainly never really talked about his love life. Of course, being gay, even twenty years in to the 21st century in China, was still cautious business. But then, like in all those American stories, don't gay men love female confidants? Then she chided herself at putting Cheng into a stereotype.

Ultimately, we can only consider the questions of a psyche's "wants" within our own selves. And even then, it's often with difficultly. The inner life can have an unclear horizon and a labyrinth of psychological forays.

Abruptly she left this sudden interior pondering (all from that apparently casual—and joking?—remark of Cheng's) and turned her attention to the virus' S protein and her nanomaterials.

In the micrographs, the viral spikes used to bind the cell's ACE2 receptors, looked like fuzzy little points around the round body of the virus. Fan could not get any photo of the spikes that showed them in further detail. But already there were detailed diagrams of the spike, which she spent some time perusing, translating these drawings into a microbiological reality. It seemed the spikes were not thin protrusions tapering into a sharp point, but a glycoprotein that was almost tree-like with a thicker top than base, a sort of microbiological canopy. Though for Fan's purposes, the difference between the base and top of the spike would make little difference—at least that is what she thought for now. What she was looking for was a variegated substrate or texture, and the drawings seemed to indicate that was the case. Of course, when you went down to the nano-level of viruses, these creations of Nature, whose size literally fell in between the wavelengths of lights, nothing was ever a "smooth" surface. Everything became a textured terrain.

Fan fleetingly recalled her conversations with Li, about worlds in the particles of atoms. She smiled to herself. It was a playful memory laced with concern about his present situation.

What nanoparticles would she weave from the virus?

She had at hand recycled materials from the vast store of e-waste that at this stage in human history was readily available, especially in a country such as China, an exponential growth of cast off electronic-based products, which had its own viral sort of proliferation. (Fan had the considered that when something abruptly spreads widely through the internet, it is called "going viral.") Before the digital age, the reality of planned obsolescence of products had already resulted in things from discarded washing machines to cars increasing the planet's bane of junk, the excreta of the post-industrial revolution, to make way for what was newer, more efficient—or just shinier. Now, in the past generation, improvements in digital products made the lifetime from the newest to no longer seen as useful a shorter and shorter period. Since the days of dial up and flip phones, there have been a succession of faster and more capable devices; and the devices they replaced, like those old washing machines and cars, further littered the planet. And if cell phones and computers were not as large as many of the products that had long been considered necessary for civilized life, there were so many of them now this factor of size was negated. Fan had seen a disturbing documentary about the e-waste heaps among which the poor were employed to sort and extract various metals and plastics, like wretches moving through an electronic hell, replete with smoke from wires being burned to glean the metal within.

Well, perhaps some good use could come from that hell. Fan set to work, beginning a process which, if she had not invented it, she had modified and refined to the point where it might be said she had reinvented it.

While she worked on through the day, a 21st century weaver, though with materials that would have been considered magical invisibles not so long ago, she had to consider the biological possibilities of her nanotapestry. It was the spike proteins that locked on to the ACE2 receptors in human cells. Even if the S proteins were no longer attached to the virus, and were woven into a mask, would their presence cause some type of unwanted reaction on the skin if her weave was to be used a medical, protective mask? Her first thought was that the presence of the S proteins might result in a novel nasal vaccine, but she knew there could be other effects that as yet could not be ascertained. Well, that was the situation with any new method of disease prevention.

As Fan continued, she felt once more how when one went down into the depths of the nanoworld—or, rather, its vastness—and existence itself was distilled further and further, she experienced the overwhelming sense (sometimes it was almost a sort of a transcendence) that all things became distilled into a world of molecules whose substance seemingly bore little resemblance to the whole they collectively assembled.

This sense that rose and fell in Fan like a wavelength, stronger at times, but always very much there, gave her an inner vision of a continuance of existence, of an indomitable presence that was, ultimately, indestructible. Years ago, she had had a professor who had been enamored of the 20th century French existentialists. The professor liked to extol the labyrinthine postulates of Sartre's *Being and Nothingness,* which pointed out that nothing in existence is ever destroyed. It was humankind who invented the concept of destruction. A furious storm rips through a town, and its residents see destruction. But the substance of everything is still *there*, merely "rearranged."

Fan had to think about this epidemic. The virus filling cells with innumerable copies of itself until that cell burst, and a new host of virus spreading exponentially through the body, was certainly, from the perspective of a host, a destruction. One that could lead to ultimate cessation of the host's life. Of course, the death of a human being, of any animal, of any insect, any animate life, plants too, was merely a matter of that animate substance being returned, as they say, to the earth, to its essential elements.

Science had ultimately been led to the acceptance of the eternity of matter itself, in a very real sense bowing to a philosophy ancient in its source.

She could not help thinking of Li, of the virus bursting from his cells. Then again, he could be ill with just a cold. –But no, she knew she was just trying to allay what intuition told her. If he was sick now, he had this new virus.

Well, he was under quarantine under the eye of the government, which had invested so much in his training. So he would be watched and cared for—because he was just that, an investment. At least that is what she decided.

What Fan could produce in the lab was only a microscale, a template that would have to be extrapolated to an industrial scale in order to be put to practical use. She had to work up from nanometers to micrometers (microns) to millimeters to centimeters, a huge leap in size; there are ten million nanometers in a centimeter. The weave she had worked with, the tobacco mosaic virus, had produced swatches of material no more than centimeters in size. But that was fine. She was not a factory; her job was to establish how it was done.

Though by the end of the day, Fan felt she had made no more than small progress. She had become accomplished—at least relatively so— in her nanoweaving the tobacco mosaic virus; the rod shaped virus had been like needles that were easily suited to this process. The S proteins of this coronavirus, just parts of a virus instead of a full virus. where like delicate shards of a whole.

She felt frustrated. And knew, when she felt like this, the best thing to do was to walk away from the work, refresh herself—until tomorrow, in this case.

It was later than she thought it was. Cheng had already left, with his driver. That amused her for some reason. Cheng was an unpretentious man; she wondered if being chauffeured back and forth made him uncomfortable. Well, he was lucky to have this in the midst of a citywide lockdown. She was a little surprised that Cheng hadn't stopped by before he left. During the past week or so, as the virus had taken hold in Wuhan, and the lab itself felt the epicenter of this outbreak, in addition to being under suspicion as the source of the virus, Fan had come to feel closer to Cheng, an older but still youngish colleague. His knowledge of and his experiences with viruses was an intellectual strength that drew Fan and even comforted her. With a mind like Cheng's, Fan felt this epidemic could be successfully confronted.

And perhaps, with Li more and more in the isolation of his training, and now under full quarantine, Fan had, with Cheng, agreeable male company without any sexual tension.

She thought of Dr. Sun, Cheng's friend, in the hospital. She had not thought of him once during the press of her day. It seemed like so much had happened since yesterday. Had Cheng checked on him? She had been so engrossed in her own problem of the S proteins—

Wuhan was a bit darker as she drove home in the winter evening. Though there were still enough lights of the millions huddled away, trying to keep themselves from a virus so minute no human eye could see it, or even feel it if it fell like rain upon the city.

After parking her car and walking to her building, she looked up at the sky. Bright Orion was visible, even amongst the light pollution that was still prevalent, lockdown or not. Fan imagined viruses falling down from the starry sky. But viruses, as least as far as she knew, were very earthbound, carried in bodies, expelled in the fluids of breathing, coughs and sneezes. In the touch of a hand, lying on surfaces. Not very celestial at all.

She scanned the internet for news. There were conflicting figures about the infected. The authorities alternately advised extreme caution and gave assurances the outbreak of this new disease was not as serious as many were saying. Fan thought again of Dr. Sun, who had confronted the secrecy of the authorities by making information public, by saying the situation had been very bad before the public was told there was something to worry about. She and Cheng should see Dr. Sun tomorrow, she thought.

It was no surprise that Fan dreamed. She had become a figure that was no larger than the nanoworld she had worked with all day, a figure that became even smaller than the S proteins. She walked on the capsid of the virus and the protein spikes were like surreal trees canopied above her. She moved among this landscape like a little girl in the strangest forest—and then this virus world plunged toward something that Fan realized was a human cell, and one of the protein spikes, one of the trees latched onto the cell. Fan realized the cell was in Li's body, and the virus that had borne her, with its forest of spikes, drove into Li's flesh, as the RNA within the capsid was "pumped" into the cell via the spikes.

She awoke in the dark. *I'll have to tell that dream to Li,* she thought. She was amused at how her nanoworld that invaded her dreaming. But she also thought again of Li, being infected. Invaded. She had to consider the dream disturbing.

The thought struck her for the first time—that if Li were sick, she should quarantine herself. But that would mean cutting herself off from her work. She just couldn't do that. She reasoned she was mostly alone at the lab, wearing a mask— She thought also if Li did have the virus, what if she had gotten it from him…what if she started an outbreak at the lab? Her thoughts went back and forth like this, but she knew she was returning to work in the morning. The virus would not stop her from using it to be woven into something her imagination created.

So, she disguised her own desire with the call of a purpose.

Chapter Eight: The Virus

20.

Li awoke not feeling well at all.

First there was a moment when he felt totally disembodied—and mentally displaced—from his situation and setting. He blinked, cleared his eyes, looked about the room. Images of the moon flooded him with almost confusing rapidity. Then he slowed them down. That city in the distance....

The moon disappeared; there was just the room. And the way he felt. He sat up, sneezed, sniffled. *So, I am sick?* He shook his head. The virus. He did not want to consider the extent to which it might claim him. He gazed without thought at the book about the moon he'd been reading before falling asleep.

The door opened. It was Lin and Yang in masks and protective gear. Li was not in the mood to see them. They looked like creatures who would do him harm.

They gave no perfunctory greeting. Lin waved the thermometer. Li sat up slowly. Yang said, "You don't look well." Li said nothing in response. The instrument passed over his forehead. He felt, irrationally, an invasion into his mind. His temperature was 101.4. Yang said, rhetorically, "So you're sick?"

"I suppose I am," said Li, not wanting to admit it.

Lin said, "We'll be back. We'll test you."

"Will I know right away?"

"Not for a few days. But you're in quarantine anyway."

Yang interjected. "You won't have any training today."

"Maybe it's just a cold," said Li.

Yang: "That is possible, but—" He shook his head, meaning that the way things were at the moment, it was likely more than a cold.

Li's protestation—or hope—that he suffered a lesser ill was weak disguise for something that bothered him more at the moment than the possibility he had the new virus: What Yang had told him, as if the pair of Yang and Lin had abruptly decided he would have no visits to the moon today. Li had always regarded them as low level guards (for want of a better word); did they have some sort of authority? More likely they had been told that if Li were ever palpably sick, his lunar training would be put on hold. But Lin and Yang definitely had an air of authority about themselves this morning.

"When are you coming back?" Li asked.

Lin said, "Are you getting lonely?" This might have seemed joking, even playful, but Li took it as mockery. He said, flatly, "No."

Yang glanced at *A History of the Moon*. "Now you definitely have time to read."

"I looked through it. It's...interesting." Li said that with apparent indifference, as if he did not want to show he in fact had been drawn into the disparate scope of the book.

Lin: "Maybe the next edition will have you in it."

Lin and Yang left. Li hoped they would not be back too soon. His head was stuffed and achy. He pressed his fingers against his forehead, massaged himself forcefully, as if trying to push out his sickness. When his hands fell away, he laughed at the absurdity into which he felt he had been so completely dropped. He had been subject to the most realistic simulations imaginable of being on the moon. Now he was in bed with a cold (he didn't want to think of it as worse than that), and, speaking of the absurd, subject to the direction of the odd pair of Lin and Yang. He imagined them talking to the voice that had called Li on the phone, communicating the fact of Li's illness. What was it that voice had told him? Decipher? Or had that been on the monitor? His memory suddenly wasn't clear.

He laid himself down and took up the book. In a chapter titled "Lunar Anomalies," he read:

The moon itself may be considered an anomaly, so it's not surprising that there are so many strange things, unexplained facts and phenomena connected to our singular satellite, our companion world.

Such as the flashing lights that people all over the world—and for the past one thousand years—have been seeing. We have a name for it: Transient Lunar Phenomena, or TLP. The flashing lights are just that: lights suddenly seen and gone in a second or seconds. Though sometimes the lights flash for a long period of time.

William Herschel, whose skill as an astronomer we've already detailed, reported a red glow near the Aristarchus crater in 1783. In 1787 he observed several TLP on different dates, and became convinced the moon was exhibiting volcanic activity at three different locations, including the region of Aristarchus. He even extended an invitation to King George III to see the crater with the royal telescope at Windsor. It's not known if the king noted any TLP.

Coincidentally, on July 19, 1969, a day before *Apollo 11* landed on the moon, the astronauts saw luminous activity on the northwest wall of Aristarchus. At the same time the crew of America's first moon mission was seeing this, two German astronomers noted similar activity from Aristarchus that lasted from five to seven seconds.

(Incidentally, this crater was named after Aristarchus Samos, an ancient Greek astronomer and mathematician who was the first to propose the heliocentric model of the heavens, in other words, sun-centered.)

It's been theorized that shifting in the crust of the moon releases certain gases that briefly give off luminescence, but at this point there is no provable cause for these lights and flashes. Just another mystery of the mysterious moon.

Li smiled wanly, chiding the author for this coy summation. Li could tell him a few things about "the mysterious moon." He put down the book. He closed his eyes, trying to drift apart from the ill feeling in his body. Lights on the moon. Signals?

Of course, what could Li really tell the author about the moon? How real were the things he had experienced—while his body was still in this room?

Li laid himself back on the cot, tried to free his body of what knew was the beginning of illness. Whenever he got sick, which was always no more than a cold, he would try to fight it off by not accepting it. How one does not "accept" illness is not something that can be precisely quantified, but that's what Li would do. Sometimes it would work. He would go about the normal things he did, and sometimes that cold would be no more. But usually, the virus would have its way and he'd be sick a few days. There would be a point when he accepted that his "nonacceptance" wasn't working. Then he would, as he once told Fan, "sink into the sickness, flow with it," as if he were both physically and psychically riding it—and thus, in some way, eventually seeing it ushered out of his body.

When he had awakened this morning he had not "accepted" his body's malaise, but that had ended more quickly than usual—probably due to a confluence of things: the fact that what afflicted him was a new virus, his strange being-there-but-not-being-there experiences on the moon, his being quarantined in this room, and just the odd presence of Lin and Yang and the fact that he had a definite fever. *So am I sick*, he said to himself. *And it's probably the virus.* He tried to think of everything Cheng had said about this new coronavirus. What Li was not accepting was that it would attack him to the point at which he would have to go to the hospital. He would not at all consider the possibility he could actually be killed by it.

Li closed his eyes and tried to imagine waves of healing energy pass through his body, cleansing it. But it was actually hard to do this for even just one full minute. His mind wandered, especially to all the odd facts he'd read in that book. Flashes of light on the moon.... He thought of those flashes pulsing in his body. He thought of the abandoned lunar city, the buildings sporadically flashing with light—as if survivors were signaling. And he had the thought, just before drifting into an anxious sleep, that if one lived on the far side of the moon, one would never see the Earth; and if you did not know the science of the situation, you could not know that the world you were on was bound in gravitational tandem to a larger and very different world. –And the further thought, now on the tenuous border of sleep and nonsleep: there are forces acting on us of which we cannot know.... He, Zhen Li, was being drawn, directed, maneuvered, whatever through something important, even momentous—and had been chosen as a figure in this passage because he had indicated his willingness to traverse the terrain upon which all this mystery occurred. But had he chosen the mystery?

Li dreamed. It seemed there was so much dreaming now. He approached the lunar city, drawn there by flashes of lights of different colors that flickered on and off, like some Spring Festival display. Reaching one building where a reddish light flickered above him, he entered and moved onto upper floors. There was the sense that he had "risen" through the building, but his dreaming did not supply how he had done this. He entered rooms; there were no doors, only doorways. The interiors of every room were simply stone, as if all these structures had not been intended for any sort of soft flesh. There was nothing in these rooms that indicated habitation. No furniture, artifacts. Even in the stone caves of Earth, that had once sheltered humans thousands of years ago, there were shards of bones, tools, even drawings.

And so his mind, his dreaming mind, took that as hint and created something to which an Earthman could be connected. He moved from one austere room to a corridor, a hallway, entered another room, and found on a wall a precise series of concentric circles, each circle fitted into larger one with an exact, repeating redundancy. Circles of thin lines, dully white. Li went up to the circles and touched them. They were minutely raised from the surface of the wall. Like Braille, he thought. Braille: like the message—warning—he had been given. Li had the sense there was some astronomical connection to the circles. If there hadn't been so many of them, he would have thought it was supposed to represent a planetary system; but no, there were just too many. And there was no central "sun"; the circles got smaller and smaller until the center of this series was just a dot. Though Li had the thought that a microscope would reveal that dot still a circle with other circles within it, further microscopic circles, further nano-sized circles within that, on and on, infinitely. He placed his finger on that center, as if he would feel through his flesh the infinite series of concentricity.

Then he realized he was not in his space suit, but walking in this deserted lunar city, with his Earthman's body exposed to the harsh world of the moon.

He awoke, his eyes looking at the blurred, beyond-world of the room, trying to sort through the dream.

He felt a bit worse. And considered that in the dream he had not felt sick at all. He felt his forehead. Yes, it was warm. He drank some water. He wondered: how widespread, within the program, was the knowledge that he was in quarantine?

Fourteen days. The length of a lunar day, a lunar night.

Thinking of the lunar city his dreaming self had moved through, he wondered what Wuhan was like now. Everyone locked away, apparently. A traveler from another world might think it an abandoned city, but, entering its buildings and its rooms, find Wuhan very peopled. And if this visitor and the people of the Earth city could communicate and relate that they were keeping themselves away from a virus— Perhaps the world of the traveler had no such thing as viruses and could not comprehend that invisible entities could keep millions in fear and hiding.

Well, did viruses and bacteria live "out there"? Li understood that human life, indeed all life on Earth could not live without bacteria, but as for viruses—He remembered conversations with Cheng, who had said that viruses had been very much part of the journey of human evolution, imparting genetic material to the human genome. What would this new virus leave us? Cheng had also said that perhaps viruses had genetic material from us, too. It was cycle of universal exchange, something perhaps that neither side intended, but to which all "creatures" here had to bow. Human beings try to put themselves apart from this constant order, humans try to order their interactions with the natural world as much as possible, but when something like a new virus comes along, it's a new ball game (as Fan said the Americans say).

But could there be worlds with no viruses? If ours is ordered so, that did not have to mean such was the case elsewhere. When the Apollo astronauts returned from the moon, they were quarantined, in case they brought had back any lunar pathogens. Of course, that twenty-one day quarantine had been of arbitrary length. If the astronauts had brought back something, who knew how long that contagion would take to show itself. The nature of the moon being what it is, it was more likely the Earthmen would shed some germs. Of course, it was not likely that anything could be shed through those spacesuits. Though humans, spreading throughout space, would ultimately bring their Earthly viruses along. Perhaps viruses needed humans to spread them throughout the universe.

Li was aware of the theory that viruses, at least protoviruses, had been brought to Earth from space, via comets and the like. Well, it would make more sense that viruses would be a constant throughout the universe, a presence not at all unusual, though dependent on whatever life that could emerge on different worlds. If a virus fell from the heavens on a lifeless world, what good would it do the virus? Unless viruses were *necessary* to kick start life.

Li picked up the book. It seemed this would be his diversion for a while. For some reason he did not want to start with page one and go on from there, but dipped in and out of it. He opened to a chapter called "Moon Changes."

The most widely known "moon change" legend is that of the wolf man, the werewolf, a man—or woman—who changes into a half human, half wolf creature during the full moon.

But the moon did not always figure in the story of the werewolf. The earliest known mention of men being changed into wolves is the Epic of Gilgamesh, circa 2100 B.C., in which Gilgamesh rejects a potential amor because she transformed a former mate into a wolf.

In ancient Greek legend, King Lycaon drew the anger of Zeus when he served him a meal with human meat—a sacrificed boy. Zeus punished Lyacon and his sons by turning them into wolves.

Li skipped a few paragraphs and then came upon if not exactly the story of a Chinese werewolf, then the unusual—and true—story of Tai Djin, the "Kung Fu Werewolf."

Born in 1849, Tai Djin had hypertrichosis—unusual hair growth. His face was covered with hair like an animal. His family saw this as a sign of the demonic; they left the child in the woods to die. A monk from Shaolin was travelling through the forest, found the boy and took him to the Fukien Shaolin Temple, where Tai Djin was raised by monks. He was also trained in martial arts and was so adept at mastering this discipline, including the Chi Ma, or 'Death Touch.' He became the first Grandmaster of Shaolin-Do, known as Su Kong (Grandmaster) Tai

Djin. He died in 1928, after teaching many pupils in the arts he had mastered so well.

Li had the thought: it was so recent that China had preferred boys to be added to their population over girls, while trying to restrict the growth of the population as a whole. What treatment would a child born with hypertrichosis receive in China today?

Li wanted to know when men becoming wolves was first linked to the moon.

In parts of western Europe, it was believed that a man could turn into a wolf by sleeping outdoors under a full moon, but it is difficult to establish an original 'first link' to werewolves and the moon any more precisely than this general location, and perhaps more difficult to establish a period when this belief firmly took hold. Certainly, the moon-werewolf link has been in existence for two or three centuries, though never more firmly established than in the horror movies of England and America during the 20th century.

It is said that werewolves are most affected by the moon under which they first made their transformation into a wolf....

Li read that the January full moon was called the Wolf Moon, with "high werewolf activity. Werewolves may team up, uncharacteristically, in packs. It is known werewolves are usually, indeed, 'lone wolves.'"

This January's full moon had already passed. Li considered that by the time he got out of quarantine it would be around February's full moon, which, according to the book, was the Ice Moon, with no particular unusual effect on the werewolf.

I guess they go back to being lone wolves.

Li was feeling more unwell. He tried to sleep. He imagined he heard faint noises outside the door. He tensed himself for someone's entrance, particularly the return of Lin and Yang. There was something perpetually annoying about them, aside from their almost comedic absurdity. Then Li wondered why he would even term them comedic....

No one entered, and sleep came.

And, of course, dreaming. Li moved through a city again, but this time it was earthly Wuhan. Above the deserted streets was a full moon. It lit the city with a beauty and severity he had never seen. Wuhan seemed washed with eternity, the phase of its human activity merely a clamor of its past, not its present, and certainly not its future. As Li walked on, his lunar-cast shadow emerging on the sidewalks before him or alongside him, he wondered at that future. Who—or what—would inhabit the city then? The virus? But no, without hosts, the virus could not continue. In that unpeopled future, the virus had passed.

Or had the population been gone not so long ago and the virus still lingered?

He entered a building, one of many offices and about ten floors. All doors opened to him easily. He walked about the deserted interiors, wondering at his own purpose. *Am I hunting the virus? Will I be the final host?*

In an elevator he ascended a few floors, giving no thought to the fact that the elevator was working. In another office he entered a bathroom—and was stopped by his image in the mirror over the sink.

He was a wolfman. A werewolf.

He peered at himself without very much surprise or shock, it seemed, touching the thick hair on his face. Then he oddly nodded to himself. He left the bathroom, descended back down to the street, and walked amongst deserted Wuhan again, looking up at the moon more often now. Perhaps the Wolf Moon had returned. He felt relaxed, even freed, apparently accepting this transformation of legend almost as if he had expected it.

Then, at the end of one block, by a big intersection, where the lights of the deserted city competed with the moon, Fan was there, waiting for him. She was dressed as she would be in the lab. Li seemed to accept her presence as if he had expected it. She looked at Li as he approached, with a slight smile, not so much one of pleasure at him being there, but an expression conveying the sense that something she had assessed about him had verified.

"So you've accepted the moon," she said as he stood before her. It was like an accusation, though Fan had spoken it without hostility.

He stepped back. Suddenly he became nervous. "No—I don't—but I'm *here*—"

Then he was apart from Fan, and staggering through the city. He looked down at his hairy hands. He was being taken over by something he had not chosen. He looked up at the full moon and with a start saw a bat dart across its light. For a moment the bat's wings made a rip of sound above him. It was a visceral sound, and it startled him.

A bat. A bat had brought the virus. He recalled Cheng's recounting of the caves of bats he had had explored, in search of viruses. Those were images of dark, receding interiors filled with fluttering or resting bats, their wings folded comfortably. But here was this lone creature in this vast, stilled city. This small creature that he could fit in his hand had shut down a city of millions. But no, a smaller "creature" had done that: the virus. The infinitesimal had brought down the large. The large host: the city.

The world was filled with invasion. He gestured to the bat—as if in recognition? But it was gone, gone elsewhere into the night. Li continued on, through Wuhan's empty streets.

He awoke. His first thought, as he rolled the dream back through his mind, was, *Where did Fan go?* He did not want to think of her roaming that desolate city.

He did not seem shocked he had dreamt of himself as a werewolf.

He sat up. He felt awful. He made himself some hot soup. The warmth felt good. He almost picked up the book again, but at the moment he did not want to be distracted by another man's vision.

The image of himself as a werewolf wandering Wuhan looking up at a full moon made Li recall his childhood, looking up at the great sky, the stars and the moon over the rice fields. His mother had kidded him, saying that maybe he was from another planet; his grandfather had once called him a moon child. Li had not thought of that for a long time. A child of Chang'e. Perhaps this was born of a sort of rebellion against the life his parents had lived, so close to, so bound to the earth and its seasons, its weathers, the toil needed to coax growing things out of the soil. Li had wanted to look upwards, outward, not at the dirt that came to his hands too easily. That mark of Earth was a bondage he did not want. He learned the Chinese and western star maps of the heavens; The Purple Forbidden Enclosure in the middle of the sky, containing the Hellenistic constellations such as Auriga, Cassiopeia, Boötes and others; the Supreme Palace Enclosure, with Virgo, Leo and Ursa Major among its realm; and the Heavenly Market Enclosure, with Serpens, Ophiuchus, Aquila, Corona Borealis, and parts of Hercules. Each enclosure was further divided into a Right Wall and Left Wall. The heavens are further divided into 28 mansions, enfolded into: Black Tortoise of the North for winter, Azure Dragon of the East for spring, Vermillion Bird of the South for summer, and White Tiger of the West for autumn. The mansions in turn were divided in into four sections of seven determinative stars, each star marking a specific direction of the compass. How precise was this star world above him. And it was an old thing that would continue its nature and course for all time, he felt. It would await him through the long years it would take him to become a man and be able to travel into its realm.

Perhaps he had been born to be drawn to the moon; he was some mix of human and star being. He didn't usually think like this, he usually saw himself as part of the human tradition to explore what was over the next horizon, but here, quarantined in the training room, he was oppressed by his dream of being a werewolf and wondered if this were not close metaphor for something integral to his psyche: a man so drawn to what was beyond Earth he not only could not be as others but showed this difference physically. He was marked.

He looked down at his hands. Of course, they were not the hairy hands of a werewolf. But Li in his spacesuit—wasn't that transformation enough?

His thoughts were running in two rivers, the stuff of dreams and the practical. He was a serious taikonaut in training, and he was traveler of more than physical worlds.

Sleep came again to Li. His illness had taken him from the regular round of day and night. His body sought as complete a rest as possible, using all its strength to heal, to pass through the violation of the virus.

When Li awoke, he was lying on the moon.

He thought he was dreaming again. It took a few seconds for him to realize that his back was feeling cold. The spacesuit's system that kept him at a livable temperature was struggling to balance the heat the poured down from the sun above him and the cold of the lunar surface that was blocked from the sun by his body.

He thought himself sitting up slowly, but in the moon's light gravity he half bounded up, almost stumbled, then stood up. He was annoyed, actually disturbed that he had been thrust back into training. He was not feeling well, he was not in the mood for—this.

He looked about. He thought about his Wuhan dreams. *I am always in solitude.*

Well, solitude belongs to the explorer. He recalled his reminiscences of childhood, looking up at the stars from the rice fields. He had already, years ago, cast himself into solitude. He realized, taking in the lunar landscape, that often, even when with others, even sometimes with Fan, he carried a solitude that was inescapable. Fan would sometimes abruptly say to him, "Li, you're being out there." It became a playful thing between them. He would smile, laugh; she would give a resigned, knowing expression in return.

Well, I got what I wanted.

But did he want this? This being alone on the moon but not really being on the moon? And if he was to be chosen for the first Chinese moon mission (he always thought it would be the first, not the second or third) he would be with a crew, not alone. A boy, a young man, might choose something unusual, something daring, but the circumstances he chose to put himself in to achieve that goal might direct him in ways not of his choosing.

At least here I'm not a werewolf.

Then again, in his space suit he could not see his hands; he had no mirror to look into to see his face. He did not feel himself laden with hair, but—

These dreams, this…sickness. He wanted to return to the room, to rest, to sleep—without dreaming. He wanted his body to feel its healthy self again.

And then, as if his wish had been someone's command, he stood in the room again, the moon gone—as if, yes, another dream. *Is my mind right, am I really having hallucinations?*

But if Li's desire had seemed to be fulfilled in the moment, it also seemed that this brief visit to the moon, was almost if he were being shown that anything could be done to him at another's wish. He had confronted a series of lunar surrealness on these very real training sessions; he had been intrigued, even stimulated as well as confounded; ultimately these events had whetted his curiosity to discover an explanation. But now, feeling sick, all that strangeness seemed too much;

and awakening prone on the moon.... He felt that almost a threat. A madness he did not want to bear. He sighed, gave himself up to his tiredness, his sickness, and drifted in that realm of illness and an interior torpor, considering in a vague but accurate way the presence of the virus in his body, that had clearly replicated enough to flood his cells, burst his cells, and continue to latch onto and replicate itself within other cells, bursting through them and continuing its passage of ravaging.

How many viruses did it take to make one sick? At what point did the scales tip from health to illness? It was probably an unanswerable question.

Trying to will his immune system to work, and work well, Li fell into a sluggish, dreamless sleep.

21.

Cheng's driver was once again awaiting him in the morning. Once again, he looked up from his phone as Cheng got in the car. It seemed everyone under thirty was neurotically attached to their phones, thought Cheng. Then he chided himself. Many forty and fifty year people were also attached to their phones now. But with this younger generation (*So I'm an old man now?* he thought) it literally seemed a part of their bodies, at least psychologically—a part of their minds.

The driver—what was his name again? Oh, Junjie. The driver smiled above the mask. What does his whole face look like? Cheng wondered. It was an idle thought that hit Cheng suddenly. He did seem to be a handsome young man. Cheng laughed at himself. He had thought so little of that aspect of life lately.

He said, "I have to go somewhere before the lab."

"Oh? Where?"

Cheng was not sure if that "Where?" might contain more than a simple request for direction. He had the feeling this driver questioned Cheng's decision to go anywhere but straight to the lab.

"I have to see someone in the hospital."

Cheng had awakened thinking of Dr. Sun, and feeling guilty that he'd thought little of the man at all yesterday. There was just so much that had been happening. He had called the hospital yesterday, gotten a terse report: "He's the same," then had gone on to some pressing work at the lab and his poor friend was out of Cheng's mind quickly.

At the hospital he told the driver, "I will try to be not too long—"

"Whatever you have to do," said Junjie. He was already back at his phone. As Cheng got out of the car, he considered it would be an interesting study to take a thousand people and actually delineate what they did on their phones every day for a month, including every call, text, etc. He suspected, indeed he was sure, that most of that time was of little consequence. Though maybe, he thought, as he entered the hospital, this was a "next step" in a new type of social bonding occurring throughout the technological world. This being connected every waking instant. Solitude had been abolished. Even now, with the lockdown, there were millions in Wuhan on every conceivable social media. Group mind? He wondered. Well, it would harder for governments to divide people now. Though if the powers that be pulled the plug on the internet...as they had, in a way, done to Dr. Sun, who had dared to post online videos about that was going on with the virus before the authorities would admit anything of the sort.

Inside the hospital, Cheng used his credentials, his affiliation with the lab in a much more forward way than he had during his previous visit. He did not want to waste time, he wanted all the new precautions to fall away before him.

"He shouldn't be having any visitors," a doctor told him, but it was a protest the doctor felt he had to make to separate himself from any wrong that might come of Cheng's presence before Dr. Sun, a protest he knew would have no effect.

So Cheng was once more by Dr. Sun's bedside. The unfortunate man had a breathing tube down his throat. *This is the step before death*, Cheng thought, but he still hoped. And Cheng did not think at all, or very little, at least, of the possibility of contracting the virus from his very sick friend. Whether this virus or other coronaviruses. Cheng had been researching this family of pathogens for so long, for so many years, from caves of bats to labs, to hospitals, that he could not think what he studied could invade his own body. He observed them, they had no power over him. Though as he had remarked to Fan, he knew this perspective was irrational—careless. Not that Cheng was careless at this moment. He wore appropriate gear, had gloves and a mask. The face on the bed looked up at him with knowing eyes. The stomach slowly rose and fell with the pulse of the machine. Cheng knew the use of a respirator meant that a cytokine storm was battering the man's lungs, the body's incredibly aggressive inflammatory response to the virus's invasion, the unleashing of the arsenal of the immune system which attacked the body's own cells. It was as if the virus had unleased a suicide response.

By Sun Bao's bedside was a pad. The doctor took it up and wrote: I AM WAITING.

Cheng raised his eyelids in a question.

The doctor wrote: TO SEE WHO WINS. AND I WILL KNOW BEFORE IT IS OVER.

Cheng nodded.

MY MOTHER WAS HERE. THEY WOULD NOT LET—

Cheng reached out and stayed his friend's hand. "I know. I had to use my…credentials to—" Bao's eyes blinked. His lips seemed to work about the plastic tube, as if tasting it, as if tasting something dire that had forced itself upon his life.

Cheng left his gloved hand on the ungloved hand of his friend for a long moment. Their eyes considered each other. Cheng had the definite feeling he would not be able to be so near him again. "I will talk to your mother." Bao blinked again. Cheng went on: "You did a heroic thing. Letting everyone know."

Now the eyes that blinked back seemed watery. The hand wrote again: HAS IT HELPED?

Cheng did not answer directly. "Everything helps now—that is truthful."

The mouth around the tube seemed to want to give a wry laugh. The lips twisted. The brow frowned. This was a face communicating an intelligence while holding itself painfully above a storm. Or within a storm.

A nurse came in. It was not the same nurse as last time. "You've been here too long." It was both an accusation and a request that he should bow to the situation and leave.

"Please, another minute." The nurse said nothing, just looked at him blankly above her mask. Cheng looked back down at his friend. Sun Bao looked up at him. It was a frieze the virus had set; Cheng and Dr. Sun Bao and the nurse, too, were merely the figures forced at random to play the roles in this scene.

"We're making progress," Cheng lied. Well, "they" were knowing more, and realizing the enormity of the powers of the new virus. But was that exactly progress? Not while the virus progressed so violently in Dr. Sun Bao.

"I will see you again." This was not a lie, but a hope. The head with the tube thrust down its mouth nodded. Cheng stepped back, felt himself drifting back, as if drawn into the safety of not being in front of a man who would most likely die. Then he turned, said an inane "Thank you," to the nurse, and left the room.

Passing through the hospital's corridors, Cheng felt himself exiting a place without hope.

Junjie looked up from his phone, nodded, as Cheng got in the car. Cheng gave him a flash of recognition with his eyes. He would have preferred to be alone at the moment. On the way back to the lab there was silence in the car, then the driver said, "A patient of yours?"

"I'm not a medical doctor." Shouldn't the driver have known this? What had he been told about Cheng? "A friend. He's sick."

"Well, he's in there, so I guess he is."

It seemed a callous response. Cheng said nothing for a moment, then said, "The virus."

Junjie's eyes widened. "That's bad. "Cheng was not sure if the reaction had been one of at least some sympathy or a sort of fear of being enclosed with someone—Cheng—who had been close to someone with the virus. Though he had not shown any particular reaction when driving Cheng to see that man who still shed the virus.

"Yes, it is," Cheng said, flatly.

That was the extent of the conversation. Cheng found himself resenting this young driver—then said to himself he was just transferring his frustration—and helplessness—of the past few days to something petty. The young man was doing a job he had been given. Cheng was doing—trying to—do a job he had chosen. And then had the feeling that the direction of his recent tasks had not been directed by himself at all.

He was happy to get to the lab. He could lose himself in the problem of the virus. As he had said to the nurse, he said to the driver, "Thank you."

Junjie smiled at him. "No problem. See you later."

Cheng nodded back. The young man was polite to him, was generally quiet. Cheng realized that his usual commute to the lab on public transportation had been a time of reflective solitude. The close presence of a stranger had disrupted that. He enjoyed his rides with Fan, of course. She was a colleague. And brilliant, Cheng smiled to himself as he entered the lab. Weaving the virus' spike proteins with recycled e-waste. Li was a lucky young man. In a way they were an odd couple, Fan friendly and drawing others in, while Li was so focused (as Fan said) on going "out there" he often seemed off the Earth when right in front of you. But they shared the quality of being intensely self-directed.

And I'm not?

Cheng smiled at himself. Perhaps what one put himself through each day, as part of the habit of self focus, was seen by an observer as an overwhelming intensity.

He had barely been in the lab ten minutes, going through his email, when Mr. 21st century Mao Suit came into Cheng's office. Cheng did not believe his dismay showed on his face, but the self-satisfied look on Dong Chao's face said, *I don't care if you want to see me, we have business.*

"Your friend in the hospital…."

Cheng really didn't like this. Too many things other than the work he should be doing were intruding. Especially this sort of intrusion. To Dong's raised eyebrows, an exaggerated expression of concern, Cheng said, "He's on a breathing tube."

"So it's serious."

"Yes," said Cheng, tightly.

Dong nodded, his air of affected concern lost. The misfortunes of the world, or any personal misfortunes, for that matter, were to be little considered. "Well, he is looked after as best as possible. It's out of your hands."

Cheng felt so many levels in that. How well someone would be looked after who defied the authorities and spread accurate information about this new virus, against all the wishes of the authorities—Cheng had doubts about that. And that "out of your hands": this official, with his Italian-designed Mao suit, was making sure Cheng knew he was helpless; from now on Cheng was to be (speaking of direction) directed by the state.

He just looked at Dong and gave a slight sigh, waiting.

"The need for a vaccine is being discussed."

"We don't even know if— We never had one for SARS—"

"Yes. We seemed to lose that threat…quickly. There wasn't a need. I don't know how much you know about it. That was before your time."

In a way, the outbreak in 2003 was, and in a way it wasn't. "I was just coming out of school." Cheng began.

"But far from being the master of your field, as you are today."

"I hardly feel a master."

"But you know you're more than good enough."

Cheng wasn't sure where this was going, and at the same time he had an intuition about it. He wasn't sure he wanted to give in to that intuition. "If you're talking about a vaccine—will this virus be a threat next year?"

"I will ask you. Will it?"

At that moment Cheng realized he had not considered any future connected with this outbreak past this winter. He nodded his head slightly. "There's a chance. Although as I said, SARS—and this virus is related to SARS—"

Dong gave his own slight nod, granting Cheng a point he would overlay with a more telling point. "We can't be so lucky twice. SARS left us—apparently. But this virus—it's connection to that very similar earlier version—"

"Version?" A possibility cracked through the strata of Cheng's thoughts: he was abruptly wondering if this new virus had not been intentionally engineered, and, like the Frankenstein story, gotten away from its creator. Fan had once forced him to watch one of those puerile American horror films inspired by the story Mary Shelley had written in England two centuries ago, in 1816. Fran had "culturally translated" the story behind the film and the book for Cheng. Li, who had been present, had offered, "Isn't the communist ideal to create a new man, one of science?"

Fan had responded, "We're all *people* of science, but we're not monsters—I hope." She had stressed "people" to confront Li's use of specific gender.

But Cheng's thoughts were drifting—because he wanted to get away from Dong's presence and whatever he was driving at. Dong was saying, "We need to be prepared, in case. We see, the way this is spreading—"

"Many cold viruses are coronaviruses. There has never been a vaccine for a coronavirus."

"Because there hasn't been does mean there will never be." Dong laughed, oddly pleased with himself. "Sounds like something Chairman Mao would have said."

Cheng made no comment to that. Dong added, "The first SARS virus—this is really a second SARS-type virus—caused more than 8,000 cases, with 774 deaths. I remember that number exactly for some reason. So high mortality. This one doesn't seem as bad—so far. But who knows? Why that virus left us by the summer of 2003—who knows. Maybe in two, three months, this will be gone. But we don't think so. One thing that made SARS' infections easier to trace, so it was easier to contain, was that people usually got symptoms in two to three days. With this virus it could be ten days, two weeks. With SARS someone got sick, they could name the people they were on contact with, relate pretty accurately their activities for three days. But when you ask someone to go ten or fourteen days back, that doesn't work. Well, viruses are mysterious—as you know, of course. We need to be more careful this time."

Cheng said, "I read that a vaccine was developed, but it was never really tested in humans."

"Yes, just animals. They used a whole, inactivated virus in ferrets, primates and mice. It seems there was some degree of immunity conferred, but the vaccine also caused immune disorders. I don't know the details."

"Did they used an attenuated virus or a killed virus?"

"I said I don't know the details."

"I think it would be dangerous to put the whole virus, whether weakened or killed—you never really know if you've killed all the virus you used—use that in a vaccine."

"That is something you are going to help us with."

Cheng looked back with barely hidden consternation. His intuition had been correct. Whether noting Cheng's expression or not, Dong was saying, "It is likely you will be chosen to lead our effort for a vaccine."

"Likely?" That not quite definite word gave Cheng hope. But Dong quickly changed that nature of his statement. "I say 'likely' to be technically accurate. But it's basically been decided we want you to head this effort."

"I think I would be more effective in researching possible therapeutics for those that are sick now. And will be sick tomorrow. A vaccine is something that can—does—should—take years to develop, test."

"That's true, that's true. But our medicine is more and more—well, modern. Isn't it? I think those development times will shorten. No, you won't come up with it tomorrow, but in some season that will come sooner than you think."

"Some season." Yes, that gave an aspect of time—but time more pressing than vague. Cheng gave a long and definite sigh. "I appreciate...everyone's confidence in me—" (Who exactly was "everyone"?) "But I am also uncomfortable with misplaced hopes."

Cheng did not like the official's chuckle. "Our country, our party is built on hope. Look at where we have come, from the days of ignorant rulers and peasants. In this century we drive the world. Our science—of which you are an example—"

"Men of science," Cheng, as if to himself.

"Exactly that," said Dong, apparently not picking up Cheng's ironic tone. Cheng almost added Fan's "people of science," but he didn't.

It's not that Cheng wasn't intrigued by the complexities of making a vaccine. But in the moments after Dong Chao left, what he was thinking about was the issue of how and why some viruses inflict their harm in a host more quickly than others. Containing a virus that did not "announce" itself soon after infection was indeed more difficult than otherwise. On one end was HIV, which could be in a host for literally years before it began to manufacture itself in the cells of the host, proliferate to the point of lysis, bursting forth from the cell and causing exponential infection throughout the body, and then there was SARS, which began to manifest its presence in days.

Every virus had its repressor gene, that kept the virus from using the cell's DNA to create other viruses. At some point that repressor cell was turned off.... (Cheng reflected on something he had thought more than once: the way in which we saw this as "on/off" might be simplifying or even obscuring the matter. But that was a side issue, if an intriguing one.) If there was only some way of knowing a person was infected before a virus manifested itself. Like predicting the weather? In a way. But not likely, at this point. The only "predictor" was if there was the knowledge that an individual had been exposed. Thus the need for quarantine. Not only for those with known exposure to a pathogen, but to treat a population as if everyone had been exposed.

Why should viruses have a repressor gene in the first place? Apparently, this was another example of natural selection. A virus that did its work too quickly, sickened its host immediately, was less likely to spread than one that could infect many before its presence was realized. Then again, if natural selection was the driving force in this matter, why didn't the viruses that announced themselves too fast just die out, or evolve, through mutation (and viruses mutate all the time) to inflict their illness later rather than sooner, thus widening their pool of infection?

Of course, there was so much, well, anthropomorphizing in all this. Just the fact of looking at the "effects" of the virus as negative. For the virus this was good; it was increasing its population. And as viruses did not usually kill most of their victims, just put them through, let us say, a malaise, and often left viral DNA in their host, wasn't this, overall, just another symbiotic relationship in the so-called grand if inexplicable scheme of things? And did viruses come away with human genetic material to pass on to their future replications? Talk about the grand scheme of things. Had there been any provable instances of that?

Of course, viruses such as Marburg have a high mortality rate; they insist on ravaging a population. The Human Immunodeficiency Virus was once like that. But now people are living with AIDS as a chronic, treatable condition, not as the death sentence it once was. Therapeutics had been eventually successful. That was the direction Cheng saw he should be researching now, instead of a long term goal (as he saw it) of a vaccine.

Or did "they" know something the rest of us don't? As in bioengineering…? Was this a Frankenstein's monster that would be afflicting the villagers of China for some time?

Later Cheng talked to Fan. "I was thinking if you try to disable—interfere—with the transcription gene…but you know even if you could make the repressor gene allow the virus to manifest quickly instead of a week or so, you would have evidence of its presence right away, deal with the infected right away, quarantine, instead of the virus spreading."

"So, the strain of the virus that would survive best would be the one with the 'best' repressor gene," Fan said. "Keep its attack hidden."

Cheng abruptly said, "I'm not comfortable being chained to creating a vaccine."

"They're recognizing your…skill."

"It almost seems—I guess it's my imagination—I'm being steered away from what I can do best."

"I always thought that when it came to viruses, you're the 'best' at whatever you have to…accomplish. And I'm not trying to flatter you."

Cheng. "I like flattery from a friend. There are just so many aspects to viruses. They don't realize—"

"We keep saying 'they.' Who is 'they'?"

"The government."

"That pays for all this."

"Are you defending them?"

"You know the philosophy of the necessary evil."

"Isn't that American, or something?"

"What makes you say that? I think it's universal."

"Well, you and your American…fascination."

"I have to visit there someday."

"Isn't there an old Chinese belief that the best action is non-action? That the world does what it does and we can't force our ways upon it?"

Fan said, "Then we wouldn't need science."

"Is science forcing ourselves on the world?"

"We find out about the world, then try to work with that knowledge to our benefit. Think of life without using our knowledge. We wouldn't even have buildings."

"I'm not advocating…non-action, just thinking—"

"You feel you're being forced to do something, so you want to…not act."

"You're probably right. But I'm thinking of *acting* on other things.

But you haven't told me about your coronavirus masks."

"It's too much at the beginning to even talk about it."

"Talk about the beginning."

Fan sighed. She had so many things in her mind—like clouds floating in the sky: tangibly there, but hard to name as definite forms.

22.

"I realize that working with plant viruses is more simple. At least you don't worry about infecting humans. I started to think, using the spike proteins, even if they are not...joined to the body of the virus...would it cause some, I don't know, interference with the human ACE2 receptors."

"But isn't your idea that the virus would in some way interact—if that's the right word—with human cells...like a mild vaccine?" Cheng suddenly added, as if hit with an obvious idea. "*You* should be doing the vaccine research."

"I want to go my way—like you. What I was just saying—that was just one of my thoughts. It's hard to describe where my mind's going. I feel like I'm trying to build a mountain by starting with a few grains of sand. Is this practical, past just the research? I'm weaving—that's how I think of myself now, as a weaver, like some old skill in this weird modern way—I'm weaving the tiniest particles: how many trillions do I need to make a mask? I was thinking of those nanobots, a million nanoscale machines weaving a million virus particles and plastic particles—some unseen factory assembly line that could create—"

"Are there really nanobots? A machine that is that small?"

"If you have parts of a virus that have different functions, why not nanomachines?"

"So, we are large scale machines and viruses are nanomachines?"

"You could look at it that way."

"Could you make a nanobot?"

"I don't think so. I'm a macrobot designing nano products." Fan paused. "Looking through the electron microscopes, the spike proteins are like little dashes of a sort of rain—and then you magnify them further—how deep into the invisible we can go now—and they are like trees. Didn't I tell you that?"

"Now, I don't think you did."

"With crowns, canopies, trunks."

"We describe these things with things we know. If we were the size of viruses, we'd say trees were like the spike protein."

Cheng's remark made Fan think again of that discussion she'd had with Li, about "life" on subatomic worlds: how the existence of a consciousness on that scale would perceive its universe. And she recalled him speaking about the miniature city on the moon. She felt the dichotomy of using her senses in both an expanded and exceedingly minute universe.

She said to Cheng, "We have machines, if you want to use that word, that go through arteries to clear out plaque."

"Wouldn't that be like earth moving machines compared to real nanobots?"

"That's true. You know, when I was talking about science…maybe what all of us are doing is believe we are getting hold of the nature, seeing into the nature of things that so far beyond our physical reach: the nano, and out there, the cosmos. I mean, how do we comprehend things like suns, black holes—or spike proteins?"

"Your Li thinks he can—what did you say, comprehend?—what's out there."

"I think Li thinks—if he does actually think about it—I mean he doesn't think about the nature of the universe as much as *going* 'out there.' The universe is a destination more than a concept. For him, I mean."

"I'd think it more a concept than a destination."

"So would I."

"Maybe you don't give him enough credit. I wonder how he would describe it."

"I just hope he's OK." Fan had related to Cheng the message she'd gotten concerning Li.

"He probably is."

Fan smiled sadly. "In science, 'probably' can be good enough, but—"

"But when it comes to love, no?" He studied Fan. "Are you in love with him?"

"Sometimes, yes. Sometimes…it's more confusion: No."

"The confusion of loving."

"I guess so."

"When he goes to the moon—"

"I feel like he's already there. He's there now."

"When it's for real—you will wish he were just quarantined in a training room and not—how far is the moon?"

"Three hundred eighty-four thousand kilometers."

"He's a lot closer now."

"But locked away. And that can seem—"

"Let's hope things can be better when he gets out."

"You think they will be?"

Cheng said, "Honestly, no. We have to go through something for a little while. Let's hope it's only a little while."

Fan returned to her nanoweaving the "canopies" of her S proteins caught in the spiraling shards of recycled e-waste plastics. It had taken much work and blunt intrusions of intuition to shape those plastics into shapes that would catch the viral proteins most effectively. She considered, during the time she emerged herself into the nanoworld, she was using technology and the remnants of technology that did not exist until well into the 20th century, while viruses have been in existence for who knew how long.

But did the earliest proto-humans have viruses? Why not? It would be hard to believe that viruses did not intrude upon human existence until the species was well along. Though Fan also wondered if there was a time at which viruses were not able to infect people—and all animals—until some mutation occurred that enabled viruses to enter human cells and so begin their work of exponential replication. Yes, imagine a time before viruses. She had never heard anyone speculate on that. According to what we all believe now, humans descended from primates, from apes, and we know those animals harbor viruses. In fact. the AIDS virus, HIV, is directly related to the simian immunodeficiency virus, SIV. So, if humans did evolve from primates, it was a passage already laden with a viral presence. Well, perhaps there was a time when viruses were not in animals, not in the animals that became primates.

Go farther back. Were viruses in dinosaurs—in the creatures before them? You weren't going to find viruses in fossils. How could these creations of Nature, smaller than the crests of wavelengths of light, be preserved, and discovered after eons?

Fan tried to recall some science she hadn't paid that much attention to at the time.

One theory was that viruses and bacteria had been in some proto-form (as much as one and a half billion years ago), then gone down two different paths. Bacteria had become more complex, and viruses more simple—or, you might say, streamlined. Viruses are protein coats surrounding DNA—and that protein can be very minimal. The influenza virus has only 14 protein coding genes.

Yet little more than a decade ago, a virus was discovered that had almost as many genes as a bacterium. Dubbed a mimivirus or mimicking microbe, it was not only larger than a virus, but one had more than a thousand genes, only a few hundred genes less than some bacteria. More of these giant viruses have been discovered since. Pandoraviruses, about one thousand nanometers in size, or one micron, have around 1,100 genes. In 2008, a pandoravirus had been found in an amoeba in a woman's contact lens. The mimivirus has 1.1 million DNA base pairs, while pandoravirus as 2.5 million. With 93 percent of pandoravirus genes dissimilar from any other microbes, some scientists consider them a fourth order of life, apart from bacteria, archaea and eukaryotes.

Science generally seeks to trace the divergent genes of species through the past to determine converging relationships between different forms of life; but the more you go back into the past, the less viable conclusions (speculations) you can reach. Go past the realm of a million years and more and it's impossible to grasp precise points along the passage of mutations over the eons.

But more recently some scientists have tried another technique, studying the folds of proteins. In the case of proteins, function follows form. Proteins are Nature's precise nanomachines. A change in their folds changes function—or disables function. While the makeup of genes has changed in species over millions of years, the fold of proteins changes much more slowly. Comparing the protein shapes of thousands of bacteria and viruses, hundreds of folds—442, to be exact—were shared between them, while 66 folds were the sole domain of viruses.

At any rate, one current hypothesis maintains that a particular protein fold in cyanobacteria was there 2.1 billion years ago, when this bacteria was fixed in the fossil record—and that 3.4 billion years ago, virus and bacteria shared a common ancestor. And the 66 protein folds specific to the virus came into being 1.5 billion years ago. Thus, during almost two billion years viruses and bacteria were "drifting" apart.

Apparently, dinosaurs and viruses were coexistent, Fan realized. Or so we believe now.

Fan broke off her musing to scan the internet about viral and bacterial relationships. And found there was speculation that a virus had been the cause—via "infection"—to alter the genes (or insert viral genes) in some proto-mammal that resulted in ordering the placental cells in the uterus so a fetus could draw nourishment from the mother instead of being excreted in an egg.

So they leave us plagues and gifts, Fan thought.

She wondered: if viruses and bacteria had "drifted' apart, and humans had had their own passage from other species, who is to say that, not unlike the theory that the universe will reverse the outward motion of the so-called Big Bang and collapse back into a point of singularity, who is to say that at some point in the distant future not only viruses and bacteria might rejoin in some way, but humans might once again, draw closer to these first sources of life, these infinitesimal creations that made life possible and continuous. She knew the human body has more nonhuman cells than human—as if we were the parasite in a nonhuman conjoining of virus and bacteria. –And perhaps, when a virus locks onto a cell, and then begins to use the cell's DNA, perhaps this is a sort of reunion, a biology repeated throughout the past and a herald of the future. We have separated but will be whole again; it's a return from a journey.

Li had told her of space craft powered by solar sails, not carrying the propulsion of fuel, but using the power of starlight. Viruses may have reached a point in the journey of life at which they had shed the fuel that our bodies and bacteria use and pass through existence by using cells for their "flight." –The purpose of their flight being replication.

Speaking of fuel: perhaps viruses sought to regain something else they lost—or should have achieved. The mitochondria that fuel our cells were thought to have once been free organisms that somehow, for some reason, joined human cells in a symbiotic relationship. Perhaps if not for the mitochondria, a virus would be there, and the human biology would be vastly different.

Fan's train of "what if" led her to consider: what if pandoraviruses continued to grow? In fact, these viruses were already larger than the smallest, bacteria, pelagibacter, that were 370 to 890 nanometers. Pelagibacter is a marine organism; as small as it is, the total weight of all pelagibacter exceeds that of all the marine life on the planet. Or so science says.

Now pandoravirus infects amoeba, which is larger than the virus. If form, or size is linked to function, a virus could not be larger than the host it infects. How could a smaller host produce a host of viruses? The cell would burst apart with the replication of just one virus. This would not work to spread the virus, whose apparent single purpose in life is to create as many copies of itself. If a virus wants to continue to be a virus it has to stay in its place, as least size-wise.

Well, the great unchecked panoply of biology and microbiology goes on. We observe and have our theories. Although, since the last century, we've entered that realm as an influence. There were those...rumors—possibilities: that the virus that had Wuhan locked down was "engineered" right in this lab. A SARS-like, bat virus that somehow got out, escaping from all the safety controls of the lab. Now that would indeed be a "Pandora" virus. And its creator or creators did not even realize what had been created. Or escaped. The moment a new thing has entered the universe is not necessarily accompanied with an announcement. Or at least one we can apprehend.

After travelling through all these thoughts, Fan felt that her seemingly imaginative weave of the virus' spike proteins and recycled e-waste was, if producing a tangible product, a useless, even a narcissistic endeavor. She smiled sadly at herself. Narcissistic? Perhaps everything we did— All this e-waste: what pronouncement, personal, business, emotional, mundane—what world, that was the sum total of us here, in this era, was not narcissistic? Even the cut and dry communications of business: important, we thought, the things that should be tended to now. And here, in the lab before her, locked into a nano-weave with a viral protein that undoubtably predated the outcast marvels or our creation by millions of years. Perhaps, in fact, a billion years. In the course of existence, our technology has been a sudden thing; and so, the surreality or reality: that an old, old thing shares the moment with a sudden and new thing—

Where is my mind going?

Fan realized she was hungry. She left her nanoworld and was soon in the lab's cafeteria.

In the cafeteria was the loud voice of someone she knew by sight, but not by name. Or if she had known his name, it was forgotten, unimportant, at least to her.

He was a thin man, maybe thirty-five, with thick, unruly hair, shaved in the back, perched on his head like some aggressive rooster. He wore black framed glasses. He was talking loudly to several people seated nearby. Fan had the immediate feeling the conversation was all his.

"I'm sure they asked everyone in the lab if we thought the virus had come from here. And you all, I'm sure said, No."

A middleaged woman across from him said, "I didn't say No. I just said I had no idea."

"And did they take that as guilt or a No?"

"Guilt? I don't think—" She looked about, as if suddenly worried, as if suddenly thinking "they" could think her guilty of anything.

But the thin, loud man was already disregarding her. "I'm sure none of our answers satisfied them," he asserted.

Fan considered this was the third time in a minute he had said "I'm sure." Whatever point he was making, he was confident no one could confound him. –Or he wasn't confident and wanted someone to redirect him?

Then she realized he was talking to her. He had turned sharply in her direction, as if he had abruptly realized the fact of her entrance. "What do you think? What did you tell them?"

Fan cocked her head, in the manner of someone who hadn't really heard what had been asked. There was a definite pause between her and him, a tension that seemed to make him nervous and for an instant amused Fan, who said, smiling, "I told them I had no idea."

"You too?" It seemed he found that hard to believe.

"How could I really know? How could any of us—at least most of us—know?" He was about to say something and she added, "Do you—know?"

The questioner was struck with his own question. He said, "I have suspicions."

"Of exactly what?"

"Of the...possibilities." He said this defiantly, as if that had closed the matter.

But Fan said, "What are they?"

He sighed. Perhaps he was suddenly resigned to the scope of his own thoughts. "The obvious ones. The virus came from here. It was created here."

"Is that what you believe?"

"I'm not sure I *believe*...."

Fan gave her own sigh. The man was just someone who wanted to make a lot of noise, and put forth the usual rumors without much knowledge. But he didn't want to stay in that position long. From being focused—uncomfortably—on Fan, he turned to the others and demanded, "So who thinks the virus is from here? We'll take a poll."

The others were uncomfortable with this. The woman said, "That's...not good to go around saying."

Fan interjected, "So your vote is that it did come from here."

"If no one else will say their opinion, why should I?"

In lieu of saying, "Who cares?" Fan gestured. It was a wordless way of saying, Let's go away from this.

She moved to another area of the cafeteria, eventually had a lunch of rice and natto and seaweed salad. Very Japanese. She was occupied in eating slowly and checking her phone. Nothing from Li. But there would not be, for many more days. She had already forgotten the man with the shock of dark hair when she looked up, saw him eating alone. The others had left his table. He looked abandoned. And a bit pathetic. Fan smiled to herself. When she finished eating, she went over to him. He looked up at her as if afraid of her return.

As if gently instructing him, Fan said, "People don't want to be pinned down in front of others about that."

"We should not be afraid of our thoughts." But his assertion was defensive, as if he were at least wary.

"People aren't so much afraid of their thoughts as cautious about speaking them." She smiled. She might have been instructing someone naïve. "I'm Po Fan."

He nodded. He seemed abruptly placated. "Wong Bai."

Fan sat down across from him. She told him what she did at the lab. He seemed intrigued, if not really impressed. Perhaps he was confused as to the connection of her research to the purpose of the lab—that is, being a Biosafety Level 4 laboratory. He told her his position was the "secure safety of biological systems." It sounded like a description he had given himself. Fan said, "So then you would know, more than any of us, if that virus got out of here."

Wong Bai had an expression of what might be called pained guilt. "Maybe it just means I think about it more."

"And with your position, do you think it's likely a virus got out?"

He looked away from her a moment, then back. "I'm not sure." This was the reverse of his "I'm sure" from a few minutes ago, but Fan did not point that out. Wong added, "I'm not the only one realizing that all this research into coronaviruses has been going on for some time—which the Americans were involved with, too, *here*—bringing all these pathogens here—was increasing the possibility that—"

"You like the word possibility, possibilities."

He shook his head. "That's all we can have."

Fan got up. "Even in science, I know."

She left him with a pleasantry that was the equivalent of "Pleased to have met you." Wong had less etiquette. He nodded, looked down. He had accepted her presence and conversation and now wasn't sure if it should be struck up again.

Returning to her work, Fan was distracted with the consideration Wong had so indelicately bruited in the cafeteria. The officials who had come to the lab the other day—so recently and yet not recently felt—had very obviously been exploring that possibility (that word again), but the subsequent days, filled with compressed events, had pushed that from Fan's mind. Imagine if all of Wuhan, Hubei itself (she had seen something on her phone: 50 million people) had been shut down because of a nano-sized pathogen that had escaped (or even been released) from this very building in which she removed herself from the macroworld and peered into and adjusted the microworld of existence. *I am in the eye of the storm and yet I can calmly go about....*

But was she calm? *What if this virus becomes a truly ravaging plague? Would a lockdown protect us?*

Fan imagined a depopulated Wuhan and the researchers at the lab emerging into a post-apocalyptic city, chastened by what a virus had wrought. Well, it was a "possibility."

When Fan returned to her work she was just not as focused. She could not help thinking she was just creating a novelty: *Get your mask made from the virus.* Youth would think it "cool," as the Americans liked to say. Or maybe, and maybe with good reason, the authorities would ban such a mask, saying who knew what would happen if people were continually breathing in particles from the virus. Her ideal of a vaccine mask could not match the controlled injection of a vaccine: you knew exactly what you were giving a patient. Of course, even a precise vaccine could not know an individual's reaction to any vaccine.

If Fan certainly would not call herself an expert on vaccines, she knew that China had become a major manufacturer and exporter of not only many medicines, but vaccines. In fact, the U.S. got most of its antibiotics from China.

Beginning in 1987, the World Health Organization has bestowed vaccines with the seal of approval for international procurement. The first China-made vaccine given the WHO nod was in 2014. And that meant big money, as whatever vaccine in question can be purchased in bulk by the United Nations International Emergency Children's Fund (UNICEF) in 152 countries.

Since the 1970s, China has instituted an aggressive vaccine producing program. By 2010, the China National Biotechnology Group had created more than 740 million doses of 34 vaccines for 28 diseases, supplying more than 85 percent of the vaccines in the country.

China took its burgeoning vaccine industry and required standards seriously. In 2007, a former head of the country's Food and Drug Administration was arrested, found guilty and *executed* for bribery and failing to ensure safety protocols.

Ensuring safety. Something about Wong Bai was nagging at Fan. She knew what that "something" was. Safety. His vague and perhaps embellished description of what he did at the lab was nonetheless clear enough to Fan; the lab had to follow very strict safety measures not only to ensure that every facet of the research done there was free of contamination, but that any potential pathogens could not get out of the lab in any way. Replaying in her mind how Wong had dared some of his colleagues (and dared seemed the word) to guess, wager, whatever on the possibility (yes, that word) of the virus that had caused the lockdown having escaped from the lab, Fan was sure now this was a reaction from something that was more than possible in Wong's mind—and Wong was worried that this might somehow be his fault.

What if it was? Fan thought. What if he were bringing it up to others, throwing it in their faces as a way to cast the blame for such an event farther from himself? He was using the conscious or involuntary psychology of asserting his own innocence with the fact that he was willing—insisting—on talking about what everyone was supposed to thwart: a pathogen released into the outside world.

He knows something, thought Fan. She had the impulse to seek him out, question him, if subtly, to use her attractiveness to ease his tongue. She smiled at that, mocked herself. This isn't some American thriller movie about a contagion. This is the real world in which things do not happen smoothly. She would talk to Wong again, just not right away.

So she tried to go back to her work. While it seemed she had proceeded at a steady pace that morning, now the going seemed harder. She blamed herself; she was not focusing. But then she realized something had changed about the spike proteins—those trees of proteins, those canopies. There was a slightly different fold to them, slight, but enough. They caught the e-waste whorls a little differently. If Fan were weaving a tapestry it might be said that she was producing two almost conflicting patterns.

She focused herself. Well, she would weave those patterns into a complementarity of opposites. She shook her head. She massaged her forehead with her fingers, as though to press on and clear something from her brain. The further one went into the nanoworld…it was as complex as anything in the macrocosmos.

She left the lab in the winter dark. She had a passing contact with

Cheng, who assured her he would be taken home by his assigned driver. He actually said that to her: "My assigned driver." Then both of them had laughed at the phrase. A moment afterward, as if he had been summoned by a cue, there was young Junjie, at the doorway of Cheng's office, in a deferential pose, apparently wanting to assure Cheng he was certainly continuing to be at Cheng's disposal, but not walking right into the office, with the bold habit of an equal.

Cheng introduced Fan, who caught the young driver giving her, for an almost imperceptible instant, an up and down glance. He wasn't bad looking…. But Fan's instant feeling was that here was someone too ready to take advantage of any situation that presented itself, take advantage in a way that would disregard the consequences to others, as long as he felt it was advantageous to himself. Fan didn't so much say these exact words to herself, it was more a stream of connected intuition, a visceral reading of the man's vibe. She formed the words of those feelings more distinctly when she got home.

And she was a bit concerned there was a young man—again, attractive enough—whom would be in a car with Cheng twice a day and could arouse in the latter feelings that would be better directed elsewhere. Fan left Cheng's sex life—which she guessed had been in abeyance for a while—outside of her concerns, for the most part. Unless Cheng told her anything specific, the farthest she would go with him was to ask about him having any romantic feelings toward poor Dr. Sun, whom Fan feared was more likely to leave the hospital dead than alive.

For a moment Fan couldn't remember: had she even asked Cheng about Dr. Sun, or just inferred? And had Cheng done her the courtesy of answering a question she had not wanted to ask directly? Oh yes, when they had visited the hospital….

And what she was thinking at home that night, before sleep…. Fan was not more or less social than most young women of her time and

place, but she knew that when she plunged deeply into her work, and especially when it frustrated her, she could easily block out people, feel little need for their company. Cheng was a good friend, easy to be with; she would never steer away from his presence. And Li— well, Fan thought at times she could be like Li, so focused on what he believed he had to do, he did not seem to need the company of others at all. Even, at times, Fan. This was something that had bothered her, but which she half accepted now. Half. The difference was Li was like that often, and Fan just once in a while. But now she felt people were intruding—in some way she could not define. Was it simply that young driver, poised so deliberately with ostensible humility at the doorway of Cheng's office that had pushed her down this track? Or Wong talking about a virus getting out? Those officials the other day had more than hinted that this was something they had to consider, but they had not seemed to have bothered Fan. Now....
It was probably an accumulation of everything: the lockdown, the officials, the empty streets of Wuhan, Wong and the driver, the changing trees of spike proteins—Li in quarantine.... Everything somehow disrupted her direction in this crisis, her self-direction.

Oddly, lying there in bed, breathing slowly and deeply to calm her thoughts, she said aloud to herself: *Nothing great is easy.* And considered, *Is that what I'm going for—greatness?* Her answer was: *Yes, I'm challenged. I have to—*

"Have to" what? She knew she had to succeed. But it wasn't necessarily at her nanoweave of viral proteins and e-waste. She had to succeed at something whose tangible nature she did not yet know.

Sometime around four in the morning, she was awakened by Mystery. He often woke her up before dawn to let him out. It was as if he'd had enough of indoor shelter and needed to roam outside again, in the dark. He would return after sunrise, before she left for work, for his morning meal.

For the first time, Fan thought Mystery must really like his nighttime rambles now, with all of Wuhan locked away

Chapter Nine: Of a Stranger on the Moon

23.

Li was sick enough to be content with just resting for the next two days, but not so sick that other things did not oppress his mind: specifically, if his illness would be held against him. Of course, it was not his fault, but to fail for whatever reason.... Never mind that he hadn't "failed," but had been forced to take a pause.

And then, he thought, perhaps this unexpected virus gave both his superiors and himself the opportunity to see how he would come out of it and continue with his training.

One morning Lin and Yang tested him for the virus. A long cotton-tipped swab was inserted uncomfortably up his nose and twisted.

"I thought someone else was supposed to do this," said Li.

Yang: "I guess they figured we're enough."

"Results in two days," said Yang, flatly.

Li continually dipped into various sections of *The History of the Moon*. And continued to read the many chapters and part of chapters out of order, scanning for whatever caught his interest at the moment. It was somewhat in the manner of those who dip into a sacred text seeking some divine direction to find what they believed they needed for hope and enlightenment. Not that Li got any hope or enlightenment from the book. Though perhaps he got more of a sense of the role the Earth's satellite had played in the psyche of human history.

In a chapter titled "Moon People," he read about the theories and outright claims that there are people on the moon. In a subheading called "A Comrade Meets the Moon Men," the author detailed the crazy but intriguing case of a Russian citizen in the 1970s, who had not only been inspired but convinced by the article from the late '60s by the scientists who had postulated that the moon was an artificial satellite created by extraterrestrial intelligences for an unknown purpose.

The story goes that a middleaged man named Vladimir came across the article in an old copy of *Sputnik* and was so convinced that this theory was definitely fact that for years afterward he both sought contact with the unknown inhabitants of Earth's artificial satellite and claimed to have succeeded in that contact. It should be noted that there are versions of this story with different last names for Vladimir—though his name is always Vladimir. A source in British intelligence, whom the author knows personally, related that this whole story is either a wholly unsubstantiated legend or that this Vladimir was providing a diversion for something covert—whose nature had never been deciphered.

This Vladimir said he built radio devices with which he claimed he had contacted the beings in the artificial moon and they had told him they had originally settled in orbit around Earth as a respite from a long star journey across the galaxy. But that respite had turned into thousands and thousands of years due to technological problems—at least that was the issue at first. These problems had taken so long to fix that the original members of that star journey had died, and simultaneously a sort of self-contained world had settled itself, created for itself a life that wanted for neither the world from which they had set out or any original, planned destination. The technological problems had never been resolved and now there was no desire to resolve them—and perhaps no longer the knowledge to do so.

When Vladimir was questioned as to how exactly the moon beings had communicated this to him—surely he didn't know their language—he said with "an electronic code" that was both "mathematical and telepathic."

And of course, no one ever saw that radio or radios or any electronic device by which these so-called communications had been effected. When queried as to the reason for that, Vladimir responded he had to guard his "connection" with these star-born moon beings because there were so many who did not want the truth of the matter to be learned. "They will let me say what I want, and most people will think I'm crazy. That's how they want it. But I've given enough information so that there will be a few people who will know it's the truth."

And then, it seems Vladimir vanishes after the 1970s. This Soviet everyman, who claimed to be a conduit to star born moon people, apparently took on both an inexplicable silence and disappearance. My contact who toiled so long in British intelligence, said this was all "a convenient distraction" for something else the Russians were doing in space, but did not know what that something was. This writer has suggested that perhaps Brit Intel was positing something nonexistent, and that Vladimir was simply just like those crazies in the U.S. in the 1950s, who claimed truck with Venusians and illuminating flying saucer rides to the moons of Jupiter.

The response to my response was: "Could be, but I've been around all sorts of wild stories and I can't help this intuition that there's method in that madness."

It seems we'll never know, only surmise—that Vladimir's claims were highly unlikely. Perhaps he simply settled into the obscurity of those who have exhausted both their imagination and a need for some kind of fame.

Li had pondered that theory about the hollow, artificial satellite that had become our moon. It was pleasing, in a way, as he moved turgidly through his sickness, to think of those science fictional scenarios, voyagers from an old, old civilization, stopping by our Earth for repairs. Then time and a change of the society within had kept them there for ages. Being apart from whatever distant mother world had been their home, they had created a new society. Perhaps they had fallen into the ennui and ignorance of the long displaced—or perhaps gained a wisdom that to move on and on through the galaxy was a needless task, that the desire to explore the cosmos may have been more a flight from making their own world aright than any need for discovery.

Li certainly had no problem believing there were much older civilizations in the universe than the human civilization that was still living through its course on Earth. The handful of celestial forays that had achieved moon landings, the space travelers who had orbited the planet, most to quickly return, even the scientists who had lived on the International Space Station for months and months—it was all like those who had gone to sea in primitive boats, but whose travels had always been limited by horizons in which the home island was still sighted. Voyagers whose intent was to always return to that island.

How long would it be before humankind could travel amidst the stars? This could surly not be in Li's lifetime, he admitted. Even if, in the coming decades, space travel technology made a fantastic, exponential leap, he would be too old by then to be on some ship passing from the solar system. Humankind still had the long road of reaching the planets.

And would he, he had to think, want to be on one of those star journeys, leaving Earth and the solar system with the knowledge he would be moving ever outward, never to return, to reach harbor, as it were, in some other section of the galaxy, the sun that had sustained him and his world's life now the dimmest star in some alien sky? Or a star too dim to even be seen? Or a star whose memory was dim, too, on the verge of being forgotten?

What will human beings be in this universe in a thousand years, in ten thousand years? Could a man of a thousand years ago imagine the technological world Li lived in? Imagine the technology that had put Li on the moon without even being on the moon?

. . .

And if Li was in a respite from his training, that technology did sporadically intrude.

He was drifting out of sleep—or drifting into it; often it was hard to tell, these past days. And, as occasionally happened, he was back on the moon. This no longer registered any surprise with him. His training was supposed to be suspended, but he thought he was being teased (taunted) with its presence sporadically—as if "they" had to remind him of their power?

He looked about, at the austere and by now very familiar surface, thinking how familiar it had indeed become. *I could give tours*, he thought.

And then he saw himself, a space suited figure, in the near distance.

It gave him a start. *I am looking at myself from here, but I am there—*

He saw himself...and yet, it was almost as if it was not himself. Of course, just as when we hear ourselves on a recording and it sounds nothing like the voice we have been hearing come from our mouths, to see ourselves move about can be as if looking at another person entirely.

Li watched the suited figure's passage; he seemed very well practiced in the kangaroo hop that was de rigueur on the moon. He thought, *Well, I guess I'm getting good at that. After all—*

But he didn't like this. Watching himself—as if "they" had separated himself from himself. The figure—himself—bent down to examine something, a rock, something on the surface; Li couldn't tell. He almost, irrationally, felt a sort of jealousy. This other self, out there, was making, well, could be making discoveries—

Li caught himself. What "discoveries" could he or anyone else, for that matter, be making in these simulations, no matter how much they seemed nothing less than reality?

So, they created another me to go out there, while I'm sick. Or are they goading me, prompting me, to get back out there, on the moon? Their moon?

Yes: "their moon." For wasn't it like that? They had created— recreated, whatever, a simulacrum so vivid that this "moon" was theirs.

Li had to think, as he had often: *What is really going on here?* There was, he felt instinctually, a definite sort of reality here. They told him he had to "decipher." If this was not real, in some way, what reality would he have to decipher? Of course, he could simply be being tested. But there was nothing simple about this. The minute city, the markings, the abandoned city—

The figure—himself—was coming toward him. Li involuntary flinched. What if one's own self stepped right up into one's very face? When you dream about yourself, does the dream-self stare back at you, as if looking in a mirror?

And then, with this approach, Li was able to see very clearly the face of this other self. It was not him at all. It was someone else.

Now Li more than flinched. He felt his blood thunder or stop or seemingly do both at once. Another person on *his* moon. It might be a moon of "their" creation, but he, Zhen Li, was its traveler. It was like being betrayed. He felt anger; he felt fear. And something else—or many things—unnamable.

Just at the point that it seemed this other appeared to walk directly from Li's vision into colliding with Li's observing body, the other veered away, not abruptly but in a direction that seemingly had been planned all along; it was only coincidence that shift in direction had occurred just at that moment.

But Li was not so sure of coincidences. As much as he was relieved this other had not bumped right into him, Li was also angry that this new visitor to his moon had veered away. As if avoiding a confrontation. Li was in such a conflict of emotions. Betrayal, anger, fear fueling a primitive instinct to defend his territory, be it only a simulacrum.

They're playing with me, they are playing with me. Testing—

But as the other moved off in another direction, Li was not absorbing the face that was definitely not him; it was as if the shock of seeing that other face needed to have that face removed from sight before Li could actually digest the seeing of it. It was a face older than Li's; a man in his forties, Li thought, say forty-five. A heavier face…with eyes intent on a list of—duties? It was bureaucratic face. The face of someone who had adhered to a routine ordered by others. If Li too had been ordered by others in his training, his nature was of an explorer. Yes, he saw himself as a strong young man, athletic (hadn't he represented his country in the international military games only months ago?)—and not unhandsome. But this man was totally the opposite of Li. It was as if "they" had placed in this virtual lunar world Li's opposite. But why?

Or is it my mind placing that man, this other, here?

There was no answer to that. Li could only keep watching. The other moon traveler continued on his way, doing nothing special but with the sense that he had purpose in his direction.

Then he was gone.

There was the briefest instant when Li witnessed the moon bare of any visitor, then the moon was gone, too, and Li was looking at the banal, immediate vista of the training room. Li felt distressed, confused—and disgusted in a way. He lay on his cot a long time, looking at the ceiling.

It was late in the day. In a few hours the lights in the training room would dim, in concert with the twilight outside, then soon the room would be fully dark. The lights had followed this rhythm since Li had been in quarantine. He was free to turn on any lights or lamps in the room, just as he would in a house at night. Usually he would turn on two low lit lamps, one by his cot, where he continued to dip into the book on the moon.

He considered asking Lin and Yang about the "other." The pair continued to show up each day, take his temperature, note his condition. He had tested positive for the virus. Li found himself accepting this with dull resignation.

At any rate, Lin and Yang communicated little, hiding whatever knowledge they had of his situation behind a flippant, even silly manner. Li knew he would ask them nothing. He did not trust whatever reply they would give, so why bother.

Li felt tired. The virus sapped his energy. Yet he had the definite feeling that he had passed the virus' utmost point of power over him. Why he felt that, he couldn't say—at the moment. In retrospect, though, in a few days, he would realize his seeing that "other" kangaroo hopping upon the moon (as if taking over terrain Li had made his own), had given him the physiological impetus to fight past the virus, and reclaim his own place on that simulacrum of the moon. Whether it was his moon or "theirs."

And, of course, Li dreamed of the other. Both Li and the bureaucrat (that's how Li thought of him) were in the abandoned city, exploring its empty buildings, its empty rooms. Not together, though. The other was always just in the next room; Li could hear him moving about. Never mind that there was no sound on the moon; it was more a sensing of sound. Or he might be a floor above Li, and Li would look up, feeling some transgression was being enacted above him.

Then there was a point in the dream when Li realized he was being distracted from the fact of, the wonder of, the abandoned lunar city. What beings had created it? How old was it? Why had it been abandoned? Were they the denizens of the hollow moon who had come to the surface after spending eons in the below-world, journeying across the stars?

Or perhaps, his dreaming self thought, those star beings had built this city as a monument, not as a place to inhabit, but a monument to the cities they had left on a home world they had departed from so long ago.

These thoughts of dreaming were abruptly invaded when Li walked out of one room and confronted the other. They were only a few feet apart. And that startled, even frightened look on the man's face made Li say to himself, *He's never seen me before. He didn't even know I existed.* Li had witnessed the other, but the other had not witnessed him. Through all the twists and turns and accents and descents in the city, Li had the full sense of the other, but the other had not sensed him.

The other's mouth moved. He was speaking to Li. But the two space suited men had no radio connection. Li tried, but could not read the other's lips. Li was frozen, not knowing what to mime with his own lips—perhaps the other could read his.

Then Li woke up. He felt as if he had seen himself in a mirror. But a mirror that had reflected back a self that was not the self the self he knew.

He sat up, by the lamp he had left on by his cot. He had fallen asleep with the light on. He usually turned it off before falling asleep. The total dark of the room, a room with no windows, that might have seemed claustrophobic to many people, was a dark cocoon of almost comfort to Li. Actually there were a few small indicators always lit on various machines in the room—like the eyes of a being watching him in the dark....

He reviewed his dream. He recalled quite vividly the other's face. The bureaucrat. But why did he think this man had to be a bureaucrat? He could simply be an older man in the country's space program. Why did Li have such a strict stereotype of a taikonaut: the vigorous explorer. The space program would undoubtably use scientists who were brilliant if sedentary.

He shut off the lamp. Before he returned to sleep, Li had the thought: *They wanted to present me with my opposite.*

He awoke as the room was lightening, in concert with the dawn outside. What was it like outside now, in Wuhan? Had the virus spread to a much greater degree? Or was it being controlled? What was Fan doing? And what about Cheng? He should be right in the forefront of this crisis. And what exactly would he be doing in this forefront?

Yes, I guess it is a crisis. While I am paralyzed here.

He picked up *A History of the Moon*. He opened to a chapter, "What Did the Astronauts See on the Moon?"

Amidst the things that we know about, the films we saw, there is—and no surprise—things that the first astronauts saw on the moon that the public was never privy to. There was a two-minute interruption in communication with Earth in which we have no idea what was said between Houston and the moon, but there are many who claim the astronauts were on another, private channel and were relaying to Mission Control they had seen flying saucer-like objects parked along the rim of a crater. This 'fact' was garnered by ham radio operators scattered around the world who say they were able to pick up these otherwise censored communications from the moon.

None of the astronauts said anything of the sort in public statements; and again, those who say NASA made sure that information was not conveyed publicly like to point to the demeanor of the three Apollo space travelers when they gave their first press conference after emerging from a three-week quarantine after their return.

(The word "quarantine" associated with moon had to strike Li's psyche, though certainly the case of those astronauts was different than his. –Or, perhaps, in some ways not.)

Instead of seeming pleased with the success of their mission, exhibiting any sort of enthusiasm or happiness that they had accomplished the first mission to land human beings on another world, each of the three astronauts was outwardly sober, somber, as if each harbored an inner concern they could not speak about.

Neil Armstrong remarked that a new age had begun.

Or had it? There were six Apollo moon landing missions, from that first one in July 1969 to the last in December 1972. But after so capably going to the moon during those three and a half years, America did not go back to the moon again. The Apollo program ended.

And the Russians who certainly by circa 1970 had the capability to send cosmonauts to the moon, did not even try. Perhaps the explanation was that after "losing" the race to the moon to the Americans, Russia saw no point in such efforts, and concentrated on a space station.

But there are those who contend that America, and Russia, too, were reacting to some 'message,' whether given outright or more subtly (but no less ominously) that the people of Earth should stay away from the moon. Those who presented the message: aliens, of course.

And of course, there is no proof of that, no matter humankind's fascination with and belief in 'moon people.' Or, the more 20th century notion that extraterrestrials came to the moon from elsewhere and claimed it for their own, and don't want humans claiming anything beyond their planet.

All this suspicion and belief that the astronauts saw something on the moon that eventually led the U.S. (and subsequently the Russians) to keep away from our nearest world is based on wholly circumstantial evidence that can easily be explained by other factors.

For instance, the demeanor of the three Apollo 11 astronauts at that press conference. Those who have seen the Earth from space, witnessed the physical totality of their home planet hanging in the void, have spoken of a change in our perspective, a realization of the self and of existence sheared from the petty obstacles and disguises of the everyday that burden us and narrow perspective. The astronauts had been sobered by seeing their home world suspended, in all its beauty and fragility above the lunar horizon. They were now three men who would not beat their breasts with accomplishment, talk about the glory of America's accomplishment—that was for the Earthbound, who could only see what they had done in an Earthbound way.

Another, subsequent Apollo astronaut, Edgar Mitchell, would often say that the venality of humankind, the machinations of politics and the murderous activity of war "look so petty" when you're out there, looking at the world on which all this insane clamoring is taking place. "You want to grab a politician by the scruff of the neck and drag him a quarter of a million miles out and say, "'Look at that, you son of a bitch.'"

Mitchell, who walked on the moon as part of the last Apollo mission, would become intensely interested in the paranormal, UFOs, and the possibility of aliens. After his retirement from the military and NASA he founded the Institute of Noetic Studies, whose mission was to investigate "how beliefs, thoughts, and intentions affect the physical world."

Noetics, from the Greek *noetikos*, deals with the study of mind and the intellect. That might seem to include a large realm. The philosopher William James wrote of how mystical states are of a "noetic quality": "…states of insight into depths of truth unplumbed by the discursive intellect. They are illuminations, revelations, full of significance and importance, all inarticulate though they remain; and as a rule they carry with them a curious sense of authority." Mitchell postulated that the universe was "a quantum hologram." In quantum holography, physicists place images, hidden objects, with entangled photons. Mitchell envisioned "a giant hard disk in the sky," a quantum Eye of God, so to speak, recording, encoding every and all matter and events in time and space.

NASA, while honoring Mitchell's contributions as an astronaut, never supported his other pursuits. And NASA did not know that during Mitchell's mission he had conducted ESP experiments—with cards, in fact. There are unfortunate echoes of magic tricks here. What Mitchell did was to have four people back on Earth try to guess the images of the cards he had brought with him. He later related that two of the four had guessed 51 out of 200; a bit above random chance that would have been more 40 out of 200. The other subjects did not do as well. At any rate, this was not a very conclusive test for lunar-sent extrasensory acumen.

The card test seemed silly to Li. But hidden objects, entangled photons: this nagged at him. He felt it had something to do with himself. He read on.

Mitchell was on the last American lunar mission. So was his crewmate, Alan Shepard, who had been the first American in space eleven years earlier. In May 1961, Shepard's flight had been, in essence, the mere blip of an adventure; he was in outer space for only fifteen minutes. The U.S. was being careful with its astronauts. In April of that year the Russians had sent up Yuri Gagarin for one full Earth orbit of 90 minutes. It would not be until February 1962 that an American orbited Earth, John Glenn (after a second 15-minute mission by Gus Grissom, July 1961). At any rate, there seemed a sort of, well, cinematic end point in Shepard being the first American in space and then on the last lunar mission. In a very prosaic touch, Shepard hit some golf balls he had brought with him across the lunar surface with a makeshift club.

Card tricks and golf balls. Yes, Li had seen that photograph of Shepard golfing on the moon. He could only think, then and now, how very American—not so much the card tricks, but the golf.

Li recalled reading that NASA had actually sued Mitchell to recover a camera he'd kept from his lunar mission. He had given it to a New York auction house, where its worth had been estimated at $60,000-$80,000. The court had ruled in the government's favor and the camera was eventually turned over to the Smithsonian.

Mitchell had argued that this motion picture camera, one of the two on the lunar module *Antares*, was to be abandoned by the government anyway, and that he was merely following the practice of other Apollo astronauts who had brought back keepsakes from the moon.

Li recalled when he had read that it did not seem to make sense. Why should NASA not want the camera back from the moon right after the voyage? Why did NASA actually go to court to retrieve it decades after the event? There was the temptation to consider the U.S. might have come to think there was film in that camera it did not want the public to see—but again, Mitchell had had it all these years. The government had not interfered in the possession and even sale of other items astronauts had brought back from the moon. Quite soon after it initiated the lawsuit against Mitchell, NASA released guidelines for protecting hardware of its lunar missions.

Li put down the book. The room was bright now. Outside, day had taken hold—in a Wuhan whose nature from which he had been isolated. For only a few days, but it seemed a long time to Li. But his noting this interior daylight and thinking about the outside world was only considered on the surface of his mind. In his depths, he was thinking about the universe, of existence itself being a sort of hologram.

What if they have pushed me into a reality that was actually beyond them?

And he considered he might forever, from this point on, be confused about what was precisely reality. He had entered a meta-perception that had disrupted habitual perception.

He stood up. He looked about the room. He had to get back to the moon.

And then Lin and Yang came in—masked as always, in their protective gear. Li found himself looking at both, as if one of them had been the stranger he had seen on the moon. But neither looked like that bureaucrat at all.

How odd, surreal. Li was in isolation, but these two entered his domain regularly. Why were they his medical keepers? They had no medical background—that he knew of. Of course, anyone can take your temperature.

"No fever today," pronounced Lin.

"You look better," said Yang.

"I feel better." Li said this cautiously.

Yang: "You'll be back to your training before you know it."

Li did not mention—and had not mentioned—that the interruption of his training had nonetheless been invaded by vivid visits to the moon. In fact, he had never told the men that his training had become so real, far beyond absorbing the progress of the rover.

"I hope so," was all he said. Then he asked, "How is it outside?" He realized he was saying this as if he were inquiring of the world outside this room still existed. "With the virus," he added.

"More people getting sick," said Lin, almost curtly.

Li thought about Fan, and Cheng too. But what he said to the pair was, "Are you worried?"

Yang shook his head; and Lin did, too. There were more than a few times when these two seemed meshed in a sort of neural quantum entanglement. Yang said, "We're careful."

Li wondered what the rest of the day was like for Lin and Yang, but asked nothing further. They left, and Li was left with...waiting for whatever would be visited upon him.

When these lunar intrusions had first occurred, there had been some resentment in him, and even fear—that his mind, his perceptions were so easily, well, taken. Now it was more a matter of being intrigued, and even tempted with expectation. "They" had taken him so much beyond those earlier sessions with the rover.

He realized he hadn't thought of the rover for some time. He had not seen it for some time. He had moved—on his moon—far beyond sight of the lander and rover. And felt no qualms about that.

Am I so comfortable on the moon now because I know I am really safe here? And then thought: *Or am I trapped here?* But that was a histrionic thought, he quickly decided. He wasn't trapped. He would not be training like this forever. Why he was so sure of that he could not say.

24.

Nothing happened for most of the day. Li was restless, impatient. He turned from *A History of the Moon* to a training manual, as if by focusing on that he could call up a "teleportation" to the moon.

It happened by mid afternoon.

The moon surrounded him; he was in the midst of it. He turned about, hungry for the view—and, it seemed, looking for something. He was standing on the surface, not merely seeing it from somewhere.

Then he spotted what he had perhaps been looking for. On the sharp edge of the horizon was the rover. He had wondered about it earlier and now here it was. As usual, it was moving slowly. Had Li's thoughts, in a sense, called it to him?

And then, as if just literally materialized, he saw the "other," near the rover, moving toward it.

Li felt—jealousy? Not quite that, but definitely annoyance. What business did this other moon traveler have with *Yutu-2*?

The other stopped by the rover. And it appeared the rover stopped too. Li had the impression there was some sort of communication going on. He shook his head. And began to move in their direction. As he got closer, the other, who had been bending slightly over the rover—yes, in the manner one leans forward to catch a quiet word—straightened up and looked toward Li.

There was an exchange of vision. Li felt anxious. In another moment he was face to face with the other, as he had been in his dream of the abandoned city. The heavy, nondescript face looked back at him calmly. It was an expression of waiting for someone to speak.

Those eyes: Li's body actually trembled. He pushed that away; he did not want to feel anything akin to fear.

Who are you? Li mouthed.

The other's lips moved. Was he saying the same thing? Li could not be sure. Then the other stretched out his arms, and in the heavy suit it seemed his shoulders shrugged. Then he pointed in a direction diagonal to them both. Li turned to look—carefully; he might be making sure the other would not strike him when he was looking elsewhere. Li saw only the lunar landscape. He turned back to the other with a question in his eyes. Who in turn gave an unmistakable gesture: *Follow me.*

It was sort of a difficult progress. Sometimes Li actually followed, sometimes he was alongside, and sometimes—because Li had stronger legs—he was ahead of the other and had to rein himself in, falling back alongside and exchanging a look with his "guide" that was meant to be both assuring and confrontational. Li felt simultaneously resentment (*Who is this man on my moon?*) and intrigued. The former emotion played with this curiosity.

And then—and Li was struck with great surprise—they were before the miniature, the minute city. Li was disorientated. Had this been the way to this? Of course, there might be many paths to the same place. And he was upset that this other was here before something that Li realized he regarded as his private discovery.

And was all the more shocked when the other brought his foot down right in the middle of this apparent model of a city, destroying its delicate presence, creating a crater of a footprint, as if a giant had leveled a metropolis.

Instinctively, angrily, Li grabbed at the other, pulled him back, a motion Li did not temper to the moon's lower gravity. On Earth, Li's strength would have been in great evidence; here on the moon, it dislodged his own balance, as much as the other's, who was now dragged across the minute city, causing more destruction.

Both men seemed to steady themselves at the same time. Li angrily gestured. He could not decipher the gestures of the other, who seemed surprised, even astounded at Li's reaction. The other gestured downward, to the ravaged city, and an expression swept across his face that conveyed to Li: *This doesn't matter.* Or perhaps it was not the gesture but a sort of telepathy, a distinct feeling that shot through Li— which he tried to reject; he wanted to keep his anger. What was this surreal guide here for—to destroy the unusual he, Li, had discovered?

The other, frowning, as if concerned, concerned with Li's sanity, perhaps, gestured beyond them, and began to move off. Li followed— or moved alongside, or ahead. In the latter position he considered moving ahead faster and faster, leaving this other, moving far ahead, into that lunar horizon. At the same time, he was struck with the resignation that he could not get rid of this other. Maybe for a moment he could, but "they" would decide on the presence—or absence—of this other lunar traveler.

So Li was not surprised, his resignation only affirmed, when they came to the boulder, its shadow slanting across the surface, the boulder with the markings that seemed like some sort of writing. At this point both men were alongside each other, and it was Li's guide who reached out, stayed Li (but not violently, with just the right amount of pressure) and seemingly guided both to a stop.

Li was tensed for some another unpleasant act: striking the enigmatic markings. ("Braille," he remembered.) But it was otherwise. The other gently crouched and began to run his thickly gloved hand over the markings, and Li saw—or was it a trick of light and shadow?—the faintest glow. As if...the other was activating the markings. Li had the sensation of some sort of vibration. Then he felt he was being forced to feel sensations that were not really there.

Of course, none of this is there—here. These were arrows of thought he would strike himself with on this moon travels, reminding himself of reality, necessary barbs he would acknowledge, but which could at the most be placed alongside the "reality" that seemed very real indeed. Just as he paced alongside this strange, sudden guide.

The other straightened up, nodding to himself. Yes, to himself, definitely not to Li, as if having gathered some depth of information that was both expected and requiring a further moment to process. *So he read the braille*, Li thought. The other turned to look at Li, and there seemed a bit of actual yearning in his eyes. Li frowned, considering this. The other seemed concerned he could not communicate—at least adequately—what he had gleaned.

Li looked down at the markings. Were they the same as when he had come upon them? Hadn't he taken a photo of them? But at the moment he did not know how to access that image. Yes, it was on the monitor in the room. (*But I am in the room, the moon here is in the room—*) He understood the previous image of the markings was being kept from him.

All he could do was look back at the other, expectantly. He communicated with his expression he was willing to accept what was next.

And so they moved on.

Li was almost expecting what was next. The abandoned city.

And his dream would come true, of him and the other in this city—
the apparent model of which the other had smashed down with his foot.

Li thought: *It's waiting for me like a trap now.*

Together they entered a building. They moved through rooms. They
used an ancient staircase to go to upper floors. Surely this city had once
had elevators—or something more advanced; where were they? Li was
insisting to himself that the abandoned city had to have been at least as
"advanced" as the cities he had known. Then he thought that just the fact
it had been erected here, a full city, if a small city, here on the airless
moon—that bespoke achievement. –Or was the city so old that had it had
been built when the moon was a different place, one more hospitable to
life? Though he knew, or at least today's science asserted, that the moon
had never been hospitable to anything like earthly life. Yet, why did it
have to be earthly life? Because these buildings, these rooms seemed
living spaces for those of his kind. And then thinking, *This is a maze, a
copy of something they are mocking me with. Testing me, anyway.*

Was it a test for this other, too? Perhaps this man was merely an
older taikonaut forced into the training Li was undergoing. Perhaps he
was in another room, somewhere, and "they" had joined him and Li in
a shared mysterious moon—

But Li could not see this other as a space traveler in training. Yes,
he was a bureaucrat; Li had decided that. But that simply could be his
prejudices, Li knew.

In this exploration (was it such, or merely random wandering?) of the
city, Li sometimes looked with great study upon the other's face, seeking
he knew not what, and other times he was so immersed in the at once
mundane and fantastical nature of the structures through which he moved.
It gave him a sort of tiredness of perception and expectancy, a feeling that
soon he would be too tired to take in much more—of this "reality."

As he continued to move about the city, usually in sight of the other, but sometimes, for a moment in a room or corridor without the other, as if gaining a few instants of stealthy privacy, Li had the thought that nowhere in this city was there any article, not a one, of its disappeared inhabitants. Not a single thing in these endless interiors that suggested the daily round of life: beds, chairs, any sort of household machines, stoves, dinnerware— He stopped himself. So perhaps this vanished race lived nothing like we on Earth. Yet this was plainly an "Earth-like city. All the interior objects, all the interior things that filled rooms could not have vanished even if this city was very old. This was the moon—no air, no weather, just the extremes of the lunar night and day. Some things, many things should have been left.

Then again, this was just another lunar anomaly in the training room.

Perhaps Li's handlers were recreating a reality that did indeed exist—on the moon; well, somewhere.

He did not lose these thoughts so much as put them alongside his attentions as he moved through these buildings, with the other usually in sight. The other would often give Li this look, as if making sure Li were still in proximity.

Li and the other entered a room in an apartment in which a space for a large window gave them a panoramic view of the cityscape and the lunar surface beyond. It was a powerful view and Li was held, and said aloud to himself, "A room with a view."

The other turned to him; he might have heard. Li was sure he had not. The other was pointing, pointing to something beyond the city, it seemed to Li. "What—the horizon?" said Li sarcastically. He was abruptly feeling he no longer wanted to negotiate the absurd; at least he needed a respite from it.

But apparently no respite was to be held. The other reached out, grasped Li's arm, and tried to pull him right up to the window. It shot through Li's mind that the other wanted to throw him out of the window. They were three floors above the surface. But with the moon's gravity, would that be dangerous? Li shrugged his arm away, gave the other a baleful look. The other's head seemed to recoil in surprise, and even insult. He pointed again to something out there.

Li looked. Was he seeing…? There were lights—but just on the verge of seeing. He had to squint; he shook his head. The lights were still there—it seemed, just on the verge of being apprehended. Like those unexplained lights sometimes seen on the moon?

He looked back at the other. The other nodded.

"There?" Li said aloud. He felt tired. He abruptly knew he had not shaken the virus fully yet. This city…he could move through all of it, and it was undecipherable. Just like the markings—that the other had made illuminated. "So you bring the lights? Bringing me to lights?"

The other stared at him as Li spoke. Li repeated himself. He wanted the other to read his lips. But the other's face expressed no understanding of what Li said.

And then the other's face seemed to grow less distinct. As if dissolving. No, it was darkening. Li almost reached out a hand—before even thinking about it, recalling it, he was trying to stay the fulfillment of his dream.

The other's face was black. Then it disappeared. Li looked into a helmet in which there was no face. And yet the other, at least something in this space suit, was pointing again, out there, to the lights beyond the city. Li stepped back, more in utter confusion than any sort of horror.

And then, like some cinematic trick, the other disappeared.

Li stood stock still for some moments. The abrupt disappearance of the other seemed a cruel turn in this continual passage of strangeness. Just as the other's appearance seemed cruel. Li had accepted—in a way—this presence, and now—

So the other had been needed to show him those lights beyond the city?

He looked, but saw the lights no longer. Or wait, was that a flicker? Again, these scattered lights—there was another (or not)—seemed another cruel continuity to push him into a passage without explanations at any point along the way.

But what was that he had read, about the strange lunar lights? Transient lunar phenomenon (TLP), which has been seen by different observers for more than a thousand years. The general hypothesis today was that seismic activity on the moon released gases that reflected sunlight. Or the impact of meteorites. But in this case Li felt the truth behind the lights was something else entirely.

And he knew "they" would push him toward it.

He sighed. He left the room where the other had vanished. He descended to the ground floor and exited. He walked about the abandoned city for a while longer, but he entered no other building. He told himself he should feel relief, but the disappearance of the other had left something unresolved.

Then he was lying on his cot in the training room. He always resented these abrupt changes of world. Again he felt resentment; but also a relief: he would rather face what apparently he had to face another time.

Time. What day is it? He couldn't exactly remember. If there was a day and night to the room, he was losing track of days.

He tried to push all that aside. He reached for *A History of the Moon*. He was looking for something specific.

In June 1178, monks from Canterbury described an unusual lunar display.

There was a bright new moon, and as usual in that phase its horns were tilted toward the east; and suddenly the upper horn split in two. From the midpoint of this division a flaming torch sprang up, spewing out, over a considerable distance, fire, hot coals, and sparks. Meanwhile the body of the moon which was below writhed, as it were, in anxiety, and, to put it in the words of those who reported it to me and saw it with their own eyes, the moon throbbed like a wounded snake. Afterwards it resumed its proper state. This phenomenon was repeated a dozen times or more, the flame assuming various twisting shapes at random and then returning to normal. Then after these transformations the moon, from horn to horn, that is, along its whole length, took on a blackish appearance.

It may be assumed this was slightly embellished. Could the moon "writhe"? Perhaps that was a trick of the atmosphere. Anyway, of note in this description, is just as there have been accounts of lights on the moon, there have also been accounts of areas becoming dark. Apparently, this sighting reports both phenomena.

Li read on.

In the 1800s there were astronomers who described the crater Linne quite differently from one another: it has a steep wall and it was five miles in diameter; no, it was not a crater at all but a sort of cloud. Others said Linne was a low mound, four miles across with a crater on top. That was the way one of the foremost of 20th century lunar astronomers, Patrick Moore, had seen it. Then in 1961 Linne appeared to Moore a crater about three miles in diameter. Linne seemed to have changed. Moore examined the crater in two other telescopes and found the same thing. Two nights later Moore once again saw Linne as rounded dome with a crater on top. Moore could only say these distinct changes had to be the result of unusual lighting events. He could not explain it any further than that.

It was in the 1960s that NASA initiated its own investigation into TLP,

Project Moon-Blink, perhaps in concert with the plan to land men on the moon by the end of the decade. NASA, as others, did not come up with any firm explanation for this phenomenon, though it did find many instances of TLP.

Li put down the book. He let sleep come. He did not dream of the other.

Chapter Ten: The Duration of Dying

25.

In the midst of a busy morning, reading papers about past attempts to make a vaccine for SARS and MERS, and not happy about an email from Mr. Mao Suit saying that Dong was still shedding the virus and perhaps Cheng should once more pay him a visit (*Why am I chosen for this? There must be something more to it*—), Cheng suddenly recalled his friend in the hospital and he was struck with guilt that he probably had not given the man a thought for a full day now. Then he remembered he had checked in with the hospital early the previous morning. Sun Bao's condition had been unchanged—which, of course, was not good. But still, since then, the pressure of, well, everything, had pushed more personal considerations aside.

Cheng called his driver. He was surprised when Junjie told him, "I'm right outside."

"You're just waiting there all day?"

"For now. Unless I'm told they need me—"

Cheng had considered Junjie might have other duties, but it seems he hadn't thought about that either, lately. While others might be pleased to have a driver practically at one's beck and call, Cheng felt uncomfortable about this young man appearing to await his needs. Because it felt more like...*He's waiting for prey.* Inwardly Cheng shook his head. He thought he had to focus some part of his attentions that were being distracted. Well, not distracted but focused on extremely pressing things. That was true, but he could not escape the feeling he was being taken away from himself.

But he had chosen a calling and it was calling on him.

Getting into the car Cheng simply said, "The hospital." Junjie nodded and started the car. As they drove through almost empty

Wuhan, Cheng wondered just what sort of person this young driver was, what were his thoughts. It seemed the only thing he was interested in was his phone—again, something all too typical of youth today. Of course, Cheng was only seeing Junjie on the job. How could he know what Junjie was like off duty? But Cheng could not help the feeling that his driver had an enigmatic nature that would not be easy to discern no matter the setting. The mask the driver always wore might be metaphor for something besides the flesh that needed to remain hidden.

After parking at the hospital, Junjie nodded without a word to Cheng as he got out of the car, who said, "I don't know how long I'll be." He had a sense of déjà vu about this, that he had said these exact words to Junjie at his previous visit to the hospital. Well, what did it matter? He felt a sense of displacement, of not entirely being himself through this entire morning. Entering the hospital, he shrugged, and thought again: What did it matter?

He had little hope and no small amount of dread in these moments before he would be seeing Dr. Sun. –And for a moment or two it seemed this visit would not happen, not be allowed. Conditions concerning the virus had only gotten worse in Wuhan, in Hubei, and the hospital had gotten more strict about visitors to those who were infected. Cheng had to confront security personnel, doctors, nurses, show his identification again and again, and threaten to have some health official call on them, a threat that was basically a lie. If he *could* get into contact with Mr. Mao Suit, would that "official" back Cheng's visit, which was for purely personal reasons? At any rate, Cheng was being so frustrated that he was descending into enacting inner fantasies of confrontation, with whatever official weight he could throw at the obstacles of bureaucracy, that he had to catch himself, and focus on being reasonable, unassailable and fully expecting his request to see Dr. Sun fulfilled.

Finally, this focus must have seen him through. He was once more in the man's room. This time there were no other patients with Dr. Sun. And no nurse lingering at the door to remind him of time. On Cheng's previous visit he would have welcomed such absence; now he did not. There was no buffer of others between him and his friend's peril. He saw a face into which tubes entered; they entered the body, too. Both the face and the body seemed more wasted than on Cheng's last visit.

Was there a point to this? Cheng had to think. His friend appeared mired in the deep sleep of illness and drugs. But when he took two steps toward the bed, the eyes above the tubes opened and saw Cheng with full consciousness. In that seeing was something Cheng did not like. It was almost—*was* it fear? As if, Cheng had the intuition, this poor man, clearly near to the state of passing from this life, in being brought from that ill, drugged, state, was seeing in Cheng the embodiment of life and realized all the more that precious condition was slipping away.

Cheng spoke his friend's name. The eyes blinked. Cheng tried to smile. "I guess it's not easy for you to talk." It seemed the lips around the tube tried to smile. It was such a subtle movement, yet so poignant, it tore at Cheng painfully. He was struck with the sudden declaration, *This is what this virus is.* It was not some nanosized pathogen borne from bats and other animals to humans, it was not a genetic sequence, the most minute, rounded invader with its spikes of protein attaching to cells. This, this man before Cheng was the flower of that attachment, that eternal cycle of a virus: attachment, invasion, conquering, reproduction, the explosion through the cell of so many viruses that in turn go on, exponentially, throughout the body, through the world. In fact, it seemed to Cheng, as he stood there, there was nothing to prevent the continual spread of any virus in its task. Of course, viruses always needed some hosts remain. If all hosts were killed, the virus would, in a sense, have no world to live upon.

Where was his mind going? To the reality, the incessant reality, of the physical truth of the world he was doing at the lab, the work he had been doing in those caves of bats. From those caves to this bed—

Dr. Sun's hand was gesturing to a pad by the bed. It felt to Cheng he looked at that gesture for an oddly long time before he understood. He handed the pad and a pencil to his friend, who had to suspend the pad above his face—there was no question of sitting up—and wrote, slowly, awkwardly and then slowly tried to extend the pad back to Cheng, but it fell from his hand, on the side of the bed. Cheng had to dart forward to catch it.

Going to be worse than anyone thought, was the message.

Going to be worse for him or everyone or both? Cheng was thinking, but he did not say that. He did say, "Do you feel any better?" He knew it was a ridiculous question, and he felt ashamed as his friend shook his head, slightly, but palpably, back and forth. It was a small motion that appeared to create pain. The eyes clenched. In a moment they opened, looked at Cheng, with an expression of surrender.

Dr. Sun gestured again for the pad. Cheng gave it to him as if surrendering a document of grave news both had already accepted. Once again Dr. Sun wrote with the pad above his head. He wrote quickly and was about to stretch out his arm to give the pad to Cheng, but he was now right by the bed and he touched one end of the pad, turned it to him, so it barely left his friend's hand. It was just two words:

"Coincidence? Ironic?

At Cheng's puzzled look, Dr. Sun weakly pulled the pad back to him and wrote—a bit longer this time. Then Cheng was gently touching the pad again, turning it to him. Dr. Sun's hand had fallen back on the bed.

I spoke about this. The government attacked me. Now I have it.

Cheng thought he knew exactly what his friend inferred, but he asked, as if shocked. "You think they did this to you?" The doctor's eyes fluttered. He took a long breath through the tube. Cheng said, "That would only—" He stopped. The doctor's eyes narrowed; it seemed he was expecting Cheng to give an excuse. Cheng continued: "You've become famous." The face on the bed, amongst the tubes and the plague, seemed amused.

There was truth to what Cheng said. As news of the virus, the many ill, the lockdown, became the central news of the moment, as the authorities admitted the nature of the situation, and as the recent efforts of Dr. Sun to confront the authorities and sound the alarm, this man here in this bed had achieved a notoriety he doubtless would have gladly done without. A fame here in isolation and clearly near death.

But had the authorities done this to him? If that were the case—and Cheng, always skeptical of paranoid conspiracy theories (after all, he was a rational man, a scientist)—not only had the powers that be now drawn attention to the fact that they had kept the severity of the virus from the public for too long, but had made it more possible the virus could be handled in an a deliberate, controlled manner. At this point, at least, Cheng believed his friend's illness had come from his treating patients. After all, the virus was so contagious. Even with strict precautions.

Cheng had given little thought to the possibility that he might catch the virus, whether from his friend or the simple fact of living in Wuhan at this time. He knew, if he saw himself a rational man, this was a bit irrational: as if he saw himself as someone who knew so much about viruses, and even this virus, as new as it was, that that knowledge protected him.

At any rate, he was thinking more about his friend's condition than the possibility that this could be himself, lying in a hospital bed, near death.

He said, "I don't think they'd go that far."

Dr. Sun seemed to not hear that all. He was writing again.

It will spread past China.

Cheng realized that he had given this scenario only fleeting thought. He had been so focused on the here and now: the virus in Wuhan. So he was suddenly forced to visualize a pandemic. He wondered if he would be at all successful in overseeing the creation of a vaccine. The road to a vaccine was a marathon. What was needed now, needed for his friend, was a sprint.

But how could anyone sprint Dr. Sun Bao out of the realm of death?

A natural, if uncomfortable pause grew up in the room. It was probably no more than a few long seconds, but it was one of those moments that one's emotions feel are long minutes. The man on the bed eyed the man standing by the bed: the man who was gripped by a great illness, regarding a healthy man. Cheng didn't know what to think in those moments, didn't know what he should be thinking, The thought came to him—and it was an odd thought for Cheng—that if he had been asked if he would selflessly exchange places with his friend, give up his life for him— Well, he wasn't that close to Dr. Sun; but here was a man that had acted heroically, defied the authorities to give the public—in fact, the world—information vital to health.

Why am I thinking this? Because life had been so upheaved. Dr. Sun was only a few years older than Cheng. Dr. Sun should not be in this bed, dying. –And Cheng was struck by that: Sun Bao is dying. Cheng's expression must have given him away (and what expression is the one that tells others you know they are dying?); his friend on the bed tilted his head slightly, as much as he was able, as if saying, *So you know I'm dying. I'm not sure I want to know it.* And Cheng didn't really want to know it. What would he say to Dr. Sun's mother?

It was too cruel. Felled by a disease, by an epidemic for which he had sounded a warning.

Perhaps Dr. Sun had read his mind. He was writing. *My mother called. A nurse read to her what I wrote. Can you call her for me? Tell her—what you need to.*

Cheng looked down at this sad request. "Of course."

His friend looked back at him as if pitying him. There was the slight nod the tubes allowed.

"I have to go." But did he? He touched his friend's forearm. The arm was on top of the blanket. The short sleeves of the hospital gown left exposed the forearm and as Cheng touched it, he was thinking, *This is a reckless farewell.* But he had been overwhelmed by and drawn to the commonness of the color and texture of the arm's flesh, the soft sparse hairs, the slight tracery of veins…. The *fact* of life, still there, insisting.

He left the room without disinfecting his hands.

Back at the car, Junjie didn't look up from his phone right away when Cheng got in. He was not wearing his mask. He appeared to need a moment to refocus on Cheng's presence. He seemed to put on his mask with deliberate slowness. "How is your friend?"

"To be honest—with myself: he's dying."

Junjie nodded slowly. It reminded Cheng of the nod Dr. Sun had just given despite the tubes.

"From the virus, right?"

"Yes." He had already told Junjie that, but admitting it again now, saying it aloud, was not pleasant for Cheng. He wanted to divert himself, to distract his distress. He said, "You looked…very absorbed in something."

"What?"

"On your phone."

"Oh. A little business I have on the side."

Cheng wasn't really that interested, but he asked, "What's that?"

"Seeds."

Cheng could have expected anything but that. "Seeds?"

"It's sort of a government project. Sending seeds all over the world." Junjie started the car.

"To other governments? Agricultural departments?"

"No. To people. Individual people. A lot in America." They were pulling out of the parking lot.

"Buying special seeds that only come from China?"

"Not necessarily. Usually no. Common seeds. Cabbage, roses, mustard, lavender. Plants, spices. Mint, sage—"

"I don't understand. Why would Americans order—?"

"No one orders them. They are just sent."

"It doesn't make sense what you're saying."

"The seeds are sent out—I'm tracking the distribution—randomly. No one orders them."

"No one orders these seeds, but the government sends them to people in America. Seeds that anyone in America can get in America."

"Yes."

"Why?"

Junjie shrugged. "I have no idea. Some sort of experiment, I guess."

"Experiment for what?" The driver shrugged again. "And you're not curious?"

"I'm paid."

"Are these seeds supposed to cause some kind of harm?"

"I don't think so, but I don't know."

"You're involved in this and you're not curious?" Cheng was plainly accusatory.

"Don't governments always do absurd things?"

"Yes. And this sounds absurd. And—ominous."

Junjie laughed. "It's just seeds. Maybe—what it probably is, is that these seeds will produce better plants than the Americans can get, and they will want to buy these seeds from China from now on. Or it could be—have you heard of 'brushing'?"

"What's that?"

"Companies send unsolicited items to people. Then put fake reviews from that person online. In other words, they are using someone's identity they've bought or stolen to boost their business. They're not really hurting anyone, though. Someone gets free seeds, knows nothing about a fake review."

"Or the seeds could be—if the government is behind it—genetically engineered to eventually harm American crops."

"I don't think there are enough seeds to do that."

"A few seeds, it's like a virus. It spreads. The seeds make plants with fruit or flowers that spread all over."

"You think I'm involved in distributing something—keeping track of it—that will bring down United States agriculture?"

"I hope not. You know something bad like that happens in one country, it goes on to infect the world."

"Like your virus, I know."

It's not "my" virus, Cheng thought. As he had in the hospital room with Dr. Sun, Cheng considered that the virus which beset Wuhan could become a pandemic. "Yes, like a virus."

"You're saying I'm doing something that will cause harm."

"Unless you know more about it, I wouldn't—"

The young driver stayed Cheng with a look that appeared to regard him as naïve. "You have a good position, Dr. Cheng. I have to get along."

Cheng frowned, not happy about any of this. "How long has this been going on?"

"I have no idea. I have been doing this for just a few weeks. Maybe that's when it started. I don't know."

Then neither spoke for a while. For the first time Cheng was wondering about the nature of this young man who so conveniently drove him about in the midst of this new plague.

.   .   .

Back at the lab he scanned the folder he had been sent about virus. That light brown icon on his desktop now had folders within folders as more information—and speculation—about the virus had grown. Cheng realized that within a month, two months., there would be too much to absorb, especially if—when—the virus spread outside of China.

In fact, it was only that morning, then and there, that Cheng saw news that the virus was indeed in other countries.

On January 13th and 16th, Thailand had reported its first and second cases. Just as Wuhan and Hubei went into lockdown, with 830 cases in mainland China and 25 deaths, the first deaths occurred outside of Hubei. The first medical professional who had treated patients with the virus died. Of course Cheng thought of Dr. Sun.

On January 24, Nepal, Vietnam, France, Malaysia confirmed their first cases.

France. It's beyond Asia.

On January 25 Australia and Thailand reported their first cases. America had its third case.

On January 26, China banned the sale of wild animals throughout the country, whether in markets or online. America has its fourth and fifth cases, in Los Angeles and Arizona.

January 27: First cases in Siri Lanka, Cambodia and Germany. The U.S. sets up screening in twenty airports. Of what exactly that screening consisted, Cheng did not know.

January 28: Hong Kong and Mongolia institute partial border closings with mainland China. (What good is partial? Cheng thought.) Japan and America evacuate their nationals from Wuhan. China announces it will welcome a group of WHO personnel to aid in research and response. United Airlines suspends all U.S. flights to China.

.   .   .

Cheng drifted back and forth between news reports and scientific research. It was frustrating that much of the science was still speculative at this point. There were facts, yes, but not enough, and one could only extrapolate from these facts to possibilities, which could only be confirmed or dismissed by further research. *By more disease and death*, Cheng thought.

His mind drifted back to Dr. Sun in the hospital.

So when he received the call that afternoon it seemed the inevitable link to his persistent dread—or simply resignation. Dr. Sun had died.

Cheng compressed the moment of receiving that fact in a deep, heavy moment of time, while the person on the other end might have thought Cheng responded without any lag: "Has his mother been informed?"

The voice on the other end, a woman's, was matter of fact. "He asked you be notified first."

Of course, so I can notify his mother. Instead of the hospital.

Cheng felt he had, through just these past few days, been given tasks—burdens—which he had certainly not sought. Not that he resented this particular duty. He accepted it would be better for him to tell his friend's mother than someone from the hospital.

He waited a few long minutes before he made the call. He said he would give himself ten minutes, then fifteen. First, he simply stared at the wall, gathering himself. Then he glanced again at the screen of his laptop, at the reports. A moment ago, he had been reading all this, and did not know his friend had died. No matter that Cheng had fully expected it. In those moments before the call, his friend was like Schrödinger's Cat; it would take an observer to coalesce the reality of life and death. But now the hospital had conveyed reality to Cheng, coalescing his consciousness into "knowing" his friend was dead.

Cheng rubbed his hand back and forth across his forehead, as if trying to release something in his brain, his psyche. He called Dr. Sun's mother.

He did not begin with the essential fact immediately—but would pronounce it soon enough. "I saw him this morning."

"I am glad they could let you see him—" As if she could be thankful only for official favors, not any outcome with her son.

Cheng cut her off, not wanting her to assuage herself, and thus be all the more sad—and bitter?—when given the truth. "He…wasn't well. The hospital just called—"

"Oh." It was not a word; it was a sound. Now she too was an observer coalescing the reality of the heart.

For an instant he did think, *What if I don't have to say it?*

He knew she understood, but he had to bluntly give the fact. (Because he was a scientist?) "He died this afternoon."

There was silence on the other end. It was not a long silence, but Cheng drowned in it, he felt subsumed. Her silence was worse than sounds, words—tears. Her silence meant that he should speak. Or he should not. His psyche was saying, *Help me give this message.* Well, he had given the message; he needed help with the aftermath.

Though Dr. Sun's mother would not flail him with the silence for any length of time. She did try to help Cheng. "I appreciate your…help. I know my son did."

Help? I've helped nothing.

She was saying, "I should call them— Arrange…."

"Yes, yes," Cheng said, relieved, wrung out. She would bear it now.

Then something he did not expect. "My son said…if…if something happened—" She drew in her breath. "A flash drive. Some information. I'm not sure what it is—though it's probably about the virus." She said that last word as if pronouncing, in a lament, the murderer of her son. "He wanted someone to see it. He mentioned your name. He held it—wanted to, he said, 'verify it,' more, but if something—like now—"

"I will of course look at anything he wanted…me to see."

"You can come; I will give it to you."

Cheng was about to say Yes, then reconsidered. "I have had some exposure to the virus. I don't want to—"

"I should give this to you in person. I am not worried about myself. Now." The mother who had lost her son had nothing left to live for? She added, "I can bring it to you. Anywhere."

Outdoors? thought Cheng. That would be safer, Healthwise. But conspicuous. Dr. Sun had confronted the authorities, and even if they had had to come around to the truth of his warnings, there would always be the residue of having been challenged. "They" would want that flash drive.

"I'll come," said Cheng. "I will keep my distance. You have a mask, I hope?"

At this point in time it was like asking her if she had legs. "Everyone has one," she said. She gave a little, sad laugh. "Everyone is used to wearing them when the air is bad, but now we have to wear them— we're afraid of someone's else's breath."

Cheng tried to give some comfort he knew was inane. "Let's hope it won't be for a long time."

She did not acknowledge his hope. "We're afraid of someone else's life. Their life might kill ours."

It was perhaps a macabre tangent from the death of Dr. Sun; anyway, it was both too metaphysical and everyday for Cheng. He said something further, which he could not remember five minutes later and said he would call her back shortly to say when he could come to see her. Should it be before the end of the day, or the evening, or tomorrow morning? He did not want his driver, the young man with the mysterious side job of the seeds, to bring him to the bereaved mother of Dr. Sun, who would pass who knew what information on to Cheng. Then again, could Junjie know anything past the purpose of his visit other than comforting a grieving mother, the friend of her dead son?

The driver would simply be outside, waiting in the car. But just the fact that Cheng would have something, perhaps something explosive he did not want this young man to even intuit, gave him unease.

Cheng considered that as a scientist he wanted to be truthful, not act like, well, a spy. Of course, modern history was replete with scientists who were also spies. Look at the Manhattan Project. They were scientists who knew the facts of their work, yet at the same time they could delude themselves with ideology. Cheng believed himself free of the later. He had no illusions about the nature of governments, including his own. He was simply glad he could use the government to allow him to do his work. He laughed soundlessly to himself. I guess the Nazi scientists thought the same thing. Not that that the present situation was anything like that.

He might as well go now and get that flash drive. He called the driver.

26.

Fan also drifted back and forth between her work, the intricacy and the depth of it, and outside distractions. The lab had more visitors. Some looked as if they belonged in the lab, at least *in* a lab, but beside the fact that she did not recognize them, they had a certain look of not belonging. It also made her think: did she indeed know everyone who worked at the lab? It was possible she didn't. And then there were those who were so obviously outsiders: men and women who wore business dress, and peered from above the line of their masks as if the masks were more instruments to hide identity than for biological protection. Fan wondered if these—at least some of them—were the "experts" from the World Health Organization. She decided probably not, as all these visitors were Chinese. Visitors from WHO would have most likely been from a variety of countries.

Fan had several of these visitors burst in upon her, inquire as to her name (as if her presence itself were questionable) and what she was doing. It was only a few days ago four "officials" had apparently interrogated everyone at the lab. –Though it seemed longer than just a few days ago. Time was so compressed now. Every day had so much crammed into it. It seemed her male questioners lingered longer; well, she was an attractive young woman. The one woman who talked to Fan appeared actually suspicious when Fan described her work, remarking "They let you do that?" Fan gave a bland but confrontational response: "What do you see wrong with it?" The woman did not answer, only shook her head and after a moment asked Fan some other questions— which from Fan's perspective were useless—then left. She did not threaten to return, or even take up the nature of Fan's work with any hierarchy of superiors. Fan considered that the attentions of these visitors, at least in her case, had been more swayed by sexual considerations (attractions, jealousy) than scientific concerns.

She had a memory. Her response of "What do you see wrong with it?" reminded her of conversations—debates—she had had with her father when she was a girl. Ever the career military man, he had always defended the government; while Fan's inclination toward science made her question everything, looking for the facts of the matter. In those discussions, which were sometimes affectionate, sometimes a bit tense, at least frustrating, it was her father who would take the tact, "What do you see wrong with it?" when young Fan questioned the way things were. And sometimes she, being so young, could not quite explain why she thought something was wrong; sometimes she just felt so strongly it was. Her father would laugh at that. "Feelings are no argument." But older she realized she could have told him—and *would* tell him, when older—that feelings tell us to look or not look at certain pertinent facts in whatever matter at hand.

Fan remembered one particular debate in which her father said she was "being swayed by emotion not to look at the facts." It was about the one child policy that China had begun in 1980 to limit population, balance population with the country's resources. That policy had remained in effect until 2015, when it was relaxed to allow two children per family.

It was a policy that fractured into many realities. China had 970 million people when the policy was enacted. By this year of 2020, China had 1,400,000. You could say if that policy had not been in place for decades the country might have easily had a population of two billion. Families had to pay fines—based on their income—if they had more than one child. Though often the authorities would look the other way if the first child was a girl. There could also be some leniency if both parents were single children. At any rate, boys were generally considered more desirable; even in this country which encouraged female doctors and scientists, it was considered that males would secure better jobs, in other words, benefit the country's economy more than females. There are stories, never quite verifiable, of more female fetuses being aborted, of female infants not getting proper health care. As of 2018, there were 114 boys born for every 100 girls in China. If you extrapolate these to the number of births per year, which has averaged about 16 million since 2002, that's a large male-female disparity.

If fines could prove a deterrent to having more children, prove an incentive to better family planning, the authorities could get very draconian about enforcement. Women who had had two children were asked to submit to sterilization. If they refused, a relative would be kidnapped and not released until the woman agreed to be sterilized. As horrible as this was, it might seem an improvement to methods used by the state not so long ago: forcing women to have abortions even up to the ninth month of pregnancy, smothering newborns and throwing the bodies in the trash. Women who worked in state run factories had to show their supervisors bloodied sanitary napkins to prove they were menstruating every month.

The policy certainly did curtail population. In the more rural areas of China, women in the 1970s averaged 5.8 children. Thirty years after the policy went into effect, the average was 1.7 children.

In those father-daughter conversations, Fan had said, "I understand it's better to not have so many people, but to punish people, fine them, kidnap relatives, to have girls less regarded than boys—"

Her father had said, "The issue of boys and girls is not right. I am proud to have you. But when you have so many people already, even if most of them understand what is best for everyone, and practice control of their families, in that large group to have even one percent resisting—that's a large number. Fan, when you are dealing with a whole country, especially China, you cannot have just an ideal—you have to have a successful method."

"It doesn't feel right to me."

"When you're older—"

"I'll lose my sense of what's right?"

Her father was alternately smiling and annoyed. "To lead the people is hard. You cannot act like you are dealing with just one person. You have to look for what is best for most of the people. If you don't, you will have situations that are not the best for everyone."

"You're saying it is not practical to be humane."

"I say looking at the whole, the collective, is more humane."

"In other words, what the individual wants is not humane."

"Often not humane for the rest of us."

So was that what was going on? Fan wondered, with this virus and this lockdown? Well, of course, in times of plague, it's the collective that matters, the survival of the tribe, not the individual discomfort that might be required to ensure that survival. But what the authorities liked to do was enforce rules, often harshly, without giving the information as to why these rules—let's say restrictions—were needed. She thought of Dr. Sun, who had confronted the authorities with their coverup of information, and was now gravely ill with the virus.

Then, as if in telepathy, she got a call from Cheng who told her Dr. Sun had died.

"I just wanted to let you know. I can't talk now. I'll tell you more later."

That drew Fan from memories of any conversations with her father and the intrusions of visitors to the lab. She returned to her work, even if she still harbored, at least now and then, the thought that what she was trying to accomplish might be no more than a nanotech novelty than producing any real useful work.

Then again, science seems to find use for any new avenue or research in the end. Or rather the world finds use for what science finds. Of course, in the present situation, if anything she was doing turned out to be useful, it had to be of use now, not later. Fan had the sense that the situation with the virus was only going to grow larger, more unpleasant.

I'm a weaver in an old dynasty, she thought, though what she wove could not pass through her hands. She visioned a cascade of spike proteins enwoven in a variegated mass of nanoplastics. The progress of this tapestry could be seen only through the electronic microscope. It was as if a blind painter moved her paints across a canvas by a n almost visceral instinct, and then, in certain moments, sight was granted and what she had created could be beheld.

In one of these moments of beholding, Wong Bai suddenly broke in upon her—an invasion of her inner sanctum. Her attention, abruptly drawn to this thin, anxious looking man, felt a surreal displacement— from a world in which she felt she had some control to one where she did not. And Wong's aspect was one that projected he felt himself under the control—at least the influence—of circumstances beyond him.

"I'm sorry to interrupt."

"What is it?" She realized she sounded annoyed. Ordinarily, politeness would have ameliorated those words with something more gently spoken, but she left it at that, as if what she shot at him were a test of his purpose and its substance.

Wong didn't seem affected by her manner. "Have you talked to these people that are all around here?"

"Several." She paused, then added with a wry smile, "Unfortunately."

"I've talked to too many." He scratched the back of his head as if his own thoughts were irritating him. "I had to—not just with one of them, but two, three, take them around, it seemed, every corner of the lab. You would think they were looking for a hole the virus could escape through."

"Does that mean they are admitting—or are we admitting?—the virus did come from here."

He nervously scratched his nose. "I don't think anyone's *admitting*…just that they want to torture us with everything."

Fan could not help poking at his obvious distress a little. "You do seem tortured. They're just being—official."

"They acted as if I were guilty."

"But of course, you're not."

"You say that as if I'm—"

Fan laughed and touched his arm. "I'm joking with you."

Wong Bai jerked back a little, almost as if frightened by her touch. Fan was about to say something reassuring, as she might to a leery animal, but he quickly said, "I know, I know. It's that they made me feel…responsible. I told you before I think the security here—You know they were working on viruses that are like the one that's making everyone sick."

"So, you're just as worried as they are."

"But I'm blaming no one."

"You just haven't found the person to blame."

He looked at her as if she had said something illuminating. Then said slowly, "It's probably not just one person, it's just that it's the way things are done here."

"And how are things done?"

"All for science, without regard to—" Fan cocked her head, waiting. He said: "Consequences."

"Scientists don't think of consequences?"

"Not enough. Not enough."

"You're a scientist. You're thinking of consequences."

"I'm not sure I'm exactly a scientist. And maybe I haven't been thinking of consequences enough."

"Why aren't you a scientist?"

"It's more that I manage what scientists do. Not exactly what they do, but contain, or make sure—scientific security, I guess. That's all."

"Sounds like enough. Sounds like a lot. You have to know what you are—containing."

He looked at her for an uncomfortable pause. At least Fan became uncomfortable. He didn't seem to feel the pause was uncomfortable at all. Perhaps he was waiting for her to go on. When she didn't, he asked, "What exactly are you doing? If you're allowed to talk about it."

"I've talked about it to everyone who's asked." She related the outlines of her work. He seemed interested. She went into more detail. He appeared not only interested but impressed. She added, "Though maybe it just *sounds*…innovative, but won't have much use at all."

"Even if what you're doing doesn't have immediate use, the *technique*—"

"I don't think there's any technique, just plodding along. The fact that I'm using part of the virus just makes it sounds better than maybe it is."

He leaned toward her a bit, as if now losing any awkwardness—or fear—he might have exhibited. "This virus, though—it's special, isn't it?"

"Special?"

"Different. From what I know, everything I hear—I hear more than I know—"

"That's a good way of putting it. I think everyone here hears more than they know."

He stopped, as if absorbing the ramifications of his own words. "There's something different about this, there is. You get the sense after a while. That's why they're so worried."

"They?"

He didn't answer that directly, but said, "They don't know what it can turn into. How far it will go. It's too new to predict."

"That's true." It was a banal statement that if brief allowed her time for her own thoughts. This man chattering away before her (it did seem he was chattering away, like a bird that had settled before her and was cawing away): he was plain, you could say homely, and his flustered aspect was not attractive—not manly at all.

Though what did being "manly" mean? Being a young woman, Fan had either thought about this or reacted subconsciously to the "manliness" or lack thereof of the male half of life. It wasn't something you could put into words. Li, for instance, was manly, though in a distant sort of way, as if his maleness were more a psychic afterthought than an insistent center of his being. In the case of Fan's father, manliness was indeed an insistent center, though a quality that could be too consciously insisted upon. If one lived a certain way, one was a man. The military had afforded him a clear path to that. Perhaps the military made it easy for one to "be a man." Not that Fan felt any special attraction for military men. If she could appreciate the stolid maleness of her father, she could be just as aggravated at how it kept him with certain parameters of perception.

Li's present status as a taikonaut in training had succeeded a stint in the military, but Fan did not look upon Li as a military man. There was an essential difference in the way Li and Fan's father saw military discipline. Most young men entering the military saw that discipline as a fact of military life, a fact to be borne: it was just there, you had to go through it. Her father had seen the purpose of discipline, how it fitted into the structure of military life, how it was necessary to its continuing machinery. Li had neither of the above views. He had embraced discipline not as a substance fitting into a larger cause, but a vehicle for himself, one that could focus him more precisely on his chosen path. Discipline would be his personal tool. He was the ascetic who took the structure the military insisted upon and made of it his own personal nature. So far, he had been correct in the manner of his embrace.

Cheng was of another type of manliness. He was plainly not the stereotype of the gay man with an affected voice and manner. As Li had once said, naïvely, "You wouldn't even be able to tell." Fan had responded, "There's a certain sense there; I can tell." She wondered, if Cheng were not gay, would she be attracted to him? He was not bad looking, if not as handsome or as athletic as Li, but he was extremely intelligent—in fact, she had to admit to herself he was smarter than Li, and he had a personality that drew one in—if one could handle his aspect of intelligence. In other words, he really appreciated the intelligence of others. It seemed to Fan that Li not so much appreciated the intelligence of others as noted intelligence as merely an aspect of a person. She had once asked him, "Just how do you judge people?"

He had said, "I don't judge them. I just note…how they are."

He did not ask in turn how she judged others. And in this moment, musing on men from Wong Bai to Cheng, she did not ask herself either. At any rate, she did realize that Li did appreciate *her* intelligence; it had made her pleased and flattered when they first met and he had told her how impressed he had been with her talk on the nano world, that it had made him look at "matter and reality" (his exact words) so differently.

Could I have a child with this man? Fan had asked herself that question once or twice—though she saw motherhood, whether or not with Li, a few years in the future. (*I'd hate to be a mother now, with this new virus.*) Her joking with Li about not wanting to live on the moon with him was serious joking. She did not see him being in space or on another world for any great length of time, but if he did come to live a life in which he was frequently or even once in a while, "out there," she knew it could be unsettling. There was the natural worry about something going wrong in an environment what could not support human life without flawless technical equipment, and there was also the sense that Li, even when with her, would always be a little (or more than a little) "out there," his spirit not bound to the Earth.

But then, that was what he was. It was take it or leave it. She would have to decide, she told herself recently, if that "negative" outweighed—or equaled—the "positive" she found in being with Li.

Though what exactly was that "positive"? He was a virile young man, but there were certainly other young virile men. Now perhaps a lot of "manly" men would feel a little overwhelmed by Fan's intelligence, but certainly she could find men who were more earthbound when with her. Perhaps, as is often the case, the very factor that made her have misgivings about Li was what drew her. Yin and Yang. It was a cliché that opposites attract. Though she would not say she and Li were opposites. Just in different realms. For her it was the nanoworld. For him it was the macroworld. The cosmos. Though, as he had once said, "The universe is made up from your nanoworld."

Fan realized her thoughts had drifted while Wong Bai was still speaking to her. Or rather he was silent, apparently waiting for her to respond to something he had said.

"I'm sorry, I was thinking of something. I really didn't hear you—"

She was afraid he was going to ask her what she had been thinking—he was the type who would, it seemed—but he didn't. He didn't even repeat what he had said. "I'm taking you away from your work."

"I needed a little break." And perhaps she had. "All these visitors—it's not a normal time."

He nodded, as if they had both agreed on something of importance, if mundane. "I'd better get back to…making things secure." He gave a rough laugh, as if mocking himself.

"We'll talk again," Fan said. Bai took his exit with a nod, as if assenting to his own departure.

If there was something more than a little agitating about Wong Bai, Fan realized she wouldn't mind talking to him again. She felt, well she couldn't exactly express it, she felt that this nondescript man held some…clue, yes, clue, to the virus. A clue to something amiss that was connected to the lab.

Researchers were of course looking for "clues" to the virus. But Fan felt there was some other sort of clue involved here. Was it as blunt and plain as some accidental release from the lab? Or something a bit more covert—but just as plain? –That the virus had been created, humanmade, and thus had to be confronted differently than had it been a natural virus?

But what was "natural"? In the reservoir of mammals, bats, human or otherwise, viruses gained and or lost genes, entered into or came out of the primal systems of those bodies like invaders in a war they had created: conquering yet altered, defeated yet altered, absorbed yet altered. Nothing, not invader or unwilling host, was the same after battle.

Wong Bai…. One could hardly connect him to battles. It would seem so, anyway. And yet…. She had thought of him as nondescript. Is one born like that, or does one become so? Fan thought more the latter. The psyche chooses its disguise for survival. Though a disguise implied that the opposite of appearances was hidden. Perhaps the disguise eventually effaces what was once hidden. The disguise becomes the essence. And perhaps, in the situation here at the lab regarding the virus, Wong Bai was feeling the discomfort of having his nondescript aspect threatened. He was alarmed, he was concerned; he was moving outside of the aspect of not being noticed for anything out of the ordinary. His agitated conversations with Fan were like appeals for some sort of assistance, at least recognition of his predicament. Though he was probably not so much consciously aware of this, but driven by an unease he was not willing to look at, let alone define.

Is he guilty of something? Of the very thing he worries about?

But then he would not be raising any alarms. –Or he would be taking the tact of severing himself from all appearance of guilt by raising the alarm?

Why am I thinking such convoluted things? It was this matter of a "clue" that Fan sensed…somewhere.

In this big, big lab she sat before her nanoworld that opened itself to her through the technology she operated so well and felt herself on a borderland of realities. The nanoworld that she saw, or rather saw the translation of it via instruments, that nanoworld living within this odd world of human affairs, its lies and mysteries.

Aren't all mysteries a path to uncover lies?

She smiled to herself. Why a smile, she did not know. She chided herself for sounding profound. Even if it was only to herself. Reality cannot lie. We tell lies in declaring we have unraveled the center of it.

She had the sense of being in some corner of a labyrinth, not recalling how she had entered it, and only recalling some recent turns of passages. She had no idea of how to reach its exit. Perhaps only time does that. As humans we "wait it out." We "ride the wave" until, without a course, we are thrown upon some stretch of sand, make our way up a bit up the beach, then fix ourselves below the sky (the same sky that was above us while at sea) and be grateful we can stand on something solid, even if the land is foreign. We are pleased to have shed the journey—the journey that seemed to have chosen us; there had been no choice on our part.

Indeed, our best skill might be just going through time, doing what we do each day, and depending on fortune or the lack thereof to resolve what course has befallen us and gain some rest in the end.

Well, all of life was like that, bringing us from this confusion, to some final beach, at the end of our time. Perhaps death was that sky, seen from the stability of the beach, while we believe in the delusion of reaching the end of those days—so, so many days—of travel, when we wanted rest...a moment's cessation, in order to *see*.

Fan thought again of Dr. Sun. She suspected that for most of us death was not sudden at all, but inexorably gradual. There were those immediately felled by eruptive, biological events, or accident, but for most of us life closed down step by step, a painful progression—or regression. The lungs breathing less and less, the blood sluggishly carrying less oxygen, the organs seemingly forgetting their functions, the mind in some cases even more damaged before this morass of decay—or holding on until the last, watching in its way, all this failure of the body. Dr. Sun would have understood more than most what the virus was doing to him. Though even he, as most of us, couldn't know all the weapons of this new virus. It destroyed Dr. Sun in ways we know, and in other ways we don't—yet. Anyway, Fan believed that someone like Dr. Sun had the full scope of his mind up to the end of his duration of dying. It would have been an awful awareness.

Late in the afternoon Fan drew back from her work, sat at her desk and slipped into a half sleep, not really out of any physical tiredness but the weight of emotion and, simply, thought. Images that became almost surreal flooded across her inner visions. She imagined herself nano sized, in the lungs of Dr. Sun, in the cytokine storm that had flooded and drowned his breathing. She moved in frightened repugnance in a sticky, clinging whiteness that soon began to cling to her, trapping her. She began shouting, then feared the life ending morass that clung to her would enter her own lungs—

She started back, withdrew from that terrible vision. She looked at her laptop, at the functional banality of her workspace with relief, focusing on the one pleasing visual object in her space, a jade plant, its simple (well, complex, really) life: its pleasing there-ness. Even without the plant, any reality would be welcome placed against the vision she had just suffered.

Chapter Eleven: The Terminator

27.

Li had his own visions which sometimes crossed the border from dreams into things he beheld or experienced that seemed as real as his journeys across the moon. One morning—or was it morning, or another time of the "day" of the training room?—he was on the moon once more, confronting the nameless other, that bureaucrat face made startling by a bizarre change in the pupils of his eyes: instead of dark and round they were slits, like a reptile's, slits a dark, glowing red. They repulsed Li, frightened him, but in the surrealness of this half sleep, half awake vision his astonishment and curiosity made him ask, "What happened?" –As if the other could hear him. The other did lean toward him, perhaps to see the movement of Li's lips more closely; so Li repeated: "What happened?" After a pause he added: "To your eyes?" He pointed to his own eyes. The other frowned, but the reptile eyes made this something other than a frown, and Li in turn did not so much frown as wince. This seemed to elicit and odd smile from the other, who simultaneously spread his arms out, as if answering Li's query with the language of the body, an answer that there was no answer, that things were just as they were—as they are.

Li turned his head away from the other and with that motion shook away that vision and or dream. He lay there, breathing slowly, looking up at the ceiling of the room.

After a few moments he reached out, picked up *A History of the Moon* and read something from a chapter titled, "A Few Basics."

Even those who couldn't care less about the moon know that it goes through what are called phases: the same phases months after month. What makes this happen? Many of you know the answer to that, but in case you don't, here's why.

The moon, the brightest object by far in Earth's night sky, has, unlike a star, no light of its own. It reflects the light of the sun. Now think of the moon in its different positions as it orbits around the Earth. Actually, it is more correct to say that the Earth and moon orbit around a common center of gravity, closer to the larger Earth than the smaller moon, but for the purposes of this explanation let's just say the moon goes around the Earth. Anyway, when the Earth is between the sun's light and the moon, the moon is full; we see its full disc. So that's the full moon. The Earth is not directly between the sun and the moon, so it is not blocking the sun's light. That is, unless it one of those occasions when the Earth does block the sun's light and causes an eclipse of the moon.

The opposite of a full moon is what is called the new moon; this is actually when we cannot see the moon at all, because the moon is between us and the sun. This is when the far side (that we never see from Earth) is illumined and the side we see from Earth is completely dark, because it is not in a position to reflect the light from sun. So, the new moon is the phase of the moon we cannot see at all.

Then as the moon continues in its orbit it begins to catch more and more of the sun's light. The visible part of the moon takes on a crescent shape. This is a waxing crescent; 'waxing' means increasing. At this point, the part of the moon that is illuminated is on the right side of its disc as seen from Earth.

Further along in its orbit, the crescent moon becomes a half moon. This is the first quarter moon, meaning the moon is now one quarter along in its 29 and a half day orbit. As the moon continues past that first quarter phase, it is called a waxing gibbous moon. Gibbous means humped or rounded.

Halfway through its orbit, the moon becomes a full moon, its entire sphere catching the light of the sun. A full moon always rises at sunset and sets at sunrise. A new moon is just the opposite, rising at sunrise and setting at sunset. Its form is made invisible by the strong light of day. You can't see the moon until it starts to become a crescent, and you can catch its form just before sunset. There is always something beautiful in the lit thin curve of the moon in the sunset sky. Though sometimes, even a good while before sunset, depending on the light, you can see a sort of "ghost moon" in the sky before sunset.

As the full moon continues on its orbit and goes past that point at which its sphere catches the full light of the sun, it goes through the waxing process in reverse. Less of its surface is illuminated. This is called the waning gibbous moon. Now the surface of the moon we see is on the left side of its sphere. This lessening of the lit surface reaches a point where we once again see half the moon's surface. Now the moon is in its second quarter. The waning gibbous and the second quarter moon are rising after sunset now, later and later into the night. Eventually the second quarter moon becomes once again a crescent, a waning crescent, mirror image to the waxing crescent, a waning crescent we see rising just before sunrise.

Li put down the book. It was interesting, even pleasing to read this step by step explanation of a continuing astral phenomenon that he thoroughly knew to the point of not thinking about it.

Then he wondered: at what point in the day of the far side was it in regard to his lunar travels? Eventually it would be lunar night for the far side. It seemed, as he recollected his adventures, the sun was always high in the sky. Or was he not paying attention? But this was something he would have noted as matter of habit. Since boyhood his attention to the night sky was a corollary to his habitual regard of the daylight sky and weather in general. Of course, his time on the lunar surface was not "real," so "they" could make it any time they wished.

Yet he had a feeling, just then, that lunar night would come. The terminator, that demarcation between night and day, would approach....

Li heard the door open. He watched Lin and Yang enter. For a moment they didn't seem real, these figures in their protective gear and masks. Li might have been having dream visions of the enigmatic lunar other.

And so he didn't say a word to them as they approached. Both gave a brief smile and nod, but they too were silent. They took his temperature. He submitted as if this was an expected part of life. And, indeed, it was.

He had no temperature. "I'm not sick now," Li said, more to break this by now unnatural silence.

Yang said, "You still can't leave for a few more days."

"How many days?"

Lin: "It's fourteen days; you know that."

"I mean how many days do I have left?"

Yang: "You mean you don't know?"

Li paused. At the moment he actually didn't know. Days and nights that weren't really days and nights—well, probably most of them were, but— He felt a tinge of fear. The reality or rather the surreality of his training had confused his time sense.

And then, before he realized he was thinking it, he said, "Who is giving these orders? You—or?"

Yang said, "What do you mean?"

"Are the two of you controlling my staying here, or—?"

Lin was angry. "Do you think we're playing a game with you?"

Li looked at the two men almost as if he hadn't really seen them before—seen what they actually were. There had always been a sense of the absurd about them, as well as an arrogance he had accepted but which he would not allow to threaten him. Yet now…. Then again, his mind, his time sense, for instance, had been, well, abused. Was he thinking clearly? There had risen in him such a strong intuition there was some sort of cruelty involved here. He had the visceral thought that it was Lin and Yang that really ran this whole training program he had been subjected to and this pose of being guards (for want of a better word) was a deception.

Li sighed and said, "How much of what happens to me do you control?"

Yang barked out a laugh. "Maybe we control that door. But you have your orders, we have ours."

"What are they, exactly, your orders?"

Yang frowned, shook his head, and looked at Lin, who shook his head in turn, as if both were communicating, *What can be done with such an attitude?*

Lin gave Li a friendly tap on the shoulder. "You'll be out soon. You can go home then. And your training, at least this phase of it, you're almost done with that, too."

"What's the next phase of my training?"

Yang: "We don't know that."

"Or you're not telling me."

Yang shook his head again. "You are getting some paranoia. That is worse than sickness."

"I am being kept in the dark."

"You train. You are in quarantine. That is very clear. That's not dark."

"Are a lot of people in quarantine in Wuhan?"

Lin said, "The whole city."

"I mean in quarantine from being sick."

"We don't know that number."

"But it's still bad here."

"Yang: "Bad enough. It's a new illness. We will all pass it soon."

"When do you think that will be?"

Yang had to laugh again. He said to Lin, "He wants definite answers from us."

Lin said to Yang, as if Li were not there, "I guess we are the only ones he sees, so…we are his connection to reality."

Li had to establish he was indeed there—here: "That might be a sad fact."

Yang said, "There are no answers now. We are all waiting. For things to clear."

Lin said, "You will be out before then and see for yourself."

Li smiled grimly. "So I guess I'm safer in here."

Yang gave Lin and knowing smile, as if to say, *Ah, he's got it now.* To Li he said, "Maybe that's your answer."

"But that's the last question—answer—I need."

Both Lin and Yang laughed in unison; perhaps they considered this meandering back and forth had reached a comedic conclusion.

Yang said, "Li, we have to go."

Li was a bit surprised. He could not remember either of them addressing him with his name. "Goodbye," he said, with a tone of mockery, looking after their departure, with an odd sort of realization gnawing at him, something he could not coalesce into words, much less understanding.

Trying to distract himself, Li returned to his reading.

A subheading of a chapter was titled "The Lunar Terminator."

The lunar terminator is that sunset/sunrise line that passes across the moon in its monthly orbit. It moves much more slowly than the terminator line of the Earth, which has a twenty-four hour day as opposed to the lunar twenty-nine day cycle. At the lunar equator, the terminator line moves at 15.4 kilometers per hour. Taking the moon's average distance from Earth, that translates to about 8 arc seconds an hour.

That speed is at the moon's equator with the terminator precisely on the lunar meridian at the quarter phrases. The farther one moves from the equator, the foreshortening causes by the sphere of the moon causes the speed of the terminator to decrease. For whatever latitude above or below the equator, multiply equatorial speed by the latitude's cosine.

At 45 degrees latitude, north or south, the terminator will move approximately 70 percent of its equatorial speed. From Earth we would see the terminator line move about six arc seconds per hour.

Why had he been thinking about the terminator before Lin and Yang had come in? Oh, yes: that soon he would be forced to meet that dividing line on an imminent lunar venture.

But that issue of time. The lunar day was fourteen days, exactly as long as his quarantine. But he had gone into quarantine after his virtual adventures on the moon had begun. And if he had a few days left in quarantine…the lunar day should be just about done. Of course, "they" would present to him whatever hour of day—or night—they wanted….

He was on the moon, walking toward the terminator, a darkness ahead of him that brought the horizon terribly close. He hesitated just before reaching this demarcation, which of course was not like an abrupt curtain, but a shading from light into dark, with the space in between an area of transition that both frightened him and drew him.

Well, no, he wasn't really frightened, just very wary of what this new venture had in store for him. He had been thinking about the terminator and now he was here. Were "they" tuned into his thoughts?

Or he was directing all this? But the miniature city, the markings, the abandoned city—he did not think of all that beforehand. And certainly the presence of the "other." All of that had sprung up before him as a surprise.

Unless my unconscious….

But that was as far as he would go in thinking about all this logically.

He did not want to go past that grey area into the darkness—so he began to walk along the terminator, with light on one side, darkness on the other, feeling one side of his body the heat of the sun and on the other the cold of the absence of the sun.

He imagined walking the whole length of the moon like this, a longitudinal journey in which he would seek—something. Yes, he had the sudden thought something was to be found.

He could not say how much time had passed before he saw the object up ahead: some sort of elliptical…craft.

A spaceship.

It was dark and dull, though one end gleamed a little being near the sun side of the terminator, while the other was almost vague, joining itself in the darkness that marked the line of the lunar night. It seemed to stretch across the area of the terminator, like an obstacle in his path. Or a gateway.

As when he had apprehended the abandoned city, Li felt no surprise. He felt curiosity, yes, but what he felt was actually more akin to duty. Here was another anomaly that was part of his training. He approached the ship and began to make his way around it, looking for an entrance.

He made is way once around the ship without finding one. He repeated his search, going more slowly this time, running his thickly gloved hands over the dull dark surface, but would he be able to discern some subtle crease that would mark an opening through the gloves?

He had almost completed this second circumnavigation when he did feel something. Then he lost it, found it again. He ran his hands along this line, a curving line, tracing an oblong that was surely a doorway.

But his touch revealed no way to open it. He pressed along the line; he pressed at various points within the area of the oblong. Nothing. Then he wondered if there was some sort of code, some sequence of touch he had to effect. Press here, then there, then elsewhere, etc. A certain order required. But that would be like guessing a sequence of numbers, the combination to a safe. There were too many possibilities.

He stood back. He told himself just to let his mind go, just to act, place his hands without thinking.

And so, of course, the opening gave way, splitting in half, each half disappearing inside the craft.

I am creating this.

Then he lost that thought too, and stepped inside.

If he had expected an airlock, as there should be in a spaceship, there was none. He did not think about how whatever air the occupants of this craft had breathed (yes, he thought in the past tense; this craft did not feel either functioning or occupied now) would be kept from flooding out of the ship.

He entered. The door closed behind him.

There was light for him to see, recessed points spaced regularly ahead of him, not bright lights, but soft and low; light just ahead of him as he moved and, just behind him, a low illumination that seemed to follow his progress, for as he moved into the depths of the ship he could see no light any distance behind him or ahead—as if all illumination were activated by sensors that needed the presence of a moving being.

He felt himself walking straight ahead for some time; felt himself going much farther than what the length of the ship had seemed when he had stood outside it, and circled it twice. He felt himself walking down a featureless corridor, with only dark walls and the lights that seemed to cocoon him.

He considered he was having a time displacement, that something in the design of the ship was disorientating him. Perhaps the lights had hypnotized him....

And then there was a doorway to his right side. He entered a room whose ceiling and far side was aglow with stars, a vivid projection of the heavens. And in the midst of the room was a sort of console with something like a panel of instrumentation.

So the ship was navigated with this projection of stars.

Too much like a movie, was Li's sudden thought.

And then he saw the back of a figure at the console.

Why his eyes hadn't fixed on that right away, he did not ask himself. The figure was bent over something on a panel. Perhaps Li had viewed the figure at first as part of the console—but he only considered that afterwards. All his attention was focused on the figure now turning to face him, a figure that had no spacesuit in this airless ship. –Or was it airless? A man in a metallic looking jumper that might have been worn under a suit. A Chinese man. *The other.*

Li actually took a step back. The other smiled, spoke. But Li heard nothing. So, there was indeed no air here. Or did his helmet just block it out? But if the ship were airless, how could this man—?

It was the other.

Li was not expecting this at all. And he was not expecting that the man's eyes still looked like a reptile's.

The other was reaching out to him, in a gesture an observer might think welcoming, meant to draw Li to him, but Li felt as if the other were about to devour him, that he was prey to—something. He stumbled back. The other then made a sharp gesture, in a very different manner, and the projection of stars in this control room changed. There was the sensation of speeding into some center, some point, some destination. Stars loomed more brightly, then fell away; stars that had not been visible appeared, brightened, then they fell away. It was as if Li, this room, this ship were travelling through the galaxy at an impossible speed. Li gripped his hands as if holding a railing, but his fists merely gripped themselves. The other was opening his mouth as if in a soundless laugh. His arms made quick movements. *He's orchestrating*, Li suddenly realized. Indeed, like a maestro wildly conducting a symphony that was a rampage of sound, the other's movements were faster and more violent, the man was wrapt in a frenzy of inexplicable purpose and the star scene speed across Li's vision more quickly, maniacally, and he felt he should hear a thundering in this plummet through space, as the reptile eyes of this other opened and closed and regarded Li as if he were not there.

Then it seemed there were no stars, the stars had been left behind, they had gone past the edge of the visible universe and the conducting arms of the other fell to his sides in sudden stillness and the reptile eyes closed and Li darted away, back into the corridor with the lights that followed him and he ran, in an awkward crazy way in the gravity of the moon, back to the entrance of the ship and though the end of the corridor showed no opening, and he could not see the outline of an opening and he felt genuine despair, then suddenly the opening was there, opened fully, and he thrust himself back out onto the moon. But while he'd been inside the terminator had moved appreciably, and the line of light was on the far horizon and Li bounded to it, through the lunar dark, feeling his suit heat up against the cold and then take a moment to reverse itself when he bounded into the light, that is, the grey area first, then into the light that the terminator had not yet claimed.

28.

Li traveled ahead quickly, preternaturally propelled by the vision of the other inside the ship and that light-speed journey through a universe that seemed to have exploded through his flesh. He did not look back at the ship. He did not want to still see it. He did not look back until he knew he would not be able to see it. When he did turn it was with literal relief: there was only moonscape. He was…safe? No, that was not it. But he did not seek words; he went on.

As he grew calmer and continued in the twilight of the terminator, he had the thought that if he stayed in this zone, he would actually not be making a straight passage but a curving one, as the zone of light moved across the moon with its rotation. He imagined watching himself from above, making this curved passage. For some reason that pleased him—as if, by keeping with the natural order of things, he was defying the rule of straight lines.

Then he laughed to himself. *The natural order of things. This is in my mind. All this*— He went on, simultaneously amused and focused.

Eventually his mind settled into a state of thoughtlessness—or, rather, thoughts fled from him as quickly as they emerged, they appeared to seek no hold on his consciousness (or if they sought it, could not succeed), and so, after they fled, left behind no memory. If we do not remember a thought, does it no longer exist? –As the things of the world exist?

Do thoughts, in fact, *exist*? They exist when we hold them, but when they are lost—?

He suddenly remembered something. As a teenager in school, during a science class where the teacher had been talking about the different states of matter, of energy, how they were in fact interchangeable and then had segued into saying that everything is energy, even the thoughts in your mind, that create electrochemical reactions in the brain.

A girl had questioned the teacher, "So if thoughts have energy, and energy is matter, are thoughts matter?"

The teacher, a pleasant, middleaged man, had been brought up short with that. With a laugh he'd said, "That's an unusual way to look at it. Perhaps they are."

That's what Li was thinking now. And thinking about how what was his in head was very real; after all, he was on the moon when in reality he was just in a room. But what was in his head was reality, too, was matter.

And if thoughts were matter, imagine how much matter each person had added to existence. Each person that has ever lived. And animals, too, their thoughts. Going back millions of years.

Perhaps the matter from thoughts was in fact the mysterious dark matter that astrophysics asserted was the most prevalent matter in the universe, more prevalent than visible matter.

Li had once had a discussion with Fan about whether animals think. Li had always felt there was certainly some level of thought to animals, but Fan, vegan Fan, had made a convincing argument that the thoughts of animals were as complex as those of humans, if perhaps in different ways. "You judge them on technology, but there is so much thought apart from that. You can't know the extent of their thoughts, just as they can't know the extent of yours. But our thought processes overlap, like Venn diagrams. We—the animals and ourselves—understand each other in those overlapping areas. Humans are so arrogant that they call so much of what animals do as coming from instinct, not thought."

Li had said, "Do insects think?"

"Why not? But insects and we have so little overlap—or none. They are so foreign to us. I wonder if they even comprehend us, sometimes."

"We comprehend them."

"That's true. But they must comprehend us. They avoid us—"

"Or bite us."

"I think what we should understand is that—just like when we say we are looking for 'intelligent life' in the universe: would we recognize it when we saw it? We are trying to look for beings like ourselves. They don't have to look like us, just do things like us."

"Technology."

"Yes. And maybe they'll have technology we can't recognize either. Do insects recognize our phones? Our internet? And do we recognize what they have? Never mind insects. We think we know birds, but do we know how birds migrate?"

"Something about the electromagnetic field of the Earth."

"There are some birds that have magnetite receptors above their nostrils, but with all the birds, science doesn't really know. There are theories they navigate by the sun and stars, recognize landmarks—that certainly takes memory and thought. Maybe with animals they have their technology more in their bodies. We have to put it outside ourselves."

"That was harder, but served us better in the long run."

Fan had had an odd look in her eyes. "How do we know what served us better until…some point in the future?"

"We don't have enough of the past to look back on?"

"Our judgements of ourselves always change."

Li's memory took itself from that tangent back to the concept of thoughts as matter. Thus, if life has increased the energy of the universe, life has increased matter. But was this not contrary to the idea of entropy—that all things in existence are in effect losing energy, winding down, so to speak?

And when we die, depart from this existence, do our thoughts, all that matter, stay here?

But *where* is that matter? We never speak most of our thoughts. So is that energy enfolded into us, departing with that matter?

But according to physics, energy can never be destroyed, only transformed.

Again, he mused on the dark matter of the universe. One theory was that dark matter formed a sort of scaffolding upon which visible matter became stars and galaxies. Li's mind went on like that, as he moved in the twilight of the terminator.

Up ahead were forms that did not seem natural to the landscape. Dark forms, darker than the landscape. As he neared, they seemed, yes, it was unmistakable, like huge, still beetles. His mind had once again been answered by the "reality" in which he moved. Of course, they really could not be giant insects, but as he neared them something on the surface—or just beneath the surface—of one of them moved; there was no doubt of it. And then one just beyond that raised what seemed like antennae….

Ridiculous: he had been recalling talking with Fan about insects, about them comprehending us, and now—

A basic tenet of horror films are giant insects: the small alien creatures that we can step on and swat now suddenly too huge for humans to stay any impulse of theirs to rend or devour us. Yet Li was not so much afraid as trying to assess this new, well, apparition, perhaps the least "realistic" thing he had come across in his training. Spaceships, abandoned cities, markings that seemed like writing, a model of a city, they could be indications that some creatures who were also space faring had been here before. Not so illogical. And even the other, the bureaucrat—but no, those reptile eyes—and now these giant insects.

I cannot be harmed. These are not real enough to—
But what was enough?

The giant beetles were in the zone of the terminator. And perhaps beyond it, too, he thought, but the dark on one side and the brightness on the other subsumed them—if they were there—in his vision.

He began to skirt the insect nearest to him. It seemed to be somewhat curled into itself. Then, as Li moved, it uncurled; a head, at least the front of its body, rose to the level of Li's head, a slit of a mouth, eyes that were as dark and as unpupiled as black knobs, and an array of feelers along the side of the face, feelers that moved in a purposeful undulation.

The slit of the mouth opened slightly. Li saw the serrations of something like teeth.

The creature moved slowly toward Li; Li moved quickly away. For an instant he turned his back on the thing, was about to take a huge bound, his legs bent, but even as he unleased the force of this push, he felt what he could only have described as a sloshing pressure beneath the ground of the moon. He felt an instant of horror—

And then awoke (it that was the word) back in the training room. He was standing right in the middle of the room. He looked at the banal walls, while the image of that creature's face stayed in memory.

The energy of thought? More matter he had created? Or someone had created.

Li sat down. He felt a strange longing to continue that journey along the terminator, as if it had had a necessary purpose that had been bizarrely interrupted by something his own memories had placed there. Memories twisted and enlarged, yes, but certainly his.

Should I be afraid of my own mind?

He considered that "they" were testing him to see if the solitude of the moon would make him crazy. Then again, the other, and all the rest—that had certainly not come out of his mind. –Though how could he be sure of that?

And all the thoughts he had thought through all of this: where was that energy, where was that *matter*?

He recalled something he had read when a student. After the first Apollo mission, an old American Indian was told about it and had responded in the vein of what was so special about going to the moon? "I've been there many times."

Li smiled wryly at that. Even if he did not actually go to the moon after all this training, he felt he had "been there."

He went through a night of odd dreams that flowed into one another; awake he could not unravel any thread of substance or succession. All that he was able to remember was that Fan had been in his dreaming— but in what way, he could in no way recall.

He realized that aside from his memory of the conversation he'd had with Fan about the thoughts of animals and insects, he had in fact not thought much of Fan lately. He considered that he was pressed so much in this surreal round of his training and he felt less connection to any prior reality.

Prior reality. Did that mean that his life before this, including Fan, was a reality to which he could not return?

Do I still love her? More importantly, he considered: *Did I ever really love her?*

He shook his head. *I will get out of this, get back to myself.*

But he felt he needed to "resolve" his present training. But what did he think he could resolve? The way things were going, his lunar journeys could be endless. He thought there had to be a limit to what they could subject him to— *But everything has to end.*

Well, it hadn't ended yet. He was soon back on the moon, walking along the terminator, once more in the borderland of lunar day and night. He actually felt pleased to be travelling along the terminator again; at the same time, he wondered if this would prove to be a trek without—without what? He couldn't say.

At one point he came to the outside wall of a crater; the wall was about a meter taller than Li. From the corner of his eyes, he noted something nearby in the wall. He discovered it was an opening. Not some natural, irregular opening, caused by eon-old disruptions or even weather, but so regular it had to be artificial.

Li accepted this as another test. He entered.

The opening became a corridor with curved walls and an arched ceiling. He moved ahead with the light from his helmet. He moved slowly, examining the walls as he continued on. He was not sure if he expected some marking, some hieroglyphic, but there was nothing.

At one point he stopped. He was not sure how far he had walked; he was not sure how long he had been in this tunnel. It had to end at some point—or maybe it just went on, tunnelling through the surface of the moon. Li had a vision of some subterranean—no, sublunar—terminator, going on and on. He asked himself what it could be terminating, what it could be dividing.

The tunnel had seemed straight, though Li knew its direction could be gently curving and he would not be able to discern that. Though almost immediately upon that thought he came to a definite turn in the tunnel. He was both intrigued and more than a little wary at this change of direction. He took that turn and began to see that the texture of the walls became somewhat different, rougher, it seemed, as if up to the point that interior of the tunnel had been well worked, smoother, but this new section had been left in a less finished state. Though once more he found nothing unusual on the walls.

Then the tunnel came to a fork: two tunnels branched off at 45-degree angles (very precise 45 degree angles, it seemed). Li stopped. He walked down one tunnel a bit, came back, walked down the other, came back. The walls of these tunnels were even more rough, as if they had just been hollowed out without any subsequent smoothing.

Li stood before this sublunar fork, weighing a choice. He decided he would walk down the length of one tunnel up to the count of five hundred, then come back and do the same with the other.

He chose the tunnel on his left. He counted to one hundred, two hundred, and on; well past four hundred he was again presented with another forking of tunnels. He repeated the process of walking each tunnel a bit, then returning to the fork. The walls here were even rougher.

He chose the tunnel on the left again. His reasoning was that he would not be confused in returning if he always chose the same direction. —As if he intuited he would come to further forks?

He did; the situation repeated itself again. And again. Li only briefly paused before continuing on. While he seemed to be going deeper into a maze, he held in himself the thought, the reality, that he was in the training room. *I could be swallowed in a black hole and still be back in that room.* But the surreality he moved in was so real he did not feel a complete confidence in that "reality." And the walls of subsequent tunnels became more and more rough, giving the effect not of artificial passages but natural caverns, added to the "reality" to which he was being subject. Sometimes the walls bulged out, so that he had to angle himself around it; here and there the ceiling was actually, and unevenly, lower than his height; he had to stoop to continue. Until ultimately he came to a forking at which both of the passages presented to him appeared a jumble of rocks and small boulders with a ceiling so low he knew he would have to crawl. He decided he would crawl as far as he could, then finally turn back. He did not have the concrete thought that he was supposed to find something at the end of all this, but in retrospect he saw it was exactly that that was driving him to continue. —While he also realized that he was probably descending in the course of his passage, not travelling in a parallel line to the surface.

Making his way, with difficulty now, through this tunnel, he laughed at himself as he was once more counting. He had stopped doing that a tunnel or so back. He reached five hundred. He stopped. Go back?

Across that rubble, again? But to travel on, over and through more of this debris—

The passage opened up, abruptly—so suddenly, so widely, Li almost felt as if he were falling forward. Cautiously he stood up, stiffly. There seemed less debris ahead. Just ahead the passage turned a bit, and when Li made that turn—

What was before him now was not only less debris but a stunning sight: crystals hanging from the ceiling and walls. White crystals with a faint play of prismatic colors as he moved his helmet's light about. He approached the nearest of these stalactites and stalagmites and suddenly realized: frozen water. Ice. He had read so much speculation about pockets of frozen water on the moon, perhaps in the shadows of crater walls, places that were always shadowed, water frozen for millions and millions of years; and, of course, water below the lunar surface. Astounded, even enchanted, Li moved amidst this underground cavern of eon-old ice like a man discovering an astounding remnant of the past, something so old that the present might look upon as legend more than anything else. He touched these descending and ascending pinnacles of ice, and in fact broke off a thin tip of one, held its almost eternal coldness in the glove of his space suit, walking on with it, as if he had taken a talisman that would protect him as he further journeyed.

The stalactites and stalagmites thinned out. He came upon a frozen lake.

He stood at the edge of the lake. It was vast. Scanning his light across its surface, he could not see its apparently far perimeter. He stepped onto the lake, a few steps, cautious. But ice could not break here, in this eternal underground cold. If it was a meter deep or a hundred, it was solid. He walked out onto the frozen surface, walked out farther, until he stood at a point at which he could not see the point of his departure.

I could be utterly lost here, forever.

He felt at some encompassing End of the universe, some point at which all of Existence had been stilled, and he was entombed within it.

But the room, the training room awaited. In fact, he was in the room right now. Or was he really? There were always two parts to his mind now: accepting the realness of what he moved through, and knowing it was not real.

He turned to go back. Or was he returning the way he had come? He really was not sure. There was so much sameness of ice. And yet he would reach some shore, find some tunnel, he was certain.

He did. He went through the hanging pinnacles and ascending pinnacles of ice, back through the tunnels of debris, the tunnel where he had to crawl, the tunnels of lesser debris—and yet the turns he made, as he made sure he was reversing his previous passage...something nagged at him. Some interior sense of cardinal points nagged at him. He was annoyed at himself that he had not counted the turns. Eventually he felt he should have been at that first, long ago fork; he stopped. But to go back, as if trying to correct his passage: that would confuse him further. He continued onward; he could continue onward endlessly—while he knew that all these adventures did end. Again, there was simultaneously assurance and disbelief in that.

No, he was certainly returning a different way. A tunnel, a corridor opened up—too wide, too wide. And as he moved within it, it grew wider. And as it grew wider it took on the aspect of the terminator on the surface: one side was dark, one side was light. Where this light came from, here under the ground, was inexplicable. The helmet's light swung over, into and through the darkness, seeing no far wall, and when he looked into the lighted side, he saw no wall there either. He walked within this division line of light and dark, and he felt, as he had on the surface, half in cold, half in heat—and the shard of ice he realized he had been holding all along, was melting. He moved more fully into the light, and held it out, and watched it melt completely: million year old—billion year old—water gone in the furnace of the sublunar day.

He walked on and walked on (or in this light gravity, hopped), a creature of lunar night and day until even in the moon's low gravity he grew tired. At one point he stood there, thinking, *How long is this session?* Then continued onward.

Could—would—they just leave him in this confusing passage until frustration gave way to madness?

But as if these thoughts cued him back to the reality of the room, he had been returned to it again, standing in four walls in a country called China, on the outskirts of the plague-ridden city of Wuhan.

Li slowly turned about, taking in the entire room. –As if he were revealing it to himself by the light on his space helmet. Of course, he was not in his spacesuit now. He wore a sweatshirt and sweatpants. He looked at the door, which was locked against him, and thought that soon he would be allowed to leave. At least that was what he had been told.

But have I finished what I needed to do—there?

He seemed to go through the next hours with no memory of what he was doing. He had no desire, at least at the moment, to read anything more about the moon. He was saturated with the moon. He slept, eventually, and dreamt, dreamt not surprisingly of the cavern of frozen water, the underground lake. He walked on it, and it gave way. Not to any flowing water underneath, but as it the lake were a thin glass-like surface that his weight had broken through. He lay there, his back on some cold ground, in these shards of lunar ice, moving his arms slowly, imagining he heard the tinkling of all this broken ice, but there was just silence. He continued to just lie there, thinking, for some reason, he needed to be discovered. As if now, he required a witness. But didn't "they" always know all details of his passage? Wasn't he always being watched? Even if usually he would forget all those constant eyes.

He brought himself back to wakefulness in the room, sat up on his cot, looked at the dark walls. It seemed he was looking to the nearness or distance of walls so much lately. He looked at the small points of differently colored lights of the electrical equipment in the room, the forever turned on machines that were all around us in the 21st century. Human beings so rarely know true darkness anymore. Li thought of the darkness of the dark side of the terminator.

If it's too dark, we cannot see. If too much light, we are blinded.

This was hardly profound, it was even cliché, but at that moment Li held on to it as if it were a revelation.

And then thought: *Did I conquer the terminator, or did it conquer me?*

Why was he thinking about conquering? But wasn't all exploration about conquering? At least that was how it had been for so much of history. To "conquer the unknown." To make it ours. Not to just go and see—to understand the unknown (even if not to understand it).

We call it space exploration, but is that really what it is?

China wanted to get to the moon the Americans had abandoned, which the Russians had become indifferent to after they had been beaten by the Americans. China had chosen the far side of the moon (Chang'e's realm?) because America had not been there.

But did China know of the abandoned city, the markings that seemed like some record left? Had Li been tasked to "know" this?

It must be a test to see how he would react if these things were real, Li thought—and yet perhaps what he had discovered (in that reality) were things the Chinese space program did not know. *The program had needed Li's imagination to find all this.*

Though he could not believe that all that surrealness had come out of his mind. Li had always had the desire and imagination to go into space, but he had never really imagined discovering things that seemed more science fiction than science. He would have described himself a levelheaded explorer. So why would his mind project such science fictional artifacts and events on the moon?

Is the moon even more in my psyche than the rest of the human race? He smiled and spoke Chang'e's name aloud. He thought of werewolves and the moon being an alien spaceship. Had he imagined greater things?

He returned to sleep. Fan was in a brief dream, telling him, "You have old depths, like that ice you found on the moon." He told her the ice had just been a thin sheet, something you easily fall through, then he corrected himself, told her that had just been in his dream, and the "real ice" on the moon was of an unfathomable depth.

Chapter Twelve: Demolition

29.

Fan was working on the specifics for her nanomask.

The fibers of combined virus S proteins and recycled nanoplastic would be around 70-80 nanometers thick. The standard N95 masks, the common gold standard for medical grade masks, can filter 99.8 percent of particles 100 nanometers in size. The most recent findings showed that the diameter of this new, round shaped coronavirus ranged from 60-140 nanometers. If virus particles are on the larger end, the N95 masks are effective, if less, perhaps less effective. But respiratory droplets, that were the main transmission route of the new virus, are measured in scales much larger than nanometers: micrometers (millionths of a meter as opposed to billionths); these droplets are usually 5-10 micrometers in size, so an N95 mask is extremely effective against such sizes.

The situation of droplet transmission and aerosol transmission was serious. Droplets are produced by talking, coughing and sneezing. One minute of loud speaking could send out thousands of oral droplets a second, with at least a thousand virus-containing droplets that could remain in the air for eight minutes. While speaking is more common that coughing and sneezing, these latter two methods result in greater possibility of transmission. A cough might send out 3,000 droplets, while a sneeze produces 40,000. And the droplets from a sneeze could actually travel seven to eight meters!

Not all droplets contain virus, but the large number of droplets from someone infected guarantee that any person exposed to such a discharge has a good chance of breathing in virus—unless that person has a mask.

So loud talkers, those coughing or sneezing, were to be avoided. And singers, too. Just before the lockdown, after a group of twenty-five college students rehearsed for a performance, more than half came down with the virus.

Fan was just coming to realize that toilets can also be a serious mode of transmission. Flushing a toilet with a viral fecal load can cause half the viral particles in the feces to rise above the toilet seat. Fan had just read an interior memo that traces of the virus had been found in mobile toilet rooms for patients—as well as medical staff areas, such as PPE removal rooms. Peak concentration of the virus in droplets of .25-e micrometer and 2.5 micrometer can remain airborne for some time, as can virus particles that settle on surfaces but become airborne again in the drafts of nearby movement.

There were cases where the virus had survived in the air for three hours. And even more disturbing: virus samples were found on surfaces in the bathroom of an apartment that had not been occupied for some time but was above an apartment of five infected people. Not only that, aerosols could also ascend not just to the floor above. Recent experiments to that effect found that flushing the toilet in a 16th floor restroom resulted in aerosols being found in the bathrooms of the 25th and 27th floors.

All this could only give Fan the impression—the reality—that the virus was permeating every aspect of the air in which she moved. She thought, *If this were ebola, we'd all be dead.* The indications were that if this new virus were indeed serious, it could not be as deadly as ebola, or the Marburg virus—but then, it was so new. *Will it become worse than it is now?*

Recently she had harbored the unpleasant notion that her work, creating her nanomask, might just be a novelty, but in reviewing all these circumstances regarding how easily the virus can be transmitted, she thought otherwise.

Apparently there were others who thought it was of worth.

Just before Fan was to come out of her nanoworld and break for lunch, she had a visitor. She was very surprised to see Cheng's driver, Junjie at her office door. Her first thought was that he had a message from Cheng. But that did not seem logical. Cheng would have called or texted her. So immediately she felt somewhat uneasy. Her brief prior contact with Junjie had left her with the sense that this was a young man on the make, someone who was more clever than skilled. She had asked Cheng how Junjie had achieved the position of being chauffeur for scientists at the lab. Cheng had shrugged, said he hadn't even thought to ask.

"So he's just there, for your use?"

Cheng had given her a friendly smile, but perhaps he had been a little offended. "He was assigned to me. Anyway, it seems he has other, well, pursuits." He had told Fan about the driver's seed dealings.

That had seemed very odd to Fan. Never mind Junjie; what was the government up to?

Today the young man was both polite and deferential. "I am sorry if I'm disturbing your work."

"No, I was just going to go to lunch."

"I don't want to stop you from that. Do you have a few minutes to talk?"

"What about?"

"Cheng told me about your work."

"Really." Why this bothered Fan she could not say.

"That can be a very profitable financial…product." He quickly added: "Because it is so needed now."

"I think it is needed, but—"

"I have certain connections…that could market this very well."

"And how do you have connections?"

He spread his hands out, a gesture that seemed shy, self effacing—and at the same time indicated he had to be humble before his extensive talents. For a moment Fan looked at Junjie without saying anything.

She had become so used to (in such a short time!) seeing everyone with a mask, she only just realized she had never seen this man without a mask. From the half of his face visible she could see he did seem handsome; but those dark, assessing, complacent eyes: yes, more clever than intelligent. She looked into them for some "explanation" that he would surely not voice.

What he did say was, "Working for the government, in various positions—"

"So you work for the government, not the lab."

"The lab is the government."

She considered that. She did not want to go through some either/or, this-or-that query. "Tell me your connections." And then instantly added, as if she did not want to hear what she intuited what would be dubious. "This would have to be tested. You could not just take it and—" She shook her head. "I have made minute—and I mean minute—samples. One whole mask does not yet exist."

"If you have established the process...and you have, right?"

"So far. The process, if that's the word you want to use, may need to be changed."

"Of course. There is always...adjustment."

She did not like that word. It intimated a change of expediency, not necessarily change for the better. "What do you get out of this?"

"Of course, a certain...fee." He had searched for that last word; it was plain he did not like it himself.

"A one-time fee or a percentage?"

"That would have to be worked out. I would prefer...a small first time fee for putting it together, then a small residual.... Of course you would be the one who would benefit the most."

"Do you have something concrete to offer me, or is this just to see if I'm interested?"

Junjie leaned toward her slightly. "I have to start to see if there is interest—in any proposal."

Involuntarily Fan leaned back a little, as if in instinctual reaction. The way he said "interest" and "proposal" gave Fan the feeling he was trying to seduce her. She said, "Did you tell Cheng you were going to ask me this?"

He gave a muffled laugh. "When he mentioned your work—he admires your intelligence, it's so obvious—I didn't think at the time of the...possibilities. Afterward, hearing all this talk about how serious this can still get, that it's starting to appear in other countries—"

"A few cases."

"There were just a few cases here—once. Just weeks ago."

Fan knew she had said that to keep him at bay. It was a useless move. She knew the virus was not going to stay in Wuhan, in Hubei. Thinking she was going to be as clever as he was, that she would appear to be playing his game, she said, "So when your connections connect to my work, do I deal with you, or them. Or both?"

"There is nothing definite yet."

"That is the feeling I have. I think you are just looking around for ways to make money."

"That what is people in business do."

"What exactly is your business? Driver, seed seller? What is the purpose of those seeds?

He did not seem surprised she knew about the seeds. He shrugged. "I am really just a middleman with that."

"It sounds ominous."

"Seeds? Ominous. That grow plants? How could that be?"

"Why to people in America? To plant something that will ruin American crops?"

"Not at all. Certain companies want to expand, reach markets. Reach American markets."

"I thought these came from the government."

"Companies and our government—work hand in hand. Each is interested in the success of the other."

"And you are interested in money."

"You say it as if I should be ashamed." He said like a challenge (with hints of more than a business seduction). Up to that moment he had fended her reactions with the practiced pleasantries of a salesman. Now he was feeling familiar enough to accuse her.

"I'm feeling something not quite right about this." She was also adding in her mind: "About you."

He spread his hands again in the self effacing way in which he had begun his "proposal." But now that gesture was less of humility and more communicated a success of character he believed no one could deny.

Fan gave a long sigh. "I said: my work isn't even in the middle of where I want it to go. And I have to go to lunch now. If I want to talk more about this—I'll tell Cheng." She rose; it was a plain sign of dismissal.

He stepped back, accepting that dismissal, voluntary or not—at least for now. But he had to give some parting words. "I hear you love America."

"I 'love America'? Where did you get that?"

"Cheng told me you know everything about America."

Fan was annoyed that Cheng had talked too much about her. "He probably said I know a lot *about* America."

"And they say to know is to love."

"To know could also be to hate." She gave him a look he could not misinterpret.

He did not seem to acknowledge her reaction. "But you and America—it's not hate."

"Where are you going with this?"

"I am just commenting on your wide knowledge. It is good to know about America: our economic...I won't say adversary, I'll say competitor. Your knowledge would serve well in the marketing. I have no great knowledge about American business."

She was abrupt. "I can't talk about this anymore now."

"I am very pleased you gave me the time."

She began to move past him, but then did not want to leave him in her office. He understood. He bowed to her, very, very slightly, as if mocking a courtesy. "I am glad I could talk with you. I will tell you soon something more—concrete."

"Take your time about that. I'm still working on what you call a product."

He nodded. He left. Fan gave a long sigh. She did not like her work, her innovative efforts, which were meant to help keep people safe from disease, described as a "product."

And why would Cheng talk so much about her to this—this opportunist? Looked at one way, it seemed that Cheng was boasting about the accomplishments of a good friend; looked at it another way it could appear that Cheng was pushing Junjie's opportunism from himself to Fan.

Who thought: what could Junjie get from Cheng? –Other than a resume point that he was the trusted driver for one of the premier virologists in China? But trusted? No, no one should trust that young man.

Fan saw Wong Bai in the cafeteria. She had just sat down; he had just entered. Fan had been curious to talk to him again, but after the uncomfortable conversation with Junjie, she was not in the mood to talk to anyone. She sighed with resignation as Wong came toward her. Once again, he seemed agitated and worried. She wondered if this was not his usual state.

He asked if he could sit with her. She nodded and smiled. Wong was too wrapt in whatever was bothering him to realize the smile was feigned. Fan expected nothing less. But quickly she was drawn in by what he said—in a broken torrent, while giving glances to either side of him and more than once turning around, as if expecting someone he didn't want near him to come upon him at any moment.

"Twice today they questioned me. I had to show them around—to every corner of the lab, practically."

"Who was it?"

"Two men. I don't think they even told me their names. But you just knew they were—you had to do what they wanted. No one came to you?"

"No. Not today, anyway." Then Fan thought of Junjie and wondered if these men who had beset Wong were connected to the driver—or rather Junjie had been emboldened by some link to them to offer his "proposal" to Fan. She said nothing to this to Wong, who went on:

"It was as if they were looking for a crack in some corner for a virus to escape. I told them again—I've told everyone—about the air pressure: lower inside than out, so that any air from the lab gets pushed back in by the air outside. They gave me looks like they didn't believe me. But they have to know that. They couldn't be coming here ignorant of—of the...." He pressed fingers to his head; he could not think of a word for a moment. Then he added: "How things are arranged here. Set up. Then they asked for records of all visitors, nonlab workers going back six months. I had to personally print that out for them. And three times I had to go to others in my department, with the two of them at my back, and ask questions they prompted me with—as if they didn't want to ask the questions themselves; or to see how I acted asking the questions. It felt to me as if they were trying to make me...break down, admit some guilt. Why should I be the target? I don't do research. I oversee—" He shook his head, he frowned. That's exactly what one of them said: 'You oversee security.' I told them this was beyond security.

I guess it didn't make sense to say that. But I was…reacting. Wouldn't you?"

His rush of words had stopped so abruptly that there was a pause before Fan responded. "I don't know what I'd say. Some men did talk to me—today and days ago, too. They seem to think I'm…safe. Not that I trust how whatever I say might be interpreted. The government wants to find something."

Wong pounced on that as if Fan's obvious observation was brilliant, and evidence of solidarity. "Something, they want something and I'm the target."

Fan did not want to encourage Wong's paranoia, however it might be justified. She said, "So there are no cracks in the wall. Everything you showed them was fine."

He looked at her cautiously. "How do you know that?"

"I guess I am assuming. Was everything…in order?"

"It was. The way I saw it, anyway. Who knows what they saw?"

"But they didn't say—"

"They don't tell you when—they don't tell you you're guilty at first."

"Do you *feel* guilty?"

"I almost do. I almost do. I'm supposed to oversee—as they said—and maybe I did let something—without knowing it—get out."

"I'm sure it didn't happen that way. If something did get out it wasn't through you, because of you."

"How could you be sure?"

"You want me to tell you you're guilty?"

"Of course not. I want something…logical to assure me."

"Maybe I can't give you that. Maybe it's just…intuition. Or the experience of having worked here long enough."

"But you're in your one section of things. It wouldn't be your fault if you didn't realize things that were happening in other places here."

"And you feel you should be the eye that takes it all in."

"It's my job. That's why they are looking at me."

"You are going in a circle with this. They found nothing. You do know that."

He leaned back, put his hands together in worry. "That's what it seems. That's what it seems to me."

The two of them looked at each other for a few seconds without talking. Then Fan said, "Are you going to eat?"

"I think I'm too…I don't know."

"Well, you came in here, so you must have hungry."

"Actually, I came in here…looking for you."

"Me?"

"Yes. I thought you might be here now. I can talk to you."

This assessment (and, perhaps, a newly grasped obsession?) concerned Fan. "Do you have anyone you are close to here?"

"Not really. That I can trust."

"But you trust me."

"Yes."

"Why?"

He smiled and gave an uncomfortable laugh. "Intuition."

"I'm…I'm flattered. But maybe you have the wrong intuition about you possibly doing something wrong."

"It's the way they treat me. That's where it comes from."

There was something universal and pathetic about Wong's obvious emotional suffering. He was an individual whose neuroses equaled his intelligence, making him at once insular and vulnerable. He would give everything to his duties and yet expected to be found wanting. It was an insecurity that made him withdraw from both friendships and success. And Fan concluded that the only reasons he "trusted: her was because she was attractive and so he had been drawn to her and because she had listened. Or the other way around: she had listened, and Wong had clung to the boon of having an attractive woman pay attention to what he had to say.

At any rate, all this time Fan had eaten nothing. She said to Wong, "I've to eat and get back. Why don't you—?"

"No, no. I've got to get back now. Or they'll think I'm not...paying attention."

"It's obvious that you are. You've got to be calm. Don't let them...whatever they are doing, you know what you did, what you do."

"I hope so." He suddenly got up. "Can I talk to you again?"

"I'm sure you will."

Wong left in a rush. Fan watched him exit, thinking on the two conversations she had today. There was just madness about everything now. It was obvious the government really believed it was likely this virus had gotten out from the lab. Even if they sacrificed someone like Wong on the altar of that possibility it would be unlikely to further anyone's understanding of the virus or any method of fighting it. More pertinent than it having gotten out of the lab was: What was the nature of it, created or natural? A key was needed, to unravel its replication.

30.

Cheng told Junjie he had to pay his respects to the mother of Dr. Sun. Junjie nodded and said softly (as if with humble approval), "Of course. That's necessary." Cheng gave him a curious look—which the driver either did not catch or ignored. Junjie's pronouncement of "necessary" seemed odd. It was as if his approval was required.

Cheng gave him the address; Junjie put it in his phone. It would be about a half hour's drive. The driver made no mention of his earlier conversation with Po Fan. And of course, Cheng made no mention of a flash drive.

The home of Dr. Sun's mother, Biyu, was on the periphery of Wuhan, where suburbs began in an area that was still considered the city. The makeup of the neighborhood must be mostly professional, Cheng considered, by the aspect of the homes here. There were a lot of trees, both along the streets and in yards. Looking at all these bare branches on this drab midwinter day, Cheng tried to visualize how beautiful this must all look in spring—which was really not all that far away. A few months, and there would be so much green.... Cheng thought about the Spring Festival that the lockdown had felled: like the spring semester in American universities that began in midwinter, the festival was but a herald of a time to come that had not yet arrived.

As for any thoughts of time: if the calendar recorded passing days, there was yet the sense that time was suspended; this virus had put the world, at least the world of Hubei, in a realm stayed by menace. Cheng could not imagine spring coming and the lockdown still being in place, everyone walking around with masks. Or, rather, he could not imagine the virus *allowing* spring to come. Of course, this was irrational. It was only because the epidemic had begun in winter that Cheng held it in his mind the virus was connected to a season—

Junjie pulled up to the house. Cheng said, "I might be a little while," adding, "I will try to not make it long." (Again, as if bowing to Junjie?)

The driver shrugged. "As long as you need." Junjie seemed to have an abstracted look, as if he was thinking about something and was more than satisfied to be left with those thoughts. Cheng had considered he should ask Junjie to come inside with him; after all, to leave him waiting in a cold car.... But it really was not that cold outside, and Junjie could idle the car and turn on the heat when needed. And Cheng wanted to be in the house alone with the mother of the Dr. Sun.

Have I accepted his death yet? Cheng wondered. He decided that whether he had or hadn't, he was, with this visit, acting as if he did. Thoughts may push to us toward this reality or that, but it is our acts that create the reality in which we live.

Cheng closed the car door behind him with so many thoughts running through him. He was a little afraid of what might be on that flash drive—as much as he was eager to receive its contents. He felt his hands trembling. He looked down. No, he seemed steady.

In the car, Junjie was already at his phone. *More seeds?* thought Cheng. The government is involved in some very odd things, and Cheng did not like the fact that his driver was connected to one of these odd ventures.

Sun Biyu was a slim woman with silver streaks in her pinned back hair. She wore a dark outfit with a dark green pattern of fronds. She greeted the masked Cheng without a mask. With delicate features, she must have looked almost ethereal when young. How is it, thought Cheng, that the young, with so many years ahead, can look the most joined to the unearthly, so much more than the old, who are actually nearest to unearthly departure? This was the first time Cheng had that realization, one that would later revisit him throughout life.

As he stepped inside, Biyu said, "You can take off your mask if you want."

"I've been around so many people; it's better I keep it on."

Both Cheng and Biyu might have considered that "so many people" included those dying from the virus in the hospital; though if so, it was a thought well under the surface of things. And at least for the moment Cheng felt more…protected (but from what?) with the occlusion of the mask.

With genuine thanks, Biyu said how much she appreciated Cheng's "intervention at the hospital for my son." Cheng accepted this uncomfortably. He felt his "intervention" had done nothing to save Sun Bao.

All he could say was, "It was so unfortunate, this virus—"

Abruptly Biyu was more angry than sad. "It didn't have to be like this. He might have been alive! If they had admitted—what was there!" Her voice was explosive, and seemed especially jarring, sounding out from the quiet nature she had projected. She suddenly caught herself. She looked back at Cheng with resignation, but still also with anger.

As if to distract herself from her feelings, she insisted they have tea. For some reason, Cheng actually felt uncomfortable at this…diversion. As if this were delaying the business at hand. But of course, he accepted and soon they sat across from each other, with a thin, polished wooden table between them. In one corner of the table was a small planter with tiny succulents. The plants were rich and green with minute needles. Cheng thought of the protein spikes of the virus.

Cheng didn't know what to say for a moment. He had taken off his mask to sip the tea. Now he felt it right that he should show her his face. "He was heroic. He let everyone…know."

With a face of stone she looked at Cheng. "Did they kill him? Or the virus? Or did they give the virus to him?"

Cheng had more than lightly considered that last possibility. But of course he did not want to add his doubts to hers. Torture enough to lose a son that should have had decades more of life. He recalled—with some inner chiding—how he had wondered if Dr. Sun X were gay.

Biyu's next remark seemed keyed into Cheng's thoughts. "I wasn't sure…how long you knew—" Or did she mean: "How *well* you knew—"?

"We, because of our fields—I'm a virologist—"

"He told me."

"Our paths crossed a few times, over the years. And then with this…." Cheng spread his arms in the gesture that said there was nothing further to say.

"So you really didn't know him that well?"

It was a question that might have levels of meaning, even if only unconsciously directed. Whether she just wanted that to be a question or a statement that could have no adequate response, she went on, as if abruptly concluding the question was of little importance:

"He said you should be the one to have this—" She drew something from her clothing and displayed it briefly on her palm. The dark slim rectangle of the flash drive was like some abstract sculpture on the delicate whiteness of her inner hand.

She put the flash drive down on the table near him and the teacup. Cheng wanted to plug that into a computer right away and pour through its secrets, but he said, with almost casual control, "Do you know what is on this? Any of it?"

"He told me it's the true nature of the virus—that's all."

Cheng let the hot tea go down his throat, then said, "The true nature being—?"

"It's manmade."

It appeared that Cheng absorbed this without surprise. He said, in an almost matter of fact manner, "Have you looked at it?"

"I went through it—quickly. Most of it…you'd understand a thousand times more than me."

Cheng picked up the flash drive. Its lightness belied what it might reveal. As if to divert his mind from what could be momentous information, he thought (as he often did) how amazing it was that so much information could be stored in such small objects. But then, as a virologist, he was inclined to such considerations. The existence of a virus, slipping in between the crests of wavelengths of light, this minute "thing" on the borderline of life and nonlife, enravelled so much information that could affect beings so much larger than itself.

Biyu seemed to study the way Cheng grasped and held the flash drive—as if to assure herself he was handling it with proper importance. Cheng said, "Thank you. I will study this closely." Though as soon as he spoke, he thought he sounded too formal.

Biyu reached out and clasped his hand, closing it over the flash drive. "Be careful with it. Bao was worried that…the government doesn't want—"

"You have a copy of this?"

"No."

"I should leave you with a copy."

"No. It's better nothing like that is here."

Cheng understood. "I will make a copy. There should be more than one." *In case something happens to me?* he thought.

At the door Cheng thanked her for the flash drive.

"I thank you. Be careful."

Once more in the grey light outside, Cheng put his mask back on as returned to the car. It was idling now; Junjie had needed the heat. His mask hung from one ear, dangling along the side of his face as he looked down at his phone. It was the first time Cheng had actually seen the young driver without a mask. He was indeed handsome. As Junjie turned to him with an absent smile, he slipped the mask back on. Cheng had the feeling that the mask had afforded Junjie the ready opportunity to hide something of himself that he needed others not to see. Yet this seemed an irrational assessment. Why would a handsome young man want to hide his face? It would be an asset to have others fully see him.

"That wasn't too long," Junjie said.

"I guess not." But in that moment Cheng could not assess time. As they drove back to the lab he touched again and again the flash drive in his pocket, his hand probing under his coat as if seeking something troubling in his body.

The only thing Junjie said during the drive was shortly after they had pulled away from the house. "How is she?"

"How can I answer that?" said Cheng, looking ahead at the road.

Junjie gave him a sideway look; why was Cheng being obtuse about a casual—polite—question? In a moment Cheng added: "Just absorbing it, for now. I don't know what else to say." Junjie raised his eyebrows, nodded, and was silent the rest of the way back, as was Cheng, who took in the empty streets and houses of Wuhan. *We did this to ourselves?*

Pulling up to the lab, Cheng said, "I've got to get back to work."

"I will see you later—whatever time you need."

As Cheng left the car he wondered, if only briefly, what Junjie did with most of his day. He had the feeling there was more to this apparently hustling young man than sending mysterious government seeds to America.

There was one file on the flash drive. Before he even printed it out, Cheng made a copy of it on his desktop, then copied that to another flash drive. Then he printed out the one document on the drive, and erased the document on his desktop. He had the feeling that would be the prudent thing to do.

He read: "As many have begun to suspect, there is too much evidence that this new virus has been created and or modified in a laboratory. The following is gathered from my own observations and research as well as that of others—whom I will not name now; that will be safer for these colleagues. I will relate number of a factors—facts— that may not have been fully explored, but certainly indicate there is a great deal that defies the official explanation for this virus, which has characteristics that a virus from a zoonotic source lack. Rather the virus has all the characteristics—at least many characteristics—of being from gain of function research.

"Gain of function research has been undertaken widely in our country in the past generation, with the ostensible aim of understanding how particular viruses evolve and so may become more pathogenic and transmissible. 'Gain of function' means exactly that: the virus gains further functionality to be more virulent and transmissible. More often than not mutations decrease the effectiveness of both viruses and more fully biological organisms. Gain of function is meant to increase the potency of viruses *in the lab* with the ideal being thus we can study how to combat possible pandemics.

"Whether this new virus becomes a pandemic remains to be seen. It is my opinion this could come to pass; certainly, it is new enough and transmissible enough to be worried about.

"Even at first glance this virus differs from SARS—which it seems immediately related to by the fact that it is being shown that the virus is more than a respiratory virus: it attacks other organs in the body. What organs, and to what extent, the future—the immediate future will show.

"It is generally assumed that this is a coronavirus from a bat. It appears very similar to a bat coronavirus discovered—produced?—by the Third Military Medical University in Chongqing. The receptor binding motif (RBM) of the virus' spike protein resembles that of the SARS protein of 2003, but in a manner that indicates the RBM was artificially altered.

"The new virus has a unique furin-cleaving properties, an unusual furin-cleaving site, in the Spike protein. The furin gene breaks apart proteins. The new virus had a greater ability to infect cells. *The site this virus has is entirely lacking in all coronaviruses we find in nature.*

"It appears more than speculation that a bat virus had been used as a template for this new coronavirus. Bat coronaviruses ZC45 and ZXC21, discovered and isolated 2015-2017 by military research laboratories (research published 2018) appear to have supplied the template for this new virus.

"The virus' Spike protein is composed of two halves: S1 binds to the host's receptors, in this case hACE2 in humans. This half of the protein has a section of approximately 70 amino acids that create the receptor binding motif. The other half of the Spike protein, S2, initiates protease cleavages to enable the virus to enter the cell."

And then, what really struck Cheng: the fact that while the S2 amino acid sequence of the new virus shares 95 precent of material with the S2 of ZC45/ZXC21 (alleged bat viruses), the S1 protein, that determines which host (bat, human, whatever) the virus can ultimately infect, has only a 69 percent match with ZC45/ZXC21.

In other words, while sharing so much material from the bat viruses, the new virus differed substantially in the receptor binding proteins that determined the virus' host.

Additionally, ORF8, a protein of the bat viruses, has a 94.2 percent similarity with the ORF8 of the new virus—while no other coronavirus shares more than 58 percent. And no known coronaviruses share a 100 percent match of the E protein with the new virus. E proteins figure in the assembly of new virions. This further establishes a connection with the new virus and these obvious templates.

Dr. Sun went on to compare two samples of the new virus found in patients from Wuhan, the two bat viruses mentioned above, and two strains of the original SARS virus. For the moment Cheng skimmed over the detailed matchup to the conclusion: the RBMs of the new virus were more likely to be a recent recombination event. Had this new SARS-like virus come from a natural evolution, it would have had to have undergone mutations which would have made a sequence matchup low, instead of high. Yet the very high (94 and 100 percent) matchup belied such a scenario.

"It is more likely," Dr. Sun went on, "that the ZC45/ZXC21 viruses (or similar viruses) were recombined with another coronavirus to create RBMs that would bind to hACE2 receptors. The host for this newly created virus would not be bats because ACE2 proteins in bats are not similar to ACE2 in humans.

"This new SARS-like virus seems to have jumped into the world fully formed, with no evidence of its existence before late 2019.

"One of the theories for a natural evolution for this virus suggests two viruses combining their genetics in one animal host: pangolins. But studies proved the RBD of the new virus is ten times more infectious to the human ACE2, than that of any coronavirus found in pangolins, showing this virus was already primed to target humans and did not need any intermediate or genetic altering host.

"It cannot be ignored that the Wuhan Institute of Virology (often along with U.S. researchers) has carried out extensive gain of function research, through which coronaviruses that can infect humans have likely been developed from coronaviruses that did not originate in humans. The institute has the world's largest collection (I prefer to call it a reservoir) of coronaviruses. It is an understatement to say that the technology for such viral creation is readily at hand."

It crossed Cheng's mind that to have a room full of guns does not mean one will commit murder. Though he could hardly argue as Dr. Sun detailed another piece of evidence in this "crime."

"There are two unusual restriction sites, designated as EcoR1 and BstEII at opposite ends of this virus' genome; these sites do not exist in the rest of the spike gene. These sites are not found in the spike genes of other coronaviruses, further indication that they have been artificially introduced."

Cheng read that "The Bat Lady," Dr. Zhengli Shi, oversaw her research team place a SARS RBM into the Spike proteins of bat coronaviruses that were similar to SARS. The spike proteins of this viral engineering were able to bind to human ACE2 receptors. And just recently The RBM of the new virus was placed into the receptor binding domain (RBD) into a SARS virus. This "chimeric" RBD had no problem binding to HACE2.

Dr. Sun went on to assert: "Finding EcoRI and BstEII restriction sites at opposite ends of the new virus' RBM, along with the fact that Dr. Shi and her associates had swapped the same RBM region using restriction enzymes, further indicated the artificial nature construct of the new virus."

Dr. Sun speculated that to disguise the fact of the virus being created artificially, the exact SARS RBM would not be preserved; there would be small changes in the protein sequence that would not affect the virus' binding capabilities

He went on to the "polybasic furin cleavage site found at the junction of S1/S2."

Furin is an enzyme that cleaves proteins: when first synthesized, some proteins may be inactive, and require the removal of sections so they can become active. Furin removes these sections, activating the proteins. The term furin is derived because it was in the upstream region of the oncogene known as FES. The gene itself is known as FUR (FES Upstream Region) and so the protein was called furin. Furin is also referred to as PACE: Paired Basic Amino Cleaving Enzyme.

For the S1 and S2 proteins to achieve their functions, there is a furin cleavage site, producing furin protease (something that breaks apart proteins) located at the junction of the Spike proteins. No other virus lineage B of β coronaviruses has a furin cleavage site—except for this new virus. Furin cleavage sites have been discovered in other lineages of coronaviruses.

"At any rate," Dr. Sun went on, "the introduction of a furin-cleavage sites would greatly increase the infectivity of the virus.

"As to the possibility that this could have evolved naturally: the only way that could occur is if a virus from a B β lineage with no furin cleaving site combined with a coronavirus that did. But if there are other coronaviruses that have such sites, there are absolutely none that have the exact polybasic sequence found in this new virus.

"The nucleotide sequence of this virus's furin-cleaving site shows two consecutive Arg residues within what appears the inserted sequence (-PRRA-), which are both coded by the rare codon CGG, which is the least used codon for Arg in the virus. Further, this arrangement is the only place in the virus where this rare codon is used consecutively, which once again suggests artificial creation."

Dr. Sun further added that any one of the above might be a one in million natural circumstance, but when taken all together, so much circumstantial evidence plainly points to, once again, artificial creation.

"This is the first part of the problem: that the virus apparently has been created in a laboratory. The second part of the problem is how did this come about?

"Labs in China, as well as Hong Kong, have led the world in coronavirus research. This is borne out not merely by the number of publications they have produced, but by achieving such milestones at being the first to isolate the SARS virus. They also identified civets as an intermediate host and the fact that the virus first originated in bats. They have enhanced understanding of the mechanism of MERS. And it is here that the world's largest collection of coronaviruses resides.

"Here are the possible steps to the creation of this new virus...."

As Cheng had quickly read through the first section of this material, he meant to go over it once more slowly, but he was now too intrigued—and anxious—to not read this proposed "how to."

A bat coronavirus would be used as a template. "But not from Dr. Zhengli Shi's collections; she is too well known. ZC45/ZXC21 are available at military laboratories—this is the most likely source. In fact, these labs might also have viruses whose existence have not been published."

Molecular cloning would enable the Spike protein to bind to hACE2, thus creating a coronavirus that would infect humans.

"This would be followed by producing an ORF1b gene construct, that encodes a polyprotein that produces individual viral proteins that figure in the replication process of the virus, most crucial being the RNA-dependent RNA polymerase (RdRp), which is prominent in coronaviruses. The PCR test (Polymerase Chain Reaction) that draws out a single region of genetic material, can amplify the RdRp gene, which is used to identify the presence of coronavirus. In fact, this family of viruses is grouped/linked.

"However, the creator(s) of this new virus would seek a particular RdRp on the sequence of this gene. The ideal choice for an RdRp gene for the new virus would be from bat coronavirus RaBtCoV/4991, discovered in 2013. The only information ever published about this virus is its RdRp sequence."

Apparently, the creators behind the new virus also wanted an "antidote" for it. The RdRp gene from that particular bat virus is "for whatever reason" the best among all coronaviruses for the development of antiviral drugs. Or, rather, is more vulnerable. Remdesivir, which is being studied as a therapeutic for the new virus, targets this gene.

"It should be stressed that if this virus was indeed artificially created, it is most likely not with the intent of harming others, of starting an epidemic, but to study the workings of new viruses that might arise—though the artificial construct of any such virus seems to belie the route of natural, mutational creation. Ultimately, it seems a research project that got out hand. And perhaps there were those among the creators of the virus who did look upon it as a weapon— though exactly how would it be employed? To unleash a bioweapon—like the wind, a pathogen goes everywhere....

"The above steps would be followed by reverse genetics to put together the genes for the spike, then tested for hACE2 binding. A plasmid with this spike would go through in vitro transcription to get viral RNA and then the development of different strains until a 'desirable' one is obtained."

Dr. Sun went on, detailing more deeply the molecular biology steps of creating a new virus. Testing on animals, especially hACE2 transgenic mice, 'sacrificed' after their lungs have become overburdened with the virus, then virus extracted from "homogenized" lung tissue, the virus reinjected in new mice—and the steps repeated for a number of rounds until a virus of great infectivity was reached.

"From my research and the input of others, the creation of this sort of virus would take about six months."

Dr. Sun concluded: "While already there is a defensive—if often sincere—overall declaration from our scientists that this virus is of natural origin and furthermore it was not created from any lab, did not escape from any lab, there are many who think otherwise, and who also note that along with the sincere apologists are those who are deliberately—for whatever reasons—trying to deflect the most likely possibility of artificial creation. It seems that several publications or papers awaiting publication connecting natural occurring viruses and the immediate ancestors of this new virus are actually and obviously fraudulent, a deliberate attempt to steer honest researchers from the truth.

"It is imperative that there be an independent investigation in the Wuhan Institute of Virology and labs that have collaborated with WIV. Unfortunately, this is not very likely to happen any time soon. Perhaps never, unless there is a change in leadership at the highest levels of government—and of science."

Cheng put down the papers and rubbed his eyes. He was more convinced than not that what Dr. Sun had related was the truth, or close enough to it. And he felt more than uneasy that he was in the midst of the "scientific process" in now combatting the virus.

He knew his talent and the extent of his knowledge—and he knew he always had the ability to deepen his knowledge. He knew his "superiors" knew this. He thought of Mr. Mao Suit; and Cheng did not like to think of this dubious functionary as his "superior." Cheng was certainly being used for his expertise; and he was also, he thought, being "used." The daily round of the past weeks: visiting that man who was continuing to shed virus; being tagged to be an integral part in the development of a vaccine; his connection with Dr. Sun—which certainly had to be known; and that driver who conveniently ferried him back and forth in the absence of public transportation.... Cheng felt closed in by duties, by a situation that was larger than himself. – While his good friend, Po Fan, was creating nanomaterials out of spike proteins and e-waste, spike proteins that he had supplied. He smiled at that. Fan seemed a pure seeker of science, happy to apply her skills and also to extend them. Well, she was young. Cheng realized he felt—and perhaps felt it even before this point—that his skills were as much directed by others as by himself.

And then he considered: If the virus is artificial, does that change the situation so much—now? It has to be dealt with, contained, treated, eventually vaccinated against— But those were the typical reactions of the medical community; it had to be considered that there had never been a vaccine developed against a coronavirus. There were attempts with SARS; those attempts failed. SARS faded away. Would this virus spread here and there and then die out? Who knew?

And then, if the virus was created intentionally, for good reasons or ill, was it a signal (a warning) of a future pathogenic creation that would be even worse?

Was there some long-range plan, under the guise of being prepared for that worse event, to create pathogens more and more virulent—out of that mad scientist hubris perhaps best characterized by the two hundred year old English novel, *Frankenstein*?

What would it be like to create a virus? Cheng wondered. Would that simple, that powerful act be in itself so fulfilling one would be willing to disregard any consequences arising out of such a creation? A statement, a *fact* of creative power that was so much greater than any disaster that could follow from it?

Cheng smiled inwardly, grimly, at himself. We have the atom bomb. Isn't that enough? Nothing could be worse than that. —Then again, a virus that sweeps through the world…the seeds of a holocaust rivalling, even exceeding any nuclear ravaging.

Six months, Dr. Sun had said, to create such a virus. If the viral creation had been released this past November (first recorded case November 17), somewhere (perhaps in Cheng's own lab) scientists had begun working last spring, through the summer and into the fall, perhaps pretending to themselves they would carefully delineate how a lethal virus could develop, and yet all the while locked in the thrill of placing their own knowledge into the "flesh" of the nanoworld of viruses, the nanoworld of molecular biology that would severely affect the many times larger animal, the species of which its creators were a part.

There was an absurdity to this; and, Cheng had to admit, more than a little madness—and, yes, evil.

Chapter Thirteen: Odysseus

31.

When Lin and Yang came in that morning, Li was just about to pick up his moon book—he felt he hadn't looked at it for a while. He considered the pair, his lone human link to the outside world for these past two weeks, with his now acquired resignation to the absurd.

And yet even the absurd could bring good news. After taking his temperature, after he once again said (as he had said the day before and the day before that, etc.) that he was feeling well, Yang told him, "Tomorrow you can leave. You've done your quarantine."

Li actually gave a happy sigh—and smiled. "Is the world still out there?"

Lin said, "Where do you think we come from? Do you think we just exist on the other side of that door, come in to see you, then vanish when we go out?"

"Even before this I wondered if either of you existed outside of this building."

Yang said, as if taking this very seriously, "We have lives, too."

Neither of the men had ever spoken of anything personal to Li; he considered remarking on that, but didn't. He just said, "We all do."

Lin: "I guess you've only had the moon life for a while."

Li knew they could not know how rich his "moon life" had been. Or could they know? "How is the virus? Is everything still—?"

Yang, still serious, said, "It's worse. And everything is still locked down, closed."

"Maybe the moon is a better place for the moment."

But both Lin and Yang took this with no expression. Of course, their faces were masked, but the eyes were enough. Lin said, "When China gets there, we'll see."

Li actually felt a bit insulted at that. He watched Lin and Yang leave.

So they don't think I've been to the moon at all. Naturally he knew he had not physically left this room for so long, yet he had some greater sense he had been a very thorough lunar traveler.

He once again read at random from *A History of the Moon*. From a chapter, "Moon Tales We Told—and Will Tell":

There have been so many stories, our many fictions that we have told about the moon. Marvellous adventures. In the 20th century we came to call these tales science fiction. Of course, they began before that century; Jules Verne naturally comes to mind, and there's the Poe tale "The Unparalleled Adventure of One Hans Pfaall." There have been stories about the moon once having a race that annihilated itself with atomic weapons; stories about lunar colonies of the not too distant future revolting against Earth; stories about robots mining the moon; and on and on.

As we know more of the science of what the moon is really like, our stories will increasingly have a more factual basis, but we will always have a fictional, imaginary element that reveals the psyche of the time in which the story is told. We project upon the future our own perspectives of the present.

The American television series *The Twilight Zone* showed strange and weird scenarios of both a present and future very much colored by the time in which the show aired (1959-1964): the Cold War fear of the other, of nuclear doom, the promise of the Space Age and also the threat of the Space Age. In one of its famous episodes the one family on the block that has a nuclear bomb shelter is besieged and threatened by neighbors to give them shelter when a broadcast of imminent nuclear attack is heard. But the shelter has limited space and resources and cannot accommodate anyone else. A confrontation on the verge of violence is dissolved when the warning that that had just been broadcast turns out to be a false alarm.

At the beginning of the 20th century Percival Lowell's canals of Mars were apparently certain evidence of a civilization bringing water throughout a thirsting world. Ray Bradbury, who brought a poetic wonder to his science fiction and more earthly fantasies, published a collection of stories titled *The Martian Chronicles*. Here was a Mars upon which a dying race of Martians were scattered just beyond the busy turmoil of the invasion of Earthlings, a Mars on which humans could breathe the air, where astronauts found replicas of the towns of their midwestern youth, where oppressed American black people could find a place of freedom. Bradbury's Mars was much more fantasy than science fiction.

Mars has always been a place that seemed to Earthlings to offer so many possibilities of fantasy. There were the Edgar Rice Burroughs stories, John Carter of Mars. But the moon is different. It has always presented a more somber image to our senses. Oh, we have those old legends of werewolves and such, but those tales were of the effect of the moon on us, here, on Earth, not of being on the moon.

The question is, what 21st century tales will we tell about the moon? Perhaps they will be as much psychological as science fictional. Until now (and likely for some decades hence) we had to imagine what it would be like to live on the moon, in a situation of total technological life support. But the end of the next one hundred years there will be human beings living that experience and they will tell their tales as something other than science fiction.

Those lunar colonies may at first have citizens from only one particular country on Earth. Which leads to speculation as to who will be first on the moon in the 21st century? Will the Americans take that honor again? Or will the Russians grasp what eluded them in the 1960s? Or will those much older civilizations, the Chinese or the Indian, make their lunar foothold before those former Cold War adversaries? –And then, perhaps the first colonies will be a mix of nationalities in the spirit of brotherhood, sort of a United Nations ideal, that occurs too little on planet Earth.

Of course, there will always be our science fictions. Perhaps the best near-future denizens of the moon will be human beings who have been genetically altered to live in a wholly technologically sustaining environment. More cyborgs than human; androids that do not share the human experience and who will write stories that parallel our consciousness but do not intersect it.

We will see what fictions and what reality that 21st century brings. The certainty is, whatever it is that will come, we can't quite imagine it now.

This comes to mind: by 1969 there had been so many stories of humans landing on the moon, especially through the 1950s and '60s; but none, absolutely none, had imagined that first moon landing would be seen all over the world on television. Not one writer, at least not one published writer, had imagined that.

Li closed the book, a book published 25 years ago, a full generation ago. And thought that world of the mid 1990s was only dimly realizing this new "thing," the internet, that would become the main form of communication and information in the first decades of the 21st century. Just as no one had imagined televised moon landings, Li believed no past writer of future tales had concocted a world whose daily bloodstream was this present electronic interconnectedness.

Li mused a bit on how a world without an internet would know about and react to an epidemic like the one that now beset Hubei, and especially Wuhan. Well, there had been a flu pandemic a hundred years ago, a time when there was not only no television but no radio, just newspapers, so information was not instantly communicated. The world had gone on, made its way, but so many, many had died—50 million people. If not an exact number, but an estimate, these are numbers the size of a European country in the early 20th century. It was also estimated that literally one third of the planet's population became infected: 500 million people.

Recalling those figures of a century ago, Li could only reflect how just a hundred years later his own country had almost as many people as the entire Earth did then.

Li wondered what new "thing" was being born now, or about to be born, that would so revolutionize human life. The same year America landed on the moon, 1969, the internet had been born, but it would be another generation before it would begin to become in common use.

Is this new virus the new "thing" this year would grant the world, and, hence, the future?

In the midst of Li's musing, he was once more on the moon.

Li felt something different this time, something different in himself that he could not explain. Perhaps because he had done this so many times before. It was not that he felt jaded with these more than virtual lunar visits; it was not that he felt annoyed that he was once again being subjected to this surreality. Perhaps he simply felt himself on the verge of something entirely apart from his previous adventures.

He also had the sudden thought: *If I get to the real moon, it can never be as interesting.*

Then he corrected himself—or at least argued with himself: *Reality has to be interesting.* And then thought: *But what is the 'real' moon?*

In the midst of these inner musings, Li realized he had not been looking at the landscape before him. And realized, with a start, that in between himself and the near horizon, were the lander and the rover.

He had not seen them for some time.

He almost felt a pang of nostalgia. He had begun his lunar journeys here, with these marvelous machines; now he had returned. The rover was moving slowly toward him, as if in welcome. Was he being recorded, filmed through those "eyes" of the rover? Was another astronaut in training seeing Li on the moon within the frame of a monitor? Of course, that could not happen, as Li was not actually "here."

The rover was right before Li and he looked down upon it, with a sort of calm benevolence. The rover had stopped, was still now, and to Li the rover felt like a pet awaiting a master's instructions. And Li, irrationally, waved his arm in a sort of pointing manner and said aloud within his helmet, "Let's go then." And the two started off, to that horizon.

Li, in his kangaroo hop, should have easily outpaced the slow-moving rover, but now the rover moved quickly, more quickly than Li had ever seen it move. He accepted this anomaly. Soon they were out of sight of the lander.

It was at the point the rover began to veer from Li's side, and move off at a roughly 45 degree angle. Li hesitated, then followed. Again it seemed the rover was acting in the manner of a pet, but now leading its master in a direction it felt imperative to pursue.

But I've always been led, Li thought. Had all his lunar excursions, if appearing to be self-directed, been in truth directed by other than himself? In the sense that he had encountered one strange thing after another, and so artifacts or events had been placed before and around him to draw him to them.

Li thought again: *I am being tested.* He wondered if there would be a point when the test would end. Perhaps, even if he should be picked to really go to the moon, every movement and act in that mission would also be a test. Yes, the mission itself would only be a further test—for what?

Every act we're being judged—for something.

Li saw the figures before the horizon, a horizon far past the one before which he had begun this lunar travel with the rover. There were half a dozen of them. They were slim, wearing spacesuits of silver grey—; but no: that was their bodies, not spacesuits. They were beings whose bodies were fully exposed to the harsh surface of the moon. Smooth bodies: the arms and legs and torso blended into each other like a metallic skin that that held itself without bones beneath or anything like that. In fact, there was the sense that they were solid, if light metal through and through, and with faces that had not so much distinct features but the suggestion of features, such as an indentation for a mouth that did not lead into mouth, a contour that suggested a nose, indentations that suggested eyes—while at the same time they looked about as if fully seeing, perceiving their own purpose of movement and easily noting that of their companions.

What were they doing? At first is seemed the figures might be in the midst of a slow, minutely practiced dance, a choreography of some abstract purpose that Li could not decipher. And at the same time their movements—which seemed both individual and coordinated—had some purpose other than an alien art. Li had the sense they he (and the rover) had come upon the figures just as they had finished some task. What that task could be was a mystery. There was nothing about save the figures, and the mandala their movements had left on the lunar surface, an interwoven tracery of footsteps. But Li could not shake the sense of something having been completed.

He—and the rover—stood there, watching, for a brief time; then the figures "saw" these other eyes, and turned in unsettling unison toward Li and the pet-like machine. Had the rover "known' what it would be directing Li toward? Well, certainly those who were directing this surreality knew. Unless, of course, something in Li's mind created all the strangeness he had encountered on the moon.

Li remained without movement as the figures came toward him and stood before him and the rover, a line of dancers in postures subtly like the gesture of a greeting.

"Hello," said Li, ironically and to himself.

And yet he felt an answer in his head. And like some of the science fiction stories he had read in which beings from other worlds communicated telepathically with Earthlings, Li received messages that were not words but more images, which he would translate into the words of his own tongue, images that had their own dance, and which replayed, as if from an outside, observing eye, his many travels on the moon, all the strangeness in which he had been caught. There was the relief of the minute city, the markings that looked like language, the abandoned city....

Had these beings been the creators of those artifacts or had they too experienced them as Li had, as explorers coming upon evidence of a vanished civilization?

In the midst of these images, one of the figures reached out a hand that suggested a hand and lightly tapped the visor of Li's helmet. He felt this as a mild shock, interrupting the flow of thoughts he had "received." He hadn't realized himself so close to one of these "beings." The figure leaned toward Li. For a moment Earthman and the figure looked directly at each other—if it could be said this figure were looking. If a stream of Li's experiences on the moon had just washed through him, now there was a clearness, all that prior time had dropped away, there was a promise of something Li could fill with his own choosing, his own direction. Li was in fact filled with the promise of choice, whereas only a short time ago, he had considered, even been resigned to a situation in which he accepted—and fulfilled?—whatever had been chosen for him.

It was as if these mysterious figures, who appeared freed from all the exact detail of human creatures, communicated to Li an abrupt path freed of the detail of others. It seemed a sort of…blessing. Li almost felt overwhelmed. He looked away from the figure, whose insistent nearness appeared to wait for some sort of recognition of the possibilities that it presented; Li looked down, to the rover at his side, upon which a dim panoply of lights played—the machine's own sort of recognition. Li wondered if the rover had "knowingly' directed him to these figures. –But that would imply Li was once again being directed.

Now the figure stepped back from him. Li felt relieved. The figures began a collective movement whose purpose Li could not understand, but there was a beauty to it. He thought once more of a dance.

Slowly the figures moved away from Li. He watched them as they receded, and almost imperceptibly, blend into the moonscape, their silver-grey forms becoming more brown-grey, until each one appeared to have literally merged into the austere surface of the moon. They had vanished, subsumed (though that was not quite the word), literally, by the substance of the moon.

What was that all about?

And yet, somehow, he knew, in a way he would not have been able to put into words. The figures had been a beckoning.

Li began to walk in the direction in which the figures had departed and disappeared, the rover beside him, like a little robot in a *Star Wars* film. He felt something cleared from the moon, all the strangeness, whether of his vision and or imagining, or the direction of others, a moon cleared of all artifacts, human or otherwise, a world unto itself, filled with its billions of years of the past, austere in its own realm of being. It was as if the departed figures had brought him across a border, freed him, granted him passage to the real and lasting moon.

Or perhaps the figures had just freed him from those previous illusions (or parallel realities) to confront an ultimate strangeness, whether real or not. After some time, Li saw, up ahead, in a sort of alcove formed by the remaining wall of a crater whose complete circumference had fallen away eons ago, leaving this shard of itself sticking up from the surface, Li saw something he could not quite believe, but accepted immediately, in the way one accepts things that at once defy belief yet are so irrevocably *there*.

He saw a woman in ancient Chinese traditional costume, her hair held back with a bone of ivory spiked through its thickness, slightly bending over small pot. It was too much an illusion, a mirage of Chang'e herself, tending to her elixir of life. Even from meters away, within his space helmet, Li felt the steam of the heated mixture on his face.

As he approached, the woman looked away from her task and turned to him. Her face was…wholly Fan's. Confounded, Li mouthed her name, and the woman smiled at him, as if she had heard what he had not spoken aloud—and even if he had, it could not have passed from within his helmet across the airless surface of the moon.

So much like Fan…. Li felt an old yearning he had forgotten. Or which he had willed to put aside during this period he had been quarantined to experience these strange sojourns on the moon. But even as he held himself in a force of present yearning (for what he did not quite know) and a sudden wash of nostalgia (as if this woman, impossibly Earth-like on the airless moon insisted on things Earthly) and present confusion, he was chagrined that he had just been feeling swept free of events and apparitions such as this but now had been presented with the acme (at least to him) of all lunar visions: the goddess Chang'e, who had left Earth to reside on the moon.

A goddess with Fan's face.

Li recalled the legend. Chang'e had drank all the elixir of immortality to keep her husband Yi's apprentice from stealing it. She had then ascended to the moon, where she could be in the heavens but still close enough to her husband to watch over him. No quite a logical reason for heavenly departure. The alternative legend about Chang'e gives more rationale for her departure. She was the thief of the elixir from Yi, drank it all, and fled to the moon where Yi could not follow.

Li recalled that Yi had been granted the elixir because with his bow he had shot down nine of the ten suns scorching the Earth. Granted the boon of the immortality elixir, he wanted to share it with Chang'e; he did not want to be immortal without her. But apparently, she was not interested in a relationship that would last beyond time.

Li had considered these legends early his training, but all that had recently occurred, made each passing day seem a long time ago. Perhaps for the first time he considered that part about the ten suns in the sky was probably a mystical exaggeration about a period of drought. He tried to imagine the Earth caught in a star system of ten suns....

But all this while Chang'e/Fan was looking at him. The drifting of his thoughts seemed an unconscious—or deliberate—drift of attention because he did not want to face the surreality of this apparition; of this current "reality."

And to assert this reality or surreality all the more, the *Yutu-2* rover, named after Chang'e's rabbit, moved to her side, the lights along its body flickering subtly on and off, conveying a stream of inner content, the essence of a pet moving to the side of its mistress. Li stood there for what felt to him a good while, looking at the woman out of myth, out of his own present, with the rover at her feet.

He said, aloud, "I'll be getting out of quarantine—so I can see you." He was talking to Fan, putting aside the vision of Chang'e—who lifted an arm, the loose sleeve of her garment falling back from her forearm, in a gesture that was approving and happy and loving. It was as if she were receiving the happy expectation of a reunion after a long separation.

While Li was thinking that this woman, on Earth, was a skilled traveler—and creator—within the nanoworld; and he thought Fan would have mined the essence of Chang'e's elixir with expert scrutiny. And yet what he said next seemed to have nothing to do with that; he was still captured with the legend of this immortal moon goddess:

"But you're supposed to be on the other side of the moon."

Not just the Chinese but other Asian cultures see a rabbit on the moon, formed from the dark mares on the side of the moon that always faces Earth.

Fan seemed to have heard him, no matter the fact of the airless, soundless moon. Her lips moved and he was able to read the words: "After thousands of years, I came to this side—with Yutu; I did not want to be looked at every evening from Earth. This is the peaceful side."

Li didn't know what to say to that. He didn't know what to do. He moved closer to Fan, to Chang'e, who smiled. Li reached out his arm, but it felt ridiculous, over protected in the layers of the spacesuit, his hand so thickly gloved.

"Take it off," she mouthed.

Li's hand dropped away. He frowned. He would not admit it, but he felt frightened. She said, "I can't reach you in that." Again she mouthed the words, but Li seemed to actually hear them.

Although these many lunar excursions had defied "normal" reality, Li had always experienced the reality of being on a world in which he needed the protection of his suit to breathe, protection against the killing heat and cold of the moon. Could he join the reality of this Chang'e who looked like Fan, who was dressed and acted as if they were both on Earth, their life-giving world?

She tapped Li's helmet—like one of the silver figures had tapped it. She smiled.

This was indeed the first time in all these bizarre (for they had been that) training sessions that Li hesitated to accept the event which had been created for him. –But how had this been created? How did they know of Fan? Wait, he had given Lin and Yang instructions to have her notified that he was in quarantine.... But this meant that "they," whoever that was, had actually seen Fan in order to create her here, as Chang'e on the moon. Then again, surely it was his mind that was creating Chang'e/Fan—

Her hand was tapping on the helmet again She was still smiling. Li began to undo the helmet.

When he removed it from his head it was as it the lunar world about him was wider, greater. His bare, unprotected face looked back at Fan's smile. He smiled back. For the first time he considered that she was not in what he had always called her "American hair style" from that old film from the 1970s. Her hair, darker and longer, and caught up in long shaft of what looked like bone or ivory certainly gave the look of an old myth—and yet, this was also just in another aspect of modern, 21st century Fan.

And he heard her—actually heard her, on the airless moon—say, "The rest. I need to hold you."

Her voice: he could not resist her voice. It filled him with both consternation and longing. These two emotions collapsed into acceptance. He placed the helmet he still held on the ground beside him; he did it delicately, as if this act might upheave the reality he was experiencing. But nothing untoward happened. Then, with much less than the difficulty he had expected, he got out of his suit and placed that down on the lunar surface beside him. He looked upon the figure it made alongside him. Li now wore only the snug thermal-like top and bottom and socks he always wore under the suit. And just as when he had taken off his helmet and the lunar vista seemed greater, more expansive, now, in shedding his suit, his body felt freed to something larger. And he felt not at all the heat of the sun that was lowered now, at the end of the two weeklong lunar day.

He was also aware again of the rover, which it seemed he had not glanced at for some time. It stood still, with alternating slightly glowing lights, like a mechanical simulation of breathing. The rover that had brought him here. Yes, Li felt something more than mechanical in that machine, created on Earth and which had been moving upon the moon long before Li's "arrival."

Before the virus. But Li shook his head at that. Why was he thinking that? Why not think of anything but Fan's arms reaching out to him, and his to hers? They held each other, their faces nuzzled each other and they kissed. It almost seemed to Li that that act of embracing, of kissing was something he had done so long ago that he had to resurrect its essence within him. While he wondered what Fan was feeling. But the expression on her face appeared of one who was in a full realm of feeling. And it made Li think, perhaps even realize that even in the past, back on Earth (had they both truly left that home world now?) there had been the sense in him that he had to make an effort to reach for something within himself, draw it up to the surface, spread it through his being when being intimate with Fan, while she possessed this essence, projected it and extended it to him, without apparent effort. She *was* this, while he had to recreate it in himself, as if to return to it each time, accept it, while she was this always.

He thought, too, in those long moments of embrace that he was enacting—and she was, too—something like those old tales of being on the moon long before anyone on Earth knew the science of the airless, austere world. Like that book had described. A time when it was believed you could live on the moon as you lived on Earth.

He suddenly drew back his face from hers and said, softly, "Where are we?"

Her eyelids fluttered, her head tilted to the side. "Just here, Li, just here."

"But it can't be…a place that we know."

It seemed she gave the softest laugh. "It's the place where you wanted to be."

Did she mean in her arms, or—? "You mean, the moon?" he asked.

She closed her eyes and breathed in (breathed in what?) with apparent satisfaction. "It's wherever you wanted to go."

"I wanted to go to the moon?"

"Yes. Don't you still—?"

"It seems I'm here."

"Seems? Don't you believe it?"

Was she trying to soothe him or mock him?

"I'm trying to believe—or not—that you're part of my training."

"You knew me before any training." Her eyes were so close to his. What orb, what world did he see in her dark pupils?

He drew back a little, extended his arms, still holding her, as if to take her all in. "But what have you've become now."

She smiled. Had she never stopped smiling? She would like him take her in. "Wasn't I always this to you?"

This actually startled him. Had he made her some kind of myth even before this? No, that was ridiculous. To him, she was the brilliant Fan, a nano researcher, explorer of the nanoworld. Could *he* be a myth to *her* in that universe?

"Just accept this now," she said.

"I'm trying to."

"Why do you have to try?" She pulled him to her again.

So he always had to try for closeness? Whether in the life before his lunar travels, or this odyssey now? He held her. He noted at the very base of her neck the fleeting sheen of metallic nanoparticles merged into her skin. This subtle glimmering in the late hours of the long, long day of the moon. They were still for a while.

He was back in the training room. This abrupt tearing way from Fan was painful, and not just emotionally so; Li felt something torn away from inside his body. He flinched, as if he had been given a blow.

For the briefest instant he thought he saw his spacesuit lying beside him, and the outline of the rover. These artifacts of human science were like markers that were so integral to him that their disappearance also felt like a great loss. It seemed to him that he had cruelly abandoned them. –Of course he had not chosen to abandon anyone or anything. He stood in the training room, sorrowed, apart from the moon.

He assuaged himself with the fact that he was leaving quarantine. He would be able to see Fan again—on Earth.

But Fan as Chang'e…. He gave himself a sad laugh. He was training for the Chang'e program; and he placed his lover in the old myth—and the rover as her rabbit on the moon. Such obvious psychology—

That night he perhaps was also given to personal psychologies assailing the inner collective of his dreams. He was on the moon—and was pleased to be in what he considered familiar territory. And just up ahead…it was a city: not the lunar city he had come upon, but a city of Earth.

It was the great city of Wuhan, its buildings and streets spread across the lunar surface. As he approached, he felt the city was as empty as the one he encountered on the moon. He was not sure if he were sad or not about this.

But it wasn't truly abandoned. Li felt the presence of the virus. It filled the city; it weighted its streets and rooms. Li walked these streets, entered those rooms, streets and rooms empty of people, yet throughout was the palpable presence of the virus—which he could not see. The virus that had been in him. He had the sudden shock of realizing that interior invasion. While he had been sick he had not visualized the virus in his system; he had simply, rationally, thought: *I am sick.* Then,

I am better. He did not ponder the innumerable viruses invading his cells, then the cells become filled as the virus took over the cell and used the cell's genetic material to create more and more virions until the cell was so filled with the newly created invaders it burst, these new virions sent out to invade more cells, on and on. Now he realized that interior horror and wondered if he had any of the virus left in him, even if he was not sick now. And wondered at the uncountable number of the virus in the city, the city without people—though how could the virus survive, now, without hosts? But it waited. He understood that. Waited in its nanoworld, after apparently have killed everyone in Wuhan. But could that happen? Literally? Yet no other person lived in this city of his dream, except himself, going through empty room after empty room, as he had in the moon's abandoned city. He did this endlessly apparently, not fearing the virus, merely disturbed at what it had left, at what it promised, wishing Fan (as Chang'e or herself or both) could be here, to guide him into the nanoworld, to reveal to him the virus, where exactly it lurked. Or did it cover everything, like a cloth, a blanket, a trillion trillion-numbered crowd of the virus, linked and invisible? Yes, Fan could show him; Fan could guide him. He might have thought Cheng the consummate virologist would be the better guide for this, but ever since he had attended that lecture by Fan he had firmly linked her to this world in which viruses and the other invisibles of existence, the things that fell in between the wavelengths of light. So as he looked out onto a deserted street from several floors up, he abruptly thought it was like the dark matter of the universe, that matter that is believed to fill up more of the universe than the matter we can see. Li felt confounded by the reality that whether virus, bacteria, the cosmological dark matter, existence is overwhelmed with more than the human eye can see—as if our senses could never comprehend enough for us to truly know nature and extent of existence; or as if the limits of our senses saved us from apprehending how much more of existence exists about us, how we are the merest sliver of—all this. How much we are overwhelmed.

And then in one room there was a man in a chair, a nondescript man, middle aged, who looked up at Li as he entered and said, simply, "I keep having the virus." At Li's startled, puzzled look, the man added, "I'm not sick—now. But I keep shedding it." He raised an arm. "Like leaves." And Li imagined a steady, invisible, constant fall of virions from that flesh. He had no way of knowing that this man in this room could be mirror to the man that Cheng had been sent to interview—unless, in his dreaming, Li had sourced a collective unconsciousness—and he was mildly alarmed, wondering if he too were shedding the virus, while the man added, "So they keep me here. I'm the only one in the city."

That shocked Li. He considered that perhaps if there was just one host the virus, any virus could survive indefinitely. He had to get out of this room, get out of this city; he did not want to become like this man, a host for— But he said to the man, "Leave. Why don't you leave?"

"I'm followed. The virus is in me."

Li thought: *He's not followed, he's possessed.* And he turned to step away, to go out of the room (while thinking he was leaving the man to a terrible doom, but what could he do?), but as he turned he saw *Yutu-2*, the rover, by his side, and he started away from it, half turned back to the man, who had now risen in his chair, and raised the arm he had raised at first, raised it toward Li, in the manner of the figure on the moon that had tapped on his space helmet, and Li stepped away from both the rover and the man and darted out of the room, hearing a whirr of machinery (Li thought it must be the rover's lights) and some calling cry from the man.

Li fled downstairs and was out on the street.

But on the street were the figures, the silver-grey figures of the moon, not together, but moving in different directions in different parts of the street; and even as they moved, their forms became tenuous, dissipating, dissolving in Li's sight. And even as they had disappeared into the landscape of the moon before, they disappeared into the abandoned, virus-infested cityscape of Li's Wuhan dreams. It was as if they had surrendered their very existence to the city—or had simply mocked Li with their disappearance.

In fact, he cried out, "Don't mock me!" He silenced himself. That didn't make sense. Then again, it did. And then he awoke.

He sat on his cot, reviewing the dream. He wanted to dissect meaning from it; he wanted to strip it from memory. He would try to leave it to the fate of most dreams: utter forgetfulness. But he had moved through so much of "real" surreality of late; he had dreams; and everything stayed with him. He laid himself back down in the dark, eventually slept, his mind this time allowing no further dreams.

32.

He was awakened by Lin and Yang. They stood over him in their protective gear. They might have been something he had imagined from the moon, but of course they were the habitual sights of his life here on Earth. At least here in this building, in the training room.

Even as he was opening his eyes the temperature gun was aimed his forehead and Yang was saying, "You're clear. You can go home today."

Li slowly sat up in bed. The eyes of Yang above his mask darted with a pleasure that seemed selfish. "Did you hear that?"

"I heard it, but do I believe it?"

Lin: "You think this is fantasy?"

Li received that with a good deal of irony. He smiled back at Lin as Yang said, "You've had a long stretch here. You don't have to come back to training until you're called. We know you need a rest."

"…don't have come back…need a rest" What *did* they know of him?

Yang continued, "So you can go home."

Lin suddenly said, as if he'd just thought of it: "How is he going to get there, though? Everything is—"

As if scolding, Yang responded, "I told you; we have a driver."

Lin and Yang left, informing Li the driver would be here soon.

In fact, the thought of actually leaving here now seemed as surreal to Li as his journeys on the moon.

While he waited, Li turned to *The History of the Moon* and a chapter he had not noticed before: "Always the Goddess."

Throughout time and many, many cultures, the moon is considered female. Why is that?

If we think of the moon as companion to Earth, its complement, would not the moon be male, as the Earth too is thought of as female—for obvious reasons: life grows up from the earth; it is the home of all the life we know. In many cultures it is the sun that is male. That too follows an obvious route in the collective unconscious; the sun 'seeds' the Earth with its warmth, so the earth of our planet can engender and sustain life.

But why a female moon? Many will say it is because of a woman's menstrual cycle; one lunar month matching that rhythm of human physiology. Of course, the moon might not just match a women's cycle but in fact create it, giving women a connection to the celestial, something beyond this world—and, ultimately, unfathomable. Ah, yes, the mystery of women….

And the moon might be looked at not so much a complement of our planet, but one of the two brightest objects in the sky. So if the sun, the most dominant thing in the sky, is male, then the moon, its counterpart, is female. And if the sun is blazing, so strong that you can't look upon it (echoes of not being able to look upon God), the moon bears a more gentle aspect, and invites our gaze without harm. It welcomes us with a certain peace.

And the sun is for the day, when the straightforward business of life is conducted; while the moon is for the night, the time that tends toward the imagination and the other worldly. Again, the mystery of woman matches the mystery of the night.

There is also this view: that any worlds that have satellites are males; those that don't are females. The sun, of course, is at the center of many worlds. The moon is a satellite of Earth; it has no satellites of its own. That would make Mercury and Venus female planets. That certainly, in our culture, fits Venus, but we have inherited the lineage of Mercury/Hermes: definitely male.

Well, our images of myth are never totally one way or another, but there is no question that we have inherited a history of lunar goddesses.

Li read of Artemis (sometimes called Cynthia), Selene, Chang'e of course, of Abuk, Ala, and Hecate, who some consider the earliest aspect of Artemis before her entry into the classical world.

Hecate has a truly dark aspect: her three-bodied form is connected to sorcery, the dead, mysteries of the night and witchcraft. It is thought her origins might go as far back as ancient Egypt, coming to Greece via Anatolia. Centuries later her name would be spelled as "Hercat" by the English.

The cult of Hecate was ongoing in Athens in the sixth century B.C.E There were shrines in homes: Hekataion, a carving of a three-bodied Hecate facing three ways. Larger Hekataions were often placed at public crossroads—to give travelers pause in the choice of passage? There was a Hekaton on the road to the Acropolis.

Hecate was also associated with dogs, which were often sacrificed to her. In Colophon in Asia Minor a black female puppy was sacrificed to the 'wayside goddess' Hecate, according to Pausanias. Dogs and puppies were commonly sacrificed to her at crossroads. Plutarch wrote of these offerings in Boeotia.

Li put the book down. He did not much care for a moon goddess that needed blood offerings. How much more appealing China's Chang'e and her rabbit Yutu.

There was a knock on the door. That both startled and puzzled Li. Lin and Yang would not be knocking. And for the past two weeks he could not open the door from the inside.

But today he could. That should have been a feeling of freedom, but instead Li felt uneasy about it—as if this were exposing him in some way. A young man stood there. "They told me you're ready to go." It was his own driver. To Li it seemed the driver had a look in his eyes that might have been amusement—or of knowing something about what Li had been through. That could have stemmed from Li's sudden feeling of being invaded.

Li introduced himself. The driver nodded. "I know." He had the manner that introductions were not necessary and introduced himself in turn in an almost ironic manner. "Fu Junjie."

"I'm almost ready," Li found himself saying, as if asking permission to be fully prepared for departure.

Not that he had to gather much at all. He would be leaving the training room as he had entered it every day—and two weeks ago. He surveyed the room while Junjie watched—as if he had to approve of anything Li might take with him.

As Li was about to exit, he picked up *A History of the Moon*.

Junjie said, "What's that?"

Li was annoyed at the question. "My book."

There was a subtle shrug from Junjie, in the manner of one who could have objected but decided it was not worth it. Li was further annoyed. Junjie walked out ahead of Li, who closed the door behind him. He had the sense that he might not return to this room for a time.

Or perhaps this was a farewell.

Driving along the outskirts of Wuhan, Li saw this border of city and suburb as a region he had been separated from long ago. There were few vehicles on the road. He said, rhetorically, to Junjie, "Still lockdown?" The driver nodded. Li had the sensation that this man was not only used to the abandoned sense of the city but somehow was involved in that abandonment. It was an irrational thought, he knew. He made the connection of the abandoned city on the moon with the present of Wuhan.

"Still lockdown," Junjie said after a pause, "But more than that." At Li's look of questioning, the driver said, "We're making sure of everyone now."

We? Thought Li.

Junjie was pointing. "Look."

Junjie had stopped for a light. Before them was a family crossing the street, father, mother, and a child, a girl of about six. Of course, each wore a mask.

Junjie said, "They shouldn't be out like that, all of them. It should just the husband or wife." Then Junjie smiled. "He sees it—"

In the midst of their crossing the street, the man was pointing up at the camera raised above a streetlight pole. Such cameras were nothing new in Wuhan or in so many places in China. It seemed that everywhere this population one billion, four hundred million was being watched. But this camera was apparently different.

"Look." Junjie raised his phone to Li. On the screen was the family, the forms of three people, each with a different level of redness filling in the outlines of their bodies.

"Heat," said Junjie. "See if they have temperatures."

Li was surprised at one thing and much more surprised at another. First that now the government not only had placed surveillance cameras all over, but temperature reading devices—and if the devices were here, at a not particular prominent intersection, they must be in many more trafficked places; secondly, and the more surprising, that this young driver was able to have the feed from those devices on his phone.

"Why are you getting this?"

Li noted the eyes smile above the mask. "I do work for the government."

"In exactly what capacity?"

The eyes now above the mask still smiled, but smugly—and cautiously. "I can't give you an exact title. I'm needed for different things. Right now, I am driving you home."

Li blinked his eyes and said nothing. This Junjie must be some official's son, let into the periphery of things, and posing as one who was more than peripheral. He asked, "So if one of them had a temperature, what would happen?"

The family was on the other side of the street and turned to walk in the opposite direction in which Junjie and Li were going. As they moved on, Junjie said, "They would be noted, and visited; given a warning to not go out again until any symptoms are gone. They might even be given the warning before getting home. Then they could even be removed to— Well, if it was just the man, he might be removed;

they'd make sure the mother would just stay home with the child." His eyes on the road, he sighed. "Too many people...to control."

Li did not like the sound of that last word at all. For a few minutes they drove on in silence. Then Junjie said, "I have to make a brief stop. Just a few minutes." The words sounded apologetic, or rather they should have sounded apologetic, but did not. Once again, the irrational shot up through Li: was this "stop" going to be something unpleasant? His mind went along the vein of: *I saw so many crazy things "on the moon"; they want to do something about me, don't want me to talk about it—*

Junjie made a left, then a right. He stopped by some small, nondescript apartments. "Just a few minutes," he repeated, got out of the car, leaving the keys in the ignition. Li had the absurd, amused thought, *So he trusts me.* Then: *Or it's a test. Like the moon again.* He realized his virtual lunar travels had marked him.

Junjie was a little more than "a few minutes," but not by that much. Li watched him walk from the building back to the car. He had a manner in his walk that Li took as more arrogance than confidence. But a lot of young men who feel in their prime walk like that. A lot, but not someone like Li, who was an athlete as well as a taikonaut in training. His explanation of Junjie was reinforced: the official's son who was enjoying too many perks, such as being able to cue into those heat sensing devices.

When Junjie got back in the car, Li ventured, "So what was that about?"

Junjie tilted his head at Li in an almost coy way. "A little personal, a little business."

Probably a woman, Li thought. The remark about "business" was to make this stop seem important.

They were almost at Li's apartment building. He asked, "So where are you going after this?"

There was an annoying laugh from Junjie. "Mr. Zhen Li, I don't ask you questions, do I?" When Li looked at him blankly, Junjie added, "I don't know if I'd even be allowed to say."

Li considered he may have been impolite in asking about Junjie's affairs and purposes, but there was such an air of easy importance about him that Li wanted to pry at this façade. But restrained himself from further questions. Though he knew that this silence would be regarded by Junjie as a psychological triumph.

Still, Junjie was driving Li, not the other way around.

They arrived at Li's building. After the strangeness of the past two weeks, Li had a brief feeling of displacement. *Do I really live here?*

As he got out Li said, "Thank you. How does anyone get anywhere today, with the buses and trains not running?"

"Most people shouldn't be getting anywhere—for a while now." Junjie's eyes smiled now as Li exited. Li noted the driver removed his mask as he put the car in reverse and then turned around. That brief glimpse showed a handsome face. That could only add to his image of himself, Li thought.

Li considered himself more "strong looking" than handsome. When Fan had called him handsome, he had responded with, "You're prejudiced. –And you should be." He would make no qualifying remark when Fan would remark on his strength. He knew he had that.

As he entered his building for the first time in weeks, Li recalled he had that book about the moon in a knapsack he had stuffed with the few things he had brought from the training room. In minutes he was in his apartment and put the book by his bed.

Do I need to read any more about a place I've been? What I've seen isn't written—anywhere.

He wanted to forget about the moon for now. He called Fan—remembering, as he tapped the numbers on his phone, how he had met her as Chang'e...on the moon he did not want to think about. But he would never forget her as that ancient lunar goddess.

Fan did not answer. Li texted: *I'm out. I'm home.*

The text came back in a moment. *Wonderful. In a meeting. Call soon.*

Li was disappointed he could not talk to her right now, but just that contact, those few texted words—it was good.

His own text—about being "home." He looked about his apartment. He had been here only since he had started training. It was not that long ago, but long enough so that it should not look as if he'd just moved in. There was hardly anything personal about it—save for an old map of the moon he'd had on his wall in his childhood bedroom. And now it was over his bed here. He had not taken it from his parents' house when he had first moved away, but on one of his subsequent visits, years later. To have it with him again was as a sort of proof that he was in the very real process of achieving the first steps his childhood dreams.

Though—ironically—the map showed only the near side of the moon. Li smiled to himself. He knew that "other side" now, and intimately, as no one else could.

And since last summer he'd had a reproduction of an old map of China that showed Beijing at the center with south at the top and north at the bottom. It was an example of how the Chinese in previous times had regarded north and south in terms of geological feng shui: one's back to the favorable south (southern exposure equals more light and warmth) in order not to be taken by surprise by the dangers of the north. –Such as the Mongols, who at one time ruled the largest contiguous land empire in history?

Li had bought the map at an open-air flea market. In answer to Fan's "Why that?" he'd shrugged. For some reason he was drawn to these old visions of one's place—a country's place—on the Earth.

But "home": where was *that*, now?

He had been so comfortable in his childhood home, by the rice fields and the great open sky that allowed the full heaven of stars at night. When he became a man he would go *there,* above, and he went to his childhood bed embracing all the comforts of a safe child. He was a child that was smart, active; but he knew, as he grew older, there was some distance between him and his peers. He was perhaps liked more than others because he was good at whatever sports were at hand, but he was never comfortable with the "natural" vulgarity of his peers, and so he stood apart from their remarks about girls and the tests of rowdy rebellion that adults at once expect and condemn. One of Li's opponents in a track meet at school, had burst out with the declaration, "He's too *good* to win." And Li did not win, but came in a very narrow second, though ahead of the one who had damned him with goodness. Not that Li had any particular satisfaction at that; there could only be satisfaction in winning. As he came to compete against better athletes, his own athletic prowess always brought him near the top, but usually not in first place. His failure to even gain third place in the International Military Games recently held in Wuhan was a great frustration. Yet there again, the difference between him and the three who finished ahead of him was small. Fan had tried to console with, "You really should have come in second." He had snapped back with, "And you think that's good?" He had said this cruelly, and had immediately apologized to Fan, who brushed it away with, "I understand, I understand." Li felt that his talents were always bringing him near a goal but not enough to actually grasp it, at least grasp it before others. It was a feeling that surfaced too often and nagged at him now, in regard to securing a place on the first Chang'e mission to the moon. He felt, in his return from quarantine, his return from those virtual visits to the far side of the moon, that he had run a race for all he was worth— but would it be good enough?

Perhaps it was that psychic distance between him and others, the inscrutable difference that was being translated into a life of second place finishes. Perhaps that came from his childhood under those stars and planets that move in their cycles over the rice fields. Rice had been the mainstay of Chinese food for centuries; and these stars and planets had moved above such fields for as long, indeed over the earth before rice had been cultivated; and Li, in his appreciation of that ancient heaven, had perhaps imbued himself with that range of time and heavenly distance, and that had been translated into his earthly life: not quite being fast enough to be the fastest on Earth, the human parade at once recognizing his abilities but saying "That's not enough," and: "You are too far from us...."

Li knew that his memories of childhood, of that childhood home, of his parents who had always encouraged him in whatever he did, was rich and good, but he knew that childhood and that place was done for him; the years had brought him a passage away from that. And this apartment here was not a home but place to sleep, a place to divide the days of training, for those short respites, the childhood map of the moon on the wall emphasizing not the comfort and goals of childhood but an artifact of a passage that could not be repeated and which was continually moving him forward, away from the safety of that path toward the moment of a decision in the present. Would he be chosen to go to the moon?

"There will always be another mission after the first," Fan had said. It was like when she had said his fourth place finish was as good as second. But he did not snap at her; he had just looked dejected. Fan had clearly seen that, but she would not give up trying to make him feel better if he were not chosen. "The odds are more against you than in any race. How many are trying for this mission? The first one?"

Li had shrugged. "A state secret, I guess."

Lying on the bed, looking at the map of the moon, with the book about the moon beside him, caught forever in childhood dreams of the heavens, Li had to wonder at other aspiring struggling taikonauts, perhaps scattered throughout the country, slogging their way through training as bizarre as his had been. Or had theirs been as strange as his? There was no way of knowing. Perhaps he had been given the most severe of mental tests. And perhaps he had not….

And if he were to be chosen and went to the moon…would he ever want to be a part of a permanent lunar colony? But that would be well after those first missions.

But could he feel at home on another world, one of the worlds he had looked up at from the childhood rice fields?

Home. He realized he should call his parents.

Both his parents spoke to him with the relief that washes away worry. Or at least most of it. He was thankful that Lin and Yang—or someone—had informed them of his quarantine.

"No, I wasn't very sick…just like an uncomfortable cold."

His mother said, "We see people in hospitals—terrible—"

Li reflected that the authorities must be allowing more information to the public. When he went into quarantine you would not see such scenes on either TV or the internet—save, in the latter case when it was posted against official approval. He recalled the friend of Cheng's, a doctor, who had been disseminating news about the virus that had not pleased the powers-that-be.

His father asked, "So is it that bad, there?"

"The city, the whole province is in lockdown—"

"We see that, we see that."

"It's almost like abandoned city. Like on the moon."

"What?"

Li realized he had let a connection too easily slip from him. "The city—it has a deserted feeling."

"So how is the training? I guess when you were sick…."

"I was still…well, going through it."

Li steered away from that. His mother came back on the line. "When are we going to meet your scientist girlfriend?"

"Scientist girlfriend." It sounded odd, fitting that title to Fan, yet it was not was not inaccurate. Li gave a gentle laugh. "I don't know. We'll have to see." For a while after being involved with Fan, he had not mentioned her to his parents; he did so when he realized it would please them—attach his absence from them more to the normal life of a young man than this abstract training to go to the moon (a destination whose passage understandably had them worried—if proud he was undertaking it).

He imagined himself and Fan visiting the world of his parents' rice fields. Fan would be at ease, pleased to meet his parents, while Li knew he would be a bit awkward. It had always been hard for him to share an intimate portion of his life with others.

He pictured his parents clearly as he spoke to them. When he had shown Fan some photos of his parents she had said, "I do not mean this to be insulting to them, but you are so much more handsome than they are. I guess when their genes mixed together— I mean they look like plain, happy people; you: you're handsome and tragic."

"Tragic?" That word had surprised him.

"I suppose I mean driven. Leaving everything behind you. Just focused on what you want to be ahead of you. There's a little tragedy in that."

"Let's see how I end before you call me tragic."

"You won't be the type who 'ends.' You'll die still going on."

"Past the moon, you mean?"

"Oh, you won't be satisfied with just the moon."

In response as to when he might see his parents again, and when they would meet Fan, Li said "Wait until all this goes away."

"I hope it's soon. Doesn't she work in that lab? They must have an idea."

"I don't think anyone does. I'm not even hearing predictions." While Li thought that he had been so separated from the daily round of life he really couldn't affirm what he had just said.

His mother said, "Well, by spring it should be over, shouldn't it? At least then."

To appease her, Li said, "Yes, in a few months, when it gets warm, it could be." And maybe he did believe that himself, at least a little. It was the primitive feeling that cold weather brings what besets us, while spring, and the return of the flowering earth, brings us release from the harsh months. Li could remember how his father always seemed pleased at the beginning of spring, even though it meant more hard work in the rice fields. –His father, standing with an old, earned pride by the moist, raw earth, smiling, a smile that seemed to be cast across the great plain of the rice fields, right to the horizon, as the sun, higher in the sky now, cast a renewed brightness upon the ageing face, his eyes blinking in a burst of raw spring wind.

And I'm going to a place that has no wind, no earth smell, no air to breathe. He considered—without expecting an answer—that his drive to leave all things earthly had been, paradoxically, created—planted--by the world of the rice fields: the worlds of the night above those fields had been so much a part of this richness of Nature he had wanted to touch them and be touched by them as much was he was interwoven with the more immediate sensations of this place, that he could not separate those above-worlds as being places that would be antithetical to physical being, to human life. The stars were a part of his childhood world, and yet so much not a part of any human world.

Another universe. But then again, Li had once read that wherever we go, we take the universe with us. We are a part of it, so even if a human being went to the very edge of the universe—well, the universe could have no edge, no end, because that human stepping past that edge would bring the universe along—

Then again, that was putting existence in all too human terms.

He thought about what Fan had said, about him needing to go on and on: "out there."

Li's musing had split his attention; he had to ask both his parents to repeat themselves more than once before the conversation ended. His father and mother both finished with admonitions to stay safe. After speaking with them Li realized neither had asked for any detail about his training. And he of course had not offered. He would have been almost embarrassed to describe having encountered the bureaucratic other, deserted extraterrestrial cities, the disappearing silver figures. He in no way did not want to relay the fact that "they" had gotten so much into his mind, manipulated it continually.

Manipulated. It was an ugly word to consider.

Lying on the bed, he looked up at the ceiling. Would he suddenly find himself on the moon again? But "they" couldn't do that from here—he believed.

And hadn't Lin and Yang said—or at least inferred—that he was to have a break from all that? That abrupt placing him on the moon and bringing him back probably could take place only in the training room.

How exactly did they do that? Did they drug me?

Li would have accepted a technological wizardly, a virtual surreality, but the idea of being drugged, of his mind being ordered—disordered—by any sort of substance, really bothered him. He prized the strength of his body and mind. A violation of either struck him to his core.

Well, they did something to me. Will I ever find out?

He picked up *A History of the Moon*. In "Epilogue:" he read:

Ultimately, what does the moon mean to us? There are so many levels to this. Just as in temperate climates there are four seasons, there are the four phases of the moon: after the new moon, there is first quarter, half, full, waning, each first and last "season" of the moon bordered by the darkness of the invisible new moon.

Li put the book down. He had gone into quarantine during the new moon. Tonight the moon would be full. He considered that as…some personal if celestial guidepost? Anyway, he was looking forward to seeing a full moon—the side that he had not journeyed upon….

He half dozed, lying on the bed. He was awakened by Fan's call.

Chapter Fourteen: Return to Reality?

33.

As usual, Fan was lost in her work. Or perhaps lost was not quite the true word. Perhaps lost to the world in a way, but her psyche very much "found" itself in this nanoworld that she had explored and manipulated for so long that it had as much reality, as much of the commonplace as the macroworld in which her physical body existed. Like an artist, she lived in both worlds at once, or rather stepped from one world to another, while others saw her only in the world from which they viewed everything.

That was a big thing she appreciated about Li: even more than Cheng, who certainly had his nanoworld of viruses alongside the larger world in which he lived, Li's pursuit of the worlds "out there," in the great remove of existence in which human beings could not naturally live, made him (at least in her estimation) have an intuition and an understanding of her submergence into the nanoworld and her emergence from it.

"You go out there, I go in here," she had said, making a gesture inferring an inscrutable interior.

"So do you think the macro and the nano have a meeting place?"

Fan had paused, then had given an almost sad smile. "They are on the same continuum."

That evening, Mystery actually let Fan hold him on the bed for a while. He purred loudly. "Oh, so you're finally enjoying this," she said. She gently stroked the side of his head. He continued to purr. Then abruptly he extricated himself and jumped to the floor, to his own bed. Fan grunted in amused frustration.

Fan's mother called. It had been four or five days since she'd spoken with her parents, who were understandably concerned with her living—and working—in a place that was the center of an epidemic. "And in that lab, where maybe it started," her mother said. "I don't hear good things about where you are."

"You only hear bad news—but we're doing good work here. Or trying to."

Fan had described her own work to her mother, who listened for a while, then, apparently impatient with too much of the science that was difficult for her to understand, she said to her daughter, "So masks, things like that—everyone expects it to be here for a long time?"

"It's too early to know that." But by now Fan thought that this virus would probably be a problem here—and elsewhere—for a year or so.

Her mother talked on: a bit about her own everyday life, asking Fan once about "that boyfriend who wants to go to the moon."

"He's not there yet, but he may be."

"At least they won't have that virus on the moon."

"Unless we bring it there."

"Why would—? Never mind, I'm not up to explanations."

That was so like Fan's mother: too much explaining made her impatient. If something was too far from being clear cut, she turned away from it. That was the opposite of Fan's father, who would continually ask questions—but he would also often not accept the answers given, even if the speaker of those answers knew more about the subject. Fan's father would question the answers to his questions, debate them. It was something that frustrated Fan, and had frustrated others, as she had seen.

As a girl who believed herself maturing into a perception of the world beyond childhood, Fan had first considered her father the dominant—and more intelligent—one in this marriage. Her mother, an attractive woman who continued to keep herself attractive into middle age, had appeared to the younger Fan as someone who embodied the superficial aspects of a career military officer's wife: more clever than intelligent, and bearing more façade than depth.

But as Fan grew older her view of her mother shifted a bit. What seemed her impatience with things beyond her own everyday world was perhaps not so much a desire to live in an easier ignorance, but the realization that she did not need to "know everything"—as her husband did; perhaps she had a degree of wisdom that had moved past the arrogance of knowledge. While Fan's father made too much of a point of "knowing" and arguing the aspects of such. Not that Fan herself didn't want knowledge and pursued it as much as she could, and also debated its aspects....

As Fan considered this, the conclusion she drew now could be distilled to this: her mother was less superficial than Fan had previously judged, and perhaps her father more so. Though she still felt her mother could pay more attention to the intricacies of things just beyond her ken—as in her daughter's work; and if her father could temper his trying to take over any subject being discussed, she could appreciate the insistent workings of his mind; he forced you to defend your position. In fact, he made you aware you had a position when you thought you were just declaring the facts.

When her mother asked, "So you think that virus came from your lab?" Fan felt defensive, though of course it was something she wondered herself.

"There's no indication that it did, so far."

The response to that was sharp. "You know they're not going to tell you if it did. Your father couldn't say otherwise."

With that introduction her father came on the phone and said, "Your mother's right—at least they would not say it now."

Fan said, almost wearily, "They wait until they find the ones responsible, arrest them, make them example."

"You sound cynical. If it is someone's fault, yes."

"So everyone could see the government is on the right side of things."

"You're too quick to fault the government—that supports your work."

Fan thought: *The government that needs my work.* She said, "Whatever happened, we're trying to fix it."

"I don't think people realize—any epidemic is a threat to the security of the country."

"So if people are sick we're going to be invaded?"

"You're just thinking of the most simple thing: war. It affects the economy, production. Things are shut down. If it happens to the whole country—"

"I think we're too big to be...I don't know. We have so many people—"

"It's a mistake to think we're safe. Look how little Japan invaded us in the 1930s."

All Fan could say to that was, "We're past that now."

Her father shifted the subject. "How is it affecting...Li, his training?"

"He's still in training." Fan did not mention he had been quarantined with the virus.

"It would be fantastic if he went to the moon. That would be something to be proud of."

Fan had to ask. "Would you want to go to the moon?" Fan heard her mother laugh in the background.

"If I were younger...maybe I'd be in training myself."

Fan smiled at that: seeing her father training for the moon. Then again, she wondered if her father's personality would be suited to the lure of going "out there," removed from the day to day routine—and visibility—of earthly military life. The routine of a taikonaut would be too, well, interior. Yes, her father was nowhere near as interior as Li.

Well, at least he was pleased at the endeavors of her boyfriend. –That was a word that amused Fan; it implied things she felt were hardly mature.

Her father concluded the conversation with the expected, "You're probably safer at that lab than anywhere else in Wuhan."

"Well, we're careful here." Though Fan was not sure about being safer than "anywhere else."

"I suppose there will be a lot of cases until spring."

Fan was drifting back to thoughts of her work. "It looks that way."

Fan was facing a difficulty with the spike proteins in her nanoweave. The furin cleavage sites broke away from the rest of the spike. At this point she did not know if this added to or detracted from her weave— or had no effect on it at all.

The recycled nanoplastics she was using now came from one of the many e-waste dump sites in China, where old computers, cell phones, etc. were turned into whatever materials might be sold—or turned into the plastics (or metals) of entirely new products.

The nanoplastics were a literal powder that was in a little square box, marked with their source: PC MONITORS, LATE 1990s.

As if these were the ashes of a living being, Fan caught herself wondering about the "life" these plastics had once contained—the information they had housed. The more metaphysical—or spiritual or delusional—might assert that the ashes of the dead, even after having undergone the passage of the cessation of all bodily function and being seared, assert that some essence of the being that once was yet remained, insistent, if transformed. So, was there perhaps not some "residue" in these nanoplastics of the information that had flowed through their hulls?

And then, think of all the information that was continually deleted from a computer. Where did that "go"? Never mind these plastic ashes—in some realm parallel to us was all this information still in existence? An existence that would be expanding constantly. Like the universe itself.

Fan shook her head. Such were the musing of scientists. Take something real, stretch it to the edge of the known, then, just beyond that was a fantasy that could lead to truth or stay fantasy, being a fancy more of the time and place, not last at all. How many angels could dance on the head of a pin? That was some Western medieval mind bender she had heard—inferring (at least to her) that angels were of the nanoworld.

Now that was something to consider. Though angels were of the West, not of the East, of the three religions that ruled most of the world apart from China. Fan had recently read an article that said 87 percent of Chinese have no religion. *Perhaps that is why we progress*, she thought. While in some places and times, if religion had supported certain aspects of progress, from art to charity, usually religion was a foe of science, at least of new science. It had taken how many hundreds of years for the Roman Catholic Church to issue an apology to Galileo?

Both Christianity and Islam came to China in the 600s. These religions would be alternately allowed, banned, allowed again, by various rulers. Twelve hundred years later there was a scholar named Hong Xiuqun who declared he was a heavenly king and the younger brother of Jesus. He had dreamt that an angel had brought him to Heaven where there was an old man and a young man. They presented him with sword and magic seal and told him he must purge China of demons. The dream had come before he had been introduced to Christianity; and when he was, he concluded the old man had been God and the younger man Jesus Christ—and the demons were officials of the Qing government. It was the impetus for Hong to begin what would be called the Taiping Rebellion that spread through the south of China in 1850. It was civil war that lasted fourteen years. Historians put the death toll at twenty to thirty million, ranking it as one of the bloodiest wars in human history. More recent historical estimates put the death count as high as seventy million. The result of this theocratic rebellion was Christianity was once again banned in China.

Hong Xiuqun died a year before the war ended, in the spring of 1864. He was in Najing, where the city had little food. Hong's heavenly decree was that everyone should eat manna. This was not the manna of the Jews, but sweetened dew and medicinal herbs. Hang gathered greens for his sustenance and eventually feel ill—not everything that grows is fit for human consumption; he died at the end of spring. There is the theory that, seeing his cause nearing defeat, he poisoned himself. He was buried in a yellow silk shroud; there was no coffin.

In midsummer Quing forces exhumed his body, beheaded and burned it. The ashes were blasted out of a cannon to make sure he would have no eternal resting place.

Fan caught herself in this wandering from the nanoworld to the large horrors of history. Whether human ashes or recycled nanoplastics, was something of the larger "body" retained? Or did extreme reduction of a larger form effect a downsizing quantum leap that utterly changed the essence of things?

She laughed at herself. *Esoteric, esoteric*. She returned to the spike proteins and the free floating furin cleavage sites.

In the midst of this, Fan had one of those moments of clarity or perception in which what one is doing is abruptly connected to something often weakly described as transcendence. The spike proteins, the nano powder of recycled generation old plastics, the information that had passed through old computers, old visions of angels, demons and the nonreligious present, Li training for the moon—it all coalesced into a tapestry as real as her intricate weave. She saw—or felt or intuited—this as a vision of energy, of universal being that varied its form but not its essence, saw, in her inner eye, all this as light, sent within and across the universe, a substance of energy/light from stars, stars in formation, stars dying, linked to the nano minuteness of the viral particles from a virus that had shut down a city. It was a passage of manifestation that went back and forth, not from one point outward, onward.

But then, what was the Big Bang, but some moment of beginning that proceeded onward, connected to that beginning only in its history? In that moment Fan suspected this was a cosmological vision that had as much to do with lineal Western perceptions as science. Speaking of religion, wasn't it much like the old religion's instant of "Let there be light"? It wasn't that Fan felt it all as a circle, with no one point of beginning, but a point of forever being, in which all forms and energy flowed, a multitude of which a human being could grasp only the slightest portion.

Yet our grasp, the grasp of humans was increasing—wasn't it?

Then again, just as one can list a multitude of numbers yet there are an infinite number of numbers beyond that (numbers never end); humanity's "increase," of being able to go deeper into the nano world and farther out into the macro universe, left a multitude of layers, minute and large, still beyond our reach.

At any rate, at the moment what flooded Fan left matters of human "grasp" only a tangent of an issue. There was so much knowing of which we only perceived the edges. As she had told Li of the nano world, he had told her of dark matter and dark energy: that the universe may be composed of much more matter than our eyes can see and our instruments perceive, the latter giving only hints of something "more" in existence that for now eludes our comprehension and taunts our awareness; while a dark energy drives the expansion of the universe— if indeed it does come from a linear beginning.

Fan shook her head, resting it against an elbow propped hand and sighed. Something in her descent into her nanoweave had prompted this. While her memories of Li talking about the mysteries of the cosmos, mysteries that we "maybe explain in words that disguise the truth instead of lead us to it," she had a vague but insistent inner vision of herself on the moon with Li: an impossible, fantasy vision, of the two of them on the lunar landscape, not wearing spacesuits, but talking as if they were on Earth, on a world in which one can breathe. It was an image that one might have in a dream, not here, in a lab.

She left her work, needing to get away from it, needing to get out of the lab. She felt more than one person eyeing her curiously as she walked outside in the middle of the day, but maybe that was her imagination, and even a sort of guilt at letting her inner vision drive her from her work.

Outside she sat on a stone bench with the lab behind her and some trees before her. In the warmer months she would often sit here, have her lunch, rest her eyes on the green trees, their leaves moving gently with a breeze. Now, in winter, the bare trees moved too with a bit of winter wind—though the wind seemed high up; on the bench, Fan barely felt it. She was warmly dressed; the cold seemed outside her, at least for now. And she was pleased at this energy in the sky above us. It was not bad day for winter. This afternoon she welcomed the austerity of the trees. In some way they matched her branching inner visions.

Branching. Branches. That was the beauty of this season: it was as if the true structure of trees was revealed: a fractal geometry that waved against a grey-blue sky. All this great reaching up, Fan thought, from a small seed. How amazing that this "bigness" could come from something so small. Then again, the human sperm and egg become something much bigger, an adult human. Was the ratio of sperm/egg to adult similar to seed and the tree?

She gave herself a silent laugh. *What is happening today?* Her usual journey into her nanoworld had released something in her. Or was the word "coalesced"?

She had read of people having these moments in which they claimed they saw, they perceived, the true meaning of life. She had always doubted not the sincerity of those claimants but the reality of their claims. Truth becomes what we believe. Or was it the other way around? At any rate, Fan was receiving no great Meaning, but a flood of the manifold aspects of existence.

She shook her head. Too much. It seemed accepted science that the mind, along with our senses (though can you separate the two?) filters out so much of existence; it would be too much to process; it would interfere with the rudiments of awareness we need to survive. Well, most of humanity now no longer lives the precarious lives of wild animals...but we still have our daily rounds that could not bear a continual transcendence. Just the fact that Fan had to leave her work before this flood of connections bore that out.

But perhaps it's good to be washed in a large perspective—as a sort of reprieve of habitual vision, to grasp a visioning that leaves a more perceptive awareness that one can take back to the everyday.

Then Fan was thinking in words no longer, but simply staring at the bare, austere, beautiful branches high in the wind. When she came back to herself, she could not have said how long she had been doing that. She looked to the sun, that ancient marker of time. It had moved, but only a little. She felt cold now; it was the cold that had probably drawn her back from her wordless, thoughtless time.

She smiled, blew out a breath the winter air made visible. *Reality.* Then, with surprise, she only just realized she had taken off her mask as soon as she had sat down here. It was as if the trees had drawn her into, well, normal. *When we didn't have to wear masks*—though that was just a short time ago. She breathed in and out, watching her breath. She let herself feel a little colder. Then, with the breathing, felt a little warmer. She thought about those tales of yogis, who could sit in the snow in a loincloth and breath themselves into warmth, their bodies eventually melting the snow around them. Or stories about a wet sheet thrown over their nakedness while they sat in the freezing cold, and, with that inner mechanism of body and mind, the latter heating the former until the sheet dried.

That might seem an appealing mastery of the flesh to attain, but Fan had also read an anecdote about Buddha: when told of a nearby holy man who could walk on water, Buddha had replied, "But for a small coin the ferryman can take him across the river."

Science is the ferryman, Fan concluded, as she got up and went back into the lab—remembering at the last minute to put her mask back on as she re-entered this place of science that had given her metaphysical visions.

Fan had been back at her work only a few minutes before she received a call from within the lab. She was being summoned by one of the department heads, but one which she felt was not exactly connected to her work.

Inside a small room Fan met a woman she had noticed only a few times before at the lab, without knowing what she did there. Now she found out. Jiang Min was the deputy director of financial operations. She was a woman in her fifties who greeted Fan with apparent friendliness, yet Fan immediately sensed this was a tactic to gain something from her—or to soften something Fan would not like.

If the former method was not directed solely at Fan but merely a habitual means of operation, the latter would turn out to be the case.

"Po Fan, your work has always been distinctive, now it seems more so. Your nanoweave, your idea for a mask—"

It was if this woman had violated a privacy. "It could be a mask, if could be many things." Instinctively Fan was broadening the scope of her work, so that if Jiang looked upon the mask with disfavor, she would not have the opportunity of a single target. And then Fan asked—she wanted to assert herself quickly: "How did you know about it?"

Jiang Min smiled, and made a gesture that seemed to be a practiced one of calming another. "It's been talked about."

Of course, some people knew of Fan's work, but not all that many. Was it Wong? Or that official who had visited one day and who had seemed both interested and complimentary? To assert herself further, Fan said (in an innocent-seeming manner): "It doesn't seem your department."

There was that smile in response. "But it may become so. Whatever wide uses your work will have—and I think it will have many…masks, first, we need more masks now. Who knows how long this virus will last? And will it spread elsewhere. These things do. It's starting in other countries. And when you have one case…more come. The thing is, does the fact of your use of the spike protein—I know the basics of virology; you have to, working here—does the spike protein in your weave enhance the effectiveness of you mask, make it almost like an outer vaccine—?"

"I've discussed that with—" Fan stopped herself. She did not want to use Cheng's name, for reasons she could not pinpoint. "With some other researchers here."

"Yes, we need to do some further research on that. Because there is the possibility—though probably not, probably not—that it could provoke infection. We just have to be sure."

"Are you telling me there is some problem with me continuing my work?"

"No, no." She was soothing a child. "We want you to continue—and give you all the help you need."

That guise of benevolence jolted Fan. "I don't know if I need 'help' at this point."

Once more the smile. "Not being a scientist myself, but working with so many, watching all the very *intelligent* work everyone here does…." Fan did not like that stress on "intelligent"; it felt condescending. As if Jiang looked on the scientists at the lab as capable of only narrow if highly regarded achievement. She was going on: "What I see is, it's easy for someone, especially if you go down a new path…to lock yourself in. To keep what you're doing just to yourself." The smile grew broader; she was both complimenting Fan and showing her the lures of an insular path, understanding how that could lead her "astray."

Fan said, "You want to make sure you are taking a viable direction before…sharing it."

The deputy director sighed. "I think it's time you share your work a little." Catching the involuntary expression on Fan's face, she added, "We're not taking anything *from* you, just widening the scope of your work that you so brilliantly started."

She spoke quickly now. "As I said—didn't I?—well, maybe not directly. There could be great use in what you are doing. Masks. We need them. Maybe worldwide."

"In other words, finance—before science?"

Jiang Min's smile now seemed to complete a purpose it had begun. "Perhaps, and it's understandable, being on your side of things, you see science as the first thing. But before any science can happen here—" She gave a wide, gesture, indicating the lab. "Before any science here or anywhere, the money comes first. Centuries ago, like the American flying a kite—Franklin—and discovering electricity from the skies, you could make meaningful discoveries outside of lab. With a telescope outside your house. But now things are so complex, advanced. All your instruments to look into your nanoworld; how we detect and eventually treat this virus—you need money for it all.

Money: science—and science of course can make money. And gives us the opportunity to do more science."

Fan could hardly disagree; but she was not pleased. "Then what is the plan?" A moment ago, she felt defiance. Now she felt resignation. She was but one mind—however brilliant—in the web of a government lab. This woman was the spider, reeling her in.

(When Fan recalled that thought later, she considered that someone had "reeled in" Jiang Min; and someone had done the same to that person. The country—life—was a series of being trapped in the webs of others.)

Jiang was assuring Fan of the wonderful plan. "To immediately have others duplicate what you do. Of course, you will have to instruct them. You will oversee—at least the science."

To Fan that sounded as meaning "the science" would be kept in its place.

While Jiang was saying, "We need to see how soon we can make this a product." She leaned toward Fan. "And that is not something that should bother you. Your work will be out in the world. Helping others."

Taken literally, those last words should have pleased Fan, but she wondered how much altruism was at play here. And she had her own selfish feelings—though she would not have described herself as feeling selfish just then. She was facing the reality of her own private world of research being invaded. Only a little while ago the nanoworld had urged Fan into perceptions of inscrutable existence; now her nanoworld would be marketed.

It was only well after this conversation that she thought of Junjie's "proposal" and wondered uneasily about any connection. Apparently, Fan—at least her work—was, as the Americans would say, a hot commodity.

It was then she got the call from Li. As she looked at the number on her phone, she smiled with a relief she did not know she had needed. "Excuse me. Just one second." Whether Jiang was annoyed or not, Fan did not care. But she would make it not much more than seconds, texting Li she was in a meeting and would call him back as soon as possible.

As Fan ended that very brief electronic contact she was smiling. "Good news?" said Jiang, her head cocked, almost coyly. Did she sense the romantic?

"A friend. He's been—" Fan did not want to say Li had been in quarantine. There was something too...negative about that. She could have said Li had been occupied with his training as taikonaut, but she does not want to give this woman any concrete information connected with herself. As it was, something special was already being invaded. Fan just finished with, "The way things are, sometimes it's hard to be in touch."

It was a vague response the other accepted, or simply thought unnecessary to challenge. "A difficult time," she said, as if agreeing with Fan. "And your work will, we hope, make it better."

She leaned forward, patted Fan's hand. Fan had to stay herself from snapping her hand back. She said, flatly, "When is this going to happen?" What she was thinking was: *When will my work be invaded?*

"We are connecting to the appropriate people. A team I think you will be happy to work with."

"And who is going to be in charge?"

That smile, now politically tactful. "You will not have to worry about...not being heard. Or having your...oversight taken from you."

It was a vague answer that Fan did not want to pursue. She fell into a refuge of silence. The woman across the desk from her did not seem to note Fan's withdrawal. Or did not care. Her smile, if remaining, took on another aspect. "Po Fan, I have another meeting. We will be in close touch." She reached out her hand. For an instant Fan took it limply, then suddenly shook the other's hand firmly. To show firmness in herself; to show…resistance? There was a note of surprise at this in Jiang's face; then it was gone.

Fan turned quickly, muttering something that was thinly courteous, and left the room.

She returned to her office, and sat quietly for a few minutes. Outside the day was nearing its end. Now that the calendar had reached midwinter, the day was a little longer than it had been six weeks ago, when the shortest days had seen the beginning of the increase of the virus, but at the moment Fan could not appreciate the increase of this time of light.

She had almost forgotten: she had to call Li.

At the beginning of the call, she was taken away from her frustration, her dejection. She realized a distinct part of her had been tense with worry at not hearing from Li for so long.

"I'm glad you had someone call me. Tell me—"

"I was afraid they wouldn't. They called my parents. too. They would have been really worried."

"Of course." Fan was intuiting that very common, expected exchange overlay something not common at all. "So you did get sick?"

"A little. It was not serious."

"You're strong. You're healthy."

"I'm hoping my mind is."

"What does that mean?"

He drew in a long breath and told her. There was so much to tell: the bureaucratic other in the abandoned city, the frozen water in the caverns under the terminator, the silver figures—on and on, it seemed…and Fan as Chang'e.

Fan was silent a moment. She was drawn back to voice by Li calling her name. "I'm here. Chang'e…. I guess *that's*…flattering."

Fan suddenly recalled that image of herself and Li on the moon, and not in spacesuits, but as they would be on Earth. This had come to her after Li's....experience. As if—telepathy? She almost told Li, but stopped. Let him be the speaker of strange things.

Then she did say, "And it wasn't like dreaming, but real?"

"Too real." Li sounded uncomfortable.

Instead, she said, "So how do you think it happened? Hypnosis?"

"There was no one there to hypnotize me. The only ones who came into the room were those two...guards: Lin and Yang." Li was abruptly quiet.

Fan knew what was going through his mind. She said, "But you don't think they could have hypnotized you."

"No, we weren't in that...situation."

She sensed he had settled on the last word with dissatisfaction. She said, "Drugs?"

"That seems the most likely."

"How do you think they got any drugs in you?"

But he wasn't answering that—she knew he would consider the prospect of having been drugged as a gross violation of both his body and mind. Li said, "Or something...artificial intelligence. The monitor simulations were real enough. They just brought me through to the next step."

"Something virtual...but that also gave you physical sensations."

"Something like that. But more. Something I can't imagine. Something new." He abruptly added, "I was being tested. That's obvious. But I want to know if they directed the illusions or did they come from me. Out of my own subconscious."

This was not a light thing to talk about. Fan said, "So your unconscious, subconscious, thinks I'm Chang'e?"

There was a slight, resigned laugh from Li. "Maybe that was the least strange thing about all this."

She gave a gentle laugh. "Maybe I'm your connection to Earth."

His echoing soft laugh sounded almost happy. "Could be. Maybe you were a return to reality for me. My mind trying to…." He searched for the word, a phrase: "Trying to assert itself."

She suddenly said, "You still want to go to the moon?"

She felt the question almost jolt him. But he seemed to answer with no pause. "Of course."

"No second thoughts?"

"I just want to find out how they did it. And how they think I…faced all that."

"If this was going on in your mind, how would they know what you faced—exactly?"

"But I feel they do. And I wonder if they did it to others. Somewhere, in other rooms, others suffered this."

"Was it suffering?"

He gave a long sigh. "I don't really know what to call it. At once I was afraid of it—not so much afraid as…frustrated; and I looked *to* it—curious. I was never afraid to walk the next step. I must have been all over that moon. The far side."

She repeated: "'That moon.' Is it *the* moon?"

"It must be. What else could it have been? Even if it was in my mind."

They were both quiet for a moment. Fan looked at the black rectangle of her phone. Through almost all of the conversation she was not really seeing this small monolith of technology but visualizing Li on the other end.

Then she heard him saying, "Will you come over here tonight?"

She said it so softly—as if she had worried he would not ask: "Yes."

"There's a full moon tonight. I want to see it…from here."

"It wouldn't be the same at my apartment?"

"Yes, but…I want to see it from a place that's mine. That I control."

After speaking with Li, Fan sat quietly in her office again, as if reabsorbing Li's words in recollection. She had the thought: Were Li's bizarre journeys on the far side of the moon more surreal than the epidemic in Hubei?

Of course, they were. There is really nothing unusual about a new virus, an epidemic. And yet, she felt something strange about it, indeed. One could even say bizarre. But she would not have been able to explain exactly why.

Chapter Fifteen: Explanations

34.

Returning to the lab, Cheng was weighted with this secret. Was Dr. Sun the only one who had parsed the artificial creation of the virus? If indeed he had been, there would probably be others who would pick up, and unwind the thread.

Cheng was indeed thinking of the aspects of that thread, his mind visualizing the microbiological world of the viral manipulation—spike proteins, cell fusions sites, messenger RNA, entry of the virus into the cell, the rapid creation of myriad virions and then lysis, the cell bursting, flooding the host with innumerable viruses.

Throughout the years of his studies and his professional career, Cheng considered this structure and progress of the virus in its process of infection and further recreation as almost the passage of music through the structure of a symphony. A symphony that was soundless in his mind— And then the sudden thought that there probably was sound to this, some nano chorus, some nano crescendo of…something, which we could not hear. Our senses were not equipped for such minute cacophony.

Cheng had always borne the knowledge that his intellect saw what most fascinated him across an impassable distance of scale—like a lover ever regarding the beloved from one side of a divide. Cheng laughed to himself. Was the virus the beloved? How odd. What did that say about him?

He tried to reach Fan, but she was at a meeting. He wondered with whom. For some reason he did not have a good feeling about that. The knowledge he had just gained (and he realized he did not doubt what Dr. Sun had outlined) gave him a streak of paranoia—which perhaps had been growing in him through these past weeks.

A feeling that was only increased by a visit from Mr. Mao Suit.

Cheng received Dong Chao with a polite smile that was combined with a resigned sigh. And discomfort that this official was not wearing a mask. It was a statement that Dong Chao was beyond bowing to the dictates of public health. Dong nodded to Cheng, in a manner that indicated he recognized Cheng's resignation and had no problem with it; in fact, he probably wanted that resignation.

"I heard about our colleague."

That gave Cheng just the slightest pause. He was going to pretend and ask "Who?"—but what was the point? He gathered himself and said, "I didn't know you knew him."

"Everyone knew—at least heard of—tongzhi Dr. Sun. A brilliant man. A little worried, perhaps, about the way things were done."

Did Mao Suit know? The "tongzhi" or comrade, seemed to assert Dr. Sun as bound to a patriotic connection that should not have been defied. On a lesser, if still uncomfortable level for Cheng, was the fact that "comrade" had been the insider greeting in certain gay quarters.

Cheng had placed the flash drive in a drawer in his desk intending to copy the file on another drive. He did not want the file on his computer. He checked himself from looking at the drawer. He suspected that Mao Suit knew Dr. Sun might know about the creation of the virus, and that Dr. Sun might have passed something of this to Cheng, but he guessed that he could not know that passage of information had been so thorough.

Cheng, blandly lying, said, "I'm glad you're here."

Eyebrows raised, the Mao Suit said, "Glad because…?"

"I have few questions to ask."

Dong spread his arms. "Ask."

Cheng felt he had to deflect an unpleasant situation that was intended to disarm him, box him in. He drew in a breath, then said,

"Throughout this, what has happened…I feel I'm being pushed along in conflicting directions."

"Conflicting?" It was an echo that was as threatening as it seemed bland.

"As if you—or someone—was trying to decide what to do with me."

"How so?"

"Sending me to check on that man who kept shedding the virus, then appointing me to head the vaccine effort—"

"You weren't intrigued with that man's situation, what it said about this disease? You aren't…proud to be chosen for something very important?"

"Someone else could have visited him. I could have read the report. Someone else is more qualified to oversee a vaccine project."

"Are you telling me you want to…withdraw from what is necessary now?"

"I do my best work in the lab. Discovering—well, science."

"We can appreciate that. But now you're required to apply your science. Isn't science supposed to be connected to the everyday world? Didn't you go into all those dark, bat-filled caves all over the country?"

"That had a continued purpose. That had a chain of steps. This seems I am being placed here and there."

"To oversee the vaccine—that is not here and there."

Cheng could not immediately argue against that. He was skirting something he could not exactly put into words. But he tried, even though he felt it could literally be dangerous to him. He said, "It's almost as if I'm being…distracted."

He had said it—almost like an accusation. The eyebrows of the other were raised again.

"We never thought of you as someone who could be…distracted." The pause before and drawing out of that last word, Dong's echo of what Cheng had said, was also an accusation.

Cheng palpably sighed. He was in it now, no going back. "I have the feeling there are things about the lab recently, the past year that—" He stopped, perhaps both afraid of adding something that would be too challenging and at the same time daring Dong to turn all this to an offhand but impenetrable official advantage.

The smile of the other was not one of self-assurance, but one that apparently presented some sort of confrontation with Cheng. A smile that said its bearer had, from habit, been prepared for such contingencies.

"Of course, we understand that anyone working here, even our top people, such as you, cannot know everything about the extensive work being done here."

Cheng was trying to think of what those officials had told him not so long ago—a lessening of phone use, and other mysterious doings that he could not exactly recall now. He said, as if with simple innocence, "I guess I'd like to know if there has been work in my field, with virus, especially the coronavirus...that for some reason I don't know."

Mao Suit said pleasantly, "Dr. Chang, I'm not sure if I know everything you know and don't know."

"Well, tell me the things I don't know."

"I said, how could I know that?"

"Tell, me what you think I don't know."

"You want me to guess."

"I don't think you need to guess."

There was a pause. The other leaned the side of his chin on his fist. For a moment he regarded Cheng like a pensive statue. Then said: "You think there are secrets. You want them."

"Are there secrets—which I should be told?"

"Should?"

"We're playing word games."

"No game, here doctor."

Now he dared. "I think you feel I need to be controlled. But you still need to use me."

"You *are* useful. And perhaps there is some aspect of control in that."

"Just tell me: is there something about this virus that I don't know—that is important to know?"

Dong Chao gave Cheng a placid stare. "Your friend thought he knew things."

"What do you think he knew?"

"That we knew how serious it was…but did not want the people to panic."

"That's all?"

"We were on his side. He was on our side—"

This was of course hardly the situation. "You really think that's true?"

"He was just rushing ahead too fast. Dr. Chang, it is not easy to oversee an epidemic in a large province."

"I'm sure it isn't. And easy to create—" He stopped. He'd said it.

Dong folded his hands together; his smile was unctuous. He seemed involved in a happy, superficial prayer. He gave a sort of half laugh. "You think this virus was…created?" Cheng was silent. "There are always rumors like that. I hope that's not what Dr. Sun told you before he…died?"

"He did not say that, no." Of course, that was technically true. Dr. Sun had not spoken that to Cheng, but his work on the flash drive had.

"Perhaps if he had recovered…." Mao Suit left that hanging. To Cheng it implied that if his friend had recovered, he would have been watched closely. Or worse. And perhaps—Cheng had to think this—that the state had made sure Dr. Sun had not recovered. Though Chang immediately said to himself, *No, that is too much—*

The two men looked at each other for a few moments. Cheng dared himself, and then said, "So you think it's just a rumor?"

"About?"

Cheng sighed. *He wants me to literally say it.* "Artificial creation." Why not, at this point, say what is?

"Well, of course that is…your purview." There was a deliberate smile. "You would know better than I do. With *your* expertise."

So now it seemed he—they—knew that he knew. Or it was part of the game? Cheng said, "So at this point…?"

"We go on. The vaccine."

"And forget?"

Dong Chao leaned toward Cheng, who had to stay himself from involuntarily moving back a bit, and said, "Nothing is forgotten, doctor, nothing."

"Nothing is forgotten—and you need me."

"Yes, both of those."

"What if I don't want to pursue the vaccine, but other…science? Related science?"

"You would not want this…prevention—for the people?"

"Of course, I want a vaccine." A pause. "So you feel this will be here a while."

Dong spread his arms, as if exhibiting the sharp cut of his Mao suit. "It appears. It appears. The indications—doctor, you know it's spreading." He stood up. "We can go around in a circle. I just came here to…."

"Yes?"

Dong laughed. "Give you encouragement." He might have been saying the simplest, kindest thing.

"To tell me my place."

Dong cocked, his head, gave a subtle smirk. Then he gave the longest sigh, like a man tired at the end of a task duty had inflicted. "If you want to put it that way…. I have my place, too."

"With more latitude than I am given."

"We are each more free and less free than we each think."

Cheng let another pause grow, then said: "Well, we've established something."

"An exchange, let's call it."

Cheng nodded. He was resigned—to being forever on guard. "Yes."

Now it seemed that Dong let another pause return and grow, while Cheng thought the conversation finished. But in a moment the other said, "It was good that you paid your respects to your friend's mother."

Cheng responded so naturally it might have seemed he was not thrown off balance by that. "That was the right thing to do."

"I hope she does not feel…aggrieved, that, along with losing her son—thinking we, the government—neglected…him."

"You didn't let him be heard. I'm sure she's not happy about that."

"And she knew everything that was supposed to be heard?"

"Again, this game. You can talk to her—although that would be…cruel."

"We would not interfere with her mourning. He was a good doctor."

"Yes."

"And a good friend to you."

Cheng felt Dong was inferring something more than the usual comradery between male friends. He said nothing but, "A good friend, yes. A comrade. And then, suddenly this does not seem a time when there is time for friendships."

Dong sighed. "Well, for a few months, at least, we'll be looking at this virus. Then it will pass. We'll have our vaccine."

"There has never been a vaccine against a coronavirus."

"Science always establishes a first time."

Cheng gave a soft laugh. "I think that is more command, than confidence."

That practiced, expansive gesture again. "You may take that as both, Dr. Chang."

As Dong Chao stood up, Cheng said, "Vaccines take time."

Dong shook his head slightly, negating Cheng's closing assertion. "Time is more compressed now. Our technology moves fast."

He left. Cheng remained still, looking at the door. *That visit was a threat*, he thought. Yet, "they" needed him. *At least enough to warn me.* That was grim comfort. No, no comfort at all, just realization. Cheng would have to walk a cautious borderline.

He knew he would get no work done today. Well, he had received so much today, though. He really wanted to call Fan, but he wondered if his calls would be monitored now, even on his own cell phone. He went looking for Fan to speak to her in person, but it seemed she had left the lab. He might as well do that, too, even if it was still a little earlier than his usual departure time. In fact, Cheng often liked to come into the lab a little later than most and stay later than most. He liked the feeling that there was not so much of a crowd of others just outside his office.

He wished he could just go home without having Junjie drive him. He considered—and perhaps not for the first time—Junjie reported on him to Mao Suit. Yes, Dong knew he had visited Dr. Sun's mother. Of course, there were other ways "they" could know, but would it not be simpler if Junjie were not only driver but spy?

He called Junjie. He would have to be on guard with him.

"I'm outside right now."

"Well, that's convenient." Cheng was not sure if the sarcasm of that was discernible. In his mind he saw Dong considering that Cheng would be upset at their meeting, want to leave the lab, and so communicated to Junjie that he should be ready to drive Cheng.

Outside the lab, the end of day was fraught with blues and greys at the horizon, as if contesting whether to allow the clear livid sunset to be seen. As Cheng was getting into the car, Junjie was putting on his mask. There was nothing unusual about that. Sitting in the car by himself, there was no reason for him to be masked. It was certainly more comfortable not to have a mask on, no matter how much one had gotten in the habit of doing so. But today, perhaps because of his tense meeting with Dong, Cheng felt there was something too practiced, too staged at this. As if Junjie were letting Cheng see his face for a moment longer than would be natural. A reverse strip tease, displaying his handsome face to the older man. Cheng for actually first time, had the startling thought that the driver might try to seduce him. Both spy and seducer. To compromise him. Whether "they" knew or not Cheng was gay—but the way Dong had intimated intimacy between him and Dr. Sun…. *They really want me bound*, he said to himself, settling into the car. He said nothing to Junjie but a simple "Hello" as he got in the back seat of the car.

And then realizing this was the first time he had gotten into the back seat instead of sitting in the front with Junjie, he said, "I've got some work to look over—need a little room." He spread some papers in front and alongside him, to give evidence of what he'd said, but this was material he had looked over thoroughly before. What he really wanted to look at, that is, reread, review, was the material on the flash drive that was in an inner pocket in his coat. This was something he did not want to be left in the lab.

Junjie nodded, and said something that Cheng could not hear through the driver's mask.

They had driven perhaps ten minutes when they came to a temperature check traffic stop. This had happened once before when Junjie had been driving Cheng, who had displayed some official credentials to the police and had been allowed to continue on, without the temperature check. But today, when Cheng rolled the window down and extended his identification to the officer, whose eyes peering over his mask seemed especially tense and suspicious, it was a different story.

"I am sorry, Dr. Chang, we have to test everyone."

Before Cheng could register any surprise or unease, the temperature gun was aimed at his head. Cheng tensed, in a moment there was a buzz. "You're fine," said the officer, who now performed his duties with Junjie. It seemed to Cheng that the young driver turned his face to the officer in an almost coy manner, but this might have been Cheng's recent thoughts coloring the situation.

There was another buzz. "You're fine," the officer repeated.

"Thank you," said Junjie to the officer, as if the latter had extended him something pleasing. Driving on, Junjie said with sideways glance, "I guess no one's escaping things now."

Whether this "spy" (as Cheng was now viewing Junjie) meant that on more than a superficial level, Cheng did take it as a not too disguised comment that he, Dr. Chang Cheng, was being watched.

He didn't like this feeling of things closing in on him like this. Maskless Mao Suit this afternoon, and then Junjie's artful—or artless—display of his features a moment longer than necessary. It was plain Junjie was a young man "on the make," as the Americans say, as Fan had related. That was distinct impression Cheng had gleaned with Junjie and the seeds. Who knew what other schemes he had working on the side?

As for possibly literally seducing Cheng.... Well, if he had met a handsome young man in circumstances other than this— Cheng had not had sex since last summer, a time that seemed far off now, not just in time but in circumstance. In fact, there was nothing so unsexual—at least to him—as this present moment: Wuhan locked down with this new virus and the new pressure he was experiencing in his work.

At any rate, Cheng was now thinking that he in turn should be watching the others who were watching him.

As Junjie pulled before Cheng's house, the young driver said, "You look tired."

Cheng was jolted out of his thoughts about Junjie by Junjie's voice. He almost felt as if the driver had been reading his thoughts. "It turned out to be a long day," said Cheng, vaguely.

Junjie turned back to look at Cheng. "After seeing your friend's mother...." He left that unfinished. His eyes seemed to say, *Tell me more.* Or: *I know you've been told—something.*

Cheng could not shake the sensation that Junjie was closing in on him. He said, off handedly (or so he tried to be), "Yes, and then some things at work—" So he in turn left something unfinished and got out of the car. He recalled the flash drive in the inner pocket of his jacket; he was surprised that for some time he'd forgotten it was there. Perhaps that was good; it had saved him continual anxiety. And yet he *should* have been conscious of it at every moment.

"Good night, Dr. Chang," Junjie called out. Cheng only half turned with his own "Good night."

Trying to settle in at home, Cheng was restless. He decided that his feelings about Junjie was transference of a larger, if undefined threat. He felt everything was closing in on him in a manner that left him no way for a safe exit. He refrained from reviewing Dr. Sun's material right away, made himself dinner and tried to watch TV.

He wanted to avoid the new, but everything else on at the moment was too inane. He resigned himself to the news, thinking, *What lies about the virus will they tell?*

A young woman outside a hospital was saying, "Originally it was thought that the time between infection and the development of symptoms was, three weeks or even more, but this seems, in most cases, to be a longer time than average. Onset of symptoms could be ten to fourteen days. At any rate, this length of time, ten days or three weeks, is long enough to hamper tracking the spread of this new virus."

The woman was earnest and serious—idealistic, thought Cheng—and so might titter on the borderline of truth and censorship. He thought this as a sudden hope, then stayed himself with the reality that her immediate hierarchy at this news outlet would keep her on track.

She was saying, "What perhaps many viewers in the city of Wuhan don't realize, is that in Hubei province other places are dealing with another virus, if a more common one: the flu. There are certainly cases of flu in Wuhan, more than usual, in fact, while in the cities of Yichang and Xianning incidence is extremely high. Some health experts are saying that the incidence of cases is as much as twenty times what it is normally."

This was something Cheng definitely did not know. There is always talk at the lab of each year's flu, but Cheng did not recall hearing anything like this. Or perhaps he had been so focused on the new virus he had not been paying enough attention. But no, that would not be like him.

"There is a question of whether this much higher incidence of flu is somehow connected to the new virus—but it is a question that no one can answer yet."

There was a brief instant during which the young woman looked back at the viewer, as if in punctuation; then she was gone from the screen. At this point, Cheng began to ignore the TV and search for further information about the response to the virus on his phone. It was rumored, but not confirmed, that President Xi Jinping and President Donald Trump had had a phone conference about the virus. "They're both hoping it will be like SARS, and just go away," was the comment of one online reporter.

It was not surprising there was speculation (well founded, Cheng considered), that the number of reported cases—and deaths—was appreciably below the actual amount. And there was the matter of how many cases had presented themselves at the end of 2019, when the incidents of this new virus could be confused with something else.

"On January 3, China reported to WHO there had been 44 cases of a pneumonia from an unknown cause. Later researchers concluded there may have been two hundred or more cases of the virus before the end of the year."

Cheng found more information about the spike in flu in Hubei. By the first week of December cases had risen 2,059 percent over the same time the previous year. Yichang had 6,135 cases and Xianning 2,148 cases. Wuhan wasn't far behind that, with 2,032.

Again, there was no scientific link that could yet be determined between the flu and this new virus, but it was likely that the flu brought many health-compromised patients into hospitals where they would be all the more vulnerable to further infection. At any rate, one health official remarked, "This huge increase of flu cases and the arrival of this new virus seems to stretch coincidence. There has to be something connected here, that we don't know yet."

Cheng thought of connections. Like the new virus, the flu virus also had spikes and was also an RNA virus. There were many influenza strains; the flu mutated easily. Yearly flu vaccines were based on scientific guesses rather than certainty. Would there be many strains of the virus that had shut down Wuhan? That would make it harder to produce a viable vaccine. Cheng still looked upon that task with the dread of a sentence—even while he told himself he should be proud that he would be aiding humanity in its fight against a new disease.

Cheng found a commentator who opined: "The advent of this new virus may call into question attitudes and a way of life that most Chinese have accepted. In general, the citizens of the most populous country on Earth have been willing to give up freedoms to the government in exchange for increased opportunities of materialism, of wealth, for increased social stability.

"But now with hundreds of millions of Chinese living in regions that have been economically—and socially—locked down by the virus, there are dissatisfactions, questions, about how the government has handled this health crisis, as well as the realization the government may not be able to keep its citizens safe. Even those, especially those, who directly try to keep us safe, are vulnerable, in fact the most vulnerable: those who directly work in our healthcare system.

"It is no secret that the government has kept secret the deaths of six doctors and nurses, killed by this virus."

Was Dr. Sun among their number? Not that it mattered, Cheng thought. In fact, he was surprised there were only six. There would certainly be others.

"A number of these healthcare workers had received a formal reprimand from the government or at least the police for trying to panic the public about this virus. –Strange job for the police. And a devious job for our government."

Yes, Dr. Sun had indeed been "reprimanded.' And had died from a disease that had come into existence only months ago, and of which he had been trying to warn others.

Cheng put down his phone, rested his head in his hands, then with tight, insistent fingers massaged his forehead. After a little while, he stopped. There was something he was forgetting. He had not called Fan. But now he really did not want to talk. What he really had "forgotten" was the flash drive. He needed to review that material. He sighed. In another moment, he was plugging it into his laptop.

35.

Li awaited Fan's arrival with a mixture of relief and enthusiasm. It seemed unbelievable that he could pass from his strange adventures on the moon to this return to his apartment, awaiting Fan. Somewhere, in the many levels of his consciousness, he contemplated the amazing fact that he could be in one bizarre realm, or simply a realm so far from the normal everyday, and that everyday realm could continue without him—and then he could come back to it.

When Li opened the door to Fan, they both stood a long moment, smiling at each other. "How's Earth, now?" Fan said, with a big smile. Li returned a wordless smile. They hugged, kissed. Li felt Fan's body against his as a further affirmation of his return. At the same time, because he had been apart from her for what seemed like such a long time, there was a newness to her presence—almost, in fact, a strangeness....

On Fan's part, the pleasure—and relief—of being with Li again, was briefly invaded by the thought he had, by his own account, experienced something very strange. Had it changed him? Then she threw off that thought quickly.

Sometime later, when they lay in bed, Li breathed happily, looking up at the dim ceiling, the room illumined by the low light of a small lamp in a corner, the geometry of the lampshade issuing a perfect round circle of soft light surrounded by a shadow that flowed out from it like a vague halo. "Earth is not bad," Li said, in answer to what seemed a long ago asked question. Fan, her head turned to him, gave him a wordless smile in return. She moved, like an animal stretching in comfort and pleasure, and the blanket slipped from her enough so that the iridescence she had tattooed upon her flesh gave a soft sheen of rippled light.

If Li had only moments ago considered Fan's presence fraught with something new and even strange, now in his eyes she had not changed at all. And why should she? It had only been two weeks since he had seen her. Yet, what Li had experienced made this separation a much longer subjective time. He had told her over the phone of his strange experiences—at least in summary; he had expected, in this so welcome reunion, that he would have related his odyssey more thoroughly; after all, was she not the one person in his life that he would want to impart fully what he had gone through? Yet, at least in this moment, it was as if what he had suffered (yes, that was the word that came to his thoughts) would interfere with his pleasure of this Now; he did not want "that" world to invade this: he had been starved for the normalcy of Fan, the feeling of her body, the sound of her voice, her very breathing. Yes, he suddenly thought, *I have not heard anyone's breathing but my own.* –It was a curious thought; in the daily round, how conscious of the breathing of others would he be? And he had seen Lin and Yang every day during his quarantine—but why would be aware of their breathing? They had always been masked. Anyway, he was so aware of Fan's breathing, as they simply looked at each other across a span of a few inches. Lovers can be so pleased with the face of the other. Looking at Fan, he recalled her as Chang'e; and when he and she had spoken on the far side of the moon....

They fell asleep for a little while. Then Li awoke with a start, as if he were supposed to be attending to something that this unexpected rest had kept him from. He looked about the room, at the small lamp, the shadow and light it threw. He looked at Fan. His gaze seemed to awaken her. She stirred. She looked back him, first in the pleasing haze of returning from sleep, then with a question. "What?"

"I have to—" But those words seemed to lead to nothing. Then he remembered. "The moon." He said that quietly, as if recall and comprehension had calmed him.

A few minutes later Li and Fan were outside, in the winter night, in the building's parking lot. Li was looking up at the moon, the full moon, which was poised just to the side of a cluster of branches from a large tree.

"It was new moon when I was quarantined. Invisible."

To Fan he appeared a man who had been rewarded after going through a dark time. "Did you think it wasn't going to be here again? That you weren't going to be here?"

"I didn't think about not being—it not being, me not being…. But it's good to look at, now." His up-looking face seemed restful—gathering in rest after a long journey.

Fan leaned against him, one of her hands wrapped around his hand, the other grasping him at the elbow. "But you were on the other side."

He looked at her. "You say that as if you believe I was really—there."

"You speak like you were."

He sighed. "So strange. How is it possible they did that?" When he considered this, he was usually distressed; now he seemed to look at this outside of himself, even philosophically.

Looking up at the moon, Fan gave a sad smile. "They seem…to have a long reach." She gave her own sigh. "It's a cold night."

"I know. Just another minute."

"You need more…seeing?"

Smiling up at the moon, Li said, "Yes, I was there." Thus he quietly affirmed something for himself. After a pause: "On the side no one sees."

"Maybe a place only *you* can see."

He looked from the moon to her—his own Chang'e. "Yes. I'm sure that journey was just mine."

"Come on. It's cold." Raising her arm, she gestured to the moon. "I will always be here. And you will probably be there again. In a more tangible manner."

"That's a strange way to put it." Her expression in response seemed to say, *How else could I put it?* He said, "Remember when we talked about minute worlds—people living on atoms?"

"Your miniature moon city?"

"Smaller than that. Your nano world. I was thinking there are probably layers, I mean levels, to the tangible. And one level really can't communicate with another."

"So you think every level communicates—within itself?"

"In its way. We think of communication as concrete messages— language. I think language is…larger." He looked up at the moon again. "Maybe just *that*—is a communication, Maybe all *forms* are a message."

Fan laughed. "You're really getting metaphysical. But it's still cold."

His face raised to the moon, Li said, "I was thinking…. All the human beings that ever lived, all the technology that's been created, civilizations that rose and fell…. All that had to happen, centuries, millennia, billions of people—for me to go to the moon. To end with me, here."

Fan held his arm. She smiled. "You're almost there. But not yet."

His smile was sweet, but from another source as hers. "I told you: I've been. There."

She gave a soft laugh, as if touched by his madness. By his certainty.

Li, still smiling, nodded, absorbing some unspoken assertion into himself. The moon had edged into the cluster of branches, their bare dark twisting forms now upon the bright disc of that world like a design. Or some hieroglyphic Li was yet to decipher. Yes, he had been commanded once to "decipher"—

They went inside. Li had so many thoughts. They flowed through him like water. The full moon above Wuhan had raised the tides of his mind. He was flooded with Wuhan dreams. Lunar dreams.

Fan had some thoughts, too. Back inside, she told Li about the commercialization of her mask weave.

"You don't sound happy about it."

"They want to use my science to make money."

"Didn't you want your mask to be used?"

"You know what I mean. They will put…an operation around my science. Take it out of my…oversight."

"Your control."

"I still have work to make it better."

"Do you feel they are going to push you aside entirely?"

Fan sighed. "I don't know. Maybe it won't be as bad as I think. Up until now it was all my ideas, my direction." And then worry gave way to the purity of an idea. "You know, I was thinking today that viral spike proteins are a great model for polymer constructions: they have both compressive strength and stiffness."

"That's a conversation you can have with Cheng."

"So you're not interested?"

"I just couldn't keep up where you are going."

"Oh, I didn't tell you: Dr. Sun died."

Li was struck solemn. Fan was confounded by guilt; it had slipped her mind. Li said, "The virus?" Fan nodded. Li pursed his lips. "Is it—was it—suspicious?"

"Who knows? I didn't ask Cheng when he told me. The government didn't care for what Dr. Sun was doing. Though I think at this point…." Her words trailed off. Her expression seemed strange and distant.

"Fan. You alright?"

"I'm getting tired of everything. Being here with you—again: a little refreshment." She gave him a sad smile.

"Is that what I am?"

She didn't answer that. "Li, I want to complain—but about what, really? That my work is being recognized? People are getting sick.

I'm not, you're not—"

"I was."

"You said it wasn't much."

"It wasn't."

"Well, you're healthy."

"I am, I think. But what they did to me: my mind. That's not good."

"You're back here. And so is your mind."

"I like to think it is. But if I go on with this—what will they do next?"

"Would you go through something like that again, to go to the moon?"

He looked at her silently. "Maybe it's just an obstacle I could not have imagined. Maybe they need a mind that...can be a little insane and still function."

"Maybe it's a little insane to want to go to the moon."

He gave a soft laugh and said nothing.

Fan had a sudden thought and asked, "How did you get back home? There's still no transportation."

"They gave me a driver."

Fan had an unpleasant feeling she did not want to recognize as unpleasant. "Was his name Junjie—young, nice looking?"

"You know him?"

"He drives Cheng regularly." Fan told Li about Junjie approaching her with his own ideas of selling her mask weave.

Li said, "You don't think that's connected to what the lab is offering?"

"First of all, it's not the lab offering, but the government. And it wasn't an offer, but a...command. But this driver—and now he's driving you. I think he's some kind of spy. At least he's, as they say in America, someone on the make."

"He might just work for the lab. Drives whomever they need to be driven."

"That may be true. But if he's driving you that's not just the lab. He's got his own plans."

"Isn't that maybe all of us? We work for the government—and want to go our own directions."

"You, me, Cheng—our own way is from our work. With Junjie…it's the work of others. He's like someone who…gathers."

"I'm not going to worry about him."

"He's like a sign of things. A part of China now."

"You're being too…academic. I think that type is in every country."

Fan looked at him. "Is your type in every country?"

"Am I a type? I'm the type that wants to go into space, that feels it's natural for the human race to do that?"

Their conversation meandered to this or that, and sometimes in a way that was somewhat uncomfortable. Then they gave up words, had something to eat and went to bed. Earlier their reunion after two weeks of separation had been suffused with longing and the erotic; now there was the simple comfort of the presence of another; each could shed in sleep the tiredness accumulated during this strange time. Before that sleep Li thought of the full moon overhead; he felt the weight of that world, unseen above his ceiling, above the roof of the building. It was hundreds of thousands of kilometers away and yet he was connected to it in a way that obliterated distance. Or simply denied it. Like that quantum phenomenon that Einstein had termed "spooky action at a distance," the state of particles widely separated mimicking each other. While Fan was thinking again of the molecular strengths of viral spike proteins woven into some massive factory produced product, the strength of a natural "weave" woven into nano threads of recycled nanoplastics bearing ghosts of information memories, an electronic hieroglyphic of polymers subsumed in the nanoworld, virus and plastic falling between the wavelengths of light by which we have known the world for all of human existence.

In the morning Li realized the moon was no longer overhead. He felt, in this new day's light, abandoned. Or perhaps he had abandoned a world that had become natural to him. He had welcomed, he had needed the evening with Fan, he had needed the contrast of a return to Earth, even an Earth, a city suffering from an epidemic; but he was truly marked now, by that moon that had slipped to the other side of the planet.

And when Fan asked him, "Do you have to go back there today?" Li was thinking of himself on the surface of the far side of the moon, when of course she just meant the training facility.

"No. I'll be called."

"I could have given you a ride."

"I guess I can have that driver."

"If you do…just be careful of him."

Li laughed. Fan both laughed and frowned. Before she left, she said, "I think Cheng wanted to tell me something yesterday—after he saw Dr. Sun's mother."

"Maybe she has some information her husband didn't get a chance to…tell people."

After Fan left, Li was restless. He picked up *A History of the Moon*. He had forgotten he had taken it from the training. He had the thought: *Is this even a real book?* Perhaps "they" had concocted it to influence him in subtle—or not so subtle—ways. But why would it be by an Englishman, published twenty-five years ago? Didn't make sense. Or did that make it more "real"? Then he said to himself, *Of course it's real—*

He was about to open it when the call came.

It was the voice that had once told him to "Decipher."

36.

"I hope you had a restful night." The voice was friendly, in a businesslike way, and had the manner of someone who spoke to Li regularly. "You were going to have another day's rest from training, but there are so many things happening in the world today—we have to use time more…quickly." (That "quickly" struck Li ominously.) "We need to have a meeting this afternoon. An hour or two."

Li felt grasped by the surreal again. His psyche was just regathering itself after his very unusual training. He felt displaced— from what he had experienced and his "return" to the more everyday world. But he had no choice. He repeated the address the voice gave him.

Did he feel better about going to a place other than the training room? Not really. Not that he would have been more comfortable returning to the place that had taken him continually to the far side of the moon.

"A driver will pick you up."

Of course, Li knew it would be Junjie, and it was. At the beginning of the afternoon Li got into the passenger seat alongside the young driver, who nodded at Li silently, as if he had been in the habit of driving Li every day, and no spoken greeting was needed at this point. Li was fine with that. He did not want to talk to Junjie; he really didn't want to talk to anyone. But soon he would be talking to someone who would certainly have a say in his future, his immediate future in the Chang'e program.

Then he realized he had to relate the destination to Junjie; though as soon as he began to read off the address, Junjie dismissed this with a wave. Well, it was obvious Junjie would know where he had to take Li—who made the uncomfortable connection of himself as a prisoner being ferried from once place of captivity to another.

From Li's apartment the drive went diagonally into Wuhan. Once more Li absorbed the fact of so few vehicles on the road. It took a much shorter time to arrive in an area in which Li would not have thought any official government business would take place. The block had a somewhat rundown aspect. There was a row of stores with small apartments above. In two of the stores were displays for items intended for the Spring Festival the virus had canceled. They seemed like things awaiting another time to be awakened.

Junjie parked in the middle of the block and indicated to Li with a nod of his head a doorway alongside one of the stores. Li could see no number on or above the doorway, and there was no address on either of the stores alongside. So Li needed that gesture from Junjie. Though as he got out, he considered: what if the driver were intentionally misleading him? It was a momentarily indulgence of paranoia that indicated he really did not want to go to this "meeting" (alongside the conviction he was being manipulated).

The door was unlocked. This seemed ominous to him, too. He should have had to announce himself via an intercom. The door opened to a narrow staircase of well worn, dark brown wood. As he climbed the stairs they creaked slightly. He found himself climbing upward more carefully, to avoid that creak. It didn't really work. At the top of the stairs, he had to turn to the right and was immediately facing another doorway, one whose top half was of frosted glass. He knocked on it lightly. He thought he heard a response from inside. He turned the knob, the door opened slowly, with a certain stiffness. He entered a small room.

A man sat at a small desk. He wore no mask. Behind the man was a window that looked out upon rooftops of variegated heights and the winter sky. The rooftops were ugly, the sky was grey and without feature. The light from the window was the only illumination in the room, though the grey window light more silhouetted the man at the desk than illumined him. It took a moment for Li to see he was around fifty, a few years less or more. He was a little heavy. It was a common face—and then Li was struck. This was the face of the "other" he had encountered on the far side of the moon.

For a moment that realization froze Li; he felt he had been trapped.

"Zhen Li." The man pronounced his name softly, rising to offer his hand. Li shook it. For an instant Li's grasp was tentative, then abruptly firm. The man, who pronounced his own name firmly, "Sung Wei," gave a look that showed he knew Li was abruptly trying to show his strength.

Sung indicated the wooden chair before the desk that seemed of the same dark wood and age as the steps. Li sat; Sung, smiling politely, sat. "Zhen Li: it is good to meet you."

Li could not say he felt the same. He nodded. "Thank you." Now there was the expression on the other's face that said he knew Li was not pleased to be here.

Sung Wei said, "You can take your mask off. I understand you've had the virus, and I've been tested recently: negative. It's better if we can talk face to face—fully face to face."

Li wasn't that comfortable taking off his mask, but he did, slowly—as if he were cautiously testing the air in the room.

Sung said, "We won't make this long. You do need some…respite—from your efforts. We just need…a firsthand report. Of all your experiences in training. Everything. What you saw, what you felt—"

"You do not know what I saw?"

Sung raised his eyebrows as if in pleased amusement. "We cannot know everything."

"But you know a lot."

Sung's smile seemed to indicate he was condescending to a child's pique. Then more solemnly he said, "Not everything, no."

"You know there were a lot of strange things."

"We understand, that yes."

"Things that you—the program—created for me."

Sung cocked his head, and his expression said, *Did we though?* "The question we need to determine at this point, is what did we, let's say, create, and what did *you* create?"

"But the program did create—for me…." Li looked back at Sung with a challenge.

"Each of our taikonauts is an individual, so we created special training for each of you."

Li sighed. At first, he might have considered his own questions and statements bold, but quickly he had embraced a sort of resignation (if not quite the accurate word) for whatever would happen henceforth. He said, "How did you do it? Was it like hypnosis? Drugs?"

Sung drew back in his chair a little. There was a pause. Li saw something wash across that face—the face he had met on the far side of the moon. Sung said, "We cannot tell you precisely at this point. We cannot tell you the How—but perhaps the Why."

Li: "So, start there."

Sung's eyebrows raised again, but not in any sort of amusement. As if Li had indeed been too bold.

Li waited. When Sung didn't immediately continue, Li said, "I met you on the moon. Anyway, there was a face in a spacesuit, another man—you."

Sung did not seem unduly surprised. "I'm flattered I was able to meet you in your adventures." His expression now was as of one receiving an intriguing fantasy. "Much more unusual than this place."

Li pressed. "Did you know you were there?"

Now Sung sighed. "No, not really."

"Not really or maybe?"

"Sometimes answers cannot be so precise."

"Can there be any answers at all?"

"Some. For both of us. Before we continue to go around in this circle, can you start at the beginning and tell me—everything?"

"I'm not sure where the beginning is."

"Yes, that is often the hardest to pinpoint. To fix. When it first seemed...strange."

Li considered. "You want everything." He said this as a statement.

"Everything."

"I recite all that and I seem crazy."

"The unusual always seems crazy. People used to think it crazy that the Earth was round. Why, you'd fall right off. You, Zhen Li, were in another place, seeing other things."

"I was in that training room."

"Elsewhere, too."

"Elsewhere."

"Definitely." Pause. "Tell me."

A pause on Li's part. "You're recording this?"

"Video." Sung waved to a wall. Li noted the camera there. There were so many cameras in China one did not notice them until one's attention was directed to them.

Li began with the miniature city on the lunar floor, continuing through all the strangeness, the apparent writing on a rock, the abandoned life size city and the other, his travels along the terminator, the underground caverns of ice, the great insect creatures, the metallic figures, and, yes Chang'e. He did not relate that Fan had been the moon goddess. He would keep some of the surreal to himself. When Li finished, he silently regarded Sung, who was silent in turn—then slowly nodded. As if all this had been expected.

Li said, "What was the purpose of all this? It seems I was being subjected to more than the moon."

Sung said, very quietly, as if to himself. "You were." Then: "We wanted you to explore more than just a dead world. We realize that as we go out there it is more than just a physical journey."

"You expect everyone who goes to the moon to experience what I did?"

"No. We knew there was richness in you."

"What does that mean?"

"There were—are—more possibilities."

"For things that don't make sense?"

Sung pursed his lips. "I'll ask you: When these…events were happening to you—did you think they didn't make sense?"

Li had to consider. "I did not think about them in that way. I was just—"

"You were receiving them, going through them…as part of your mission."

"I'm not sure I can attach the word 'mission' to them as…I did what was required? In the moment?"

A smile, of—approval? "That's a fair way of putting it."

"I don't think I'm putting any of this well. Even when I recite to you—everything."

Sung laughed. "We know you can never tell everything. Oh, not deliberately. We just know that is impossible."

Li was not sure what Sung meant, though he sensed a meaning behind that in some way—and did not want to continue in this vein. "I don't know if I even want an explanation now…." Though he did. "I just want to know how I'm judged. Will I go to the real moon?"

"I understand." Sung said this as if he really did understand. "Even after all that—you're willing— But an assessment can't be fully given at this time."

"Give it to me partly."

"You did well."

"And?"

"And you did well. Better than most, I'm sure."

"But better enough to be the best?"

"This is still—there are others in training. Though the field has narrowed." Sung leaned forward a little. "You're still in it."

Li sat back. "So that's my...reward."

"A curious way to put it."

"The race goes on. I still run. Do I have other tests?"

"I don't even know enough about that to tell you."

Li gave a long exhalation. "So...I tell you so much; you tell me nothing."

"We have given you the opportunity to go to the moon. No one human being could leave this Earth without an entire government program providing every conceivable technology. We give you that, you have to give us your experience."

"Conceivable and inconceivable. I have not been to the moon— yet."

"In a way, Yes; in way, No."

Silence again in the small room. Looking out of the window behind and to the side of Sung, Li saw several birds fly swiftly over the rooftops, swooping down with a shift in the wind, then rising again. In a moment they were out of sight. Sung noted Li's glance and looked back at Li with a question. "Birds," said Li, with a faint smile.

Sung smiled back, "As much as they can fly, they are still bound to Earth, too."

Li sighed. He felt he had been talking with Sung a long time. "You give me no…reflection of what I have gone through."

"I'm sure your meeting with Chang'e is unique."

"And is that good or bad?"

"I'm not sure. It could show you are too prone to mythology; or you could be the most bold. The one most viscerally connected to what we need to do."

"Is the government prone to mythology?

"We are not having—I am not having—an academic discussion."

"They named the program Chang'e."

"You would rather have another name?"

"No, I like it. I didn't think about it one way or another at first, but now—it fits."

"Fits your meeting with Chang'e."

Li's resignation to what he could only by now call a bureaucratic madness allowed him to rest his head in his hands, then push them back across his temples, as if sweeping all this surreality aside. He said, "I wonder if others will meet her."

"You fear her—fidelity?" Sung laughed. "I have a feeling you are unique. Or maybe it's just that you have a unique model for Chang'e."

Li thought about Fan. She was the woman in his life, but there was really nothing in her, well, essence that should have recalled to him Chang'e. Li sighed once more and said, "I wish I could say, I wish you could say, something that would make all this more clear."

"You have been clear enough." Sung seemed genuinely encouraging.

"It makes me think—you don't even need to send anyone to the moon. You can just have all those taikonauts in the program believe—think—they were there."

"You thought you were there, but you knew you weren't."

"With a little more…convincing—from whoever—"

"You walked into a room, not a rocket."

"But perhaps our scientists have invented teleportation. You walk into a room, and then you are on the moon."

"We are not dealing in deception."

"That means everything I experienced was real?"

"Didn't you ask that?"

"At this point I'm not sure."

"You know about quantum theory."

"Enough."

"Real or imagined. Real *and* imagined. You can't be sure, I mean you can be both, either—until an observer collapses the event with observation."

"But wasn't I the observer? Or is it you?"

"I'm not the observer. I'm just the one relaying—at least recording—the message."

"I don't have a message; I'm babbling."

"A person might be given a code he can't decipher. He relays it to those who can."

"You told me to decipher."

For an instant Sung seemed taken aback at that. "It wasn't a command, it was a suggestion."

"So I come back with no deciphering, just image after image." Abruptly he added: "Why did I see your face on the other man I encountered? I didn't know you."

"That is a great mystery."

"You planted it in me?"

"There are also theories that we can remember the future."

"Is that what the Party thinks?"

"There are those who are quite forward thinking."

Li shook his head. "Did you give me all your crazy fantasies? Someone else's crazy fantasies?"

"They were all yours."

"You trained me—I trained myself—in fantasies?"

"I just told you—" Sung stopped, and seemed flustered. "You've talked me around into some corner."

"That's what I feel. Maybe you're in the trap, too."

Sung's laugh now was defensive. "No, Zhen Li, I am not in a trap. You're not in a trap. From my perspective, you have met challenges that none have. I can't guarantee your future in the program, but can say you haven't failed."

"But you can't guarantee I've succeeded."

"It's not success that we need. It's...maybe there is not a word." He took a deep breath. "I'll say this. Every 'strange' thing you saw, except one, had to do with the idea there were—at least there had been—intelligent life on the moon: writing, the city, figures. Intelligent others. Except for the ice caverns, your underground terminator, you saw others. I suppose the insects were 'others,' too. All this evidence of others. Even when you saw me—as you believe. It was always others—except in the sublunar depths."

Li took a moment to consider. "I guess that is true." Sung nodded. Li added, "And that means?"

Sung shrugged. "Perhaps humans are not prepared to conceive of the lifelessness of other worlds. We need some...reflection."

For a moment Li thought of those fantasies of life on the moon and Mars, detailed in that *fin de siècle* English book. He said, "I didn't expect to see those signs."

"Intellectually, yes, but not emotionally. We cannot leave our emotions on Earth. We take them with us always."

Li would have never expected a government official to say that. Regarding what was expected or not, he looked at Sung Wei as if seeing someone he had not anticipated.

Sung stood up. He extended his hand. Li, jolted out of what had become a seemingly endless dialogue, rose slowly, to shake hands. This time he did not assert his firmest grip, he simply matched Sung's. He didn't care at this point. The interview—debriefing— had left him dispirited. He had considered his efforts in the program to be dedicated and noble. He felt not so much mocked as sidetracked, blocked.

Sung said, "You will have a few days' rest. We will contact you. You have earned some time."

Li thought this would be "time" during which he would wait for something he was not sure of at all. He slowly moved to the door replacing his mask as he did so. At the door he turned to Sung Wei and asked, "Just who is this driver, Fu Junjie?" Involuntarily he felt the mask protected him from what might be thought an impertinent question.

"He is not a good driver?"

"I didn't say that. He seems, from what I see, everywhere."

"I have nothing to do with him. And all I know is that he seems a useful young man."

Li nodded, as if he could not have expected any more of an answer than that, and left the room. His feet felt heavy as he went downstairs, as the wood once again creaked below him. He recalled the lighter gravity of the moon. Not only had they led him through all they had, but the physical reality of the lunar world has also been so vivid. So real. It still clung to him.

As Li expected, Junjie was replacing his mask when he saw Li approaching the car, putting down his phone to do so. Li felt Junjie was reporting on him to someone. He felt an urge to ask, but did not. He only said, "I hope I wasn't too long."

As Junjie pulled into the street, he said, "I'm sure you were as long as you needed to be."

That annoyed Li; it sounded condescending. He was about to respond but didn't.

They were stopped by a light. Near one corner a deliveryman was unloading some boxes from a small truck. There were more deliverymen than pedestrians in Wuhan these days.

Junjie suddenly said to Li, "Look at this." He aimed his phone towards the deliveryman, as if taking a photo; and it was a sort of photo: Li heard a click from the phone, then Junjie displayed the image to Li. There was the form of the man, a form filled with different shadings of color.

"Body heat," said Junjie. "You can tell if someone has a fever."

Li of course did not know Junjie had done something similar with Cheng. Li felt the driver was both trying to impress him and to warn him. Warn him of certain powers? Li said, "How do you have that on your phone?"

"The government. I need to be safe."

"Have you used that on me?"

Junjie nodded. His eyes smiled. It was a complacent smile. "The virus is dangerous. But I heard you had it."

"And who told you that?"

"I'm not sure I can say."

"You tease me with what you know but can't say."

Junjie said, flatly, "I'm sorry, I should not have— But I need to be safe."

"We all do," said Li just as flatly, then was silent the rest of the way back to his apartment. Junjie was silent, too. Was he embarrassed that he had been...impolite? Or just worried that he had said too much, given too much of himself away by demonstrating the heat tracking capabilities of his phone? Was this young driver more than he seemed? Or just wanted to display himself as being so?

But this gnawed at Li only a little while. He gave it up. It was all…unsatisfying. His "interview" with Sung Wei, the mysteries of Junjie—the mysteries of his training. When they pulled up in front of his apartment, he mumbled something to Junjie as he got out, more a sound than words, barely looking at the young driver. He turned around only when he heard the car pull away, and looked after its metallic body briefly glinting in the dull grey light of winter. That glint, from sun on metal, made him think of the lander and the rover on the far side of the moon, and he experienced a sensation that might have been called nostalgia, but which was not, a feeling he did not try to name, let alone analyze.

37.

Fan, Li and Cheng drove about for a while before Fan parked near a half-completed apartment building whose construction had been halted by the lockdown. The area around the building had been leveled, probably in preparation for further construction.

It had rained lightly that morning; now the sky was clearing. It was half sunny, half cloudy; the clouds seemed to unravel before the blueness above. The skeleton of the building, a framework without walls, was like the form of something which, when completed, might become other than originally planned. It rose into this sky of shade and sun, glistening with the rain that had not yet dried.

In a sense the three friends might have felt they were on the cusp of a similar possibility, torn in venues of light and dark. The original course each had taken appeared about to be altered. Or had been altered.

Fan turned off the car, said to Li beside her and Cheng in the back, "Well, this is deserted enough."

Cheng said, "Isn't the city deserted enough?"

"Even more so here."

Cheng: "Are we in hiding?" Though he surveyed the landscape without obvious worry.

Fan laughed. "I just wanted to stop." She smiled back at Cheng. "I've been thinking so many things, I just wanted to catch up to them." She nudged Li. "You're quiet."

Li nodded to the unfinished structure. "I might have seen this on the moon."

Cheng, who had been filled in on Li's visionary far side lunar adventures, said, "It does look...abandoned."

Fan said, "No, just not used yet."

Li looked back at Cheng. "That was it. It wasn't so much I found things abandoned. Now I have the feeling those things—the city— had been set down like that: it had never been lived in."

Cheng: "Just for you to be...confused?"

Li shook his head with resignation. "I must seem like that: confused."

"No, you seem to explain it very exactly."

"I don't explain it; I just relate it." He returned his eyes to the building. A cloud that had hidden the sun for a moment now revealed it. Li squinted in the sudden light, at the glint of the building. "I wish I knew what they were planning."

Fan said, "I think each of us want that. From our different positions."

Cheng shrugged and slightly smiled. Li affectionately squeezed Fan's shoulder. He pointed at the building. "Look at the birds." A dark flock of birds darted through the large, now sun-laced framework of the building, then gathered themselves in the sky, small dark bodies among patchwork clouds, and abruptly flew away. Li thought of the birds he'd seen outside the window where he had been interviewed (was that the word?) by the very earthbound "other." Of course, he had added that experience to what he had told Fan and Cheng, but not such fleeting particulars. It is those little moments of perception, those little things the eyes catch, the minute aspects that weave through an experience that seem to have nothing to do with the experience, yet are held privately in that moment and which are rarely related.

Watching the birds, Fan said, "They're free." Li had to recall the other in that grey little room saying that birds were bound to the earth. But he would not echo that. He too wanted the birds to be free—if not of Earth, at least of humans.

Cheng looked up at the birds, saying nothing. He was thinking of something quite apart from the visible.

There was another set of eyes that came on the scene and was very concerned with the visible. A police car pulled up alongside them.

Fan sighed. Cheng audibly groaned. Li gave a resigned laugh. "The birds have the right idea," he said.

A young officer got out of the car. His eyes above the mask were concerned.

Fan rolled down the window, gave the officer a polite smile, as he said, "Is there a problem here?"

"Not all. We were just talking."

The officer leaned forward, to look into the car. Li looked back without expression: Cheng gave a slight nod.

"Identification." He said this blandly, with the indifference of routine authority.

Fan handed over hers; Li and Cheng passed theirs to her; she gave them in turn to the officer.

Who was already frowning as he looked at what he'd been given. Two from the lab, and then there was Li's...

He said to Fan, "Did your lab send you here?" He looked back at the uncompleted building. His gaze said: *You have no reason to be here.*

"We were just driving, talking about…work. Needed to stop—save gas."

The officer nodded at this surely vague response. Then he held Li's identification apart from the others. "Is this—the space program?"

"I am a taikonaut. At least training to be."

The officer's eyes lit up. It was plain that beneath his mask he was smiling. His manner utterly changed. "That's—fantastic. I'd love to do something like that. That's something to be proud of."

Li, who normally let social opportunities slide right by him, grabbed onto this one. "It's very thorough training. Not easy." Fan was amused. She had never seen Li milk his position. For Li, this was practically boasting.

The officer said, "You might be on the moon someday."

"That's what I'm in training for."

"Wow. That's incredible." He gestured happily. "Please wait a moment." He darted back into his car, came back with an iPhone and a piece of paper.

"I just took a picture of your identification—for unofficial purposes. I'll show this to everyone when you're on the moon."

Li laughed. The officer might think Li happy at the officer's excitement, but both Fan and Cheng could see he was a little discomforted now. Especially when the officer extended the paper to Li and asked for his autograph.

He held up his hands to the officer, palms out. "I'm not sure if I should do that." But the officer tilted his head slightly and there was a look in his eyes—as if he were abruptly wounded. "This is just for personal use. I really admire—"

Li's discomfort was confounded by the man's apparent sincerity.

He took the paper and wrote his name, somewhat slowly, not with the habitual speed one usually signs one name. There was caution to this act.

"Thank you, thank you," said the officer, taking the paper.

He turned back to his car. "Be careful, be safe. Good fortune in your work."

As Li and Fan and Cheng watched the officer drive away, Cheng said, "If they were all like that, we could have the run of the city. At least you could, Li."

Li was at once smiling and worried. "He has a photo of my identification, my signature—"

"For personal reasons, only," Fan laughed. Then was serious. "I'm not sure if it's good or bad, but who expected that?"

"Who expects any of this?" said Li, frowning.

Cheng reached over the back of the seat, and slapped Li on the back. "Well, you're a hero to one man."

Fan, still serious, said, "That's exactly it. None of us expected...."
Cheng: "What?"

"What's happened to us. To our work."

There was a pause. Cheng said, "We were always involved in something larger than each of us. None of us could have been doing what we've been doing without the government behind it."

Fan: "I've been reminded of that, I think."

Li said, "But we've been working—I've been training...thinking things were in a certain direction—"

Cheng: "Is there any guarantee of direction in science?"

Li: "We should be guaranteed the right to—" He couldn't find the word.

Cheng said, "I guess we're realizing freedom is limited."

Fan said to Cheng, "So you really believe the virus is artificial?"

"It's hard to convince me of something a hundred percent, but I'll say I'm at ninety percent on this. Dr. Sun's work…seemed to cover everything, seemed the most logical path to what is happening now."

"You have any idea who could have done it?"

"I think a number of people have the knowledge—and resources—to have created this."

Fan had to ask: "Could you have done it?"

"If I had the intent—and put the time into it: yes."

There was a sad certainty to this the others absorbed as an irrevocable weight. Li said, "Maybe what's more important is where did it get out from? The lab? Somewhere else?"

Cheng: "The lab would be most the most logical place."

Li: "Intentional or accidental?"

Cheng drew in a breath. "I'm thinking now—or is it that I just want to believe—accidental."

Fan asked, "So how would you think that accident would happen?"

Cheng said, "Like a true accident. Someone walked out of the lab with it, not knowing. Either infected with it, or carrying the virus somehow without knowing."

Li: "Don't all of you work with the protective gear, things like that?"

"For the most part. But nothing is foolproof."

Fan said, "I wouldn't be surprised if it was the driver of yours. He has a total air of carelessness, along with a juvenile cleverness. It seems he is everywhere, and free to be everywhere."

Cheng laughed—defensively. "*My* driver? He seems to be attached to the rest of you, too."

"I'm suspicious of him. He comes to me, wanting to market my mask; and then the government wants it. He's the one who drove Li to that weird debriefing."

Cheng said, "There is something dubious about him. When he

told me about that scheme with the seeds to America—"

Fan: "Maybe the government is sending the virus to America with those seeds, but it backfired. It hit us."

Cheng sighed. "It's in a lot of places now. It could go from epidemic to pandemic. You really think Junjie spread it?"

Li said, "I think we're putting too much on him—because we're exposed to him. We see something unpleasant in him, he seems everywhere, his attitude is...metaphor?—for something essential we don't like. He represents something: an aspect."

Fan gave Li an affectionate tug on the chin. "Very good analysis."

Li said, "Cliché, but I think that's what it is."

Fan: "The new China: jumping on every material opportunity."

Li: "At the same time, it's possible it's him."

After a pause, in which the three of them squinted upward at another showing of the sun through clouds, Cheng said, "Whatever he is, it looks like he's going to be my driver through this lockdown."

Li: "I'd rather he'd not become mine."

Another pause. The skeleton of the building glittered again, if less so; the morning's rain was drying. Fan said, "So what are we all doing—now?"

Cheng made a resigned sound that could not be called a laugh. "Move through our duties. For me it looks like it's going to be a vaccine; and I think that's going to be more than just a few months' work. Fan, you're going to be part of—the foundation of—creating a special mask—"

"I'm just not ready to be interfered with yet."

"Is that science talking, or your feelings?"

"Intuition—which is more than just feelings."

Cheng nodded, whether accepting that or just noting it, Fan wasn't sure. Cheng said, "Life goes faster than we'd like to allow."

"What're you—Confucius?"

"Just a tired scientist." He shook his head. "So what path are you going on, Li, on the way to the moon?"

Li did not look at either Cheng or Fan, but to the towering skeleton of the building. He found himself wishing the birds would return. He found himself getting lost in its shadows, its exposed shadows, its dark places—dark, but so exposed. "I don't want them to take my mind; they've been too deep into it."

"Maybe," offered Cheng, "you have to overcome what they are doing to you to really get to the moon."

Before Li could respond to that, Fan said to him, "Will you really be satisfied when you get there?"

Li looked at her as if startled—and confused. He said, "I never thought of getting there as satisfaction. It was something I was supposed to do. Something—essential."

Cheng said, "Destiny? Fate?"

Li: "Something, I chose, though."

Fan said to him, "What will be essential after you get there? Mars?"

He smiled at her sadly, sharing with her a private understanding. "I won't know what comes after, until it's done."

There was quiet in the car. Cheng said, "That's exactly what we all have to find out. After it's done."

Fan said, "What is 'it'?"

"Our duties. Our mission. Whether we created them or the government. In this situation we're all responsible."

Li sighed. In a moment he gestured to the building. "I had a dream that Wuhan was totally deserted. That building reminds me. What if this just becomes a plague city?"

Fan said, "This is not a thousand years ago. We can fight disease now. In so many ways."

Li touched her face. "You'll have to give me your first mask."

Cheng said, "I reserve the second. Then Wuhan will bear your work."

"And you'll create the vaccine to protect us."

"We can hope."

Li said, "It's good to have something exact. Not—" He gestured to the sky.

Fan said, "You're the one who chose—you said."

"Accepted. Or accepted a passion that has no exact reason."

Cheng: "The universe isn't exact. You have to accept that."

"I already know that madness. I'll look at it again."

"You'll live. Somewhere." Fan moved across the seat and kissed him on the cheek.

Cheng abruptly interrupted this tender moment. "Li, did you ever consider the virus might have affected your mind? Or maybe in combination with something they did?"

Li jerked his head about, startled. "Do you think that's possible; a virus could do that?"

"Ordinarily I would say No, but this, especially if it's created— No, I'm being too…imaginative. That would be beyond anything we know."

But had he retracted that possibility because he knew it would be too unsettling to Li: having both Nature and science unhinge him?

There was a silence in which they were all uncomfortable. Cheng had to stress, "No, that's just not likely. Forget that."

But the thought had been planted. Li stared at the building, not looking at the others. The building seemed dull now—or, no, softer in the sun…. He was thinking: *I will hold on to my mind. They won't—*

Li's attention was abruptly caught by one lone bird suddenly flying in, then out of the building. Li linked himself to that bird diving through this construction of another species, whose essentially reality it could not comprehend—like himself encountering all that strangeness on a lunar far side that someone— or himself—had imagined....

Then he considered that birds all over the word fly about and perch on buildings, accepting and using the presence of these heights as habitually as they use trees. We all use, every organism uses, what is there.

Fan returned to the wheel and started the car. They moved slowly away from the uncompleted building, traveling once more through emptied Wuhan. At this moment each of them found this emptiness assuaging rather than troubling, a buffer of a lack of activity before the nearing time when unusual duties would be demanded of them. While the most vital questions, would, perhaps, remain unanswered.

38.

Fan got back to the lab after lunch. She was hungry and was glad the cafeteria was almost empty; there were just two other workers there.

As she sat eating, she was at once thinking and not thinking of the morning with Li and Cheng; it was as if her mind and her emotions were on two parallel tracks—and she was lost somewhere in between.

She looked up the entrance of the cafeteria not so much because she heard someone entering but more because she sensed it; in fact, Wong Bai seemed to have entered carefully, as if not wanting anyone to notice him.

Then, in the next instant, he saw Fan, smiled, and walked over to her. Fan was a mixture of annoyance and curiosity; she would have preferred to be alone for a while, but on the other hand saw Wong as a source of further (if cryptic) information.

He said to her immediately, "I just had to get away from everybody—" Fan was about to respond that she was in a similar mood, but he quickly went on: "I'm glad you're here. I just found out—" He turned to look behind him, in an almost comic, pathetic way—looked at the door, at the scattered others in the cafeteria. He turned back to Fan and said, "I just found out, I was told—I can't verify—but it seems the truth to me—"

Fan was both cautious and hopeful (it seemed a moment for conflicting moods): "What?"

Wong leaned forward, spoke in a low tone and quickly. "You've probably heard some of this—rumors—"

"What?"

"Many people weren't happy with all this gain of function research. That it could be dangerous."

She waited for him to continue. Wong drew in a breath, said, "At the end of 2017, scientists and health officials from the American Embassy in Beijing saw a presentation by a number of our scientists—some from the lab here; and a study that was in partnership with the American National Institutes of Health. About bat coronaviruses connected to the origins of SARS. The purpose of the study was to ultimately protect against an outbreak of a similar virus in the future.

"Some of the researchers believe they had found the cave of the bats who had spread SARS. And some researchers said they'd found three new viruses with spike proteins that were especially efficient at locking onto ACE2 receptors in human cells. That's what caught everyone's attention—and that these viruses were now at a Chinese lab, in Wuhan: this lab.

"At that point the Biosafety Level 4 lab here was still new. It was completed in 2014; didn't go into operation until the beginning of

2018—two years ago. The Americans—and scientists here—were concerned about how these pathogens were being handled. In 2018, Americans researchers met with scientists from the lab, met with the 'bat woman' too—"

"Shi Zhengli."

"Yes. She said after this new virus broke out, she was worried it had come from the lab. But after her own investigation she said it hadn't. Or had to say. She did say she was surprised this coronavirus had broken out in Wuhan, not in southern China, where those type of bats live."

Wong stopped, glanced about again, though in a less obvious manner than before. "I should get something. So it doesn't look, you know—"

He got up. Fan deliberately did not watch him as he got a cup of coffee; she continued eating her food. When she looked back up as he returned. she tried to make it casual, unconcerned. She realized she was taking on Wong's covert manner. Or, specifically, trying to disguise something covert.

Wong slowly took a sip of coffee. "Apparently our people—at least some of them—were very frank with the Americans...who were told—by us—that there weren't enough scientists, technicians to operate the BSL-4 as it should be. It wasn't safe enough."

Fan recalled reading that the BSL-4 lab here was built away from any flood plains and that moreover, it had been built to withstand a magnitude 7 earthquake, which was taking safety seriously, as the area was not known for earthquakes. At any rate, there would be no BSL-4 pathogenic release due to a natural disaster, no Fukushima of viruses.

"Some diplomats reported to the administration in Washington that the lab needed help, that they were working on dangerous pathogens that could infect people as SARS had.

"These reports—concerns, requests—weren't classified, though the public never saw them. And no one from the U.S. State Department responded."

Fan said, "Someone told you all this? Who?"

"You know I can't say. That could be dangerous to—I won't even say 'him' or 'her'."

Fan wondered if it might even be the "bat woman." But it probably wasn't.

Wong continued. "It probably had a lot to do with relations between the U.S, and China not being very good by 2018—Trump's trade wars: I don't know all the details. I hate politics."

"I know what you mean."

"When the virus did break out, a lot of Chinese were saying it had been brought over by the American military in those military games."

"I know that, too."

"I realize I'm telling you a lot you know, but I have to go over the whole thing to—you'll see. Here's what it comes down to. It appeared our researchers were concerned, publishing their research, and even asking the Americans, the international scientific community for help at the Biosafety Level 4 lab. But this gain of function research, to increase a virus' ability to infect, had a lot to do with bypassing natural mutations; it did raise the possibility that some tragic lab accident could occur. The Obama administration was worried enough about that to issue a moratorium on gain of function research. That might have affected U.S. participation with the viruses in Wuhan, holding back on what they, the Americans, were doing, but we, the Chinese, would still go ahead. Eventually the Americans found that our people were moving on with their gain of function research in a more extensive way than even most of us realized. Such as studying the effect of SARS on mice genetically altered to have human AEC2 receptors in their lungs. They've been doing this for some time."

Wong abruptly stopped. "Does this surprise you?"

"No, it doesn't." For Fan this was just basically further addenda to what Cheng had told her. But Wong did not know what Cheng knew.

Wong seemed a little disappointed that Fan was not as enthralled as he might have thought her to be. He said, "It wasn't just the scientists here. It was connected to the military."

"I guess that's not surprising either." *Or should it be?* Fan thought.

"And there's the rumor—there're so many—about some form of the virus being stolen from a Canadian lab. Our lab had connections to Canada's National Microbiology Lab. Two scientists from our lab were literally escorted from that lab for reasons never disclosed in July last year. The story is that a Chinese scientist took the virus from that Canadian lab, brought it here, re-engineered it."

Fan said, "That doesn't make sense—if we have all the bat viruses here, why would anyone need to steal it from Canada?"

"I thought of that, too. Has to be some reason why the Canadians threw out Chinese scientists, well, two specific scientists, Xiangguo Qui and her husband Keding Cheng, and a number of Chinese students. They all had had security clearance.

"There were different stories. Apparently earlier in the year the Canadian lab had shipped samples of Ebola and Henipah virus to our lab for gain of function research. Canada does not prohibit gain of function research, but doesn't (at least officially) do it; it's considered too dangerous. When this came out, the shipment of the viruses to Wuhan, it wasn't looked on favorably. But it went through official channels, it was approved. Ebola is Xiangguo Qui's field. She developed a treatment for it, ZMapp. Her husband worked on

HIV, *E.coli* infections, SARS—which is, yes, a coronavirus.

"The Canadians say that the removal of our scientists had nothing to do with the shipment of those viruses. And they insist there were no coronaviruses shipped to Wuhan. That was a big rumor online. One video about this on TikTok was viewed more than 350,000 times.

"So what was the reason the Chinese were removed from that lab?"

"No one is officially saying. Well, they are just saying it's a possible policy breach, which is saying nothing. So far, there is nothing more about it. Maybe they were learning something the Canadians didn't want them to learn. Or trying some sort of dangerous experiments."

He looked down into his coffee, then looked up, almost coyly. "There were viruses shipped from the Canadian lab to the lab here—no coronaviruses. At least that we know of. Two vials each of fifteen different viruses. Ebola was one of them."

"That's one of the deadliest viruses in the world. How were they shipped?"

"That's the big problem. You know there are strict protocols for that. Apparently on the Canadian end, or the Chinese who were on the Canadian end, were going to send it in 'inappropriate' packaging, I don't know exactly what, but on our end here, concern was expressed. In fact, Ebola and all the rest were about to go onto an Air Canada flight, not packaged the right way.

"Then I guess they repackaged it, sent it on Air Canada from Winnipeg to Toronto then to Beijing. That was the end of May, last year. So from Beijing to here." Wong shook his head, took another sip. "No one's sure if the removal of our scientists was just about that package or some issue with the virus we're seeing now. There were definitely concerns about Qui's trips to China. Was she passing on information the Canadians did not want share? Did she know things the Canadians didn't know, and was sharing that?

Fan sighed. It was obvious the current epidemic had been tainted—and covered up—by politics, a web of expedient political perfidy that would probably be never fully unraveled. And what Wong was telling her—it was more an embellishing of stories of which she had already heard fragments. Though she was not sure she had heard about American concerns regarding gain of function research prior to the outbreak.

She said to Wong, "Well, what does all this make you think—now?"

"It must have come from here, from the biosafety lab."

"And you are still worried you slipped up, could have stopped it from getting out?"

Wong blinked, looked down into his coffee. Fan waited. She thought perhaps her question had been cruel.

When Wong looked back up at her, he smiled. It was the smile of a man who had passed through some pain but now how freed himself from it—or had surrendered to it? "I have stopped putting the blame on myself. Not that I really blamed myself. But I considered it. I considered it."

Fan placed her hand on his. "There's so much unknown here. Blame isn't necessary. It's distracting."

Wong smiled at her. Certainly he was pleased at her consoling touch—which she had withdrawn, discreetly. He said, "Blame should be necessary now, but not on people like me. And yes, we shouldn't be…distracted."

There was a pause between the two of them. Wong finished his coffee.

In a moment he got up. "I'm sure there will be more to learn. I've got to get back—"

Fan said nothing, just smiled and nodded. She watched Wong walk to the entrance. But before he reached it, his passage was blocked by three men, two in suits, one in a lab coat. One of the former addressed Wong. He stopped, and was plainly tensed. Fan had never seen any of these men, even the one in the lab coat. Each of the men said something to Wong, who appeared to respond carefully. Fan could not hear the exchange. One of the suited men made an unmistakable a come-with-us, gesture, and Wong exited in the midst of the three men. It was an ominous departure.

Fan looked on, dismayed. She thought, *We're all going deeper into this. Am I watching his disappearance?*

Speaking of deeper.... Back at her work, Fan descended into the nanoworld: coronavirus spike proteins and the infinitesimal particles of recycled plastics. She considered, *It's like I'm hiding here.* She thought about Li once musing on life on the minute world of subatomic particles. She realized an irony: it was *she* who was living upon and within minute worlds, perhaps seeking a safety beyond the human in those places falling in between wavelengths of visible light.

Chapter Sixteen: The Rate of Departure

39.

Cheng's mind kept being drawn went back to the technical aspects of creating a new virus—this virus that had Wuhan in lockdown, and was inexorably now seeping outside the country.

Back at the lab, Cheng nodded absently at colleagues and even walked right past one who turned and called out his name jokingly to jar Cheng's attention. Cheng mumbled a quick apology about being pressed with something—and he was.

Inside his office, he sought the records of the reservoir of viruses that had been researched at the lab. He'd made use of this source often. Now he was asking himself, *Why haven't I looked at this since—?*

He was shocked to find the TEMPORARILY UNACCESSIBLE notice on his screen.

Not one analysis of any of the viruses the lab had researched was to be found.

He stared at the computer. "No…" he said aloud, his voice trailing into the silence of realization. Then, softly aloud: "How obvious could they be?"

For the moment outrage was larger than caution. He called Junjie.

The driver seemed startled that Cheng was calling him at this hour. Certainly it was too early to be leaving. And more startled when Cheng demanded, "I want to speak to your boss."

"My boss?" Junjie seemed genuinely confused.

"The one who assigned you to me. Mao Suit. Dong Chao."

As if disassociating himself from someone who had committed a crime, Junjie said, "He is not really my—"

"Junjie." Cheng said the name loudly, and threatening.

In fact, Junjie said, "You do not have to threaten me." Cheng made a guttural noise. Junjie gave a defensive sigh. "Give me a minute. I will text you the number."

In much less than a minute Cheng had the text.

"Who gave you this number?" demanded Dong. And yet there was already something mocking in his voice.

For an instant Cheng had the instinct to protect Junjie from authority, then he considered that mercy worth more than its object. "Your driver."

Dong said slowly, "I'm not sure I gave him permission for that…."

"What happened to the viral library?" Dong was silent. Cheng went on: "The listing, the cataloging of the research here. All the sequences."

As if he were being reminded of something utterly banal, Dong said, "Oh. They're…being reviewed."

"Reviewed for what?"

"Information, of course."

"Information you don't want me to have, other people to have?"

"Why would you think that?"

"You're playing games with me. Again."

"It will be…restored to access. For everyone."

"With certain deletions?" There was a chuckle from Dong, a condescending chuckle: Dr. Chang Cheng was being foolish. And perhaps Cheng was being foolish, in challenging Dong Chao so openly. This short exchange was throwing him off balance with its blatant duplicity. But he collected himself to add, "You want me to lead a course to a vaccine. How can I, when there is such obvious—" He searched for the word. He could feel Dong cock his head at the other end, waiting for Cheng to dig himself deeper into a rancor that could easily undo him. Cheng's only asset—protection—were his scientific skills.

"Such obvious…secrecy."

"You will be given the information before you know it. What you call secrecy, we call caution. You friend, Dr. Sun, he was not cautious."

"Are you saying the government killed him?"

Dong actually sounded shocked. "Dr. Chang, of course not. He was an unfortunate victim of—"

"The disease the government wanted secret as long as possible."

There was a long exhalation from Dong Chao. "We go in circles. You will have your viral catalogue. Just not today."

Cheng looked at the dark rectangle of his phone as it went silent. He sighed, went back to his computer, spent an hour or so searching the lab's data base, as if what had been suddenly missing could be found somewhere in that invisible matrix of information. Though he knew it as useless, and it was. Shaking his head back and forth, trying to relieve the tension in his neck whose stiffness he was only just realizing, he picked up the phone again and called Junjie.

"I'm leaving."

"Oh. That's early."

"You don't approve of my schedule—which is my own making?" Though Cheng realized it was less and less so.

There was a pause. Junjie did not respond to that, but said, "Did you speak with Dong Chao?" He plainly wanted to know if he would suffer any repercussions.

"I did. And please don't ask me what about."

"Of course not." How sincere he sounded. But now, after the conversation he had had earlier with Fan and Li, and the discovery that the viral catalogue had been removed from any access, Cheng really felt that Junjie, "his driver," represented something not at all good. Could Junjie have actually taken that virus out of the lab? Sent it off with seeds to America? Not likely. Anyway, Cheng still needed him for transportation.

That afternoon, that need would be translated into silence as Junjie brought Cheng home. Cheng had given him an emotionless nod when he'd gotten into the car; Junjie mumbled something in greeting. For the entire ride neither spoke. Then, when they were minutes from Cheng's house, he said, "Are you still doing those seeds?"

"Not lately." The driver looked surprised.

"So all finished."

"Unless...well, I don't know."

Cheng nodded, as if he had some information on Junjie the latter could not divine. The driver's eyes looked worried above his mask as they pulled up to the house. Cheng nodded as he got out, just as he'd nodded when he got in.

"I will see you tomorrow, doctor." There was a sort of hope in that look, as if the awkwardness of today might be effaced tomorrow.

Cheng made no reply as he walked to his house.

Inside he sat hunched over on a sofa, looking out on the winter street. He felt at the edge of some absurd and malevolent conspiracy. Or perhaps it was simply amoral. What does a virus know of our...outrage? And the handlers of that plague...perhaps they had come to mirror what they had dealt out to others.

The weekend came and Cheng, on impulse, took out his bike from a shed in the back of the house. In the warmer mouths of the year he took sporadic, lone bike rides that were a welcome relief from his day to day work. Being out in the open air and the light, and moving via his own strength was an assuagement of the very interior life he had lived for so long.

He rarely biked in the winter. But today was mild for winter, barely any wind, and the sun was bright. And he needed to move his body, to in a sense outrun the turmoil in his mind.

The metal of the bike was cold to his grip. Though soon his hands inside his gloves would be warm. He wore a loose puffy jacket and a dark scarf. He had a on a mask, as usual.

But as he biked into the less crowded sections of the suburbs, he thought: *I don't need this*, and slipped the mask into a coat pocket. And he recalled the lone cyclist he and Fan had seen in the first day or so of the lockdown: a man, like some herald or messenger, moving through a town stilled by an epidemic. Cheng did not feel himself similar to that unknown citizen; he did not see himself involved in any imitation of brotherhood; rather he was undertaking a sudden journey apart from anyone and everyone else.

The lack of activity about him could only increase that feeling. Only occasionally did a car pass, and only twice did he see someone on the sidewalk. One of these pedestrians, a slim middleaged woman with a thick hat pulled just above her eyes, waved at Cheng; it was like the signaling of one person to another, each caught in large circumstances. Cheng returned the slightest nod, perhaps too subtle for her to catch, and pedaled on. He felt himself both insulated and exposed by the stillness of these streets. He dared himself to absorb the protection of that stillness.

As he stopped by a traffic light a police car pulled up beside him. Cheng was prepared to be questioned, to be asked for identification—or certainly questioned as to why he was not wearing a mask, but the officer merely nodded at him from the driver's window and drove on when the light changed. Cheng laughed to himself. *Perhaps I have a look of authority.* Or perhaps the officer subconsciously sensed the insular world that Cheng carried in his being, and knew there was no reaching out toward it; it would be useless to question or order it.

While Cheng was not questioning or ordering himself. He was simply moving along, turning here and there sometimes, now in neighborhoods which he had seldom visited. Though if they were largely unknown to him, he recalled the location of a park and reached it easily enough, where he travelled upon a hard curving path that led to an elongated pond. Its water was a dark green, almost black. He stopped, got off his bicycle and sat on a wooden bench. He thought he was glad it was a wooden bench, not one of stone, which would be cold.

He looked out on the water. There were several dark ducks at the far end of the pond. The water was a green-black and the sun gleamed upon it. Cheng stared at this strip of brightness on the water until he had to close his eyes for the glare. He sat there awhile, eyes closed. When he opened his eyes, he saw that the ducks were now on the far shore, at the edge of the water, sunning themselves. Cheng thought it was amazing how some animals could live through the harshness of the winter. Even if their bodies were adapted for cold in a way human beings were not, in Cheng's eyes there was something more to it. Did their psyche and hence the body simply accept the cold and so were better able to move through it, even if that cold did constitute a struggle for flesh and bone? Human beings, at least modern human beings (which now means most human beings alive throughout the world), look upon cold as an inconvenience to a threat, and know there is a warm house, a warm apartment, a warm workplace to go to. They pass through cold on the defensive, not accepting it. Not that Cheng felt he should be accepting it. He even shivered a little at the thought. He knew if he sat here for any length of time he would grow cold, no matter the mildness of this winter day.

He looked back up to the sun—carefully. Now he considered how amazing—or frightening—it was that everything here, that all existence on the Earth depended on, in fact came from this very sun. He had been grimly fascinated to read when young that if the sun suddenly went out no one on Earth would know for eight minutes, the time light takes to travel from the sun to Earth. *I could sit here and the sun could already be gone.* This was almost an adolescent amusement. But all these mighty struggles of life here, the eons of life on Earth, the first creatures of the sea, of the land, the dinosaurs, human beings, this present world of supercities and technology, this virtual group brain of the internet...and the viruses, his viral world, Fan's nanoworld, dependent on that continuing star. *We live on a precipice.* And yet all the aspects of life, from the weather of this winter day, this ground below, the virus that was being borne in this city, had such psychic weight, the essence of a forward moving life that manifested in every aspect of our grasp, and our illusions.

Cheng pulled his hands down across his face. *The sun is not going anywhere, I will still be beset by Mao Suit, the virus itself and Junjie's seeds. I can sit here and perceive the metaphysical, but can never be freed from my poor position of perception.*

Cheng got back on his bike. He rode around the park a little, disturbing the sunning ducks when he passed by. They clucked and honked and dragged themselves back to the surface of the dark water. *Would they have been more disturbed by my thoughts?*

He exited the park, biked back home, arriving in the latter part of the afternoon. He had been traveling though deserted neighborhoods for many hours. He felt a good tiredness, of effort spent outdoors. As the sun set outside—he saw a livid horizon from a window—he was on his laptop with the flash drive plugged in, going slowly through the steps of the created virus, following that path like a soldier on a mission. It was as if Dr. Sun had left him with a course not only to follow, but a course to attack. Dong Chao and his ilk may be hiding further pertinent, very pertinent information, but did not Cheng have the most pertinent information of all? Who was one up in this absurd game? The world of the virus was apart from our machinations—but no, it wasn't. It had become our tool. While so much of it struck back at us. Even if we had created a virus, it killed us in return. What metaphysic could be parsed from that?

Later that evening, when Cheng entered a dark room and was about to turn on the light, he paused at the sight of the moon in the window. He moved to the window, then raised it, along with the storm window.

(When he had first bought the house Cheng had found it poorly weatherproofed and had quickly had storm windows installed. He had heard many visiting scientists complain of the lack of weatherproofing in many of the city's older homes and apartments.)

The winter night air hit Cheng; he did not find it unpleasant. He looked up at the moon. It was a little past full. *Li's moon.* He laughed aloud. Apparently, Li had claim to it now.

The relief of the afternoon's long bike ride gave Cheng the tiredness to fall asleep quickly, but the ever present virus gave him dreams that were elusive and fragmented, whose portions he could barely recall on awakening. There was a semi-clear vignette of him by the ducks on that far bank, pointing toward the sun. One of the ducks looked up, honked something, a long deep sound that seemed to shake the streak of sunlight on the water. It was a declaration to which Cheng in his dream did respond, but, awake, he had no idea what he'd spoken—or if he had spoken words at all, or had just made an echoing animal sound, apart from the language of his kind.

40.

Li shut off the lights in his apartment and looked out at the moon. It was beginning to wane, but a quick glance at it would give the appearance of still being full. Of course, Li, cued into all things lunar, was all too well aware of the terminator starting to edge along the right side of the moon.

This loss of the full moon saddened Li. He had been excited to see the full moon when he'd gotten out of quarantine, but now he did not want to witness its demise. He laid himself on his bed, turned on a lamp and without thought picked up *A History of the Moon* that was on the night table.

The last chapter in the book was "A Possible Future?"

We take for granted that in the nearing future humans will establish bases and then colonies on other worlds—colonies that may become planet nations. And we realize that life on the moon or Mars or the moons of Jupiter will be very different than life on Earth, as humans maintain a technology utterly necessary to keep them alive. But what we seem to give little thought to is how that type of existence will definitely change the psyche of those humans, especially, those who will be born on those other worlds. They will live under a different sun, a different day/night cycle (then again underground cities can keep to a 24-hour cycle), and the presence and maintenance of that multitude of technology, that constant success of life support will seem the most natural thing, as artificial as it will be (at least to us Earthlings).

Think of a native of the Amazon rain forest three hundred years ago, and think of the modern city dweller on the cusp of the 21st century, living among a complex of millions of people and a soaring architecture. You could say the obvious: that human of the rain forest is very close to Nature, in fact, is almost wholly ruled by it, while our modern urban homo sapiens is more ruled by his/her structured society. A structure that goes beyond custom, to train schedules, traffic rules and financial markets. The forest dweller would see all this as absurdity, indeed, a terrifying absurdity.

And if the citizens of the 21st century, who will face the intrusions of changes and crises we can only poorly predict, can conceive of humans living on other worlds, these citizens of the new century may well be as that rain forest human of hundreds of years ago in how far their psyches will be removed from those who will be born in the sight of Saturn's rings and understand "home" as a warren of heated, lighted, oxygenated tunnels beneath the surface of Titan. They will have become otherworldly humans, who may have also been genetically engineered to be more adaptable to these non-Earth worlds, to the light of a distant sun, beings perhaps half welded to machines and who may watch videos of Earthlings circa 2000 in the same way as we ponder—or only indifferently glance at—drawings of "primitives" circa 1800.

The exploration and venal conquering of so much of the globe by Europeans in the time they liked to call "The Age of Exploration," was effected on a planet on which the same air was breathed by everyone, whether in London or Borneo. Now the only similarity in what Earthlings and otherworlders will breathe is the fact that it will be sustainable oxygen. But on only one world will it be freely found; on all the other worlds it will be strenuously created and distributed. Again, perhaps I circle and repeat: the humans that will live on other worlds, that will be born on other words will become, naturally, appreciably different from the nature we so easily call human nature. In what way, and to what degree, we can only loosely predict—and for which we can plan for only in an almost comic way….

Li sighed, put down the book. He thought of the conversations he'd had with Fan, about living in some lunar colony, and his assertion (realization) that his nature was to go "out there," explore, but to return. He would not be one of those Earthlings transformed into an otherworlder. He would be Earth's astral messenger bringing back some shade of the reality of the worlds beyond Earth.

He slept, and fell into—of course—a dreaming sleep.

He was in a colony on a moon of one of the gas giants. He was with a woman who was definitely not Fan, who was not even Chinese. She was pregnant with Li's child. Li was telling her they had to get back to Earth. "I'm not going back there, with those governments. Especially yours. My child isn't going to grow up under dictators." Li argued and argued, but in the dream it seemed he could not even hear his own words. He did remember, though, before the dream left him, shouting at her, "I have to go back!"

And she shouted at him, in great fury. "It's about you then! You're bound to Earth!"

Li awoke from this greatly disturbed, as if his own subconscious had revealed to him a great weakness. As if the rice paddies held him more than the stars. There was nothing wrong with wanting to be the explorer who would return, go out, return again…but if he had a child "out there" should he not honor that circumstance, the beginning of another world's heritage, another human branching out, reaching out—from the rain forest?

He sat up, rubbing his fingers upon his brow. He had fallen asleep with the light on. His tired eyes grew a little more awake. He picked up the book. He read, from the same chapter:

The moon is slowly moving away from the Earth. Very slowly, about 3.8 centimeters (1.5 inches) per year. That appears to be the rate now, but in the past, it may have been greater, and may have been aligned with great changes in Earth's climate and geography. And the rate might have been much less—only .13 centimeters—or more: as much as 27.8 centimeters (10.9 inches).

This "lunar retreat" as it's called, is affected by the oceans of Earth. The moon's gravity upon our waters creates a tidal bulge, which in turn effects a gravitational effect on the moon. As the Earth spins faster than the moon, this bulge pulls the moon along with it. At the same time the moon's gravity pulls back on the Earth, which slows the Earth's rotation. But all this gravitational back and forth in the end pushes the moon a little farther from Earth.

Yet whether less than two centimeters or close to thirty, it would take an eon for this "retreat" to be noticeable. (In astronomy, an eon is one billion years.) Though the farther the moon gets from Earth, the rate of "departure" would increase steadily.

And so, this writer's mind considers:

That theory about the moon being a giant spaceship from another star system, a ship that had become the Earth's satellite for who knows how long— until the descendants of the original voyagers had come to feel that position in the universe, in gravitational dance with Earth, as "home." Well, think ahead a billion or two years, the moon drifting farther and farther from Earth, its rate of retreat increasing with distance, until the moon is out of our solar system, a world that is in no star system at all, wandering through the galaxy, the inhabitants of our former satellite in a world dependent on no sun, an orphan world in the cosmos. The inhabitants of this world, our old moon, would be so utterly different, so "other" that they would look upon 21st century humans and the forest native as no different from each other.

Li gave a grim laugh and put down the book. He just lay in bed, hardly thinking at all. Then he picked up his phone and found himself looking at a video someone had taken of Wuhan's empty streets. It was a short video, taken at twilight. This was Li's reality, not of a child on a gas giant's moon or some alien race adrift in the galaxy. That was too far away from what Li lived in now. If he simply got to the moon it would be amazing, never mind any world farther away than that. This all could be true for some future, but it would not be his future. The strongest reality now was this virus; upon that fulcrum the future would be moved.

He continued to watch the video of the city's deserted streets. He considered this was not unlike when he watched the footage from the

Yutu-2 rover before his training had become so surreal.

Here and there a light went on in a building. Whether those stray lights were signals of submission or defiance might be interpreted only by coming events.

I had that virus. I have its antibodies. Does that mean I'm free from its captivity?

The video ended as a street corner was turned and down the length of a long block the last color of the winter's sunset was seen—and it struck Li as if this were a sunset that he *was* viewing from another world—

He caught himself. *It's just not the world of rice paddies I saw as a child in the last century.* He was marking himself as of this time, of the virus and that sunset, the virus that had possessed him and the sunset that marked another day of the city's lockdown, a place and time before the imminence of pandemic.

About to call Mystery for his evening meal, Fan heard a blaring noise from the courtyard. Opening the window, she saw her cat shoot across a section of browned winter grass, apparently escaping from the erratic movement of— Fan had to look twice. It was a small dog-like robot, on four legs, maybe twice the size of Mystery, with a speaker horn atop its "head," shouting out, over and over, "Stay inside, sanitize. Defeat the virus."

Meanwhile, Mystery was scampering up the ivy, plainly unsettled by this artificial creature. He shot inside, over the windowsill, in record time. Laughing, Fan grasped him. "Scared you?" The expression Mystery returned was plainly that.

Fan watched the dog robot—dogbot?—move about the courtyard. Her immediate thought was: who had unleashed it here? The repetition of its message was irritating. Other residents thought so, too. From one window a soda can was flung at the dogbot; from another window came some other object. Both missed their target.

In a moment a man came out of the courtyard entrance of Fan's building, swearing as loud as the dogbot was proselytizing, scooped it up (its legs kept moving) and took it from the courtyard. Fan moved from this rear window and looked out a front window that viewed the street. In another moment the man emerged and roughly threw down the dogbot on the sidewalk.

Like a real animal it seemed to sway for an instant, regaining its balance. Then it took off down the street, spreading its official message.

As she watched it, Fan was reminded of Li telling her about the drone that had chased the unmasked old woman back into her house at the beginning of all this. She reflected it was not all that long ago.

She returned to the kitchen to feed Mystery, who was mewing as always, as if he had already forgotten the strange thing that had disturbed his rounds. "It's a new world, Mystery. At least for now."

Later that evening, she held purring Mystery as she looked at the waning moon from the courtyard window. The courtyard of this new world was quiet now; Fan took peace in that silence and the inner contentment of her cat's pleasure. This would shore her up for this night, against tomorrow. As for the days following…. What would the coming spring contain?

May 2020-April 2022

JERRY CIMISI is the author of *The New Man, A Novel of 9/11*, and *The Plastic Islands, An Eco-Tragedy*. His work frames how people confront large events of their time, events that will become historical turning points. He can be reached at cimisijerry7@gmail.com